Sarah Veitch's widely-praised novel *Subculture* was published by Palmprint Publications in 2000. Her four previous best selling CP books *The Training Grounds*, *Lingering Lessons*, *Different Strokes* and *Serving Time* are by another publisher and reprinted in their Erotic Classics range. Sarah's punishment-for-pleasure features regularly appear in British spanking publications and she is an agony aunt for a CP magazine.

Characters in books act without risk - but in the real world please practise safe sex.

First published in 2001 by
Palmprint Publications
PO Box 1775
Salisbury SP1 2XF
www.palmprint.fsbusiness.co.uk

All characters in this book are fictitious and any resemblance to real persons, living or dead, is purely coincidental. So if you think you recognise your sister you are wrong.

Palmprint Publications are too busy disciplining their employees to consider unsolicited manuscripts. Manuscripts will not be read or returned.

ISBN 0 9537953 1 4

Printed and bound in Great Britain.

CORRECTIVE MEASURES

Stories of Submission

Sarah Veitch

Contents

Author's Introduction

Versions of some of the following stories first appeared in the magazines *Erotic Stories*, *Februs*, *Janus*, *Kane*, *Obey* and *Privilege Plus*, proof that the short story is still alive and kicking. The story *A Pony Tale* first appeared in the anthology *The Best Of The Guild Of Erotic Writers* published by Cherry TCK. Two of the published stories had very similar names involving derriere puns so I've retitled them.

These stings-in-the-tale mainly demonstrate men correcting suitably deserving women. A few involve authoritative females correcting other females - and there are a couple where it's a man who cringingly accepts the protracted shame and pain.

Each story involves adult corporal punishment which the miscreant reluctantly consents to. I will always speak out against adults correcting children or criminal/domestic violence.

The settings vary from Victorian England where an irresponsible young governess is taught the error of her ways by the frustrated Mistress Of The House to a modern charity auction where a diffident young female is fully harnessed as a pony girl.

The mini-novella *Re-educating Ruth* first appeared as a four part serial in *Privilege Online*. It's set in Amsterdam, in a rigorous House Of Correction for adulterous women. Ruth leaves England to live there at her husband's insistence as it's the only way she can compensate for her various acts of infidelity.

Ruth is originally convinced that she can win over the Dutch Correction House workers with her sexuality. But she soon finds that they're immune to her charms and are merciless each time she fails one of their many tests. Soon she and the other infidel beauties are pleading for forgiveness as they buck under the lash...

Re-educating Ruth

Ruth let herself into the house, her pubis still tingling from the afternoon's adultery. Male voices coming from the lounge suggested that her husband, Franklin, and a colleague were already there. 'Only me,' she called breathlessly.

As she hung up her jacket, Franklin appeared in the hall. He wasn't smiling. 'Ruth - there's a gentleman here to see you,' he said. He turned and went swiftly back into the shadowy chamber. Her arms starting to prickle with uncertainty, the twenty-two year old followed him in.

A dark-suited male stranger sat at one end of the elongated black leather settee. He was sipping from a glass of amber liquid. 'Sit down,' the stranger said. Ruth blushed, but stood mutinously before him. *How dare he tell her what to do in her own house.* She looked at Franklin for support, but his eyes were blank with an unusual indifference or held-back rage.

'Am I to assume that our guest will be staying to dinner?' she asked, shifting her weight from one high suede shoe to the other: she didn't usually encounter coldness like this. Men usually looked at her long straight black hair, wide brown eyes and ready-to-laugh full mouth and started smiling. And they lit up some more when they gazed upon her thirty-six inch breasts and incongruously slender waist. Rightly or wrongly, people were usually nicer to you if you were pretty. So why were this stranger and her spouse being so hateful now?

'Is the gentleman here for dinner?' she repeated, fluttering her right hand in the direction of the impassive tall male newcomer. Franklin gazed at her insolently for a few seconds more. 'Karel Kromhout is here to give you a really sound spanking,' he said, smirking as a deep blush suffused her facial contours, 'But first we've a video for you to see.'

Mr Kromhout pressed the play button and the video recorder whirred into life. To be specific, it whirred into showing her *sex* life. Ruth licked her suddenly sand-dry lips as the familiar rented room filled the screen. Damn, there was her lover, Stephen, sitting on the bed, sipping a martini. She watched as a recorded version of herself sashayed through the door and kissed his neck.

Their strange guest pressed the pause button,. then he patted his lap.

'Karel Kromhout works in a House of Correction for adulterous women in Amsterdam,' Franklin explained, 'He gets especially annoyed with disobedient flesh that keep him waiting.' He jerked a thumb towards the door which led to an already-darkening October night, 'But if you'd rather leave our home forever, Ruth, then you're free to walk away.'

Walk would be the figurative word, Ruth thought, staring from one impassive male face to the next. Franklin would keep the car, the house, the very clothes she stood in. She only earned a few pounds for working in a florists two mornings a week. The twenty-two year old envisaged a Franklin-free life: she'd have to go to one of those hostels for the homeless. Surely a spanking from this Dutchman was better than living on the streets?

'Alright, you win,' she said, striving for indifference. Nevertheless, she cringed inside as she approached Karel Kromhout's knees. The prospect of prostrating herself over them was prodigiously shameful. Especially with her husband watching, a man who had previously treated her with respect.

'I didn't plan to be unfaithful,' she whispered.

'Over,' Karel Kromhout said.

Ruth stood stock still. 'It was meaningless.'

'Get over my knee now or leave your husband's house.'

Whimpering, the young woman bent at the waist and lowered herself until her entire body was supported by the settee, save for her tummy which settled in the stranger's lap with the utmost reluctance. 'I was flattered by Stephen's advances,' she mumbled in a last plea for clemency, 'I just got carried away.'

'Just as I'm about to carry away your panties now,' Karel Kromhout said.

Ruth shivered throughout her slender frame as she felt his hands pushing up her black pencil skirt and rolling it over her waist to reveal her black stockings. She felt her toes curling of their own volition as he removed her high heeled shoes.

'At a later date I may order you to keep these on,' he said, letting the footwear fall to the floor, 'A girl tottering about on stilettoes with a very red bum can be exceptionally appealing.'

What the hell did he mean by the phrase 'at a later date', Ruth asked herself. 'I've only agreed to a spanking,' she said quickly, lest he be planning to make her parade around the house wearing only her pretty patent shoes.

'We'll see just what you're willing to agree to once we've had a serious chat about divorce lawyers,' Franklin said.

The twenty-two year old breathed shallowly but fast as she felt the Dutchman's fingers tracing the tops of her lace-topped stockings. She whimpered as he unclipped them, then rolled them down her sunlamp-goldened legs.

'Can't I keep some of my clothing on?' she muttered raggedly.

'Yes, your upper clothes for they nicely accentuate the globes that I'm going to be thrashing,' Karel Kromhout said.

Ruth closed her eyes and her lipsticked mouth. She'd say no more for now. Her words only seemed to be exacerbating the situation. My God, she was stretched over some Correction House worker's lap wearing only a pristine white T-shirt and a pair of cream silk pants.

And it felt as if those same pants were about to come down. Ruth tensed her thighs as she felt her chastiser's fingers brush the waistband of her briefs. 'Nice,' he said, 'But I like a bare bum even better. I can watch its colour deepening as I spank.'

'Can't you use your imagination?' Ruth snapped. She knew that she wasn't being wise, but she just couldn't help herself - this was so demeaning. She had to show this chauvinist that she could give as good as she got.

'Oh but I'm very imaginative,' the man said, and his English was controlled and perfect, 'When I have a disobedient girl tied down on a punishment stool I am very ingenious indeed.'

The twenty-two year old wriggled about as the stranger dragged her panties over her orbs. The change of air currents told her that her bottom was now completely naked. All she had on to protect herself from his scrutinising gaze was her T-shirt under which she wore a half-cup silk bra.

Karel Kromhout lifted his right hand. Ruth tensed her bottom muscles and inner thighs. The video switched itself off as it always did after the pause command had been held for five minutes, and the TV screen went blank.

'No matter,' said her tormentor, 'I'll give you a warm-up spanking, then we'll have ourselves a little X-rated viewing, then I'll tan your adulterous hide some more.'

'I wish...' Ruth tried to find the words that would begin to put this situation right. 'Franklin, I love you, and I'm really sorry,' she said, hoping that her husband was still in the room and was feeling merciful.

‘Maybe some Amsterdam-style correction will show you what contrition really means,’ came her husband’s flat hard tone.

The settee ran the width of the room, and she was facing away from him. She couldn’t tell if he was a few inches from her exposed bum, or quite a few feet away.

‘I’m scared,’ she muttered, putting her hands back to cover her exposed extremities.

‘Mr Byrne, she’s trying to protect herself. You’ll have to tie her hands in front of her,’ the Dutch Correction House worker said.

The settee creaked. Her husband’s shadow fell across her - then he knelt so that his face was close, their gazes parallel. ‘Stretch your hands out, Ruth,’ he said.

Ruth did as she was told. The last thing she wanted to do was upset Franklin further. Maybe if she took her spanking without complaint he’d let her keep on being his wife. She watched as he took off his silk tie and wound it around her wrists several times before knotting it. Now she could no longer protect her sentient cheeks.

Ruth felt Karel Kromhout pull back one of his arms, and knew that her chastisement was beginning. She flexed her buttock muscles, then flattened her tummy against his lap as sensation exploded across one defenceless sphere. ‘Aah...’ she started to gasp out, but the sound was cut short by another echoing imprint. Ruth kicked her bare feet against the leather of the settee and yelled.

But the bastard seemed imperious to her wails. She felt his large palm crashing down upon the centre of first one disarmed sore cheek and then the other. His thick fingers toasted the sides of her twitching arse.

‘Ow. It really hurts. Not so hard,’ Ruth muttered over the spectacular slapping sounds.

'Just like you hurt me by being unfaithful,' Franklin's cold voice said. For a moment she'd almost forgotten his existence - all she could think about was the strong heat in her soft bare bottom. But now, as the Dutchman spanked on, she tried to appeal to her loving spouse.

'Franklin - I'm sorry,' she gasped, the slaps raging down on her backside making coherent thought difficult, 'Never be unfaithful to you again.'

'You won't after I've finished re-educating you,' her chastiser said. Her husband said nothing. Ruth writhed as the Correction House worker spanked her full force. His palm lashed on and on whilst she squirmed and whimpered. He spanked her till her small buttocks felt like baking coals.

'I'll say and do anything,' Ruth gasped piteously, 'Please, sir - I'm so sorry.' To her relief, her tormentor stopped.

'Let's make this naughty girl watch an even naughtier video,' he said, carefully turning her head to one side, then patting it gently. Ruth focused with difficulty on the TV screen as he aimed the video control at the underlying machine. Immediately a recorded version of herself and Stephen, her lover, came into view.

'Late as usual,' Stephen teased on the video tape, 'You'll have to be tied up to make atonement.'

Ruth watched as he tied her totally naked form spreadeagled-style to the hotel's four poster bed.

'How often did you screw him, Ruth?' Franklin asked.

Ruth wished that her husband was sitting near her head rather than near her bum which was still hellishly exposed for future punishment. If only she could make eye contact, could make the cute faces that usually meant that he forgave her anything. But, tied and positioned as she was over the stranger's lap, she could only entreat her angry spouse with her voice tone and her words.

'Just the once, darling,' she murmured, for in the video she was wearing the pencil skirt and jacket that she'd worn today, so figured that her spouse had only proof of her latest act of adultery.

'Start spanking her again,' Franklin said.

'But I swear,' Ruth started, 'You can see that I'm wearing this skirt and jacket, and...'

'I had that tape made up three months ago,' her husband said.

Damn! She'd met Stephen six times in all, once a month for the past six months on the day that Franklin had his headhunting trips. She might well have worn her most flattering outfit more than once.

'Three times then?' she amended, but it came out like more of a query than a statement. She shivered as her tormentor switched off the recorded tape and raised his right hand again.

At the first buttock slap, new warmth spread over painfully-established heat. Ruth drove her belly and pubis forward, then had nowhere else to go but reluctantly backwards. She bucked like that for several minutes as the muscular man continued to conquer her denuded cheeks. 'Oh please have mercy, sir,' she whispered as the spanking continued, 'Please, please, please!'

'On future occasions when I sense real regret in your voice and actions I'll stop punishing you, but today your correction isn't negotiable,' Karel Kromhout said.

'If I had my way right now she'd be corrected with more than your palm,' Franklin cut in.

'Your wish is our command, sir. She'll squirm under the whip, cane and tawse during the next few months,' the Amsterdam Correction House worker explained.

Was he really going to whip her? Ruth lay heavily across her tormentor's knee and felt extremely contrite about cheating on her spouse.

'Now where were we?' Karel Kromhout enquired.

I was wishing you'd go to hell, Ruth thought. Aloud she said: 'I was... apologising very sincerely for all the wrongs I've done, sir, and promising never to repeat them again.'

'You won't repeat them after six months in the House of Correction,' her dominator murmured, raising his hand.

'You can't make me go. That's kidnap,' Ruth blurted out, tugging with new levels of trepidation at her silken wrist bonds.

'Oh, you'll only be coming to my Amsterdam discipline centre if you ask very nicely,' the older man countered, hoisting her small red cheeks higher upon his lap.

'Forget it,' Ruth spat out, 'I'm happy here in England. I never want to...' But she didn't get the chance to say that she never wanted to live abroad, for the Dutchman started spanking her helpless hemispheres again.

At last he stopped and turned the video on. Ruth watched dazedly as she was fucked by her lover who'd left her tied to the four poster. Stephen so loved his bondage. He'd tied or cuffed her wrists and ankles on all six occasions they'd met.

'Stephen, do you do this with your wife?' she'd murmured, knowing from the especially-swollen rod between his legs that he didn't.

'No, she's strictly into missionary with the lights out,' he'd said.

'So, you like being tied up do you, Ruth, my dear?' the Dutchman asked now, as he caressed her soft curved flesh.

'Not really, I...' That was true. The tying up bit had scared and unnerved her. But she'd liked letting Stephen take control.

'Why let him bind you, then?' Franklin asked. His voice was heavy with hurt and a simmering anger. Ruth wished that she hadn't bruised his heart and his ego. She'd only wanted one wild day a month with her lover, and had been sure that she'd never be found out.

'He... it was just different,' she answered lamely.

'Appealed to her latent masochism,' the spanker amended, kneading her blazing globes.

What was he, a disciplinarian or a shrink? Ruth forced back the retort. Her husband was talking again. She wondered if her spanking was over at last.

'Has being touched by you got her all sexed up, Mr Kromhout?' Franklin asked.

Ruth sensed from the movement around her that Karel Kromhout had shrugged slightly. 'She's your wife, so if you'd rather check for proof yourself, sir?' he said.

'No, she obviously enjoys being fingered by strangers,' Franklin murmured, 'So be my guest.'

Suddenly the most delicate of touches butterflied its way across her sensitive clit. Groaning with desire, Ruth pushed her pubis blindly towards the pleasure-source, craving for it to be repeated. Instead she felt a finger trace around the rim of her sexual space.

Please let him put a finger in. Please let him put a finger in. Her mind started up an inner chant of frustration. *Please let him...* A satisfyingly thick digit was inserted in her vulva and she relaxed and parted her thighs a little more. Was Franklin still watching? Maybe he'd see how wet and open she was, and he'd want to have hard and driving sex.

'As you can see, her vulva gets grovellingly needy when she's thrashed,' the Dutchman murmured, withdrawing his dripping finger, 'I think we can re-educate her until she genuinely repents her adulterous ways.'

If only they wouldn't talk about her as if she wasn't there. Ruth lay, motionless over the older man's knee and wondered when he would touch her pleasurably again.

'Go over and offer penance to your poor cuckolded husband,' the Dutchman said, half-lifting her then pushing her gently back till she sat on the settee, her hands still bound before her. Ruth twisted awkwardly around till she saw Franklin sitting a few feet further along from her and coldly gazing her way. She started to stretch her bare feet towards the floor, planning to walk over and stand before her spouse, then kneel in front of him. 'No, just wriggle along the settee on your belly,' Karel Kromhout continued in a casually commanding voice.

Worse and worse. Wincing as her warm tummy made contact with the cool leather of the settee, Ruth humiliatedly began to wriggle towards her husband, using her feet to help increase her speed a little. Not that she was keen to show him her vulnerable contours - she just didn't want to upset him further by being too slow. And every movement which took her nearer Franklin took her further away from the despotic Karel Kromhout with his painfully effective large right palm.

If only both men weren't staring at her partial nakedness. She could sense Franklin's full frontal gaze, even though she refused to confront it. From his vantage point he could see her nipples pressing into the settee leather through her thin bra and T-shirt as she writhed. The Dutchman, on the other hand, was behind her and closest to her rosy rump, which tensed and untensed with each crawling move.

At last the twenty-two year old's vision focused on Franklin's trousered leg. She hesitated, psyching up her voice and words and courage. Then she wriggled over the few inches that separated them and manoeuvred herself with effort over his immobile lap.

'I'm really sorry for what I did, Franklin. Your friend spanked me so hard,' she whispered.

'He was a stranger to me until this week,' her husband said coolly, 'He's not a friend.'

'Then why...?' She wondered if it was wise to start asking awkward questions. But Franklin relaxed back against the settee, and seemed to want to talk.

'Remember young Pete's twenty-first birthday?' he asked. Ruth nodded: Peter was a junior engineer in Franklin's electronics firm. He worshipped Franklin who was a mentor figure to the shy young man. 'Well, a few of the lads chipped in twenty quid each to give him a really special coming-of-age present,' her husband continued, 'Two hours with a high class escort girl in her Fantasy Chamber rooms.'

'First I've heard of it,' Ruth muttered. Then she realised that she'd better be nice whilst lying under his fingers. 'Not that you have to tell me everything,' she added submissively.

'I didn't tell you because Peter didn't want anyone outside the firm to know,' Franklin said. He traced an exploratory finger down the deep crease of her arse, and Ruth shivered with lust and humiliation. Her husband teased the crack some more. 'Anyway,' he went on, 'When I went to the Chamber to pay the woman she showed me a room with a one way mirror for guys who like being watched whilst they're being punished. You know, an additional humiliation sort of thing.'

Tell me about it, Ruth thought sarcastically, but she kept her council. She was in no position to start answering back.

'Anyway, I said jokingly that I'd bear the room in mind if my wife was ever disobedient,' Franklin continued. Ruth heard Karel Kromhout give a short low laugh. She shut her eyes, sure that Franklin wasn't laughing. For a moment he'd been delightfully caressing her silky thigh backs, but now he'd obviously remembered how unfaithful those thighs had been.

'Somewhat to my surprise,' the electronics entrepreneur went on, 'She admitted she knew of a place which re-educated grown ups. She said that it belonged to a friend of a friend and was based in Amsterdam. When I found out you'd been unfaithful to me I went back to the woman and she gave me The Correction House's e-mail address.'

'So you paid Mr Kromhout to come here and chastise me,' Ruth muttered ashamedly, wishing for the fortieth time that they'd let her keep her pants on for her spanking. How long must she lie here like this displaying her small hot cheeks? She twisted her head back and was shocked to see how finger-marked red they actually were.

'Franklin, I want you inside me,' she whispered pleadingly.

'You've already had a man inside you today, you little whore,' her husband said.

Was it really only this afternoon that Stephen had tied her to the hotel bed and thrust pantingly inside her? That act of adultery seemed very far away. 'I know, but... it's you that I really want,' she continued, lifting her sore hips and parting her legs in a take-me gesture.

'And I can't forgive you until you've atoned for your crimes in a Dutch Correction House,' Franklin answered unrelentingly.

'But I... How long would I stay there?' Ruth muttered, as her impassive spouse untied her hands then set her firmly on the floor.

'Depends on how good you are,' Karel Kromhout explained.

'And you'd be the one... re-educating me?' she asked, putting her freed hands over her tenderised posterior and trying to massage the deep down heat away.

'Myself and two others,' the Dutchman admitted, 'One of whom owns the Correction House.'

'All men?' Ruth prompted shyly.

'All men,' the Amsterdammer confirmed, 'And the adulterous students are all female so you'll have instant friends.'

Ruth stared from the Dutchman to her husband then back again. Both of them were obviously awaiting her answer.

'Would I be... you know... chastened every day?'

Karel Kromhout shook his head. 'Only when your behaviour warranted a meeting with our numerous canes and clit-teasing devices and multi-thonged whips.'

This bastard certainly knew how to shame. Ruth flushed at his blatant words. 'But if I'm perfect I'll never be punished?'

'You, perfect?' Franklin raised his eyes.

Damn them all - she'd live an exemplary six months so that she didn't have to taste the cane, and she'd have a Dutch holiday into the bargain. She'd act as if she was contrite but would still remain in charge. Ruth smiled with mock submissiveness at the unusually hard-hearted Franklin and at the hard-palmed Karel Kromhout. 'Alright, gentlemen, I'll go to the Correction House,' she said.

******

Three weeks later Ruth stared out of the aeroplane's window as red streaks appeared in the 6am sky - a foreign sky. The glow reminded her of how Karel Kromhout had spanked and spanked until she'd pleaded with him to spare her burning buttocks. Now she was going to meet the pitiless specialist again.

'Almost there,' Franklin said matter-of-factly, glancing at his watch.

'Will you miss me?' Ruth asked. She so wanted to regain his husbandly approval.

'I'll miss the old Ruth - the one who was faithful,' Franklin said tautly, 'I'm hoping that after a few sound thrashings I'll get the old Ruth back.'

'She's back now,' Ruth countered quickly. She risked a light touch of his hand, but he hadn't responded to her advances since finding out about her unfaithfulness. He'd rarely spoken to her or even smiled. 'I phoned Stephen the day after... the day after Mr Kromhout visited us,' she continued as the aeroplane neared Amsterdam, 'And told him our affair was over. I've ignored his phone calls since.'

'You still have to be thoroughly re-educated by the experts,' her husband said coolly, slapping one large palm against the other, 'So that you don't commit the same offence again.'

'And you'll come back once a month like you promised for conjugal visits?' she persisted, feeling her sex canal aching with frustration. How she longed to be caressed and held and kissed by her husband again.

'Yes, I'll return to visit and to see videos of you being birched and leathered,' Franklin said in the same terse voice which he'd used since she'd cheated on him, 'Believe me, I wouldn't miss it for the world.'

The plane landed, then they boarded a train to Centraal Station. Justus Lederwaren, the second trainee Master, met them there and led them to his very big car.

Even Franklin whistled when he saw it. 'Maybe I should become a trainee Master myself,' he said, patting the bonnet as if it was a pedigree pup.

'We have to be on call to re-educate the girls twenty-four hours a day if they're disobedient,' the Dutchman answered, 'So we charge the husbands commensurate fees for our service. It means that we can afford the finer things in life.'

'Am I costing you lots of money?' Ruth muttered to her spouse, thinking about cost for the first time since agreeing to be sent to the Correction House.

'It'll be worth it,' Franklin said gratingly, 'If it stops you spreading your legs for a stranger again.'

Ruth swallowed hard and got quickly into the back seat of the car. There was no point in apologising to Franklin again - he wouldn't listen. Only when she'd been fully retrained would she have a chance of regaining his favour and his love.

'I'll learn my lessons and come back to you fully cleansed of my sins,' she whispered awkwardly, 'Really I will.'

Her new trainee Master drove through increasingly quiet streets. She watched the Amsterdam landscape change, then gazed at the Dutchman's broad firm shoulders. Franklin sat beside her, but just talked about the country's industry with the other man.

Finally they drove along a lane until they reached a hotel sized multi-windowed building set in its own tree-lined grounds.

'Here is the Correction House,' Justus said simply, indicating the reddish brick edifice with its wonderful yellow sandstone sculptures, 'The other girls have been expecting you, so breakfast awaits.'

Breakfast was prime ham, Edam and crusty bread, eaten overlooking a circular duck pond.

'It's beautiful here,' Ruth said with genuine enthusiasm as she admired the verdant view.

Justus Lederwaren looked pointedly at his cup and a small brunette rushed over to pour him a coffee and top it up with a liquid which looked like cream. 'The entire building, apart from the punishment chambers, has been furnished to promote tranquillity,' he acknowledged softly, 'I'm sure you'll especially love your room.'

'I half expected to be sharing a dorm,' Ruth admitted, adding the cool white liquid to her own fragrant cup.

'We're not heathens,' the man said, smiling, 'No, people need their privacy. You'll have your own sleeping quarters, ensuite shower and bath.'

Ruth finished her coffee, then had a second and a third. It combined with the nutritious food to waken her up. She felt dynamic.

'Right, if you show me to my room I'll unpack,' she finally murmured, standing up and reaching for her case.

Franklin frowned. The Dutchman looked at his watch. 'You can unpack later. There's a disciplinary session about to begin.'

Ruth stared at him open-mouthed, then her hands crept back to cover her skirt-clad haunches. 'But I've just arrived. Surely you aren't going to...?'

'To punish you?' Master Lederwaren continued, 'No, you're merely required to watch.'

'But I don't want to watch,' Ruth objected, staring at the coffee pot as if it could absolve her.

'It's a requirement of the House that some punishments are observed and commented on. It's more shameful for the wrongdoers,' the Correction House worker said.

He stood up and stepped around the side of the table, then took Ruth's nearest upper arm.

'You are welcome to watch too,' he told Franklin politely.

'Try stopping me,' Franklin grinned.

Ruth dragging her feet, all three of them walked out of the breakfast room, went along a corridor and down a very narrow but steep flight of stairs.

They reached a door with a sign which said Punishment Chamber One. Justus pushed open the door and Ruth saw the tethered inmate. The blonde girl was completely naked, and was tethered standing in the shape of a cross. She had her back to the watchers - and her bottom. She was securely held in place. Leather cuffs around her wrists were connected to an overhead beam which held her arms out in a V shape. Her ankles were similarly cuffed and fastened to a beam on the floor.

For a moment Ruth was only conscious of the girl's taut nether cheeks and their obvious vulnerability. Then she became aware of another presence in the room, and saw Karel Kromhout standing to one side.

'So we meet again,' he said to Ruth, and his eyes spoke of how intently they'd once feasted on her buttocks. And his smile told of how he wanted to bare her bum some more.

Not knowing what to say, Ruth turned back to Justus Lederwaren and to Franklin who were both staring at the female's waiting orbs.

'Sit,' the Correction House worker commanded, pointing at a bench along the wall and staring at the twenty-two year old. Ruth sat. Justus turned to Franklin, 'You can sit too, or you can inspect this naughty girl more closely. She's to be chastened for sneaking out to a late night club and flirting with men.'

'She's got a lot worth flirting with,' Franklin said hoarsely, sidling up to the squirming female, then walking around her, 'A good arse and a great pair of tits.'

'Agreed, but they should only be for her husband's delectation,' Justus Lederwaren said, 'After all, they don't have an open marriage. She's here because she committed adultery, so to have her compound the offence by last night's club trip means that we have to whip that wilful rump.'

Ruth licked her lipsticked lips at the mention of the word whip. Then she nibbled at the inside of her mouth as Karel Kromhout walked towards a range of implements hanging on the wall across from her.

'Talking of whipping,' he said easily, 'I think we'll use this riding crop on Geri's tender spheres.'

Ruth focused on the braided coiled whip. It had several tails of heavy dark leather. She didn't know if it had the traditional nine tails, and didn't want to get close enough to examine it. The naked culprit was obviously also staring at the crop, for a slight shiver ran through her spreadeagled body and she tensed her helpless bottom cheeks.

'Yes, you're nervous now,' Karel Kromhout said, walking towards and behind her, 'If only you'd been nervous yesterday and hadn't sneaked out to that corrupting nightclub.'

'It was a dare,' the girl muttered nervously. She sounded Swedish. 'Ryka dared me,' she forced out.

'We know that,' Karel Kromhout verified, 'And she's to be dealt with next.' He stepped closer and stroked the girl's taut globes. 'But our newest resident, Ruth, is here to watch a girl being disciplined. We thought we'd show her your bum being whipped because it always writhes and colours so prettily.' He patted that same bottom then traced the curve under the waiting cheeks. 'Ryka makes a lot more noise than Geri when she's wriggling under the riding crop, but her backside never gets as adorably hot and red.'

'Please - not too red,' the Swedish girl whispered, as a glistening trail began its ponderous journey from between her labial lips.

Karel Kromhout smirked coldly. 'Very red and very hot indeed.' He stepped back and lined the whip up with the centre of the waiting bum. 'So red that it resembles a crimson apple and feels like a well baked peach.'

'What if I promise to be a good girl?' Geri pleaded, a slight lisp entering her accented question. In answer, her Master launched the leather thongs through the air.

'Aah,' the blonde girl gasped. Ruth watched the whip's tails bite into her tender flesh. Both buttocks tensed then untensed in a manic dance that continued for thirty seconds.

The girl jerked her naked arse from side to side. Thin pink lines appeared, tapering off in all directions. Another line of moisture dripped from her quim.

'Please, Master, how many?' she whispered throatily.

'I haven't decided yet,' the Dutchman said. He contemplated the marks left by the tails, then pulled back the merciless punisher. Then he applied it to the helpless nether cheeks again.

'I'll reform,' the girl muttered.

Karel Kromhout shook his head. 'That bottom promised to reform when it first arrived here. Since then I've lost count of the number of times I've had to thrash it hard.'

'Bet you haven't,' quipped Geri in a lightly sarcastic tone, and the correction worker pulled back the leather crop again. He whipped the bare bum in front of him four times in quick succession, and the owner of the bottom yelped and writhed unproductively in her bonds. 'Sorry,' she breathed, puckering up her bare bum then untensing it again before repeating the gesture, 'Master, I'm really, really sorry that I was rude.'

'Sorry that your arse deserves a whipping, not sorry that you almost cuckolded that poor husband of yours again,' Karel Kromhout said, stopping to caress the whip marks. His lascivious attentions made the bondaged girl squirm some more.

'I can't help... It's just...' Geri broke off, obviously searching for more suitable words. The man stopped fondling her bottom. 'I want to be a loving wife, to stay with one man. But then I see the single girls going out on the town and getting chatted up. I want that too.' She shrugged the little she could in her spreadeagled position, 'I love the admiration and attention that a stranger can give.'

'But we've met your husband. *He* loves and admires you,' Justus Lederwaren cut in from the bench beside Ruth and

Franklin. As if remembering that there were several strangers behind her, the stripped girl wriggled anew.

'Yes he loves me, but... well the love of a new man is more exciting,' she admitted softly.

'In that case, as we've said before,' Karel Kromhout concluded, 'You should divorce your husband and remain a free agent for a while.'

'But I like being married,' the blonde girl protested, tensing then untensing her adulterous parts in an agony of pain and frustration, 'So I'm really trying to cheat less on my spouse.'

Her Master sighed. 'My dear, until you learn to stop cheating completely you're going to find your arse flinching under my whip.'

He raised the crop again and applied it smartly to the waiting orbs six times in quick succession. Geri wailed and moved her bum the little she could.

'Does it really hurt?' Ruth whispered to Justus, feeling appalled yet fascinated.

'Of course it hurts,' he answered, 'See the way her soft cheeks flinch beneath the lash?'

'Isn't that brutal?' Ruth mused out loud.

'No, just firm,' the trainee Master replied, 'After all, she knows she can avoid all punishment by obeying the vows she took when she married. And all the girls who are here have been chosen because on some deeper level they respond to CP.'

'I won't respond,' Ruth cut in fiercely.

'You already do,' Karel Kromhout answered without even turning to face her, 'You were soaked like a sponge after I spanked your bottom three weeks ago.'

'That's because... because I'd just come from my lover,' the twenty-two year old countered hotly.

'Believe what you like,' the Dutchman murmured, 'I'll prove otherwise when I next haul you over my lap.' He returned his attentions to Geri's defenceless bum. 'Where was I? Oh yes, disciplining this recalcitrant trollop.' He applied the whip to both glowing hemispheres, flogging the curvy underswell so that the girl moaned and pushed her pelvis forward the little she could. 'Do you still want to flirt?' he asked coolly, 'Still want a stranger's thick cock inside you? Still long to stroke another man's balls?'

'No sir,' Geri half-sobbed, 'Only want the cock of the man I married.'

Karel Kromhout smiled and shook his head. 'Oh sweetheart, you'll say anything when that pretty bottom of yours is getting a roasting. If only you did as well in our psychological examinations. Truth is, those exams show that you're still naive and deceitful, that you need to be soundly chastened for a very long time.'

'I know, sir, but not now, please - it stings so much,' the Scandinavian girl said piteously.

'I'll give you four more lashes for complaining too much,' the Correction House worker answered, 'Then we'll see if you're a good girl by conducting one of our little tests.'

A shudder ran through the girl's flesh at the mention of the word tests. Her body trembled.

'I hope you've been learning self control,' Karel Kromhout added, applying the whip again.

'Aaah. Yes, Master. I won't do anything without permission,' the blonde gasped tensely. She shook her hips from side to side as if to shake off the lash.

'Time to go dancing, sweetheart,' the correction worker murmured, applying the riding crop four more times and making Geri jig about and yell.

When her whipping was over, Karel Kromhout dropped the implement but left the girl tethered in place.

'Testing time,' he said, moving his strong body into a crouch on the floor. He did something to a circular handle on the beam between Geri's spread thighs and a black shaft slowly elongated from the ground until it formed a phallus that was three feet high, its head near the blonde girl's labia. 'Now for an exquisite little adjustment or two,' the man said. He smiled, then moved nearer to the Swede's nude body. Ruth watched in eroticised fascination as he parted Geri's labial lips.

Even from where she was seated she could see that Geri was very wet, her pink fronds swollen. She groaned when the trainee Master touched her, then rubbed her sex against his hand.

'Bad girl,' he said lightly, 'This isn't your husband's hand, and you've just been telling me that you only want to enjoy sex with your husband. I'm not convinced that you can pass our little test.'

'I'll pass,' the girl gasped hollowly. Ruth wished that she could see her face rather than her buttocks. But Franklin seemed to be enjoying the hot sore view.

Now it looked as if the emphasis was going to be on the hot. As everyone watched, Karel Kromhout manually lengthened the phallus until its penile head nudged against Geri's sexual slot.

'In a moment,' he said to the tethered adulteress, 'You're going to near Nirvana, because I'm going to switch this on.'

He stood back and contemplated the scene, then shook his head. 'Justus, can you get me a collar and attachment clips? She doesn't have enough downward movement this way so the test isn't scientific.' He smiled at the waiting blonde woman, 'After all, your hot quim needs the option of bearing down.'

'I won't bear down, Master,' Geri said fervently, 'Not unless you tell me to.'

'Oh believe me, sweetheart,' Karel Kromhout said, 'I won't.' He looked over at Franklin. 'Sometimes she's allowed to climax on a machine like this, aren't you angel? Her pussy loves it. She comes so long and loud.' He sighed and shook his head, 'But last night she was a bad girl, and has a bad pussy. So its pleasure obviously has to be denied.'

Justus Lederwaren approached Karel Kromhout and handed over a studded black appendage and something which briefly caught the light. Ruth craned her head forward to see what the man was holding.

'Get a good view, love,' Franklin said crudely, 'You could be next.'

'Only if I do something wrong,' Ruth muttered. She'd promised herself that she'd behave like an angel to avoid giving Karel Kromhout the opportunity of pulling down her pants.

'Oh, you'll do something wrong all right,' her husband countered, 'After six years of marriage I reckon I know you pretty well, and I'm willing to make a bet on it.'

Ruth swallowed twice then sat more firmly on her bum. She still felt at risk, so curled her hands around the bench to hold herself in situ. She was so glad that she wasn't in Geri's place.

She watched as Karel Kromhout unfastened the Swedish girl's wrist cuffs from the beam.

'Swing your arms about for a couple of minutes before I bind them in a different position,' he said gently.

Geri swung her hands back and forward twice, then moved them around to cup her reddened buttock cheeks. 'A bad girl isn't allowed to touch her punished arse,' Karel Kromhout added, moving behind her quickly. With equal speed he slapped her protective hands away.

Then he picked up the collar from the floor. It had silver studs on the outside, was the kind of thick collar worn by a large dog like an Alsatian. As the watchers watched, he slid it around Geri's throat, and buckled it in place.

'It doesn't hurt,' Justus said, looking over at Ruth intently. 'It just makes her feel more slave-like and it gives us an appendage on which to fasten her wrists.'

He handed the glistening accoutrements to Karel who fastened them to the leather band. Ruth could now see that they were chrome hoops which linked the girl's wrist cuffs to her collar. Now her legs were still tethered apart to the floor, but she looked as if she'd put her hands behind her head.

'She couldn't stay like that for long. It's not comfortable,' Justus Lederwaren said, looking at Ruth and then at Franklin.

Karel Kromhout laughed. 'But I suspect that she won't have to, that her pussy will betray her really quick.'

'It won't, sir,' Geri whispered. She twisted around as she said the words, and looked pleadingly at Karel. Then her eyes focused on Ruth and Franklin, and she blushed some more. 'I won't come without permission,' she muttered, her nipples stiffening, 'I just won't.'

'That's what your upper mouth says. Let's see what those lower lips want,' Karel Kromhout said in his usual crude voice. 'Now what can this little switch do? I really must press it and see what happens,' the man continued. Geri groaned. She was obviously familiar with the switch's purpose and with its long term effects.

Karel Kromhout pressed a button lower down the phallic machine and the entire thick rod immediately started vibrating gently. Its effect on the bound girl's sex centre was obviously quite strong. She exhaled hard and then pushed her body against the machine so that a quarter inch of it disappeared inside her eager sex tunnel. Ruth watched the black cock entering the white and inner-pink quim.

Geri wasn't watching herself being turned on - but she was obviously feeling it. She sagged slightly at the waist and moved her bound arms forward a little way. Now that she'd impaled her rim on the machine she didn't seem to have the willpower to rise off it. Either that, or the blissful sensations had robbed her spreadeagled legs of their remaining strength.

'Does the bad pussy like that?' Karel Kromhout taunted, walking in front of the tethered girl.

'Y-e-s,' Geri said through breath, the word a drawn out whimper. Ruth watched the girl's bum cheeks closing more tightly together as she flexed her thighs above the arousing machine.

'But the pussy knows that it mustn't come, that it must learn self discipline,' the trainee Master added gloatingly. In answer, the blonde girl groaned. 'I didn't hear the pussy's reply,' Karel Kromhout continued in a low clear voice.

'I'll... try not to... come,' the Swedish infidel said, her buttocks twitching like they were being stung.

'Because what happens if you do come?' the Dutchman prompted, picking up the riding crop from the floor and running it insinuatingly through his fingers as he walked around her excited nubile frame.

'I'll be sorry,' Geri gasped out. There was an almost unbearable sexual frenzy in her voice. Her spread thighs trembled.

'How sorry?' her tormentor queried, lashing the whip against the floor so that the sound echoed through the Punishment Room. He repeated the question in a voice as soft as silk. 'Mm, my sweet? How sorry will you be? How sorry will your arse be?' But Geri seemed to be lost for words.

Justus Lederwaren joined Ruth and Franklin on the bench.

'Will she fail the test?' Ruth asked.

'What do you think?' Justus answered, raising his eyes heavenward.

Ruth imagined how she'd feel if her own sex was positioned over that devilish machine. The vibrations would thrill the rim of her vulva and emanate up, up, up, also spiralling to her clitoris. Her labial leaves would be resting on the oscillating head. The resonance would send signals which said almost, almost, almost, and in desperation she'd bear down on the thick shaft a little bit.

Ruth looked back. Geri was indeed moving more greedily against the phallic machine. Her sex seemed to suck another half inch of the black cock in and hold it captive. A light sheen of perspiration now coated her back and shoulders. Her bum was still crisscrossed with zealous cruel red.

'Please let me come,' she whispered in a lust-filled voice.

'Permission denied, girl,' Karel Kromhout said laconically.

'But I need to...' the Swedish girl pleaded, squirming more urgently against the tool.

'Do you need to come as much as your hot bum needs a thrashing?'

'No, please. Got to... can't bear...' The girl seemed to reach some point of unthinking need, and lapsed into her native Swedish. Then each sinew of her nude body stiffened and she cried out and convulsed in ecstasy against the pulsating machine. 'Ah,' she gasped out, 'Ah, ah, aaaaaaaaah.' Her fingers moved spasmodically against her own hair, her arms moving the little they could courtesy of the wrist bonds. A trickle of perspiration seeped from under her collar and made its shiny way to her glistening back. 'Ah,' she said again, 'Uh, uh, uh, uh. Jesus!' Ruth knew that the contractions which follow orgasm were taking place.

When Geri's ecstatic cries and overjoyed writhing eventually stopped, Karel Kromhout switched off the pussy-pleasuring implement. Then he undid the cuffs from the collar and from her slim wrists, and she put her arms around his neck and held on tight. Next he unbound her ankles and rubbed her spreadeagled legs.

Ruth stared at the Scandinavian girl's taut thighs and wet-look pubis. Watching this whipping and quim-based teasing had made her feel so strange. Part of her had hated watching the naked girl's buttocks reddening. Another part of her had wanted to see.

'Does she... Will Mr Kromhout use the riding crop again because she came without permission?' she asked, her voice strained.

'Personally I'd cane her,' Franklin said, slapping his palms together hard.

Justus Lederwaren looked from one to the other. 'No, her hindquarters have suffered sufficiently for today.' He cast an expansive hand around the room with its many devices. 'I'm sure Karel will come up with a punishment which doesn't involve her bum.' He looked back at his contemporary, who was now ordering the girl to bring her spread legs together and stand in place.

'Shall I leave the Punishment Chamber now?' Geri murmured hopefully.

'Yes, but you have to be chastened first for obeying your sex core rather than your brain's directives,' Karel Kromhout replied.

'Please, not my... not my haunches again,' Geri whispered. Her hands fluttered towards her posterior.

'No more whipping today,' her trainee Master said detachedly. He looked at Ruth, Franklin and Justus sitting on the bench, then turned the naked girl around until she was facing them, 'Geri - you're about to greet our visitors intimately.'

Geri made quick eye contact with Ruth then looked away again, her face suddenly turning more florid than her bottom.

'Don't be shy, sweetheart. They've already seen you squirming on a plastic cock and shrieking to the heavens,' Karel Kromhout continued, 'And they've heard you admit that you've fucked men other than your husband since you got wed.'

That was *her* crime too. Suddenly Ruth couldn't meet the fairer girl's eyes, or look at her hard-nippled breasts or her gently trembling tummy. She stared at the floor, then cast a quick glance at Franklin, only to find him staring at the blonde's shaven pubes. Damn it. She, Ruth, had turned her normally loving man into a woman hater. She wished again that she could undo her adulterous acts.

'Your punishment is to show the strangers your rebuked arse,' the Dutchman said. Geri toed the floor with one bare foot, then she glanced at him, her eyes beseeching. 'You're the one who likes to show off your charms in nightclubs,' her Master continued, 'So show Mr and Mrs Byrne your bum and tits.' He clipped one of the chrome rings to the collar which the girl was still wearing and pulled her slowly over to the three people seated on the bench.

Justus Lederwaren immediately stood up and addressed everyone in the room. 'I'll just prepare Ryka next door. I'll give you the guided tour before we actually cane her.' He looked at Franklin, 'We often tether a girl in the punishment position for a few minutes before we chastise her. Gives her time to reflect on her most floggable crimes.' He smiled, 'Obviously we leave one of the other girls in the room so that she can be freed if she feels ill or needs to go to the bathroom. Sometimes they start playing with each other and earn extra stripes.'

Franklin half-nodded. He was still staring up at Geri. Ruth risked a glance in the same direction and saw the desire and shame vying for supremacy in the girl's eyes.

'Show the nice man what a misbehaving backside looks like,' Karel prompted, moving the collared girl closer by the chrome ring. He kept up the tension until the girl was facing sideways to Franklin's lap.

'Get over my knee now,' Franklin snapped.

Ruth jumped in surprise at his words and his tone. She was glad that they weren't directed at her, felt sorry for Geri. The Swedish girl looked at his trousered legs, then swiftly obeyed. Ruth shifted along so that no part of her body touched the girl's head or outstretched arms. She didn't want to see which parts of the naked girl her husband groped.

'Ruth - cup Geri's full breasts,' Karel Kromhout instructed, 'Feel how much Franklin's touch excites her.'

Both Ruth and Geri groaned and bit their lips. 'I can't,' Ruth whispered. She put her hands behind her back. She'd never as much as kissed another woman on the cheek, far less cupped her chest.

'If you don't,' Karel warned, 'You'll take her place between the oak beams and dance under my whip.'

The twenty-two year old remembered how Geri had looked, naked and spreadeagled. She wasn't ready for that level of dishonour yet. 'Alright, I'm doing it,' she whispered, sidling back along the wooden bench then staring down at Geri's bosom. Marshalling every ounce of her resources, she opened her hands wide then placed her palms under the girl's large round tits. Each breast felt surprisingly warm and undeniably smooth, almost silky. Ruth looked down and saw the pinky-brown nipples elongating at her touch.

She turned her attention to Geri's face. The Swede's eyes were shut, her full mouth twitching with cowed humiliation. That twitch intensified as Franklin began to speak.

'Those whip marks are still hot,' he murmured, and Ruth could see that he was tracing the crop's feverish lines. 'But there are places in between that haven't been warmed yet.' He fingered the marks some more, intensifying their redness, 'If *I'd* been whipping you then you'd have had a much sorer bum.'

'Yes, sir,' Geri whispered in a compliant voice. The cropping or the orgasm had rid her of her earlier sarcasm. Now she just wriggled on her bare belly across the man's suited lap.

'And I'd have made you touch your toes and ask me very nicely for the cane,' Franklin continued, fondling the dark crease between her naked buttocks, 'How many strokes would you need before you started to beg very sweetly? Six? Seven? Eight?'

'After the first stroke, sir,' the naked girl replied with obvious feeling.

'She dreads the cane most. It really hurts,' Justus Lederwaren commented, coming back into the room. He looked pointedly at Karel, then asked 'Join us on the guided tour?'

Karel shrugged, 'No, I'll go and have a word with Ryka.'

'Just talk her down, then,' Justus added, and Ruth could hear the underlying tension in his voice, 'Don't start the caning till we all get back.'

'Would I?' Karel laughed as he made his way towards the connecting door. Justus helped Geri up from Franklin's lap, and they started to make their way towards the Punishment Chamber's exit on the other side of the room.

'I hope I never have to go through what you just did,' Ruth whispered to Geri looking at the fairer girl's soundly thrashed posterior.

'You needn't if you learn well here,' Justus Lederwaren answered, holding open the door.

For a moment Ruth felt secure, knew that she could ride the storm of her adultery. Then she heard Karel Kromhout's voice reach out to her from across the room.

'But if you don't learn quickly enough,' he warned, and his tone was full of gloating and anticipation, 'Then I'll give you the harshest caning that this House has ever seen.'

******

The next day Ruth showered and dressed then walked shyly to the breakfast room and helped herself to thin brown bread and thick yellow cheese slices. As she ate, she reread the timetable she'd been given for the ensuing week. At 10am today she'd to attend Room Five for a seminar on *Couples And Trust* then was to have one-to-one instruction with a Master for the remainder of the day.

The English girl reached the appropriate Seminar Room and listened for a while. Animated voices came from within it. At 10am Ruth knocked and a male voice called 'Come in.' Ruth obeyed the command and was pleased to see that Justus Lederwaren was leading the discussion. He seemed genuinely nice when he wasn't handing Karel Kromhout the whip. Five females, two of whom she recognised, sat curled in five overstuffed armchairs around him. There was a spare armchair to one side and Ruth quickly claimed it as her own.

'Trust is the quality which allows a couple to separate without anxiety for various lengths of time,' Justus was saying, 'It means they can have various freedoms. That's why the fabric of a relationship splits when that trust is betrayed.'

'Ergo you shouldn't get caught.' The speaker, a girl with auburn curls, laughed loudly.

Justus smiled back mirthlessly. 'Amber has only been here for a week,' he said to Ruth, 'She has your droll Scottish sense of humour.'

'I'm English,' Ruth said belligerently, 'It's not the same.'

'It's the same in that you both have small rumps that will redden beautifully under my tawse,' the trainee Master said, 'And you'll both beg for mercy.'

'Want to bet?' Ruth mumbled under her breath. She felt the humiliated heat rush from her nipples to her pubes. She played with the top fastening of her white silk blouse and moved her legs into a crossed position. When she finally looked at Amber she could see the other girl had also blushed hard.

'As you're both newcomers,' Justus Lederwaren continued, 'I'll overlook your rudeness this once in order to continue the discussion. Now lets get back to the topic in hand.'

For the next forty five minutes Justus asked questions and made observations. He turned to Ruth at the seminar's end. 'Franklin mentioned you hadn't been to Amsterdam before, so would you like to see the city now? Think of it as your first one-to-one counselling hour.'

Hardly able to believe her luck, Ruth said yes. They went sightseeing. They shopped. They ate at an Indonesian restaurant. Ruth could see admiration in his hazel eyes.

After lunch he walked her to the Red Light District, beginning to give her rules as they approached. 'You'll see half-dressed prostitutes in the windows, but show respect and don't stare at them too blatantly.'

'Why would I? I'm heterosexual,' Ruth replied.

'Oh, and don't take photographs in the area or someone will smash your camera,' the man continued.

'I don't even own such a thing,' Ruth lied, her compact camera mere inches away in her bulging shoulder bag.

A dark-skinned female of around twenty-five sat behind a large rectangular pane of polished glass. She wore a luminous white bikini, the incandescent material squeezing her Galia melon-sized breasts and pulling tautly across her hips. Three youths and a couple passed by, walking slowly. The dusky girl smiled at no one in particular with lips stained red.

They moved on to the second window. This girl was smaller and paler, looked more like Ruth herself. She was dressed in a fishnet body stocking which showed off her slender waist and oval buttocks. She tossed her hair back over her shoulders as Justus walked by.

'How much do they charge?' Ruth asked, intrigued.

The Correction House worker shrugged: 'Depends what the customer is looking for.' He grinned at her, 'They're straight here, though, so don't start having any dyke fantasies or hoping for three in a bed.'

'I've never had a lesbian fantasy,' Ruth replied indignantly. It was true. She'd never understood how one woman could finger and fondle another. It was such a forbidden and unlikely love.

'I'm sure we'll find out what really turns you on in due course,' the Dutchman said.

Ruth shrugged, her attention drawn to two near-naked women in the next window. Maybe she could take girly photos here and sell them to a newspaper for a fee? It would be great to feel that she was capable of earning serious money, and it would mean she wouldn't be destitute if her marriage failed.

'Watch the only clean show in a dirty business,' one of the sex club managers called from an open door. Justus stopped to talk to him. Ruth surreptitiously worked her camera up to the top of her shoulder bag then transferred it to the inside of her jacket which she swiftly buttoned up.

With the lens peaking from between her buttons, she took her first shot.

Justus said goodbye to the man, and they crossed the street. Ruth snapped a tall blonde pouting girl in a champagne silk body stocking. She photographed another who was wearing a black basque and matching thigh length boots.

'I know of your camera,' Justus Lederwaren said matter-of-factly, 'So you might as well stop breaking the rules this minute. Your bum will get a roasting when I find a suitable place.'

'You mean back at the House?' Ruth muttered, looking around to make sure that no one had heard him.

'No, here in the Red Light District,' the trainee Master replied.

'But there are people around and...' The English girl trembled at the thought of having her bum bared in public.

'You should have thought of that before you ignored my orders,' the Dutchman countered, 'That rebellious little arse won't wait.'

They reached a sex shop and he marched her in. 'Can I rent a booth?' he asked loudly, 'Yes, one for couples.'

'Choose your video,' the man behind the counter said mildly, indicating the tape-crammed shelves.

Justus shrugged, 'Oh any video with a naked girl being whipped will do nicely. It'll mirror the thrashing I'm about to mete out.'

The shopkeeper stared at Ruth with new interest, and she felt the colour rush to her miserable face. 'Justus, please don't,' she whispered, looking up at him and widening her eyes in a sweetly pleading gesture.

'When I give you a simple order and you defy it you have to be thoroughly rehabilitated,' the man replied.

'Then spank me in the Punishment Chamber, not here,' Ruth begged in her quietest voice as Justus marched her towards a curtained doorway.

'You disobeyed a trainee Master. I'm going to do more than spank you,' Justus replied. To Ruth's shame he stopped by one of the flagellation-magazine racks and began to unbuckle his belt. A couple who were in the process of selecting a video turned and stared at Ruth with open-mouthed curiosity. The man in particular seemed to be assessing Ruth's chinos-clad bum.

'Alright, I deserve to be chastised. Let's go inside the booth,' Ruth muttered with genuine urgency. She'd die of shame if he bared her bottom out here in the middle of the shop.

The booth was painted cream. The puckering hemispheres on the screen were a hard-caned red. Ruth suspected that her own facial cheeks were equally hectic. She looked up at the squealing correction which was taking place on the video, then looked down at the long wooden seat which ran along one wall.

'Strip,' Justus said.

Maybe she could turn this into a more mutual seduction scene. Ruth gathered her mental resources. 'Wouldn't you rather undress me?' she whispered, sidling up to him and pulling his hands onto her breasts.

'Strip now or I'll double my belt before I use it on you,' Justus Lederwaren replied coolly, 'And make each stroke twice as hard.'

He was only a trainee Master, Ruth thought, so he probably wouldn't give her too stringent a chastisement. Then she remembered with a low pull of dread that the merciless Karel Kromhout was ostensibly a trainee Master too.

Ruth put her fingers to her trouser buttons then hesitated, overwhelmed by uncertainty. The Dutchman took the buckle of his belt and began to bring it warningly towards the other end.

'Please don't double it. I'm stripping,' Ruth said. She pushed the metal button through the hole, then tugged her zip down with trembling fingers. Justus Lederwaren's impassive gaze remained fixed on her face. The English girl manoeuvred her feet out of her shoes, then pulled her socks off. Her chinos fastenings flapped back, but the garment stayed clinging to her hips.

'Remove those trousers this instant,' the Correction House worker said.

'Been a while for you, has it?' Ruth muttered sarcastically. She knew that it hadn't: he'd watched Geri and Ryka being whipped.

Justus leaned against the wall, the thick belt trailing from his right hand. Ruth looked at it then awkwardly pulled down her beloved white trousers. She removed them completely, then stood there gazing over at the man and trying to look as if she didn't care.

'Pull down your pants.'

Ruth licked her lips, but knew that arguing was useless. If she refused to obey him he'd probably parade her, half naked, through the outlying shop. 'Pants coming down,' she replied, trying to add a jokey flavour to the conversation. But her Master just stared at her and didn't laugh.

The thin grey carpet wasn't a feast for the eyes or the imagination, but Ruth stared fixedly at it as she hooked her fingers into the waistband of her panties. She continued to gaze downwards as she pulled off her butterfly-motif briefs. Now only her white blouse remained on her body, covering her upper arse cheeks and half of her pubic hair.

'Tie your blouse up high around your waist,' her tormentor continued, 'We don't want it flapping down to cover your small soft bottom.'

'Speak for yourself,' Ruth muttered, then she saw the look in his face and hastened to do as she was bid.

When the twenty-two year old had finished knotting the upper garment in place she felt horribly vulnerable. Especially when Justus Lederwaren ordered her to face the wall. She did so, and sensed that he was assessing her newly-bared bum and naked thigh backs. Any second now...

'Sit on the bench beneath that coat hook,' the Dutchman said. Surprised, Ruth looked around at him and Justus jerked his head in the appropriate direction. Maybe he wasn't going to chastise her after all. Ruth felt an odd deep pull in her stomach, part relief, part disappointment. A tiny fraction of her psyche had wanted to know how a belt-based punishment felt.

The twenty-two year old smiled at the trainee Master, then walked to the bench which ran along one entire wall of the video booth. She sat down gingerly, knowing that the plastic would feel cool against her bare bottom. She folded her hands in front of her so that they covered her pubes.

'Now swing your legs up and back,' her hazel-eyed trainer continued. Ruth looked at him blankly. Justus sighed. 'Like this.' He hunkered down and took hold of her ankles then brought them slowly up and over her head, holding them in situ. Her twitching nether cheeks were now totally exposed. 'Let's bind these naughty legs out of the way,' Justus Lederwaren continued, and Ruth peered through her thighs to see him removing his cravat and using it to tie her ankles together. He then bondaged them to the wall's high coat hook then stood back to admire the fleshy view. 'You may want to put your palms down on the bench rather than keeping them in your lap,' he said conversationally, 'That way you'll have something to grip onto when the leather sears your cheeks.'

Ruth heard his words, but couldn't quite translate them into action. Her entire being had become focused on her hugely-displayed haunches. Her eyes, peering through her upended legs, were fixed on Justus Lederwaren's belt. Somehow she'd envisaged being put over his knee and given a leathering. She could have wriggled against his manhood and gotten him hard...

'How many strokes do you deserve for lying to your Master?' the Dutchman asked.

'Four?' Ruth asked. She wasn't feeling hopeful.

'Four it is. And how many for taking photographs of the window girls?' the man replied.

Damn! Ruth had wanted a total of four lashes, but her helpless rotundities were obviously going to taste a great deal more. 'Another four?' she muttered, flexing her ankles to relieve the slight pull on her calves and shoulders.

Justus Lederwaren nodded. 'That sounds fair.' He paused, looking contemplative. Ruth shivered, awaiting further instruction. 'And two for trying to talk your way out of this punishment. And two for not stripping the instant I told you to,' the Dutchman said. He smiled. 'That's twelve of the best, but if you touch your punished flesh you'll get extra. We have to teach these adulterous globes a measure of control.'

Ruth had no defence, and knew that an apology wouldn't save her from her fate. She sucked in her breath, watching the man step backwards. She closed her eyes as he pulled back the belt, then opened them wide and yelled as the first band of heat streaked across her creamy soft skin. Her bottom did a little jerky dance on the bench of its own volition, but her bound ankles ensured that she wasn't going anyplace.

'My dear girl, with movement like that you'll never need aerobic exercise,' Justus said lightly.

Ruth felt a low rush of pudenda-based pleasure and a sweeping shame. 'I thought that you liked me,' she muttered piteously.

'I do like you. That's why I'm doing this,' the older man replied. He lined up the belt again, and Ruth pulled in her arse cheeks the little she could in her displayed position. 'I like you enough to want to make you a better person,' her tormentor said.

'I'll be better,' Ruth yelped, wishing that he wouldn't stare over at her helplessly exhibited pussy folds.

'No, you'll just try to look better - to not get caught out again - if I stop chastising you. If I continue to teach you self discipline then you'll ultimately lead a more honest and worthwhile life.'

'It's for my own good, you mean,' Ruth said sarcastically.

'Yes, your extremities will hate it but your character will thank me for it,' the Correction House worker said.

He pulled back the belt again. Ruth cried out before it touched her and Justus Lederwaren stayed his hand and smiled coolly.

'Save the histrionics, my dear. No matter how much you yell you're getting twelve of the lash.' He contemplated her hugely-displayed bum, 'Don't worry. I spend my life chastising soft young buttocks. I know how much you can take.'

'Psychic, are you?' Ruth muttered. Then the belt came down and her words turned into a wail of impotent perturbation. Her position prevented her from examining her posterior, but she could feel that he was toasting the fleshiest part of her nether cheeks. Though the leather stimulated her poor arse to the utmost, her main misery was caused by the ongoing shame.

The man dropped the belt and moved forward, then hunkered down at her rear. 'Let's see how hot you are so far,' he said, and brushed his fingertips along one of the wide long belt marks. Lust immediately coursed through Ruth's lower belly, spreading through her pubis and inner thighs. She groaned and tried to jerk her thrilled mons upwards, her sex tunnel suddenly begging to be filled. All pride gone, she writhed helplessly and whispered 'Please enter me, sir.'

'Easy,' Justus said, 'You're nowhere near deserving pleasure yet.'

'Please,' Ruth muttered hollowly, the need for an orgasm almost overwhelming her.

'Please warm my bare cheeks until they become more thoughtful?' Justus Lederwaren mocked. He reached for the belt and stood up, holding it near the silver buckle. A few seconds later Ruth howled as she tasted stroke three. Again she jiggled about on the bench and again the man waited until her movements eventually slowed to mere bottom-twitching. Then he laid on the fourth stroke and the fifth.

'I'll never photograph the window girls again. I'll do anything you say,' Ruth cried, temporarily meaning it.

'I told you that I'd stop when you'd suffered all twelve, and you're just about to taste the sixth one,' the Correction House worker said.

Ruth flinched as she heard a scuffling noise in the corridor outside. 'Who's there?' she asked sharply.

'Maybe a customer or the shop owner making use of a peephole,' Justus Lederwaren replied.

At the shameful thought Ruth found that words almost failed her. 'You mean, someone's watching us right now?'

'Yes - I'm sure the shop owner enjoys watching a disobedient girl getting her pants pulled down and her bottom reddened,' the impassive Dutchman said. He moved closer and ran a knowing finger down the swollen wet folds of her labial lips. Ruth moaned loudly and tried to buff her hungry fronds against his fingers, but he immediately pulled his hand away. 'Now where was I? Ah, yes, admonishing your wilful backside.'

The wilful backside quivered and quaked then relaxed slightly after the sixth stroke, which wasn't as bad as expected.

'Because you've a greedy little hole you're able to endure a more agonised arse,' Justus Lederwaren explained. He fingered the belt. 'We've done tests in which we stroke a girl's pussy before we take the cane to her. She howls less when she's thoroughly sexed up.'

Ruth shivered. She hated this man knowing that her quim was begging for it. She wanted to retain a vestige of control.

The seventh stroke cruelly crisscrossed two of the others. Ruth did her inevitable baying dance on the bench and tried impotently to pull her ankles free of their pitiless bonds.

'You're making too much fuss. You're beginning to anger me. I'm going to lay on the next four in quick succession,' the Correction House worker said softly, then he lashed the leather strap into her disarmed buttocks in a quiver-making quartet. Each sound effect in tandem with her movements, Ruth grunted, groaned, whimpered and finally yelled.

'Only one to go,' the Dutchman said consolingly when her sore globes had at last calmed down. He stopped and fondled her all over, then stood back and put his head assessingly to one side. 'Mm, a nice unfluctuating scarlet. I know how to administer a thorough thrashing, firm but fair.'

Ruth thought that he'd behaved like a male chauvinist pig, but she kept her council. With her ankles bound and her bum raised, she wasn't in a position to make him into an enemy.

Justus Lederwaren doled out the last lash across the centre of her tautly-held cheeks. Ruth squealed at the strange mixture of sore heat branding across her bum and covetous heat spreading throughout her sex curve. Her hands opened and closed convulsively on the plastic bench.

'I'm sorry I disobeyed you,' she whispered, hoping that she could make amends and earn permission to cup her anguished flesh for a few seconds, 'Really, sir, I'm remorseful about being bad.'

The trainee Master smiled what Ruth hoped was a forgiving smile. 'Such humility deserves a little reward,' he said. He knelt between her legs and lowered his middle fingers until one was inside her, the other just touching the flesh above her clitoris. 'There you go, sweetheart. Just rub against my hand like a bitch on heat.'

'Don't you want to...?' Ruth muttered, trying to move her thighs further apart to indicate her empty sex tunnel.

'No, the rules state that only your husband can make love to you,' Justus Lederwaren replied.

He removed his hand from her sex lips and Ruth whimpered at the loss of contact. 'But it's a month till Franklin returns for a visit,' she said.

'Exactly. Your crack will be begging for it really sweetly,' the trainee Master said impassively, 'You'll appreciate even the slightest thrust.' He put his fingers close to her bud. 'Well, what's it to be, dearest? A little light fingering's all that's available - will you frig yourself against my fingers like a little animal or spend the day entirely without release?'

Beyond feeling proud, Ruth lifted her pubis the little she could and used his digits to stimulate her dripping furrow. Her pinkish fronds had been swelling from the moment he told her to remove her panties, and now near-ecstasy thrilled through the curve between her thighs.

'Your butt may dance away from the belt, but your clit is doing the cha-cha,' the man said crudely. Ruth whimpered with increasing need and squirmed some more. 'Pity we don't have a mirror in this booth,' the man continued, 'I'd really like you to see your straining thighs and bright red backside.'

Ruth cried out into the booth as her orgasm began. Justus kept his hand immobile whilst she rubbed frenziedly against it. Ruth's sex felt like it was on fire by the time she pulled her mons tenderly away.

'Please hold me,' she whispered, 'Oh please, please, please, sir.' She felt gratified and close to being loved when he freed her ankles and obliged.

For a few moments he sat on the bench and cradled her near-nakedness, Ruth kneeling up to keep the plastic bench away from her well-thrashed buttocks. At last he kissed her hair then pushed her away. 'Time we continued our sight-seeing trip.'

Ruth nodded and got onto the floor, stretching one languorous arm out towards her chinos. She smiled at the man who'd given her such pleasure. 'Shall I get dressed?'

'Not in those, you won't,' her trainee Master replied.

His voice tone had gone firm again and Ruth looked up at him in confusion. 'I don't understand.'

'It's simple. You're supposed to be learning how to be a faithful wife, yet a moment ago you beseeched me to fuck you. If you're going to behave like a tart then we'll have to dress you as one.'

'I'm not a tart,' Ruth said, stung.

'You're not, deep down, but your behaviour sends out mixed signals. You're thoughtless and impetuous,' Justus Lederwaren explained. He walked over and tilted her head so that she was looking up into his intelligent hazel eyes,

'You foolish little girl, you'll have to learn more self-disciplined ways.'

'I could learn whilst wearing my chinos,' Ruth chipped in, fingering her favourite trousers and gazing hopefully at her trainee Master.

'You'll learn much better with an exposed sore rump,' the Dutchman said.

He picked up her chinos and pants, crumpled them into a ball then walked towards the door holding both garments.

'Leave your blouse tied up like that,' he said, 'I'll be back in a moment. Watch the video and be glad that it isn't you up there.'

The booth door closed. Ruth turned her post-orgasmic attention to the screen. Her climax had been so intense that concentration was now difficult. She half registered a scarlet-arsed female convict writhing over a woman prison warder's knee. God, it must be awful to have your panties pulled down by another woman. That way you couldn't cocktease...

As she watched the dominatrix sort her submissive out, Justus Lederwaren returned with a bowl of warm water, a sponge and a small hand towel. He also held a large black carrier bag which she suspected contained her jacket, chinos and pants.

'Thought you'd appreciate a clean up,' he said genially, 'Before I show you the further wonders of Amsterdam.'

Silently chiding herself for her self consciousness, the blushing twenty-two year old brought the dripping sponge to her equally dripping folds and sponged away the secretions from the rim around her entrance. Then she dabbed herself dry with the towel, washed her hands and stood up.

'Say hello to your new outfit,' Justus Lederwaren chimed. From the depths of the bag he produced an A-line black lacy miniskirt, glossy black shoes and a pair of charcoal hold-ups. 'They're all in your size. I checked. Put them on.'

'But these are sex shop clothes. They're for wearing in private,' Ruth muttered, staring at him in amazement.

'Well, you offered your body to me a few moments ago, so you're obviously not a private person,' the Correction House worker replied.

He held out the skirt. Ruth reached out and took the soft small scrap and let it run through her fingers. After a moment's hesitation, she stepped into it and pulled it up, fastening it at the back. The hem ended near the tops of her thighs, but was wide at the end so rarely touched them. Ruth stepped forward and could feel the shifting air currents against her bum.

'Now for the hold-ups,' Justus Lederwaren said. Wordlessly Ruth accepted the suspenderless stockings. She eased them up her legs slowly. They felt like silk. 'And, finally, the shoes,' her trainee Master continued. He set them on the carpet. Admiring their sleek lines, Ruth pushed her silk-clad feet into them and stepped forward then realised she still wasn't wearing any pants.

'Can I have my briefs back?' she asked softly, figuring that they were with her other clothes in the carrier bag.

'No, you offered someone other than your husband your sex, so now you can show the world your sore bare bottom,' Justus Lederwaren replied.

Ruth swayed on her heels. 'But I'll get done for indecency in a public place,' she protested.

'Depends on how breezy it is outside and how carefully you walk,' the Dutchman said. He put his head to one side in what Ruth now knew was a characteristic gesture. 'You've got both hands free so you can always hold down your skirt.'

'I'll look odd,' Ruth gasped out.

'Well, you've been acting odd. It seems fitting.'

'I hate you,' she added petulantly.

'Really? A few moments ago you were begging for my cock right up you as you wriggled against my hand.'

Ruth flushed anew and found herself lost for words. Justus Lederwaren opened the door of the booth and she walked reluctantly in front of him into the main section of the sex shop. There was a man looking through the Watersports shelf.

'I've never understood how a man can enjoy pissing on women,' Ruth muttered to Justus Lederwaren.

'Hey, you're the one whose pussy wets itself when your arse is leathered,' the Correction House worker said in an exaggeratedly loud voice.

The man turned and stared at them both, his mouth agape. Ruth cringed inside and out, then walked around the displays of Group Sex videos. She'd never understood that particular fantasy either, but she didn't intend to say.

'Everything all right for you, was it?' the shop owner asked.

'Nice and toasty,' Justus Lederwaren replied, patting Ruth on her all too visible backside.

The two men grinned at each other as if sharing a joke. Ruth stared at the plastic phalluses in the nearby glass case as if her life depended on it, then turned to look at the vibrator shelf.

'Sweetheart, have a flick through the whipping videos whilst I talk to the man,' the Correction House worker ordered.

Ruth followed his pointing finger. If she did what she was told she'd have her back facing all three men, and she suspected that they'd be able to see a centimetre or two of her reddened lower cheeks beneath her skirt.

'Don't want to,' she muttered, crossing one high-heeled leg behind the other and staring at the ground.

'She's shy,' Justus Lederwaren explained, 'And new to strict training.' He touched the belt around his waist with obvious inference, 'Ruth, would you rather watch another video inside the booth?'

'Christ, no,' Ruth knew that she'd be watching it with her ankles tied to the coat hook above her head. She knew that the sound affects would come from her mouth as he thrashed her already-tenderised bare bottom. 'I'll look at the... at the videos,' she said. She walked with tiny movements across the room, trying to lean back so that her short skirt covered the source of her shame, then she tried to remain tilted in that position when she reached the required shelves.

Womanly bared bums flinched beneath leather crops and under braided long riding whips. Female faces showed that strange blank mix of humiliation and desire. Ruth felt the fast-becoming-familiar pull at her belly, and wondered why the images excited her this way. Maybe she was just missing a man's caresses? It was ages until Franklin's first conjugal visit was due and her neglected quim ached...

******

Three sex-free weeks later Ruth was window-shopping on a sunlit Amsterdam street when someone gently but firmly pulled her into a doorway. 'Stephen!' she muttered in pleased amazement, staring at her debonair British lover. If she hadn't committed adultery with him and been found out, she wouldn't be here now.

'We can't...' she started, but despite her best intentions, she thrilled as his strong appreciative hands slid round her waist.

'I had a private detective eventually trace your flight here but then the trail went cold,' he said. He held her very tight and Ruth could feel her nipples hardening, her inner core expanding. God, it had been a while. 'I've been walking the streets here for a week,' he continued avidly, 'And showing your photo in bars.'

'I'm not supposed to...' Ruth cut in, then realised that she couldn't bear to tell him about the Correction House, about the disgraceful unveilings. 'I'm staying with Franklin's friends,' she lied. 'So we'll have to meet secretly,' she continued in a stronger voice.

'I can live with that,' her lover said and ran his hands down her haunches as if he was assessing a show horse. 'You shan't escape from my tongue and hands again.'

I don't want to escape. I just won't get found out, Ruth told herself as she slid her hand into Stephen's and let herself be led to his luxurious hotel. *I'll only see him occasionally and I'll be discreet.*

A grim-faced correction worker watched the couple from across the road. Did Ruth really think that she was allowed out to shop unchaperoned? He sat in a cafe for two hours until she emerged again then followed her back to the corrective house.

After her evening meal that night, Ruth was summoned before the house's formidable Disciplinary Committee. Six trainee Masters and the establishment's owner were sitting behind a magisterial table. At the end was a tall stern woman that Ruth didn't recognise.

This time there was no point in making excuses. 'What are you going to do to me?' she asked, her hands creeping backwards to protect her vulnerable extremities.

'I'd like to tether you to the trestle for a thorough paddling,' Karel Kromhout answered, 'Then arch you over the punishment rack to taste my riding crop on the bare.'

'And how would you like to re-educate her, Justus?' the owner asked softly.

'She's most shamed by the prospect of being thrashed by another woman,' Justus said evenly, 'Which is why I've invited Sadie, my rigorous friend.'

Ruth bolted for the door, but the tall woman raced after her and held her fast. 'Sweetheart, I hear that you want to preserve your marriage. We won't tell your husband of your latest adultery if you accept a thorough tanning from me.'

'Is there no other way?' Ruth stalled.

'No - take it or leave it.'

What choice did she have? She didn't want to lose the luxurious way of life she enjoyed in Britain. She didn't want to lose her husband and her home and have to start all over again. Ruth nodded her head, feeling very apprehensive but resigned to her punishment. 'Okay just get it over with.'

'If only - it takes a long time to thrash out persistent adultery,' the Amazonian woman said, flexing her large right palm.

Karel Kromhout laughed hoarsely. 'Start with the cane, Sadie, and give her more stripes than a zebra. It gets quick results.'

Sadie smiled mirthlessly - but Ruth had nothing to smile about as she felt the older woman yanking down her jeans and protective panties. 'Not yet, Karel, her flesh is too soft to immediately bear the rattan. It would slice her tender globes and it's one of my rules to never break the skin. No, I'll spank her for a good half hour first to prepare the skin before applying the rod.' To Ruth's chagrin, she hoisted her, bare bummed, over her shoulder. 'Right, love, lets get you to the Punishment Chamber so that Auntie Sadie can sort you out.'

She'd survived being spanked by Karel Kromhout, and even thrashed by Justus Lederwaren, so surely being finger-whipped by a woman wouldn't hurt as much, Ruth told herself as she was carried into the main chastisement area.

Sadie sat down in an armless chair, still holding Ruth tight. 'Stretch out your arms and legs, dear,' she said. Ruth did so. Sadie beckoned to one of the others who had clearly followed behind to see the discipline session unfold. 'Can you fasten her wrists and ankles to the rings in the floor?'

When Ruth was firmly held in place across the stronger woman's lap, Sadie issued another instruction. 'Justus, can you bring me a leather spanking glove with a hardened palm?'

Ruth's main view was of the carpet, but she caught a quick glimpse of the heavy black glove as it was carried past her. 'Auntie Sadie's going to make little Ruth very sorry,' the older woman said.

'I'm already repentant,' Ruth mumbled awkwardly.

'You'll be kissing the glove and begging for forgiveness by the time I've finished with you,' came the contemptuous reply.

The spanking which followed felt more like a wood-based paddling. Each slap of the heavier woman's hand sent the younger girl's buttocks flattening inwards, only to bounce back again a redder shade. Ruth couldn't see her own anguished movements - but she could well imagine them. To make matters worse, Sadie kept up a relentlessly disparaging commentary. 'Oh, your tender young buttock didn't like that. Ouch, nor did its neighbour. Oh, that little bum hole is puckering up at the thought of what's going to happen next.'

Eventually she stopped the relentless whacks and took off the glove and caressed Ruth's flaming spheres for long cringeworthy moments. 'Right, angel, let's get you over the whipping stool so that your bum's nicely presented for the rod.'

'I've never been caned before,' Ruth whispered as the woman marched her towards the slanted tall stool.

'It'll make you squirm like you're being stung. And you'll certainly sing for your supper,' the dominatrix said.

Again Justus helped to position Ruth in place, whilst Karel Kromhout and the other trainee Masters watched lasciviously from the sidelines. 'Put a cushion under her tummy to raise her to the maximum,' Sadie said.

'Gee, thanks,' Ruth muttered.

'You can thank me in a moment. First, ask nicely for stroke one,' Sadie said.

'Please give me stroke one,' Ruth muttered shamefacedly into the middle distance.

The cane flashed against her extremities and she yelled loudly, her arse on fire.

'That was an extra stroke for not trying hard enough. You're still due the full twelve,' her punisher said.

'What do you want me to say?' Ruth muttered, squeezing her bum cheeks hard in a futile bid to shake off the anguish.

'Say something like "Please warm my naughty cheeks till I absolutely can't bear it." But don't use these exact words. Use your imagination,' Sadie said.

'Please birch my bottom till it trembles,' Ruth whispered then was told to repeat it loudly for the benefit of the listening crowd.

Thereafter, the first official stroke emblazoned its way across her prepared flesh and she wailed long and hard in protest. Then she looked for the words to ask for stroke two. 'I deserve to flinch under the rod again, Mistress.'

'Yes, you do,' Sadie agreed, standing back and lining up the hellish rattan. This stroke went lower than the first and livened the most sensitive part of a female posterior, where it curves under to meet the thighs.

Ruth squealed and squirmed against the cruelly-positioned cushion and promised loudly that she'd never cheat on her husband again.

'We're just going to talk about the shade of your arse for the next hour,' the cane-wielding woman warned, 'Now how much hotter do you think it's going to be?'

'Very hot,' Ruth whispered nervously, skulking about in situ.

'Practically sizzling,' Sadie agreed.

She swished the rattan across Ruth's tender divide so that Ruth gave a prolonged groan and arched her haunches the little she could before flattening her belly back against the whipping stool. She could tell by her movements that she must look like the back end of a weakly bucking horse.

'Such a pretty picture,' the dominatrix said, 'You'd almost think that arse was trying to escape from me. Doesn't it realise that it has to stay?' She caned Ruth again then snapped 'Answer, girl.'

'Yes, Miss.' Ruth sought out further humiliating words. 'I have to stay to taste the cane till it gives me the sorest bottom. I have to learn humility,' she said.

The cane swished down and down and down. By the twelfth, Ruth was reduced to helpless sobbing. 'I'll never commit adultery again,' she whispered, 'I'll be the perfect wife.'

Justus Lederwaren approached her and kissed the top of her head. 'Dear Ruth, if only. You haven't been progressing at all well so Sadie's going to train you at her own Chamber in the annexe for a while.'

'You mean I'll be alone with her? Please, anything but that,' Ruth whispered as the other trainee Masters lifted her from the whipping stool. 'She's so very strict.'

'Exactly. She'll soon leather you into tip top shape,' Karel Kromhout cut in.

As Ruth snivelled on the ground, Sadie approached her and buckled a dog collar around her neck. 'Let's take you for walkies.'

‘Have these with my compliments to help you control her.’ Karel Kromhout fastened spreader bars to Ruth’s wrists and ankles so that she couldn’t crawl too fast.

‘What are you going to do to me?’ Ruth mumbled as she crawled in front of Sadie on her leash, heading for one of the doors at the far side of the building.

‘I’m going to teach you to sit up and beg, to give a paw, to be a good little dog,’ the stronger woman said.

‘And if I won’t?’ Ruth’s pride fought against the humiliating orders.

‘If you don’t you’ll get your arse tanned again and again.’

And suddenly Ruth knew that the previous weeks had been a mere rehearsal for the training that was to follow, that her real re-education had just begun...

It Could Be You

Chloe cheered as the wind-powered town clock struck midnight. A snowflake fell, bringing forth another excited roar from the drunken crowds. There had been so much global warming of late that a flurry of snow was a cause for much rejoicing. The New Year was off to an auspicious start.

'Let's go wild tonight!' Emma whooped, slugging back another half tin of lager. Chloe hesitated, wondering what her best friend had in mind. Emma had the courage of a thirty year old revolutionary, even though she was a hair extension consultant aged twenty-two.

Now Emma started to steer her away from the Hogmanay crowds. 'I know how we can get access to The Game,' she said excitedly, 'Big Game. We're talking thousands if your numbers are called.'

'And we're talking about the sorest backsides in Christendom if we get caught buying a ticket,' Chloe replied in a tense low voice. She shivered at the thought of publicly baring her bottom. She'd never had a spanking, far less a thorough caning before. And the State Caning Machine seemingly ignored a female convict's pleading, was supposed to stripe her cheeks the hottest red.

'Hey, it's the New Year. Do you really think that the Anti-Betting Boys in Blue are going to be out looking for the likes of us?' Emma scoffed haughtily, 'We just need one big win and we'll never have to work again!'

And so it was that Chloe found herself following her friend down a series of tunnels to an enormous factory basement. Emma muttered a password, and the girl on the door beckoned them in.

Both girls bought ten tickets each then crossed their fingers. The hour passed slowly. They sipped cranberry juice cocktails as they waited for the lottery winners to be announced. 'This is the last time I'm coming here,' muttered the bearded man at the next table, 'My brother got a state caning yesterday. You should see the colour of the poor guy's arse.'

'Is it true that they can vary the severity of the caning machine?' Chloe started to ask with bashful curiosity.

'Ssssssh!' everyone else said as the successful numbers appeared on the satellite screen.

'Damn,' Chloe muttered a couple of minutes later, crinkling up her tickets, 'I haven't been lucky.'

'You certainly haven't,' said a voice in her ear. 'I'm from the Anti-Betting Squad. The disciplinary rod awaits.'

Twenty minutes later Chloe watched through a glass panel as Emma was led into the State Caning Room. A uniformed male policeman held her right arm and marched her towards the automatic mechanical punisher. 'Disrobe from the waist down,' he said matter-of-factly, 'Then bend over the whipping stool and grip the lower bar to hold yourself in place.'

'That's easy for you to say,' Emma sulked. Her fingers fumbled against the button of her jeans, then she reluctantly pulled down the close-fitting denim. She shrugged the garment off then hesitated, her fingers on the waistband of her silken pants. 'Couldn't I just keep my briefs on, Mr Policeman?' she asked humbly, 'The material's thin so it would just be for modesty's sake.'

'Section 2A of the Bottomley Act demands that the illegal gambler be naked of posterior,' the policeman answered, staring at her with mild impatience.

'What if I don't comply with your rules?' Emma shot back. Chloe was glad to see her friend showing such verve and spirit. She wondered if she'd be so brave when her own turn came.

'A failure to comply with the rules can lead to extra hard cane strokes,' the man replied, 'And we have three bachelor security guards who are very eager to undress a naughty young delinquent,' he added with a smile. 'Their fingers have been known to stray up vaginal and anal passages as they pull down a recalcitrant girl's pants.' He looked at her own tautly-knickered crotch, his eyes assessing, 'Shall I call them all in?'

'No - please don't do that.' Emma licked her lips then turned her body so that her stomach rather than her arse was towards the restless official, then she slowly pulled down her bikini briefs. Chloe could see apprehension in her friend's blue eyes - apprehension and a cautious excitement. Emma was obviously rising to the challenge of all this.

'Bend over the whipping stool,' the officer said again.

Emma took a deep breath then obeyed him. Chloe watched her friend's bare bottom quiver slightly as it neared its painful fate. What must poor Emma be thinking and feeling? She, Chloe, just wanted to escape.

But that would earn her further correction for resisting arrest, so all she could do was watch her friend's chastisement. Watch and learn, knowing that this striping would fall on her own small buttocks next. 'Ten strokes for the purchase of ten lottery tickets,' said the robotic overhead voice which presumably always passed sentence, 'First time offender, so State Caning Machine is to be set at level three.'

The policeman did something to a square machine at one side of Emma's bum. That same bum twitched, obviously aware that its punishment was growing nearer. It was a wonderfully smooth and defenceless bum, Chloe thought, with a rush of lust and shame. At the moment both hemispheres were a uniform creamy shade, a firm peach of perfection. A tiny part of Chloe's psyche wanted to see the flesh striped a glowing red. Emma had gotten her into this fix, she told herself with a little rush of devilment. She deserved to writhe under the swishy cane.

'Stroke one,' ordered the robotic voice. Chloe looked back to see that Emma's fingers were tightly gripping the low bar of the punishment stool, bare feet resting in the grooves of the crossbar. It was a position which elevated her extremities to their utmost, resulting in an erring and very sorry looking bare arse.

'Let the official punishment commence,' the policeman said. As Chloe stared, a long judicial cane came mechanically out of the machine. Obviously Emma couldn't see it. She sensed or heard it, though, for her body puckered up some more. The cane was attached to a metal arm which seemed inordinately flexible. That same arm pulled the rod back, back, back, then whacked it forward into Emma's waiting flesh.

The twenty-two year old's bottom jerked and both slender thighs stiffened for at least ten seconds, then Emma seemed to push her tummy more fully into the wooden stool. The muscles in her bum tightened then slowly relaxed again as they realised the first cane stroke was over. After another few seconds her shoulders also untensed.

The mechanical cane seemed to know that the transgressor was ready for cane stripe two. Either that, or someone watching the punishment was pushing the activator button. Whatever, the long rod struck again and the state's newest prisoner yelped and groaned. A second thin pink line appeared on the undercurve of Emma's pale bum, below the first stripe. They were almost parallel across the twitching creamy flesh. Chloe winced in sympathy for her friend but still watched, mesmerised. 'She's wriggling that arse so prettily,' a male voice said.

Chloe looked around in shock and surprise. It was an older policeman who had spoken. He was standing behind her and staring fixedly at the punishment scene. 'I like a backside with a bit of life in it,' he continued, watching through the glass as Emma's bum wriggled under the rod again, 'Especially one as cute as this.'

'She's my best friend,' Chloe muttered, wishing that the man wouldn't talk so crudely.

'Then you can compare red stripe marks afterwards,' the fifty year old replied with a lazy grin.

Chloe stared back at him with wide eyed apprehension: 'I've never been caned before, far less in public. Isn't there another way...?'

'Are you offering me a good time?' he asked, clear interest lighting up his eyes.

Chloe hesitated, not wanting to have full sex with the man yet longing to control the situation. 'I could please you with my hand,' she murmured, curling her ringless fingers into an inviting sheath.

'Oh dear, trying to bribe an official with sexual favours. That's perverting the course of justice,' the man said sadly, 'Which earns you another two sore strokes.'

God, no! She'd tried to wriggle out of her ordeal and only succeeded in making the situation worse. Chloe pushed her weight down more firmly on her pencil skirt clad bum as if to make access to it difficult. 'But that makes twelve. It'll be agony,' she moaned.

'You should have thought of that before you broke the law, young Miss,' the policeman said.

Knowing that he was right, Chloe moved her gaze back in time to see the mechanical rod being lined up with Emma's lower half again. The poor girl had been getting caned for some time and her bum looked like that of a luminous zebra. Now it tensed and quivered as she waited for another judicial stroke.

Chloe licked her lips at the thought of her own nether cheeks being so vulnerably displayed. The shame must be daunting. *At least it's not personal,* she told herself. *It's an impartial machine which lays on the cane.*

Emma took her last stroke and lay over the stool for a while whimpering quietly. It was clear to both watching policemen and to Chloe that she'd never break the anti-gambling law again. Gently the policeman who had been overseeing her punishment helped her up and steered her out of the gallery. The older man then turned to Chloe. 'Time for your flogging, girlie,' he said with an eager grin.

Together they walked towards the newly vacated whipping stool. 'Let's have that skirt and those panties off,' the man continued. Remembering what he'd said about procrastination, Chloe reluctantly removed her skirt then pulled down her pants.

'State Caning Machine has malfunctioned. Have paged all electronic engineers to report for duty to fix it,' the robotic voice of the intercom suddenly said.

'Paged all engineers? There's only two of them,' the official laughed, rolling his brown eyes heavenwards.

'I thought that *lots* of people wanted to be engineers,' Chloe gasped with growing dread.

The policeman shrugged. 'They did until the government stopped giving out university grants.' He smiled. 'Nowadays we've a very small skilled workforce. Speaking of which, what do you do yourself?'

'I record talking books,' Chloe said.

'Thought you had a nice voice,' the officer replied amicably. He slapped one palm against the other. 'Well, now it's about to squeal.'

'But I thought the caning machine was broken?' Chloe said, looking hopefully at her discarded skirt and panties.

'It is. Means I have to use manual intervention,' the policeman replied.

'You mean you'll cane me by hand?' the twenty-two year old muttered, taking a step back then covering her bare bum with her spread-apart small fingers.

'It's a difficult job but someone's got to do it,' the older man confirmed with a sardonic look.

Worse and worse. Chloe searched for ways to delay her punishment a little longer. 'Can't I come back when the machine is fixed?' she asked.

'No, correction must be carried out within six hours of arrest,' the official said. He put his hands on her naked cheeks and started to steer her towards the whipping stool, 'Best get the striping started. Your friend's eager to see the show.'

The twenty-two year old's belly tingled with excitement and ongoing shame. 'You mean Emma's watching?' Chloe asked, peering fruitlessly at the one way window. She'd half enjoyed watching her friend receive a state caning, but she felt quite different now that her own rump was on full display.

'Yes, public humiliation is part of the corrective process,' the policeman explained, 'Usually we have queues waiting to see the wrongdoers taking their canings. It's only because its Hogmanay that the public gallery is almost bare.'

Bare like her bum. Chloe looked for a way to take the warden's mind off the birching she had due. 'Why is buying a lottery ticket so terrible?' she asked quickly.

'You're obviously too young to remember the year two thousand,' said the man. He sighed. 'I was born that very year, so when I was older my parents told me all the details. I knew then that I wanted to stamp out such gambling vice.'

He bent Chloe over the whipping stool. 'Right, girlie, raise your arse in the air whilst I tell you the rest of the story. That way you'll connect the crime with the punishment even more fully and hopefully won't be foolish enough to repeat the offence.'

Slowly Chloe wrapped her hands around the stool legs and placed her feet in the grooves. Her bottom was displayed like the full moon and felt hugely vulnerable. 'I really am sorry,' she whispered ingratiatingly.

'We find that criminals are even more sorry once their bums have been warmed,' the official added. He ran a palm over Chloe's naked haunches and she shivered with pleasure and the fear of pain.

'As I was saying,' the man continued, 'When the lottery began in the mid nineteen nineties it was supposed to be a bit of fun, an occasional diversion. Unfortunately the organisers hadn't allowed sufficiently for human weakness and human greed.' He adjusted Chloe's naked haunches so that they squirmed more centrally on the stool, 'Some people started spending most of their income on tickets and scratchcards, then they'd shoplift to make ends meet. When they still didn't win they started to rob people of their savings in order to buy more lottery tickets.'

'So law and order was breaking down and the lottery became illegal,' Chloe muttered, wondering how her bare bottom looked to the watching man and woman, 'Thanks for explaining all the anti-betting propaganda. Now I understand.'

'If you'd taken the time to understand before then this naughty backside wouldn't be facing a roasting,' the anti-gambling policeman said in a heartfelt tone.

His words seemed to remind him of her fate. Leastways he walked towards the cupboard and brought out a long thin cane with a thicker curved handle. 'Twelve strokes coming up,' he warned, walking up behind her exposed soft curves.

'Couldn't you just settle for the original ten?' Chloe muttered.

'No, your proposition was lewd. Being punished for it will stop you becoming a woman of easy virtue,' her dominator said.

'Yeah? And what will it take to stop you being a sadist?' Chloe asked jeeringly.

Then she squealed and shoved her tummy into the whipping stool as the cane whacked against her bent-over cheeks.

'This is state-sanctioned chastisement. Would you rather go to prison?' the man replied.

'Christ, no,' the twenty-two year old gasped with feeling.

'Then ask nicely for the second stroke,' the policeman said.

The room fell silent as Chloe mused over this latest demand. 'What if I don't?' she asked, not wanting to say the words which would immediately continue her chastisement.

'If you don't then my arm may get annoyed and may start to cane harder,' the official replied.

'Don't cane harder,' Chloe yelped, already hugely aware of her inaugural stripe. She marshalled her resources, reminding herself that humiliation was part of the rehabilitation process, that it was for her own good. 'Please sir,' she whispered ashamedly, 'I deserve a second sore swish of the cane.'

The official obliged. Chloe felt the rod heating the centre of her small soft globes. She drummed her feet against the stool's grooves and wailed for thirty seconds. In truth the pain was bearable but she was already thinking ahead to how she'd feel by stroke twelve. 'I clearly haven't lost my touch,' said the man, 'Both stripes are very comely. But there's far too much white flesh left...'

Chloe shivered. She knew that he intended to redden each centimetre of her unclothed orbs. She wished again that she hadn't broken the law, hadn't listened to Emma. Remembering that her friend was watching, she resolved to act unfazed.

'I don't hear you begging for stroke three,' the policeman said.

'That's because I haven't said anything,' Chloe muttered. The man laid on the third stroke immediately and she groaned.

'Did that one sting more than the others, my lawbreaking friend? You brought it on yourself,' he said softly.

'Please, sir,' Chloe whispered, 'I've been a naughty girl who deserves another stripe.'

She winced as the official put that same red band in place. Now she was a third of the way through her punishment. She wondered if Emma was enjoying the naked view.

'Now where shall I put the fifth stripe?' the policeman said.

'Surprise me,' Chloe muttered. He was such a gloating bastard that she felt obliged to verbally fight.

To her shame, the man took her at her word. 'Well, I could aim the rod at the tender area above your legs,' he murmured thoughtfully, 'That makes your bottom jerk real hard before it gets back into position. Or I could warm you just a little further up so that one stripe lies beside the next.' He hesitated, and Chloe sensed that he was lining up the cane with her cheeks again. She pushed her tummy more fully against the whipping stool's seat. 'One part of me wants to toast a new section of buttock just to see the line appear,' the man continued thoughtfully, 'Another part wants to make an existing mark a more heated red.'

Striping a new section of her arse obviously won, for the guilty party felt the man laying the cane on a previously untouched centimetre of her raised bare bottom. She muttered obscenities under her breath as he applied the long thin rod to her creamy right sphere. 'Now, now, be nice to the kindly policeman,' he mocked, doling out the sixth stroke to her left.

A moment later he swished on the seventh and the eighth. Chloe could tell that he wasn't moving his arm very far back - but then he didn't have to. She was finding out that even a small swish of the cane thoroughly disciplined her sentient helplessness. What on earth had possessed her to break the law when she'd known that a caning was the penalty? She'd just never envisaged baring her bottom like this.

The ninth stroke landed on the delicate crease above her thighs and almost unnerved her. Chloe gave an animalistic little cry and started to rise. She scrambled awkwardly to her feet then put both hands over her punished haunches, rubbing furiously at the latest pain.

'Section 5B states that...' the policeman started, jerking his finger towards a set of rules on the wall. He looked at her steadily. 'If you don't bend back over the stool of your own accord you'll get two extra lashes of the tawse on your naked bum.'

'But it's so sore already,' Chloe whispered, holding her stinging twin rotundities.

'Of course its sore. It's punishment, isn't it? If you'd been sent to prison you'd lose your freedom. This way you only lose your dignity for an hour.'

An hour of the cane. Chloe's lower lip trembled. 'Can't I have an early pardon or something?' she asked, 'I admit that my behaviour was wrong.'

'Your friend Emma took her ten strokes. You've only had nine and you're making a fuss,' the official said sternly. His features softened, 'If you ask for the remaining strokes real sweetly I'll apply them at level two rather than level three.'

'I'll ask sweetly, sir,' Chloe promised in her most sincere yet breathy voice. The man looked at his watch and tutted loudly. Anxious not to keep him waiting, she turned and faced the judicial whipping stool.

Bending back over it took all the resources she possessed. For a few moments she'd held her bum safely in her cupped hands and massaged away the anguish. Now she had to obscenely display it again.

'Don't be shy. I've been warming that arse for the last half hour,' the officer said with a shallow laugh, 'I've seen it wriggling like an earthworm.' Chloe wondered if he taunted the male culprits with equal verve.

But she didn't have time to muse over the workings of the man's mind. She had to concentrate on getting through her official chastisement. 'Let's hear that bum begging for its tenth correction,' the policeman said.

Chloe sought for the most debasing words, knowing that they'd make her disciplining lighter. He'd made it clear that if she shamed herself he wouldn't lay on the judicial rod so hard. It was fair in a way, she thought. After all, the object of the exercise was to make sure that she didn't become a repeat offender. If she was thoroughly humiliated she'd never play the illegal lottery again!

'I've been very bad. I need the cane. I deserve it,' she muttered stiltedly.

'Not so coy next time,' said the man, 'Say something like "Sir, I deserve a hot sore reddened arse".'

As Chloe searched for the words, he applied the tenth stroke to the pinkened centre of her hapless flesh.

The twenty-two year old yelped, then searched for the phrases which would result in a lighter eleventh mark. 'My bare bottom's so sore, sir,' she whispered, 'That I'd give anything to sit in a tub of deep cool water.' She hesitated, then continued contritely, 'But I know that you're going to make it a hotter and better arse.'

'My cane will do that,' the policeman confirmed, 'It's a tool of transformation. Especially when I swish it just *there*.' He whacked it against Chloe's curvy underswell, and she moved her hips from side to side then forced them to still into position. 'I'm just wondering,' the official continued, 'Where to apply stroke twelve?'

Chloe tried to find an answer that her chastiser would like. 'That's up to you, sir,' she murmured, 'After all, my bottom is yours for official punishment.'

'And is that bad bottom sorry?' the man prompted, his voice holding a rueful smile.

Chloe's tone was heartfelt even to her own ears: 'Yes, sir. God, yes. It's very sorry.' She shivered as she felt the rod being run up and down her curves.

'Your soft pale skin has turned hot all over,' the policeman said softly, 'It's making me angry cause I can't find a single white space.'

I could take a raincheck, Chloe thought, but she daren't say it. Instead she waited, her reddened bottom sticking up in the air.

'I can't hear you,' said the man.

Chloe sucked in her breath. 'Sir, I've broken the law and...'

'No, your *naughty backside* has broken the law. Let's not be bashful. Let's call a disobedient arse by its proper name.'

The girl exhaled. Damn, he was going to shame her till the very last cane stroke. The man was such a cad.

But the cad was wielding the cane and her body was a vulnerable raised target. She'd humiliate herself to reach her sentence's end. 'Sir, my bottom's been really bad. You were right to make me pull down my pants and bend over the whipping stool. I'm asking you nicely for a last sore taste of the cane.'

'How can I refuse such a cutely said plea?' the official murmured. He squeezed her cheeks preparingly for a few moments then Chloe felt the rod heating the place just above her thighs.

'Aaah!' she gasped, then lay there for a while after her disciplining ended, feeling the strength flow back into her upper limbs.

After tea and sympathy, the two friends left the building. They'd walked three streets when they saw a slightly younger girl buying illegal raffle tickets. 'Don't do it,' Chloe said, rushing over to her and knocking the ticket book away.

The girl looked alarmed then scornful. 'What's it to you? You're not the anti-betting boys.'

'No, I'm a recent ex-offender,' Chloe sighed.

'Took a bit of a spanking, did you?' the girl jeered, 'I'm not scared of a slapping.'

Chloe shifted from foot to foot: 'It was much more than that.'

She hesitated, hating the prospect of further displaying herself. Then she decided that her actions were an act of true philanthropy, were for the greater good. Slowly she turned round and bent forward until her hands were touching her toes, her head hanging. Then she lifted up her skirt to reveal both scarlet globes and murmured 'It could be you.'

Pretty In Pink

'I'm sorry, Ma'am - the tray just slipped from my hands,' Betty-Ann whispered as she knelt on the floor surrounded by the Master's best crystal. If only she hadn't been daydreaming again. 'You can cancel my days off for a year!' she continued, mind searching for a suitably shame-free punishment. She knew all too well what could happen to disorganised young serving wenches' bums.

'Just fetch the razor strop then set your belly across the kitchen table,' the Housekeeper snapped, beginning to sweep up shards of crystal decanter, 'And contemplate the whipping you're about to get.'

'As you wish, Ma'am.' Betty-Ann curtseyed low, then hesitated, wondering what a thrashing would feel like. She'd been a servant in the Big House for three whole years, which was ample time to see the razor strop used on various pleading backsides. And the Housekeeper was well known for short temper and her especially strong right arm.

But to delay would just earn her a further welting. Obediently Betty-Ann walked towards the door of the kitchen, praying that she wouldn't find Cook or any of the serving wenches loitering. To be chastened by the Housekeeper was abasement enough, but to be disciplined whilst others employed at The Big House looked on...

The razor strop was two feet long with a rounded end. It was fashioned of thick brown leather. The twenty-one year old stared up at it for a dry-mouthed moment, then she unhooked it from its place on the wall. Gently she ran her middle fingers along its length, feeling the frayed texture caused by its slapping against luckless bottom after bottom. Men and women in senior positions were always punishing the more junior staff.

She, Betty-Ann, had only been punished once before, and that had been by a hand which doled out a thorough spanking. She'd been eighteen at the time - it had been her first week here. The long hours and the early morning winter chill had gotten her head quite muddled, and she'd put bleach in the cottons when she was supposed to use starch. 'But I can't read, Ma'am!' she'd protested, as the grey-haired Laundress pushed up her skirts and pulled down her pants.

Unswayed, the older woman had bent Betty-Ann over her bony knee, and started slapping. 'You should've taken a telling,' she'd replied, 'Starch is in the red urn, bleach in the blue.'

That spanking had hurt so much. The Laundress had had big hands - rough, wash-toughened hands. They'd felt like sandpaper on Betty-Ann's tender spheres.

Having her naked cheeks spanked had made her quake. She'd blushed and kept her head right down. She'd stared at the cold slate floors and tried to think romantic thoughts about finding a husband. But after a moment or two of hard slaps she'd only been able to think of her poor sore backside. She'd let out a sob, and the Laundress had said 'Stop snivelling or I'll really give you something to cry about.' Betty-Ann's howls had seemed to enrage her: she'd lashed especially hard at both buttocks after that.

Now, as Betty-Ann lowered herself over the kitchen table, she wondered what the razor strop would feel like. How many strokes would the Housekeeper give her? How long would the pause between the whackings last? Some of the girls ran up to their attic rooms after they'd tasted the cane or the birch, and when they came down again their faces were all soft and relaxed and they seemed gently contented. Betty-Ann couldn't imagine what caused that.

She was very aware of her rough serge bloomers being on display now that she'd lifted her own skirts up as she'd been told to. Would the Housekeeper mock their thin cream countenance? They were all she could afford. The bloomer legs went halfway down her thighs, which would afford her poor extremities some protection. She'd seen Daisy the Seamstress taking the belt once and the leather had struck low and pinkened her plump white thighs.

It was warm here in the Kitchen. Betty-Ann flapped her arms to create a draught. She knew one part of her was about to get warmer. She'd seen the other maids touching each other's red rumps and marvelling at the heat. She'd been such a good girl until now that she'd never had to endure such a thrashing, had never known more than a few harsh words from the senior members of the House.

'Been thinking about what's coming to you next, have you?' The Housekeeper marched in. Her heels made angry clicking sounds on the flagons. Long years of being in-service had added a brisk seniority to her tone.

'Y- yes, Ma'am,' Betty-Ann stammered, raising her pleading large eyes to meet the woman's, but keeping her face down against the table top.

'At least you've got your skirts raised and the strop ready,' the forty year old continued, 'First instructions of mine you've carried out properly this week, you dreamy girl.'

'I'll do better,' Betty-Ann whispered. She tensed her buttocks as the woman moved behind her and picked up the hellish strop.

'You'll do better with a well-warmed bum. Never fails with the other serving wenches.' She pushed Betty-Ann's skirts even further up her back, and pulled her bloomers more tightly against her bottom, 'This thrashing isn't just for ruining the Master's best brandy goblets, you know.'

'Yes, Ma'am. I understand that, Ma'am.' The last thing Betty-Ann wanted was a rehash of her last fortnight's crimes and their possible penalties.

'You put away the china in the wrong cupboards. You've been late lighting the fire of a morning. You've let the silver service sets get tarnished. Why, if the Master was to hear...'

'He's heard!'

Both women jumped and turned their heads in the direction of the rich low voice. Betty-Ann shut her eyes seconds after they feasted on her employer. Behind her, the changing currents of the air told of the Housekeeper's long low curtsey: 'I'm about to remind the girl of her duties, Sire. That is, if it fares well with you?'

Betty-Ann held her breath: what would the man say? He'd always been such a generous and understanding employer. But she was guilty of so many recent wrongs...

'You use the strop on her bloomers rather than on her bare seat?' The man sounded intrigued. Betty-Ann cringed as the lord of the manor walked round to stare at her extremities. He was a good looking man of some thirty-eight summers. Most of the older girls in the Big House hoped that he'd look on them with especial favour some day. She, Betty-Ann, had always worn her best frilled cap and apron in his presence. Now he was staring at the thin creamy bloomers which Housekeeper had pulled tight against her rear.

'Yes, I strop her over her cami-knickers, Sire. It spares her modesty a little, Sire. And the strop is hard enough even through the material to teach her rump the error of its ways.'

'Go ahead then, Miss Krell. I'll just pull up a chair and watch you put her through her paces.'

Oh, this was degrading! Betty-Ann trembled as she heard the scrape of the kitchen stool's legs on the floor. She turned her head to the side and squinted back. Her usually kindly Master was sitting about three feet behind her bum. He was looking at it with coolly academic interest.

'If you'd rather...?' The Housekeeper held out the leather punisher to him. The waiting servant held her breath.

'No, no. I've been hearing reports of her many sins this past month or two, so after you've taught her the work ethic I intend to discipline her myself.'

Worse and worse! Betty-Ann bit her lip at the sire's cold words, then she opened her mouth and gasped as the strop lashed her unsuspecting right buttock. The gasp turned into a squeal as the woman walloped the knickered orb five times.

'Let's make the other cheek the same, shall we, love?' she murmured gloatingly, and Betty-Ann shuddered anew as her left globe was treated to the same fiery focus. She ached for permission to put her hands back to protect her lower self.

'Ask the girl why she's been so lax,' the Master said.

'I know that without asking, Sire. She's been walking out with Jackson the carriage driver. Keeps her out to all hours on her day off, and she sneaks out to the yard to see him when she's supposed to be following my instructions in the house.'

'Is this true, girl?' the lord of the manor enquired.

Betty-Ann shuddered, but knew that whispered lies would simply earn her a sorer bottom. 'Yes, Sire, but I'm really sorry, Sire. From now on I'll concentrate fully on your employ,' she said.

The man laughed low in his throat: 'As the person who gives you food and a roof over your head, I'm glad to hear it. But for now I just want you to concentrate on the horrid stinging strokes that Miss Krell has been forced to dish out.'

'Yes, M'Lord,' Betty-Ann squealed as the Housekeeper laid on the strop again. The leather hit low down her thighs, sending her cami-knickers flattening against the curves of her cheeks.

'A dozen!' the Housekeeper said with some satisfaction, 'Sire - should I thrash her more?'

'No - I'll take over now.' Betty-Ann bit her lip. 'Stand up and face me, girl,' the man continued. Betty-Ann got up carefully from the table and turned his way. Staring at the ground before him, she smoothed down her skirt in an absent-minded gesture. 'You won't be keeping that over your haunches for long,' her Master said. He looked her up and down. 'Go into the sitting room and push the three chaise longues and the armchairs back against the wall. I'll join you in a moment.' The girl hastened on uncertain legs to do what she was bid.

Ordinarily she loved this room, adored its heavy purple velvet curtains and chintz settees, but now it was to be the scene of her further ignominy. If only she'd obeyed Housekeeper's earlier warnings and caught up with her sleep and her chores. A Master could thrash his servant very hard indeed: it was the rule of the land, it was a house rule. She'd been lucky to lodge with a Master who didn't dole out whippings for each small misdemeanour. But now...

She curtseyed almost to the ground as the man strode into the room. 'Sire, I've cleared a space as you asked.'

'Good girl, now fetch the whipping stool and bring it here.' He pointed to the area she'd cleared on the carpet. Afraid yet curious, Betty-Ann went to the cellar and brought out the low wooden contraption with the padded top.

With difficulty, for it was both heavy and ungainly, she carried it back into the vast sitting room and put it down where the chaise longue had recently been. The Master smiled at her approvingly then he tugged the bell that called for every member of staff to assemble in the room.

The butler came first. His eyes didn't even flicker when they rested on Betty-Ann's flushed face: 'Can I help you, M'Lord?'

'You can stay and watch this lazy disobedient girl take her thrashing.' As the kitchen staff, gardeners, pageboys and wardrobe women hurried through the doors they were told the very same thing.

At last the entire staff was assembled round the walls of the room. 'You're here to watch me make an example of Betty-Ann,' the Master said, 'As most of you know, she was a quality serving maid until six weeks ago, when she started walking out with a certain gentleman.' Jackson reddened and hung his head. Betty-Ann looked away from her embarrassed beau. 'I'm a fair man,' the Master of the house continued, 'I overlooked the decline in her work, her increasing lateness. But today she ruined a crystal gift from a friend in Germany which can never be replaced.'

A low murmur of disapproval filtered from the staff, and several of them scowled at Betty-Ann and shook their heads. 'I'm going to put paid to her laziness and daydreaming now by baring her bottom for six of the cane,' the man added. He turned to the blushing servant girl, 'Get in place over the whipping stool and raise your skirts.'

Not looking at the others, Betty-Ann obeyed. The padded top seemed to push up her tummy in the centre so that her buttocks felt raised and slightly spread. 'Now pull down your knickers,' the gentleman added matter-of-factly. Never had she felt so ashamed.

Yet she daren't disobey him. Slowly Betty-Ann pulled the well-washed garments to her knees to reveal her posterior. She was glad that she was facing away from the watchful women and men.

'Stroke one coming up,' said her Master's voice. She felt the currents of air around her backside change, then a burning line was branded over her sit-upon. Betty-Ann gasped at its unexpected intensity, but kept her bare bottom in place. 'Stroke two,' added the man. This one went lower than the first, left the area feeling even more tender. Stroke three warmed the plump backs of her thighs.

'I'll be a good maid from now on, sir,' she cried out, as she sensed him line up the rod for the next lash.

'You'll be better after half a dozen of these have seared your rump, girl,' the man retorted. Betty-Ann closed her eyes tightly as she realised he was going to dole out all six.

The fourth was the unkindest cut of all. It seemed to retrace its predecessor's harsh glow, redoubled the hotness at her poor leg tops. Acting on instinct, Betty-Ann scrambled backwards then leapt to her feet.

Flushing hotly, she held her sore bottom and stared at the assembled staff. The Housekeeper shook her head. Jackson looked away. The butler winked lasciviously. Slowly Betty-Ann moved her gaze towards the Master. His look showed disapproval, disappointment. He'd been such a kind employer so far...

'I'm sorry, Sire. I'll take the last two strokes and extra ones for getting up without permission, Sire,' she mumbled, apologetically. Shuffling back to the punishment trestle, cami-knickers now at her ankles, she got back into place.

Lifting her skirts up again was the worst part, as, for a few blissful moments, they had flapped down to conceal her naked haunches. Now she reluctantly pulled each layer back to show her shy striped cheeks.

'So pretty in pink,' the lord of the manor said softly, 'Can I inspect these parts more closely later on?'

'Yes, Sire. Whatever you say, Sire,' Betty-Ann whispered, her feminine core flooding with both mortification and arousal. Even Jackson had just tumbled her in the carriage by lifting her petticoats, had never seen her nether parts fully bare.

But for now her bare bottom was all that the man wanted to see. The maidservant winced as he further tenderised her small buttocks with stroke five. It pained her curviest parts and made her squeal and wriggle. He laid on the final lash just above the section where arse curves in to thigh. 'Betty-Ann, come lie across my knee and let me inspect my handiwork. Everyone else can go.'

Was this better? Worse? Wonderful to get rid of her shaming audience, awful to have to lie over his knee!

But he was her Master - it was her duty to please him. And a small increasingly womanly part of her wanted to please him in every way. He was so handsome, normally so kind, so thoughtful and learned. If she could only win his favour again...

'I'm waiting, Betty-Ann.' He still sounded stern. Trembling she pushed herself off of the punishment stool and approached him, keeping her gaze trained on the ground. He patted his lap and she sensed from his voice that he was smiling, 'Let's have a look at that pretty pink bum.' Trying to let her mind go blank, she put her palms on the carpet, laid her tummy against his knees and stretched her bare legs back.

'Does it hurt?' he whispered, running a manly finger along the thigh-based welts.

Betty-Ann opened her mouth to say yes, but found the sharp pain turning to a hot spreading pleasure. His touch was silky and sure and suggestive. Jackson's stolen squeezes had never felt like this. 'It feels better, Sire,' she mumbled as he continued his deliciously arousing ministrations.

'What about this bit, Betty-Ann?'

He touched the very kernel of her femininity, and sensation after sensation thrilled through her loins. 'Rub against my fingers, girl,' he ordered and, beyond words, she did so again and again, aware of the wet heat and a heavy pulsing spreading over her thighs. It was followed by a rush of pleasure so intense that she feared that she might faint.

'Uh,' she heard herself cry, and her voice sounded hollow and somehow unearthly, 'Uh, uh, uh, uh, uuuuuuuuuuuh!'

'You're not the first girl that's taken a fancy to the cane,' the man murmured. Betty-Ann had no idea what he was talking about but she relaxed over his knee as he stroked the hair that flowed from her cap.

'So,' he murmured after a while, 'Has Jackson enjoyed your ultimate delights?'

'Yes, Sire. Will I be caned for letting him, Sire? He said I would cause strain to his manhood if I didn't offer my treasures every time.'

'Did he now?' The Master sounded amused. He stroked her soft bare bottom until she wriggled anew, 'No, you have a right to walk out with whoever you wish. You'll not feel the rod for that - only for household negligence.' As he toyed with her caned hot cheeks, Betty-Ann found her womanly parts getting excited again.

The Master seemed to know. 'Would you like us to take mutual pleasure?'

'Yes, Sire. I would Sire,' Betty-Ann murmured. Her hidden places yearned once again to be greatly pleased.

'Then lie on the carpet on your punished little bottom and spread your lovely legs nice and wide.'

His words brought the heat to her face - and to the flesh between her thigh tops. Such a strange shamed rapture. Betty-Ann did as she was told and watched the lord of the manor unbutton his pantaloons. Then he put his weight on her and slid slowly forward. Oh, that was nice, much nicer than what Jackson did. She gazed up at him with near love as he started to tease her with each thrust.

'I think it thrilled you, baring your bum for the others,' he murmured. His words were mocking and merciless yet they caused her sex another rush of sensation. She closed her eyes. 'I think a tiny part of you has always liked looking at the other maid's hot red bottoms. Deep down you've always wondered what it would be like to feel the tip of my cane.'

'Yes, M'Lord,' Betty-Ann muttered, licking her lips and burying her face in his shoulder. She couldn't quite look at him, not with the wild wet elation throbbing through her again.

'I may have you tied to the Maypole in the Village Green for further misdemeanours - take my riding switch to your poor bared backside.'

'Yes, Sire. My bottom is yours to punish as you see fit, Sire.' The image combined with his dexterous thrusting made some inner heat in her body expand and the rapture made her cry out and cleave to him, fingers tightening on his strong back. That seemed to excite her Master for he clutched her full breasts through her house dress and pushed strongly into her body, grunted, then declared himself well spent.

******

She'd spent a long time being pleasured, then... Shari opened her eyes and found them excitingly close to those of the Regression Hypnotist. 'I was a maidservant called Betty-Ann in a far-off century,' she said, amazed that she was able to recall every detail of her past existence, 'My Master was angry at me for a misdemeanour. I was being soundly caned...'

'Yes. I know.' Mr Myers the hypnotist had always been an authoritative and somewhat daunting man but now his gaze seemed even more relentless than usual. Shari realised belatedly that she was kneeling rather than sitting on her chair, her slender arms over the back of it, and that she'd somehow lifted up her skirt and pulled down her pants.

'My God,' she muttered, 'I got so deep into the regression that I actually started to undress myself for a caning.' She blushed as she felt her own sexual wetness on her thighs.

Dazedly she moved her hands back to smooth down her skirt. 'No, leave your bottom bare,' Mr Myers said, 'I have to reprimand you, Miss Dean. That cheque you wrote me last month bounced to the ceiling.'

Shari shivered as she recalled how she'd deliberately cheated the man. Part of her had wanted to test him a little, make him slightly angry. She'd wondered if he'd take her in hand.

'I could just write another,' she whispered, hugely aware of her vulnerable bare bottom. The hot weight rushed to her pubis as she stayed obediently in place.

'No, some experiences are meant to be repeated through several lifetimes,' the man murmured. He unbuckled his thick nubuck belt, and lined it up with her expectant buttocks, 'And you'll look so pretty in pink...'

Bottom Of The Class

To: Robert Banks,
Senior Lecturer in English Literature,
Newtown University,
Newtown.

From: Stephanie Weeks,
Third Academic Year Student,
Room 179,
Student Accommodation Block,
Elm Row,
Newtown.

12th January, 2001

Dear Robert

Just a note to say that I've decided on the subject of my thesis. It's going to be *'The Erotic Subjugation Of Men And Women In Literature From 1800 To The Present Day.'* My course book tells me that I can enlist your help as my main tutor, so let's get reading lots of punitive prose!

Thanks in anticipation and all that jazz,

Stephanie Weeks

15th January, 2001

Dear Ms Weeks

Can I suggest that you reconsider your subject matter? I'm honour bound to support you if you persist in this choice but must state that it isn't a subject I know - or wish to know - anything about. Can I suggest a dissertation on *'Social Mores In The Novels Of Jane Austen'* or *'The Use Of Coincidence In Thomas Hardy's Prose'*?

Mr R Banks, BSc Hons, MA

16th January, 2001

Dear Robert

I'll stick with the submissive stance. I read that subservient sexuality appeals to very strong men and women. Guess it's a sort of catharsis, a reversal from taking charge of everyday events. Don't know much about bottom birching in books, but I'll be reading all about it from now on. I've just bought a pulp fiction novel called *Bare Buttocks* to study. I'll leave Austen and Hardy to your more conventional swots.

See Ya,

Steph

22nd January, 2001

Dear Ms Weeks

I acknowledge receipt of the volume (one hesitates to call it a novel) that you left on my tutorial desk. I'll peruse same as my remit demands.

Mr R Banks

30th January, 2001

Dear Rob

Wow! There's masses of red-bummed literature once you know where to look for it! I've found this little shop in a lane behind the Wet Fish Store. It's got a whole wall devoted to off-with-her-drawers CP. Did you know that the Victorians were into flagellation? The woman behind the counter sold me four books in which young ladies were made to bend over the kitchen table to get their bottoms warmed. Often the Mistress of the House would pull down the maid's pantaloons whilst she sobbed with humiliation, and would birch her naked bum. Not that they just used birches. Sometimes a Mistress would spank her staff's quivering buttocks with a judicial rod or paddle or a hard-backed brush. This was erotic for the woman administering the thrashing - but not for the punished serving wenches. I'd rather have been a home owner than a servant in these whip-happy times. How about you?

Steph

1st February, 2001

Dear Ms Weeks

I'll read the Victorian literature you sent me as soon as I've finished the latest issue of *National Geographic*. Thinking myself into a particular role would be futile speculation. What is CP?

Mr R Banks

2nd February, 2001

Dear R

CP stands for corporal punishment - usually the tanning of female bare bottoms. Does that shock you? I'm a free spirit, me! I've just taken out a subscription to *Scarlet Spheres Quarterly*, which deals with the caning of naughty grown up girls. I tried to get one dealing with men as well but it was sold out. I can write about the importance of 'assuming the position' in my dissertation: the girls are usually made to unveil their arses then touch their toes to await their caning or bend fully over a desk. I'll send the mag on in a couple of days, once I've studied its viewpoint, vocabulary level, underlying themes and so on.

Isn't life wicked?

S

7th February, 2001

Dear Stephanie

That quarterly you send for research purposes was indeed enlightening. Sent in plain paper too, I hear? It was nice to see such thought-provoking articles on the subject of female submission, and know that one can learn of this subject without recourse to the gutter press. The editorial was intelligent and provocative (slip of the pen - I mean thought-provoking) and the pictures were tastefully shot. Re the section of your dissertation that relates to how the naughty girl is posed: perhaps you'd like to extend the paragraph on her tractable position by looking at her obvious shame and confusion? How exactly does she feel as she bends over her Master's lap?

Best Wishes,

Robert

9th February, 2001

Dear Robert

It's not really appropriate for me to look too closely at the submissive girl's true feelings. After all, I'm dealing with her depiction in literature, so my main focus has to be the aims of the writer vis-a-vis the words on the page.

Stephanie

11th February, 2001

Dear Steph

The undernoted incident happened last night. My palm is still stinging! I'll send a reader's letter to *Knickers Off* magazine, of course, but wanted to tell you first, given your interest in CP. Are you familiar with *Knickers Off* mag, by the way? It's a hundred pages per month of girls being leathered by the four-tailed tawse and wooden paddle. The miscreant tells the story of how it feels to remove her own pants for a hiding, an element which was missing in your own more modest text.

Anyway, back to last night. I came home to find Mrs Banks reading my *No Panties For Petunia* trilogy. Have you read any of the three? It's about an Edwardian maid with a very stern Master. Anyway, my wife was reading it and the scent of burning ratatouille was drifting down the hall. 'My God, you must have been reading for hours to burn such a dish,' I muttered, snatching the book away. She had the grace to look ashamed. I mean, we have an arrangement. I give endless lectures on Dickens to homesick eighteen year olds and she feeds me at 5pm and swirls around cleaning the conservatory with new improved Flash.

I was angry at not receiving my meal, and asked her to make me up a cheese and pickle sandwich. As she cut the Edam I told her she'd have to accept a tawsing or else I'd dock her spending money for the next six weeks. I should add that I've kept a three tailed tawse from the days in which I taught at a private school. I'd been given one by the headmaster, but had never used it as I believe it's a form of bullying to punish kids. But my naughty wife agreed that she deserved a buttock-warming - and I'd been picking up lots of clues from books and magazines!

'Lie on the bed and remove your tailored trews,' I ordered. She flushed a little, but did exactly as I said. 'Now edge those silken panties off,' I continued, 'And imagine how this tawse will feel on your bare backside.'

It's a funny thing, Stephanie, but watching one's spouse remove her knickers in order to receive a leather strap is totally different to watching her undress for regular intercourse. I feasted my eyes much more hungrily on those suntanned spheres than I ever had before!

'My God, woman - you've obviously found time to lie under the sun lamp,' I berated her, 'No wonder the standard of my dinners has been so bad.'

'You've always got your nose stuck in a Bronte book. I didn't think you cared about what you were eating,' she muttered, looking back at me with obvious challenge.

'This tawsing will show that I care a great deal,' I said.

I then flicked the leather against her waiting right orb. She flinched - it had obviously stung a little. I repeated the punishment on her left buttock and she jerked again. At this stage I was feeling my way, you understand - trying to find a level which would impart a firm lesson yet not reduce her to anguished tears.

Anyway, I upped my swing a little and Mrs Banks reared up a bit and put her fingers back to cover her pinkening haunches.

'Bum getting sore, is it?' I murmured.

She nodded and looked at me warily. 'It certainly stings.'

'You've neglected your chores. You've ruined a meal. It'll have to sting a lot more. You realise that?' I said.

'Since when was I supposed to run an Ideal Homes Show?' my dear wife muttered sarcastically as she got back down on her tummy on the bed.

I ran the tawse over her waiting arse cheeks and told her how much it was going to hurt. I talked of the exact shade of red I'd make her bottom. She squirmed about in embarrassment, but I could see the wet sheen of lust on her inner thighs.

'Where shall we whack this nice thick leather strap? Will I lash it here or here or here?' I taunted, touching each centimetre of her smooth expanse.

In the end, I toasted the tawse against the lower portion of her naked cheeks. She howled as she received the next six strokes of her whacking. 'I'll now give you four more in quick succession,' I said, 'And then your punishment's over with.'

I was as good as my word - though I gave her a minute or so between lashes to rub the sting away and put her hands to the front again. At the end of it she was very clingy and we enjoyed an hour of conjugal bliss.

Hope you can use this account in your work, Steph - or at least in your social life!!!

Master Rob

17th February, 2001

Dear Mr Banks

Your musings (I hesitate to use the word letter) are of no use to a serious thesis. I'm now reading French texts on S/M (in translation) to try to get a more global feel for this most serious theme.

Yours Sincerely,

Stephanie Weeks

19th February, 2001

Dear Steph

Sorry to hear a tawsing isn't quite your bag! How do you feel about a husband caning his wife's bare bottom? Mrs Banks couldn't get the ratatouille casserole clean (it's a Wedgewood) so I had to discipline her curvy rump again.

This time I put her over the kitchen stool. She wasn't half wriggling! Even as I pushed up her skirt she was telling me how sorry she was. I think she may have tasted the cane with a former lover, as she seemed to know in advance just how much it would hurt.

Once her underskirt was similarly out of the way I yanked down her pants. Her buttocks quivered as the cool air hit them. They knew that the cane was also about to hit them as I picked it up from the floor.

'You must keep a clean house. It's all I ask,' I said clearly, 'Otherwise you'll be getting regularly acquainted with the rod.' I striped her bare bum for the first time and she made a little noise like a kitten. 'Save the sound show,' I murmured, 'Your arse has been long in need of this.'

I think she recognised that I spoke the truth - either that or she was hanging on for the pleasure after the punishment. Whatever, she stayed obediently bent over the stool, though her hemispheres jumped and jerked about a bit.

I then moved slightly further back and laid on the cane again. It produced a fuzzy pink mark, that was darker at one end than at the other. Anxious to achieve a more uniform shading, I changed my stance and again applied the rod. Mrs Banks yelped and her bare bum twitched for many seconds. It was a wonderful sight.

'You know that it hurts me to do this dear, don't you?' I murmured sweetly.

'Just get it over with, you bastard!' she said.

Well obviously I had to tan her arse for such foul language and for not showing proper wifely respect.

'Next time you're naughty I'm going to bend you over the garden fence and cane you in front of the neighbours,' I warned her sagely.

'You've changed so much in the past month, I wouldn't put anything past you,' she said.

After that she mainly said 'ah' and 'ow!' as I experimented with the rod on her naked haunches. I was business-like without being brutal in giving her a hot, sore, quiveringly reddened bum. Afterwards I held on to her twin rotundities as I gave and received pleasure in the usual marital way.

Talking of pleasure, Steph, would you like to swap my copy of *Rhona Tastes The Rod* for another CP novel? The cover picture's gone a bit sticky, but you can still read the text.

Here's to submissive bums quivering under the dominant cane!

Rob

23rd February, 2001

Dear Sir

I withdraw my original dissertation idea and request no further correspondence into this matter. I will now study the theme of *'Poverty In Dickens Texts'*.

Sincerely,

Ms S Weeks

Saddle Sore

'I'd like to hire a bicycle for the day, please.' So saying, Suzie looked round the shop at the scooters and trikes. Millport's sunlit sea front was just made for cycling, and almost everyone on the island travelled by bike. She'd cycle to a sandy picnic spot then freewheel on to the Museum and the Aquarium. She'd...

'Sorry - no adult bicycles left,' the man behind the counter admitted with a grimace. Suzie felt the pull of disappointment drag through her 38DD chest. Having such a chest sometimes got her what she wanted. Hopefully she squared back her shoulders to accentuate each exuberant inch.

'Not even a teenager's mountain bike?' she murmured, putting one foot behind the other and leaning backwards to draw attention to her small-waisted five foot body.

'Fraid we've just a few models left for the little kids,' the shop owner said.

He picked up his Hire Records Book and Suzie noticed his strong sure hands and long sensitive fingers. 'We've a few available tomorrow if you want to book early,' he offered with a smile. He looked, Suzie thought, like a thirty-something version of Bryan Ferry. He looked too poised to be running a bicycle shop. Regretfully she shook her feathery short fair hair. 'I live in Glasgow - got the bus to Largs then came over here on the ferry. I'm just in Millport for the day.'

For her find-the-good-side-of-being-single day. She'd been manless for three mood-changing months and had taken this trip to cheer herself up - a solo adventure. She'd planned to cycle and read in the sun then cycle some more. Without a bike she was just another young woman wandering along unfamiliar roads - not an unfettered spirit. *With* a bike she was free-wheeling, more intensely alive!

'What about that one?' she exclaimed, suddenly noticing a large wheel poking through the door leading to the staff room.

'That's my tandem,' said the man, 'I've spent the last six weeks doing it up for my next door neighbours. Tomorrow I make the sale.'

Suzie felt her spirits and her breasts lifting: 'You could hire it out to me today, instead. They'd never know.'

'But it's meant for two,' said the man.

'I've seen one person riding them before,' Suzie countered. She unfastened the first three buttons of her top and flapped at the collar, 'It's so hot standing here. I need a good long ride.'

Taking a deep breath, she stared challengingly up at him. He had silky-looking dark brown hair, a pristine white polo shirt and a subtle tan. He was around thirty-five, thirteen years older than herself and sexy with it. 'I'd take ever such good care of things,' she added, walking up to the handlebars and running one small finger along their hard length, 'You'd see.' For now she suspected he was just seeing her sun-kissed thighs below her frayed denim shorts, her cute red-and-white sneakers. She took her purse from her back pocket and murmured 'Please?'

The man hesitated, then looked fully into her eyes. 'My assistant should be here shortly,' he said, and his gaze was curiously enigmatic, 'After that I can vacate the shop and take you out on the tandem for the day.'

Five minutes later they were speeding along the coastal road, the cycle shop owner on the front seat of the tandem. He said he was called Bryce Neeson. He said he owned three cycle shops and a bistro-style restaurant.

'Millport cuisine?' Suzie teased, as she sat on the backseat of the bicycle-built-for-two and gazed at Bryce's muscular shoulders.

'No, Italian. And it's in Glasgow,' Bryce said. He was full of surprises. He was full of... authority. Suzie didn't realise quite how much authority until she damaged his beloved bike.

It happened just after their picnic lunch. 'Let me ride the tandem on my own for a bit,' Suzie said, not expecting him to refuse.

'No, you could steal it,' grinned Bryce, lying back on a moss-softened rock and folding his arms behind his head and stretching each sinew.

'We're on an island,' Suzie countered, 'I wouldn't get very far.' She gazed at his relaxed sensuous face and had a sudden urge to kiss him. Instead she challenged 'Try and stop me!' and leapt onto the front seat of the bike.

She pushed down hard on the pedals, shot forward - and hit one of those dips or bumps in the road that seem made to unseat the unwary cyclist. Seconds later the tandem toppled sideways into the yellow-flowering bushes, and Suzie fell into a patch of long coarse grass. Adrenalin surged through her system and was replaced by hot shame as she emerged from the flora unhurt but undignified. 'Are you alright?' Bryce asked, taking hold of her right hand and pulling her back to the road and then nudging her back gently to the picnic site.

Suzie sat down. 'Yes, I'm fine.'

But the tandem wasn't. Bryce wheeled it over to her and gestured at its buckled front wheel. 'Look what you've done,' he said, sounding like a dog trainer talking to an unruly pup, 'You'll have to be punished.'

'Punished?' Suzie stared up at him for a startled moment, then blushed and looked away. 'But it was an accident!' she muttered, 'I didn't mean...'

'Didn't mean to ruin the work I put in on the machine?' Bryce raised a heavy dark eyebrow, 'Didn't mean to leave us stranded miles from the shops without transport? Didn't mean to disobey?'

Suzie bit her lip. She had to salvage the situation, and fast. Taking a deep breath, she pulled back her shoulders and stuck out her breasts and smiled up at him tremulously. 'Perhaps I can make it up to you some way, Mr Neeson?' she said. He was an attractive man whom she'd already fantasized about kissing. If a kiss led to a fuck, then what the hell?

'You can make it up to me by accepting the spanking of your life,' Bryce said, marching her behind a bush then taking hold of her nerveless wrists in one large hand.

'You wouldn't dare,' Suzie gasped. But by the time she formed the word 'dare' he was already pulling her over his knee with effortless agility. 'Not too hard, then,' she muttered, legs stiffening with tension. She was surprised by the sudden rush of heat to her defenceless groin.

'I'll decide the severity of your thrashing and how long it lasts,' Bryce said. He stroked her small round bottom through the frayed denim shorts, and Suzie shivered with shame and excitement.

'Isn't it a cute bum? Wouldn't you just like to kiss it?' she whispered, refusing to be lost for words.

'Oh, it's very cute and I may kiss it better after I've made it hotter than a roasted chestnut,' Bryce said.

'We could just pretend that you've spanked me,' Suzie continued, thrilled yet terrified that someone might cycle past and hear her being chastened.

'Oh, I've no time for games, you silly girl,' the business man replied.

Suzie pursed her lips together and held her breath as she felt him pull back his hand. Then she felt it ricochet down on her denim-clad backside. *There, that wasn't so bad,* she told herself as Bryce repeated the spank on her other cheek. Her bum felt quite pleasantly warm, then warmer. Eight spanks later it started to tingle. After twelve spanks it started to smart.

The twenty-two year old wriggled and flinched as Bryce laid an especially stingy slap over the crease of her arse.

'Ouch,' she muttered.

Bryce repeated the spank in the exact same place: 'Save your entreaties for your bare bottomed spanking,' he said in a matter-of-fact voice.

'You mean you're going to strip me?' Suzie queried, desperately trying to remember if she was wearing her satin push up lingerie or her staid white sports bra.

'I'm going to take off your shorts and pull down your pants, yes. I've no intention of baring these breasts that you've been pushing towards me all day.'

So he knew she'd been teasing him. The fair haired girl stared mutely at the grass as his words permeated her brain. She'd broken his beloved bike and he was immune to her bosom-based charms - there was no way she'd escape severe punishment.

'But what if someone peers through the bushes and sees us, sir?' she whispered plaintively.

She sensed that Bryce had shrugged: 'They'll see a spoilt girl getting the hot bum she deserves.' He sat straighter and raised his knees so that her bottom was more on display than ever. 'That reminds me. They'll see you taking a thrashing on the bare.' He stroked Suzie's backside through the covering of the shorts. 'Unbutton them yourself and take them down now,' he ordered.

'And if I don't?' Suzie demurred, realising that she'd never before felt quite this vulnerable.

'Then you'll get double the thrashing I'm already planning to mete out.'

The girl grimaced at the grass under her nose, then decided to do as she was bid. After all, her bottom was already uncomfortably warm. If she enraged him, who knew how much hotter it was going to get?

'I'm doing what I'm told, sir,' she muttered, undoing the metal button and wriggling her hips from side to side as she shrugged her bum free of the protective shorts. She felt Bryce edge them down past her knees, her calves, her ankles, then completely discard them. Now she lay over his lap clad in her top and her white bikini pants.

'Now pull down your panties,' Bryce ordered.

Suzie tensed at the shameful prospect. 'Couldn't you just spank me over them instead? They're really thin and...'

'No, I want to watch your arse redden and wriggle,' the inflexible business man said.

'The redness would show through the white. You'd feel the heat...' Suzie searched for further persuasive words. She couldn't bear to think of him coolly appraising her naked buttocks. Moreover, she could feel the swollen need between her thighs, suspected that her labia was glistening wet.

'Oh dear, such insubordination from a bicycle vandal and a sexual tease,' her tormentor said. 'Now your punishment will last twice as long and will probably be three times as painful.' He squeezed her worried hemispheres through the taut bikini pants, 'Next time you visit me you'll be much more obedient.'

The man took conceitedness to new heights. Suzie let out her breath: 'Trust me - there won't be a next time,' she said.

She heard his amused knowing snort, then felt his sure fingers on the waistband of her pants, was aware of the warm sun caressing her flesh as he pulled the garment down to expose her derriere. 'Dear me, this bum's hardly even pink. What a fuss you've been making,' he exclaimed, running a palm over the twitching flesh.

Suzie levered herself up with both hands and twisted her head back to see her bottom: 'It looks red enough to me.' She contemplated the smudged florid palm prints that adorned both previously creamy cheeks.

'It's not a real spanking until you've taken it on the bare,' Bryce continued, as if speaking to himself. His palm rose and fell. The smack echoed through the air. Suzie yelped and hid her face in her hands and prayed that they wouldn't be discovered. The second spank overlapped to sting the back of her right thigh and she automatically put her hands over her punished leg.

'Oh dear, that's bad. That's very bad,' the tandem owner murmured, taking hold of her wrists and edging them away.

'But it hurts,' Suzie muttered.

'Like it'll hurt my reputation and my wallet to fix that bike,' Bryce answered firmly.

Suzie sighed and told herself that she'd better accept the rest of his bum-based retribution - maybe then he'd give her pulsing crotch some much-needed relief. Somehow the close proximity to this man was enlarging her clitoris. Despite the hated spanking she longed for orgasmic release.

'Alright, I won't touch my bottom again,' she muttered, trying to manoeuvre her wet sex so that it rubbed against his leg.

'You're right, you won't touch your naughty bare cheeks because I'm going to tie your hands in front of you,' Bryce answered.

'Got to find them first!' Suzie gasped out, quickly tucking both arms under her body. She was damned if she'd make things easy for the man. Still she trembled as Bryce stroked her exposed nether globes with cool detachment: she knew that a really hard spanking was due.

Then she quivered with a different feeling all together as he turned his ministrations to her soaking crotch. 'Such a drenched little pussy,' he murmured, 'So horny.'

'You could slide right up me,' Suzie offered, longing to taste his penis rather than his palm.

'Mm? I'll think about it for dessert,' Bryce said amusedly, 'Remember that the main course on this picnic is your heated arse.'

He circled her clit and she groaned and pushed down hard.

'Easy,' he muttered, 'Put your wrists in front of you now if you want more clitoral stroking later.'

Suzie numbly shook her head, then he stopped pleasuring her bud and she knew she'd do anything to gain the ultimate ecstasy. 'Alright, you bastard, tie my hands,' she muttered, pulling them out from under her body and putting her wrists together. She watched heavy-liddedly as he used the belt from his waist to bind her extremities so that she could no longer protect her bum.

Bryce began to stroke that self-same bum, obviously revelling in its every twitch and wriggle. Aroused yet afraid, Suzie writhed helplessly over his trousered lap. 'How many slaps do you think each bare buttock deserves for being so wicked?' he asked conversationally.

Suzie stared at the ground then screwed up her face in humiliation: 'Surprise me!' she said.

The suddenness of the next spank did indeed take her by surprise. Bryce seemed to dole it out at an angle so that it stung the centre of her left cheek, with the stinging aftermath reaching the deeply sensuous furrow. She gasped at the impact. Gasped again as five more spanks slapped down. 'Ah, Oh, Uuuh,' she muttered, tensing her poor bum cheeks then just as quickly relaxing them. As Bryce continued to berate her bum it seemed to take on a life of its own.

'Please, stop - I can't bear it!' she muttered.

'Someone who really couldn't bear it would say please *sir* at the very least,' Bryce replied, stopping to palm her heated hemispheres.

'Please sir, then,' Suzie added reluctantly - crawling had never been her style.

'Oh I think this bum can get hotter than it has so far,' her tormentor continued, hoisting her lower half higher into the air. Suzie twisted her head back and gazed wildly at her stinging buttocks. They looked scarlet enough to her.

But Bryce seemed to know what he was doing, the perceptive pig. He lifted his right hand and toasted the sensitive line where arse meets thigh. The slap seemed to beat a path to her craving clitoris. Suzie whimpered and writhed.

'Please let me come, sir - I'll do anything,' she muttered, spreading her legs invitingly.

'I may want you to stop talking or to cease wriggling,' Bryce warned.

'I will, sir,' Suzie shouted as he doled out four more spanks on the bare. The irony of her words hit her belatedly, but she was too aroused and ashamed and confused to laugh at them.

'Oh dear, you're not obeying me very well. It's lucky I'm in a good mood,' the businessman answered, moving his fingers to her juice-slicked space. He slid one finger then a second inside and kept them there.

'Oh thank you! Oh yes!' the twenty-two year old sighed feverishly. She sucked in her breath, 'Sir, I love your fingers up me. But if you'd like to thrust your cock inside...'

She waited, each sinew tensed. He was an unknown quantity. He might not want to enter her pleading body. He might not think that she deserved his manhood yet.

'Ask a little more beseechingly, my sweet,' her new partner murmured, 'Beg real pretty.' He returned his dexterous attention to her clit.

'Want... Need...' His ministrations reduced Suzie's vocabulary to a monosyllabic mumble, 'Please,' she added gutturally, 'Oh sir, *please*!' She heard his zip go down, felt him roll her off of his lap and on to the grass, still on her tummy. He turned her head gently to one side presumably so that his weight didn't press her face into the ground.

Then she felt his welcome firm body on top of hers. 'Shall I ride you like a tandem, nice and slowly?' he whispered sexily, 'Or will I drive you hard and fast like a mountain bike?'

'Slowly, please, sir,' Suzie muttered, craving the type of long languorous cock strokes which usually brought her to a climax. She groaned with desire as Bryce slid all the way into her welcoming duct. He eased in till the head of his shaft lightly teased her cervix. Then he pulled almost out before repeating the progressive pleasure-drive again. And again and again and... Soon Suzie was pushing her scarlet buttocks back to take him deeper into her front, her nipples pushing through her blouse to brush against the grass as she wriggled on her belly. 'Oh yes, oh yes, oh yes!' she gasped deliriously and promptly came. The rapturous waves seemed to flood her belly and her groin for long suspended moments. And Suzie knew with sudden clarity that she never wanted to experience orgasm without spank-based foreplay again. Bryce obviously felt the same, for he groaned loudly into her hair and convulsed against her, making little grunts of ecstasy as his fingers tightened on her breasts.

Afterwards they fixed their clothing then lay dozing in the sun. 'I'll have to go in an hour... the ferry,' Suzie murmured at last.

'I'll take you there,' Bryce offered, kissing her hair.

'How?'

He nibbled firmly at her earlobe before answering: 'On the tandem, of course.'

Suzie sat up and looked at the nearby bike: 'But the front wheel...'

'I've a bicycle repair kit in my rucksack. It'll only take ten minutes.'

Suzie let the words swim round her sensation-saturated brain: 'You mean the bike will be fine, that I got punished for nothing?'

'You got punished in order to enjoy the best orgasm of your entire existence,' Bryce said.

'I reckon you enjoyed it too,' Suzie smiled. They seemed to be equal again. Equal with one difference - she was the only one that was saddle sore from thigh to waist. 'You're a total bastard,' she added playfully, then winced as Bryce frowned.

'I'll punish you for that remark next week,' he said.

'Next week?' Suzie repeated. She realised she'd spent much of the day echoing this man's words in a tone of disbelief or wonder.

'Yes, when I come to Glasgow for the weekend.'

'To see me?' She cuddled close to him, again feeling sure of herself.

'Well, to tan your arse, my dear.'

Suzie blushed and leaked a little more sex juice and looked away. 'I might manage to fit you in,' she said loftily.

'And I might manage to deepen the shade of that supercilious little backside.'

Touche. Bryce fixed the tandem and went in front, with Suzie virtually standing on the pedals in order to keep her hot bum off the saddle. She tried to envisage Bryce and herself in her bachelor girl flat. Would he spank her with his strong right hand or thrash her with the big wooden kitchen spoon or with her fibreglass riding crop? Only one thing was certain - soon after he arrived she'd be riding much more than his bike.

From Russia With The Lash

'Your Russian clients are here!' Rick's secretary smiled.

'I'm ready for them!' Rick lied, adding a few hasty words to his notebook. He knew that the Smart Card Seminar he was about to give was pathetically weak. But how would these Russian bankers know? They'd never even used smart cards before, far less understood the technology. He could bluff his way through.

He got to his feet as the two Russian strangers strode in. Called Grishna and Myka, they looked magnificent in well-cut grey skirt suits. They were six inches taller than he, and two crushing handshakes confirmed their easy power. Interest flickering inside his parched brain and moistening Y-fronts, Rick returned to his chair.

'Tea and coffee are on their way,' he smiled, 'But can I order you anything to eat, ladies?'

'Just chip cards, perhaps!' Grishna said. So she knew the term *chip card*, the less usual name for a smart card. Rick wondered what else she knew about his technological theme.

'I thought we'd start with the smart card's history and fundamentals,' he grinned, beginning to trot out his well-worn introduction.

'We know the fundamentals already,' Myka, who seemed to be second in command, said.

'And we know all about the major market sectors and the successful application areas to date,' Grishna added.

'You do?' Rick swallowed hard. He felt as if a big spotlight had been shone on him and he'd been found to be wanting. This presentation was to last for eight hours, so how the hell was he going to fill in the rest of the day?

He looked helplessly at Grishna's coiled black hair and dark red lips. Her long nails were a matching glossy red and equally daunting. She leaned forward impatiently and her jacket fell open to reveal a close-fitting white blouse which showed the twin curves of her full firm breasts. 'Tell me the smart card's implementation vis-a-vis my business,' she ordered, 'That's why we're here, after all.'

Rick's brain raced to rediscover the little he knew about Russian banks. 'Well, the phone lines often go down in Russia, right? And that holds up transactions. But with a smart card you can still get an electronic funds transfer at point of sale.'

'And?' Grishna prompted.

'And...?' Rick looked pleadingly at Myka, the less dominant of the two women, for help, but she obviously wasn't fully on his side. She stared back at him with impossibly dark eyes, her small breasts rising and falling beneath her grey striped waist coat. Her hair was long and loose and framed her watchful face.

'Tell me about proposed future applications,' she ordered sharply.

'Oh, and we need to be convinced about the security aspect,' Grishna cut in.

'Of course, ladies,' Rick stammered out. He strung together a few vague sentences, stopped talking as neither nodded or smiled.

'I understand than the phenomena has taken off in Japan,' Myka sighed, 'Have they had to face any problems that would also affect our own country?'

'I... um... very possibly,' Rick said. He tried to recover his theme, 'In Britain we use the card in garages and shops and there are plans to...'

'We know all this. We need a Russian perspective,' Grishna replied. She glared at him until he looked at the floor and toed the plush blue carpet. When he dared to look back she glared at him some more. God, why hadn't he researched this seminar instead of enjoying three hour lunches? He hadn't expected them to be quite so aggressively supreme...

'Maybe I could just say a few words about multifunctional payment cards?' he muttered weakly.

'Maybe you could just admit that you've wasted our time and money,' Grishna snapped back. She stood up, all toned calves and angry black stilettoes. 'Lead me to your Managing Director. I'm going to suggest that he dismisses you,' she said.

'Please, no,' Rick blurted out, genuinely appalled, 'Anything but that.'

'Anything?' Grishna asked softly. She paused, 'In that case tell your secretary you don't want to be disturbed, and lock the door.' Rick obeyed her instructions, his hands and voice shaking slightly. 'Now take off your trousers and lie over my knee,' Grishna said.

For a moment Rick forgot to breathe. There had to have been a breakdown in translation. 'What did you say, please, Miss?' he stammered.

'Remove your trousers. I'm about to spank your idle bottom,' Grishna said.

'And if I don't?' Rick muttered, overwhelmed at the shameful prospect.

'If you don't I'll see that you're fired,' the Russian professional replied.

He knew when he was beaten - or was about to be. Hesitantly Rick undid his belt and reluctantly pulled down his trousers. He pulled them off along with his socks and shoes. He noticed that his underpants said Wednesday when this was in fact Thursday. How had he let himself get so out of control?

'Get that arse over my lap,' Grishna snapped. Myka pulled her chair closer, obviously keen to have a ringside view of the action. Shivering, Rick bent himself across the taller woman's knee. Her legs felt firm under his and when she ran a palm over his underpants her hand was equally forbidding. 'I'm going to give you the spanking of your life, young man,' she said.

Determinedly she started to pull down his Y-fronts, and Rick felt his bum cheeks tense. He hoped that his crack was really clean, prayed that she wouldn't tease it open with her fingers. He was so totally upended that she could do anything she liked.

'I'm really sorry that I didn't prepare for the presentation, Miss,' he whispered anxiously.

'Your arse is going to be *exceptionally* sorry,' the Russian bank manager replied.

She dragged his underpants from his legs, then sat there, presumably staring down at his naked hemispheres. Rick could sense both his buttock muscles giving the occasional involuntary fidget. He knew without looking up that Myka was also staring at his jerking pale rotundities. Presumably she also wanted him to receive a reddened arse.

'Is there nothing that I can do or say to salvage the situation?' he muttered piteously.

'Just don't whimper as you're thrashed as it usually makes me hit harder,' Grishna said.

Moments later Rick felt her palm crash into his bare backside. God that woman knew how to administer a spanking. As he caught his breath he felt her hand whack into the other buttock then warm the first globe again. Spank followed spank followed spank in a merciless torrid rhythm. Rick gasped and squirmed and kicked his little legs. 'How much longer, Miss?' he whimpered, his poor buttocks glowing. At that moment someone twisted the handle of the door.

Rick froze in situ over the woman's knee.

'It's locked,' she reminded him coolly. 'Ask who it is then, fool,' she ordered.

'Who is it, please?' Rick croaked.

'It's Shelley,' came his secretary's voice, bewildered.

'We won't be long,' Rick said, wishing it were true. He stiffened in surprise as Grishna dumped him onto the floor. 'Is my punishment over, Miss?' he muttered into the carpet.

'Hardly,' said the Russian woman, 'I've barely started yet.' She pointed to his lower clothes, 'Put those on then tell your secretary that I've left vital documents back at my hotel room. You're coming with me so that I can finish roasting your arse.'

What could he say? The alternative was instant dismissal. Hell, his superiors would probably spank him themselves if they saw how poor his Smart Card Seminar was. Obediently Rick crawled towards his underpants, his red bum sticking up like a beacon. He dreaded the prospect of it receiving additional heat. 'I may be gone some time,' he muttered to Shelley as he left the building flanked by the much taller Russians. Their sleek hired car was outside.

Myka drove and Grishna sat in the front seat. Rick huddled, chastened, in the back seat. He was glad of the soft cushion for his poor spanked bum.

When they reached the hotel, Grishna went straight up to the desk. She spoke, smiling and gesticulating, to the manager. After a few minutes he nodded and handed her a keyring. 'Come - we go to the gym, boy,' she said.

'Why are we...?' Rick started nervously.

'Don't answer her back or your bum will suffer doubly,' Myka murmured as they entered a deserted corridor and Grishna took hold of his ear. Rick yelled and forced himself to keep close to her to save any further pull on his poor earlobe. He was glad when they reached a tan door and went in. A small gym containing a padded horse, climbing frame and exercise bike met his gaze. Grishna locked the door behind them, then turned queryingly to Rick: 'Unless you'd prefer hotel guests watching your bum start to beg?'

'Please Miss, no,' Rick said. He wondered if he should fall at her feet and kiss her glossy black shoes or her firm ankles. But she looked so tall and stern that he didn't dare. Instead he forced an ingratiating note into his voice. 'Shall I lie over your knee again Miss with my pants down? Would you like to tie my naughty hands?'

'No, this time you're to lie across the gym horse,' Grishna snapped.

Obediently Rick approached the exercise device. He could see that it would take all his energy to climb on to it. He turned back to his superior, waiting for the order to unveil his lower half.

'Strip!' she barked.

Rick froze in place. 'What, everything?'

Grishna nodded sternly and Myka grinned.

Was there to be no end to his shame? Tremulously Rick unbuttoned his jacket and shirt and set them on the bench, then he pulled off the rest of his clothes till he was totally naked. 'Not much of a man, are you?' Grishna murmured, walking up to him and jabbing a sharp finger at his nipples and chest. Rick forced himself to accept her merciless jibing. 'His bare bum's going back to its normal colour,' Myka said.

'That will never do,' Grishna parried. She pointed to the gym horse, 'Boy, get your arse up there pronto!' How did she know words like pronto? Her English - and her command of him - were very good. Rick scrabbled to pull himself up onto the padded back, but his arm muscles failed him. His testes wobbling, he took a little run at the horse. This time he got a better hold and succeeded in levering his naked body onto the contraption. Behind him he heard the women's sarcastic applause.

'Look into his eyes, Myka,' Grishna said, 'Keep me informed of his expression. I want to know which lashes really hit home.'

'Even the spanking hurt,' Rick said hurriedly, afraid that the word *lash* implied a whipping. Could he endure having his bottom soundly flogged?

Grishna walked until she stood in front of his face. 'See this belt?' she asked, stroking the thick leather cincher which emphasised her rigid waistline, 'It's going to hurt your helpless bare cheeks for a very long time.' As she started to unbuckle it, Rick groaned. The belt was broad and black and soon coiled in her hands with undiluted cruelty. He could envisage the wide stripe it would leave on his defenceless small arse. 'Grip the sides of the horse,' Grishna said, 'We don't want your fingers coming back to protect your chastened posterior. And remember to stare into Myka's eyes after every lash.'

Grishna disappeared in the direction of Rick's twitching bum. Myka took her place at Rick's grimacing head and gazed at him with wide eyes that seemed to sparkle with excitement. 'Thank her for each stroke and she may go easier on you,' she whispered awkwardly.

'No whispering, Myka, unless you want to be similarly stripped and whipped,' Grishna warned.

Myka blushed and hung her head. 'The bad boy is now ready for punishment, Ma'am,' she said a moment later, patting one of Rick's hands softly. Rick closed his eyes, and immediately his entire focus centred on his naked orbs. They were so hugely exposed and helplessly vulnerable. If only he'd done the work that he'd been paid to do. 'Please use your belt on me, Mistress,' he whispered obsequiously. Then he jerked and swung his hips from side to side as the Russian goddess obliged. God, she packed a powerful swing. His flesh felt fervent. Rick writhed piteously over the padded horse.

'He's moving his lips a lot,' Myka observed, 'He looks like he's wincing, but I don't hear him thanking you for that much-needed lash.'

Belatedly Rick remembered the drill. 'Thank you for... for laying on the lash, Miss,' he forced out, 'I'll be the perfect host from now on, and...'

'And you'll tell me how much you deserve the second stroke,' Grishna said.

Rick grimaced. 'He's making a face,' Myka informed. She stared into his eyes with almost hypnotised fascination, 'Is she thrashing you really hard?' she whispered throatily, 'Is your arse ablaze?'

The executive nodded. Aloud he said 'It's only right that I taste your belt again, Mistress.'

'I plan to whip you into total submission,' his dominatrix said.

The third lash went lower than the previous ones and stung the region where his cheeks met his thighs. The heat seemed to ricochet through to his naked cock. Rick reared up, spread fingers reaching back to hold his sore extremities. He caught Myka's warning glance and quickly got back in place. 'We'll have no more such insubordination,' Grishna murmured, palming his spheres with a firm cool palm which clearly meant business, 'Else I'll find your puckered arsehole and make you suffer all the more.'

As her words faded Rick felt a hot streak of pain emblazoning its way across his flanks in a diagonal searing. Again he instinctively put his hands back to cover his heated flesh.

'That's it - I've had enough. You obviously need a reminder of who's in charge before you receive the rest of your thrashing,' Grishna said tautly. She pointed to the nearest corner. 'Stand there and put your hands upon your head.'

Slowly Rick got down off the horse then immediately rubbed again at his well-disciplined areas. Noting Grishna's glare, he hurriedly did as he was bid. He stood there till his elbows ached, waiting for further instruction. He could imagine both women staring at his dangling balls and hotly chastened cheeks.

At last his Mistress said 'Now walk around the room.' Rick started to lower his arms but she snapped 'Hands still on your head, fool!' Rick walked the wooden floorboards, his manhood at uncertain half mast. 'My, but that's a sad looking specimen,' the Russian woman sneered. Her colleague gigglingly agreed with her. 'Bring it here for our further attention,' Grishna said.

Rick walked nervously closer. To his chagrin, his phallus grew longer and harder. 'I do believe he likes showing the winkle off. Or maybe he'd rather we looked at it rather than concentrating on his posterior?' Grishna asked.

'You must concentrate on whatever you like, Mistress,' Rick whimpered. 'My tongue is at your service, and begs for permission to kiss your intimate flesh.'

'Only use that tongue to speak when you're spoken to,' Grishna warned. She pointed to the exercise bike, 'Press your apologies for balls against the saddle and start pedalling. Just remember how my belt will feel if you dare to stop.'

His balls contracting with the shame of being so talked down to, Rick did what she required. The cool saddle felt hard against his flesh, and each cycling movement brought pain and pleasure to his testes. Rick gasped and groaned as he circled his naked legs.

'Now crawl to the climbing frame,' his dominatrix bid.

'Crawl?' Rick croaked. Immediately Grishna crossed the room and grabbed him by one nipple.

'Crawl, boy,' she repeated, pulling her fingers slowly down.

'Yes, Ma'am.' Rick quickly got in place on the floor and started to move one arm then one knee forward. Grishna slapped twice at his rump before he crawled quickly away.

When he reached the foot of the climbing bars he didn't know what to do next. 'Stand up,' the Russian bank manager ordered, 'And grip the highest bar you can reach, boy.'

Rick stretched almost on tiptoe in his efforts to please. Maybe if he did exactly what he was told, she'd be merciful. Maybe she wouldn't correct him further with her thick broad belt.

'Turn your head,' the woman instructed. Warily Rick did just that. Grishna was holding out the belt to him. 'Kiss it nicely and ask for your remaining four strokes,' she said.

'Four?' Rick repeated dazedly. He moved his lips against the strap. It felt slightly warm and was about to warm his arse yet further. As a delaying tactic, he kissed the punisher again.

'Face the front now,' Grishna said. Rick sensed that she'd stepped back. He scrunched up his bum cheeks in the hope of making them a smaller target. 'Untense that bare bottom or I'll untense it for you,' she angrily warned. Using all his willpower, Rick let his cheeks relax into a smooth and very punishable canvas. Seconds later that canvas received another biting stripe. Rick did a little whimpering jig on the spot but managed to keep his fingers on the climbing bars. He mustn't make his stern Mistress enraged.

'Please dole out another hard lash whenever you see fit,' he muttered when his latest bout of squirming was over.

'I'm just enjoying the view for a moment,' Grishna said. She ran the thin end of the belt down the crevice between his cheeks and he writhed and moaned loudly at the sudden sexual excitement. 'Does the naughty boy like that?' she jibed.

'It's too much,' Rick admitted, squirming on the spot.

'That's a pity,' the Russian murmured, 'For I'm about to do it again.'

Rick felt her exquisitely returning to tease his nether crack. He almost took his fingers off of the bars but sensed that she wanted an excuse to punish him further. 'I'm staying in position. I'm doing what my Mistress wants,' he said.

'Myka - come and watch the way his arse wriggles,' Grishna purred.

Myka left her position near his face and moved away out of sight, her high heels tapping. Moments later the belt edge electrified his buttock furrow and another teasing hand played over his balls.

'Oh please, it's too exquisite,' Rick begged. He wanted to protect his testes, anus and cheeks but daren't let go of the climbing bars. Again he danced frenziedly about in place.

'I think he needs a harder lash that'll really give him something to cry about,' Grishna murmured.

'He certainly needs a lesson in obedience,' Myka agreed.

Rick waited, knowing that the sixth lash was about to fall. When it did he jitterbugged about, still holding on to the gym bars. 'It's so hot and sore,' he whimpered, gyrating his well-flogged cheeks.

'You should have thought of that before you short-changed us on the presentation,' Myka's voice murmured. Rick heard a new note enter her voice, 'Can I belt his bum, Grishna? I'll put the lash where you say. I'll be really firm.'

'You said that in Spain and ended up hitting the poor man with the buckle,' Grishna replied.

Rick held his breath and wished that he could hold his arse. He wondered if Myka's arm was as strong as Grishna's was. Would he find favour by kissing their shod feet or their wondrous clitorises? He wanted to please both women, and to take their minds off correcting him with the belt. He searched for the most ingratiating words. 'You must do what you want with me, Mistresses,' he murmured throatily, 'I'm totally yours to command.'

'Really?' Grishna queried. A new level of anticipation seemed to enter her voice, 'Myka - fetch the lead and studded collar from my suitcase,' she ordered. Rick glanced over his naked shoulder in time to see Myka leave the gym. 'I carry a leash in my suitcase in case I meet a stray pup like you,' the Russian woman continued, 'So that I can take it for a nice long walk.'

'I'll walk to heel if that's what my Mistress wants,' Rick forced out, feeling a strange mix of subservient joy and shame sweep through his torso. His traitorous phallus rose quickly up and stayed.

Soon Myka returned looking expectant and happy and flushed. 'Hands and knees, dog,' Grishna ordered.

Swiftly Rick obeyed. He felt the collar being buckled around his neck, and a slight pull of the leash started him walking. Grishna strode slightly ahead, holding the tether's other end. Myka walked behind, no doubt staring at his scarlet bum spheres. Her voice was a tremulous whisper: 'Can I lash him, Grishna, please?'

'Oh alright, give him one,' Grishna said.

Rick yelped as the leather stung his upper thighs. He crawled faster, faster, faster. Obviously enjoying his discomfort, Myka seared him with the belt again.

'That's enough. I want to give him the last two myself,' the other woman murmured, 'I think I'll have him stretched out over the wooden bench.'

She marched Rick to the long low seat. Obediently he lay his belly and chest across the wood, his hands and feet stretched out on the floor, his bum fully accessible.

'Can I play with his bum hole and make him wriggle?' Myka asked hotly. She was obviously getting into her stride.

'He knows that if he wriggles he'll suffer for it,' Grishna said matter-of-factly, 'And his arse cheeks look more than ready to beg.'

'Yes, they'll beg, Mistress,' Rick whimpered, 'They'll beg to be spared the last two hot strokes of the belt.' His psyche wouldn't respect her if she let him off with anything, but his sore bum felt obliged to try.

He cried out as someone teased a fingertip around his anal rose, causing the pink flesh to pucker. The finger went in a little way and he cried out some more. He wanted to come but he feared that if he did they'd make him lick it all up and swallow it. Or they'd parade him around the room on his collar and leash again.

'Lift your bum back so that you're pushing against my finger,' Grishna snapped. Slowly Rick arched his back and raised his bare bum: the feeling of being invaded intensified. 'Further,' his superior ordered, 'Again. Again!'

Gritting his teeth, Rick obeyed his Mistress to the letter. His rectum now felt very stretched indeed.

'Your finger's in up to the knuckle,' Myka whispered with obvious pleasure and admiration, 'And his bum hole's all twitching and tense.'

That very tension made Rick want to squirt again. He snuffled as he tried to stay in place.

'Stop snivelling boy. The last two stripes aren't negotiable,' Grishna warned, slowly withdrawing her digit. The ruthless strap whizzed down and Rick belatedly thanked her for the gift. 'Now ask especially nicely for the final essential leathering,' his stern Mistress said.

'I've been... a bad boy. I deserve a tenderised blushing arse. You were right to lead me around like a dog and tease my bum hole.'

'Keep going. I don't feel that you're really debasing yourself,' Grishna said.

'I know I'm not worthy, but I long to lick your clitoris, Mistress,' Rick continued.

'No, you're not fit to do so, but I might let you lick my rectum,' the cruel beauty replied. She brought the lash flaring down across the centre of his upturned cheeks and Rick at last broke through into true submission. His attempts at control deserted him and he felt free in his slavery and somehow released.

'I beg for permission to kiss your anus, Mistress,' he whispered submissively, and putting his compliant tongue to her buttock cleft, he licked and licked.

A Taste Of Her Own Medicine

'Three bottles of aspirin? That must be some headache you've got,' Tracy joked, handing the bottles over the Pharmacy Counter.

The woman laughed: 'They're for various sets of neighbours. Half the street's got flu!'

'Hope you don't come down with it,' Tracy added, summoning her brightest smile and voice tone. This Saturday job might lead to a full time position if the customers liked her - and if her boss was pleased with her work.

He wasn't an easy man to please was Adrian Wells. He liked well-cut pure wool suits and gold cufflinks but loathed informality and fun and instant friendship. She'd only gotten these few hours a week out of him because his elderly assistant had been hospitalised.

'I could go full time,' she'd offered.

He'd quirked the eyebrow above one intelligent brown eye: 'I want a pharmacist that's trained.'

'Could take day release classes.' Though she was small and blonde, she'd soon show him she wasn't a bimbo.

'Let's see how you cope with Saturdays,' he'd said coolly. She was coping well whilst he was out on official business now.

The tinkling of the shop bell heralded his return. 'Sell much?' he asked.

'There's been a run on that new perfume and a woman bought three bottles of aspirin.'

'Three bottles?' She watched his forty-something features tighten, 'We're not allowed to sell such large quantities to the one customer, as you should know.'

'But it was for other people...'

'Doesn't matter who she *said* it was for! These are health regulation guidelines. We mustn't provide the means for a suicide.'

Tracy snorted a laugh. 'That's ridiculous! She could go to the chemist along the street and buy a second bottle...'

'That's not my problem.' He turned away, clearly brooking no opposition, 'Take off your pharmacy coat and deposit it in the back shop. As of this moment, you're fired.'

'Please don't!' Tracy took two quick steps back to stand in front of him beseechingly.

'You've jeopardised my working life so now I'll jeopardise yours. You have to take a taste of your own medicine. It's only fair.'

'I know but...' She licked her lips, 'Problem is, I've taken out a Hire Purchase agreement on a car. If I lose this job I'll end up in debt.'

'Then you should have learned your Employee Rule Book thoroughly.'

Tracy searched for the words that might appeal to his vanity as he clearly didn't have a better nature. 'Mr Wells - Sir - If you give me a second chance I'll try to learn from you thoroughly from now on.'

'You'd still have to be punished,' her employer said, scrutinising her from blue velvet hairband to patent black heels.

He still planned to penalise her, then. 'But if you dock my wages I won't be able to keep up my car payments.'

'Then we'll have to take the penalty out on your backside.'

His voice tone was calm. She felt her own pulse race. 'You mean...?' He had to be joking.

'A spanking for failing to follow pharmacy guidelines.' He pulled up his suit sleeves and she noticed he had worryingly large strong hands, 'Then a taste of my nice big belt on your bottom for not immediately taking responsibility for your mistake.'

Silence filled the shop. Her heart was beating so hard that she could no longer hear the passing traffic. 'How... how many?'

The dark-haired businessman flexed his palm. 'Let me see. I think I'll spank you for ten minutes, then use my belt six times.'

If she wanted to keep her job she didn't have much option - and a tiny part of her was hugely curious. Tracy hesitated, then decided to get it over with: 'Okay.'

'As it's your first time I won't expose you to an audience.' Striding across the room he put the CLOSED FOR LUNCH sign up, pulled the blind down and locked the door. Then he dragged a low stool into the centre of the room and sat down, looking over at her expectantly.

If only she could pay for her error in a less shameful way. Tracy shifted her weight from foot to foot as she stood behind the counter. She hoped he'd come and get her rather than make her walk towards him like a reluctant sacrifice.

'Get your witless backside over here.' She looked at his waiting lap. Damn him, and damn her own actions. She'd memorise the bloody employee handbook before she made another sale. Her calves shook slightly as she crossed one behind the other. 'If I have to come and fetch you I'll double the spanking time,' her employer said.

'Alright.' Her voice had gone tiny, lacked breath. She shuffled slowly to his side and put a steadying hand on his shoulder. Then she bent herself down, down, down and stretched over and out. She swallowed hard as she sensed him staring down at her clothed posterior, quivered as he stroked her taut spheres through the pharmacy coat.

'We have to partially bare the bottom before we can fully chasten it,' he murmured easily. She hadn't counted on this.

'I hadn't thought... is it really necessary?' she said in a husky tone.

'Oh, I think so.' He was clearly enjoying himself. 'Reach back and pull up your pharmacy coat to reveal your skirt.'

'I'm not wearing one,' she admitted, wondering if that was also against the rules. She had a feeling Adrian Wells was going to make her chastisement a prolonged one.

'Why not?'

'It's so hot in the store that I just wear a bra and pants beneath my white coat. After all, it buttons from neck to knee.'

She felt his fingers part her stockinged thighs, exposing more flesh. 'What a pity for you! I was going to dish the first few spanks out on top of your skirt to get your poor bum used to the soreness. Now you'll feel my palm on your pants from the start.'

She gasped as he suddenly raised his arm and warmed her arse cheeks hard six times. 'That was for not lifting up your coat when I told you to. I haven't started your proper thrashing yet.' He lifted his hand again, 'I'm still waiting! You'll get extra unless you show me your panties now.'

Breathing fast, Tracy reached back her fingers and pulled up the white cotton coat to reveal lacy white micros. They were thin and small and would afford her smooth bottom little protection from his ruthless hand. She shivered as he gloated over the quivering view and her bottom twitched with shame.

'I'm going to enjoy spanking this recalcitrant arse for ten minutes,' Adrian Wells said casually, 'And as my palm strikes your cheeks each time I want you to think about how good you'll be when making future sales.'

'I'll be good *now*!' Tracy muttered, hardly able to believe that this was happening. She stared dazedly at the lino, felt her boss shift her posterior higher upon his knee.

Then the slaps began. She jerked as the first one hit the middle of her right cheek, flinched as it was followed by a whack to the left that similarly warmed the centre. Further spanks heated the helpless lower curve of her rear. 'Stop wriggling, girl. I've hardly started yet.' The man rained stinging smacks on every defenceless inch of her thinly-pantied buttocks and naked thighs.

'Oh! Oh! Oh!' The hot pain built and built. Tracy pressed her tummy hard into his lap to make her bum a less tempting target. 'Ah! Ouch!' Her world was reduced to two stinging orbs and half-articulated words and cries. She tried to reach her palms back, but he gripped both her wrists in his hard left hand and continued the spanking, warming her buttocks over and over again.

At last he stopped. It must be over. Tracy let out her breath and allowed her body to rest more heavily across his lap.

'That's the first five minutes doled out. Five on the bare to go,' her governor said.

Tracy heard her own voice rise to an apprehensive whine. 'But my bum's on fire.'

'I hope you're not going back on your word?'

To do so would probably bring dismissal. 'No, sir. No.'

'Good girl. I knew these bad little buttocks would want to make amends.' Tracy closed her eyes as he pulled down her pants, wincing more as a shadow loomed in the shop doorway. At least he'd locked the place. She'd never get over the shame of it if anyone saw her being walloped like this!

Never get over the surprise of how much a spanking could hurt either. She'd had no idea her bottom would feel this sore.

'Kick your pants right off.' She did as she was told, feeling her big toenail scratch against her opposite ankle. The scratch was as nothing compared to the heat in her small firm bum. 'Mmm. That's coming along nicely,' her corrector said.

She squirmed as he stroked her newly-bared tender cheeks, wriggled as he ran a tormenting finger down the dividing furrow. God, that was exquisite. If only he'd keep touching her like this she would surely come.

'Let's show you the error of your ways.' Adrian Wells lifted his palm again. Tracy grimaced, then yelped as the slap came down on her disrobed soft contours. A spanking felt and sounded much worse on an exposed arse. She could hear the sound echoing in her ears, winced as one whack was followed by another. He smacked her wriggling extremities again and again and again.

'Please... no!' She got her right hand free and curled it around his calf, tensing and untensing her fingers in rhythm to the thrashing.

'Stop complaining or I'll really give you something to cry about.'

'So hot and sore...'

'The spanking is almost over. You'd be stupid to give up now.'

She wasn't going to be stupid any more. She wasn't going to give him the satisfaction. She could take it. She clenched her teeth and closed her eyes and tried to drive her body forward to escape his palm's reddening slaps.

'Lucky I'm not doling out extra slaps for wriggling, isn't it, my foolish beauty?'

'Yes, sir,' a writhing Tracy said.

At last he stayed his palm. 'There, aren't you starting to feel better?'

'Yes, Mr Wells,' Tracy muttered doubtfully. Her buttocks and the backs of her thighs were blazing and her nose felt clogged.

'Only six of the best to go,' the pharmacist added, tracing the stinging crease.

Six...? Christ, she'd forgotten about the belt. 'I could please you in other ways,' she whispered seductively.

'Please me by not getting us struck off the pharmaceutical register,' Adrian Wells said. Was he made of stone? She reached five exploratory fingers back and found a satisfying hardness, cried out as he slapped her hand away.

'How dare you presume!'

'I thought that you might like to...'

'You rarely think - that's the trouble. Meditate on appropriate employee-boss relations whilst I warm your arse with my belt.'

'Couldn't we have fun first?' The smacks had brought fiery need to her groin. Her labia felt swollen.

'Any more lewd suggestions from you and you'll take that spanking all over again.'

She'd do anything to avoid such shaming pain. 'No more spanks, sir,' Tracy whispered, putting her spread fingers over her baking bum and keeping them there protectively.

'Think of this moment next time you're tempted to make a mistake.'

'I will, sir, I swear.' She'd say whatever it took to get herself free of his lap, free of this punishment.

'Then get your belly over that counter now.'

That wasn't quite what she'd had in mind. Still, only six lashes to go. At least it wouldn't last for ten whole minutes. Dazedly she pushed herself back from Adrian's merciless knees. She got carefully to her feet, keeping her white coat tucked under her armpits, guessing that to let it fall down over her bottom would earn her extra strokes.

Turning towards the counter, the young woman caught sight of her bottom in the large wall mirror. Both globes had a hot scarlet centre, with blurred slightly lighter red prints where his fingers had landed on the sides of her hips and on her thighs. She put a palm to each buttock, feeling the heat against her hands like a sign of surrender, a sign of her previously-repressed submissiveness.

'I won't put soothing ointment on at the end if you're slow,' her employer said, unbuckling his belt. He doubled it and flexed the worn leather. Tracy stared at the thick black band, and felt a sudden urge to kneel and kiss its length. But she wouldn't give the man the satisfaction of knowing he'd gotten through to her, that he'd won.

'Is this what they mean by counter service?' she muttered, pushing her tummy against the glass top then flinching back a little. 'Oh, it's cold.'

'My strap'll soon warm you up.' She hoped her already-toasted flesh wouldn't be able to feel much more. 'Get that belly flat. Push those hips out. There, that's better.' Better for who?

Only six strokes, she tried to reassure herself. Only... The first lash hit the full bent-over swell of her backside and she registered the cruel cut, followed by its furiously smarting aftermath.

'Oh. Ouch. I...'

'Keep gripping the counter. Stay in place.'

She'd show him. She could take another five. She was a grown woman. She knotted each muscle in her backside as she sensed him draw back his arm then tensed some more as his hands returned to caress her waiting nether cheeks.

'Relax that bottom now or I'll give six extra strokes to your inner thighs.'

'I... can't!' He flicked the end of the strap warningly at her stocking top and she found that she could force herself to obey his orders. With effort she turned her rear end into a smooth waiting canvas then yelled as he laid on the second stroke.

Her fingers left the counter. She straightened, then got back into place. 'Lucky for you that you recovered yourself. Failure to obey the rules will always result in punishment.' She knew that already, Tracy thought, waiting for the belt to sear her bottom again.

He took his time, as if enjoying making her wait. What must she look like, her pharmacy coat tucked under her arms, her bared cheeks sticking into the air like a reluctant offering?

'A pretty picture,' her boss mocked as if reading her mind, 'The picture of a girl who knows she needs punished long and hard.' *A girl who knows she needs to orgasm under her own or her lover's fingers*, Tracy thought, rubbing her pubis against the glass.

'Now where will I land the third lash? On that jiggling lower flesh or upon your parted thigh tops?' The thigh tops would hurt the most, but Tracy was damned if she was going to tell him that.

'Answer me, girl.'

'Wherever you think fit, sir.' There, that should floor him.

Lightly he mocked her answer: 'Wherever I think fit.'

He brought the belt down over the centre swell, marking her buttocks into quartets: he'd obviously had lots of practice. Had there been other disobedient Saturday girls treated in this way? Half a thrashing to go, Tracy told herself bravely.

'Tell me how sizzling your bottom is,' her exacting boss said.

Tracy nibbled at her lip. Jesus, he liked his pound of flesh, this one. 'It's... very hot indeed.'

'It's going to get hotter still, isn't it?' He swung back the belt again, kept it held against his waist, a silent warning.

'Yes, sir. Unless you decide I've had enough, sir. It's up to you.'

'Mmm, it is. I suppose we could do a little test to see if you've learned obedience. What do you think?'

He was probably out to trick her. She didn't trust his tests. 'I'll take the last three strokes, sir.'

'Good girl. Don't put your hands back, remember, to protect your bum.'

'I won't.' She dug her fingers into the edge of the smooth surface and willed herself to stay in place. Her buttocks throbbed. Her legs stung. One lash had wrapped itself round to sting at her belly. He laid on the fourth stroke at the crease where bum meets thigh.

'Aaah,' Tracy cried out into the misting glass. The skin had tightened so that it felt as if the strap was still in place. God, he was merciless!

'Thank me for the fifth one,' he said, administering it firmly to the flesh further up.

'Thank you, sir,' she whispered when she'd recovered her breath, 'I know I deserve the sixth one.' Maybe he'd get it over with quickly and she could skulk off to the toilet and play with herself.

'Oh you do, you do. Getting me into trouble with the authorities. Denying the charge.' She felt Adrian Wells unemotional palms kneading and stroking her helpless bare bottom.

'I'll be the perfect assistant from now on, sir.' *Just use your belt on me for the final time and get it over with.*

She tensed up as he stepped back, willed her nervous hindquarters to relax, looked round as he pulled the belt back over his shoulder. 'Master, I beg - not that hard.' She hadn't planned to use that word. It had just popped out.

'Only teasing. I'll be especially lenient because you've recognised me as your Master,' he said, and brought the strap forward before flicking it with unbearable accuracy at the divide between her cheeks.

'Right, lie over my lap again whilst I apply some cooling lotion.'

She'd rather apply some labial-heating hands... Still, he was the boss, was *her* boss. Today he'd made that painfully clear. Staring at the ground, she walked over to his now seated form and again bent over his knee, wincing as he caressed her trembling buttocks. Then he squeezed a cold rose-scented balm over them and she sighed with relief.

Oh, that was nice! Moisturising and cooling, and... She wriggled anew as he worked the lotion into the crack of her bum, rimming her arsehole and sending all the little hairs into erogenous frenzy. Didn't he know that was a sensitive place which made her squirm?

'Stop moving about or you'll anger me,' her employer said.

'But I can't bear...'

'Who's in charge around here?'

'You are, sir.' *In charge of my libido.*

'Then do exactly as I say.'

Tracy summoned up all her willpower, then he caressed her craving conduit again. Jesus, that was so thrilling. She twitched and moaned despite herself.

'I really won't warn you again.'

'What if I can't help it?'

'Then I'll have to bring in my riding switch from home and use it on you next Saturday.'

'Saddled or unsaddled?' she whispered, trying - and failing - to blot out each teasing caress.

'Bareback, I think.' He was using his thumb pad to trace her writhing rectum.

Tracy closed her eyes tight and whimpered. 'I'll do my best not to move without permission, sir,' she gasped. But her best wasn't quite good enough, for after two more minutes of having her bottom furrow fondled she pushed herself against his fingers and hugely and pleasurably came.

Girls On Film

'Fancy an early night, Maris?' Richard Kearn slid his hands over his wife's front and thumbed her under-jumper nipples. His spouse patted his knuckles affectionately, then peeled each hopeful digit away.

'Sorry, Richard - I've been on my feet here since 2pm. I'm knackered.'

'On your *back* more like!' laughed Karen, her assistant, hurrying to re-stock the comedy video display.

Richard looked from one woman to the other as all three of them got ready to leave the closed-for-the-night video store that his wife ran. Maris and Karen were the only ones who actually worked here, but male customers came in every day. Did he have a rival who was secretly shafting Maris in the back shop? She had so little time for him sexually nowadays...

As Maris went to fetch her coat, he sidled over to Karen. 'On her back, you said?'

'Uh huh.' The girl seemed to be having second thoughts about her disclosure, 'We... get these videos in and take turns watching them during quiet times. Some of them are Triple X.'

'And she... *relaxes* herself?' He'd always gotten on well with Karen but talking to her like this was something new, exciting yet awkward.

'Course she does. Wouldn't you?' the wide-mouthed twenty-six year old said. Then she reddened slightly, and dipped her head forward till her shaggy elfin-cut hair covered her face.

Richard heard the click as his wife closed the safe, and knew she'd be out in a moment. 'Maris isn't on till lunchtime tomorrow, is she?' he queried.

Karen nodded.

'In that case I'll call in just after you open and get a list of her favourite movies. I can buy them for her birthday as an additional treat.'

The next morning he was there as promised. 'For God's sake don't tell her I told you,' Karen said, producing a handwritten list. Richard felt the surprise prickle down his back and up his prick as his eyes scanned the scented lilac pages: *Bernadette Bares Her Bum For A Birching. Tania Touches Her Toes For Merciless Mistress. Chloe Tastes The Cane.*

'But these are *spanking* videos!' he all but yelped.

'Well... all types of punishment. We bought the first one for... um... a bit of a laugh when this independent rep came in.' The girl's words were brave but her tone was halting, 'Maris has been mail-ordering them ever since.'

I've been concentrating on my wife's tits when she really wants her arse warmed, Richard thought with a pang. He'd have to give her a spanking for not being honest with him about her sexual preferences. That would give him an excuse to chastise her buttocks for the very first time. He could bend her over the settee and pull down her knickers when they got home tonight. And then...

He mused some more. But by 10pm she'd have stroked her swollen clit whilst she watched this *Theresa Gets Soundly Thrashed* film that Karen was now showing him. And it might be too much too soon if he roasted her little bottom out of the blue. Well, out of the red... Richard thought about it as he stared down at the type of film which made Maris hot and wet and desperate. Maybe she'd take his new dominance more seriously if he made a spanking movie of his own?

Karen came through for him again. She was a special girl - most accommodating. 'Keep my face out of the frame, and don't tell Maris I had anything to do with this,' she said as she let him into the store a few days later at 8am.

'I'll say I borrowed her keys and let myself in,' Richard reassured, setting up his camcorder. He winked and grinned in the hope that she'd keep looking at his face and not notice his big-as-it-gets erection, 'I'll tell her my over-the-knee victim was a friend of a friend!' He manoeuvred his various props till they were exactly as he wanted them. Now they could begin.

'I'm looking at a wicked little bottom and imagining that it's *your* bottom, Maris,' he murmured into the camera. He stroked the smooth suntanned bum over his lap, 'It's a bottom that deserves to be whipped severely, one that should be warmed without mercy,' he continued. Karen shuddered and he saw her breathing move to a faster and less even rhythm.

'A wifely arse should spare some thought for the cock of its husband.' Richard caressed the small high globes with enjoyment and lust, 'Oh, the woman doesn't have to be available twenty-four hours a day, but the clit should *sometimes* wait for the man rather than always resorting to its own fingers. That's why we're having to punish the soft bottom now.'

He held up a warning hand as he contemplated the rest of the feminine rump: 'No, don't say anything. Anything you say may be taken down and used in evidence against you. Well, it already has, seeing as I've just torn your lacy knickers away.' He squeezed the helpless orbs then fingered the equally smooth backs of thighs and pubic mound, 'I've stripped you because I know how shy you are about strangers seeing your bum, and because it'll hurt more. Anyway, I like to spank a woman on the bare.'

Richard straightened his knees so that the body across them had its bottom raised further, and the nether cheeks under his palms seemed to move restlessly, and Karen sighed.

'Yes, you *should* be worried,' he murmured gloatingly, prolonging the humiliation, 'Should be concentrating on just how much your backside is going to sting.'

He drew his right hand back to his shoulder, then let it lash fully down. Karen gasped and moved her position markedly. The second buttock slap made her shudder even more. Richard laid on the third across the same cheek, then repeated the whack upon its equally helpless neighbour. He placed the fifth spank over the deep dark arse crease, and she moaned.

'You've made me angry, Maris,' he said, looking towards the camera lens, 'So I have to do this for a long, long time. I may have to spank you daily.' When his wife replayed the tape it would look like he was directly addressing her.

He laid his palm over first one buttock then the next. 'They're not nearly hot enough, my dear wife. When I pull *you* over my lap and take down your panties I'm going to toast your bottom much more than I can ever warm this one.' He emphasised his words with six more spanks, 'I mean, all these nights when you've turned away from me in bed and complained you were too tired, when all the time you'd worn out your pulsing little clit by playing with yourself.'

Pushing the well-spanked bottom from his lap for a few moments, he fetched Maris's toiletries bag which he'd sneaked out of the house that morning. Getting into the scene more fully, he took out her dressing table brush with the conveniently paddle-like hard back - then he spent ten more minutes making the helpless waiting arse under his palms a fiery red.

'Cut!' Karen whispered at last. Though the word was a small and simple one, her voice trembled.

'I'll be home soon to deal with your buttocks, Maris,' Richard said to the camera, 'And the only thing I want you to do with those sexy little fingers is bare your disobedient bum for my cane.'

When he'd gotten the video edited and packaged, Richard popped it into the postbox knowing it would arrive within the next three days at the video store. Maris wouldn't be able to resist watching it when the shop was quiet. Thereafter, she'd spend the entire day knowing that her man was going to punish her stringently, and the arousal would build and swell between her legs...

The next day he went into the store knowing his wife was doing the later shift. 'As a thank you,' he said, handing Karen a bunch of three dozen scarlet carnations, 'After all, I couldn't have done it without your help.'

'You mean the mannequin?' She sniffed delicately at the many-petalled flowers, 'It was nothing. My sister's dress shop contains dozens of the things.' She grimaced, 'Though getting that red lipstick off its buttocks after you left was quite demanding. I had to resort to using turpentine!'

Richard grinned at her. 'I had my work cut out too, when it came to the soundtrack. You made some odd little sounds when you were watching - like tiny whimpers and sudden indrawn breaths. I had to edit them out and just leave my own voice on the voice-over. After all, you weren't supposed to be in the shop!'

'I know! It was just...' Karen shrugged, and turned away.

'What? Did it upset you? I'm not some overgrown bully or anything, Karen. I'm doing this because you've told me that's what Maris wants.'

His wife's assistant paused. For a second she kept her back turned, then she moved round hesitantly to face him, pupils dark and dilated.

'It's not that... I suppose it was exciting to watch you spanking those womanly curves.'

'You mean you're also...?' He'd seen Karen as the *dominant* type if anything.

'I guess. At least, I like the videos. Something about the way the girls squirm then put their hands back to try and protect their bums.' She gulped air, 'I mean, they lisp "No more, sir" but their sex is so wet that you know they don't really mean it.' She took a deep breath, 'And I suppose some women want at least one spanking just to see what it's like.'

You learned something new every day. After doing his stint as a Hotel Chef that evening, Richard drove slowly home. He could hardly see, he was so tired. Small wonder, given the earlier sexual sessions he had had.

'Maybe I should thrash you for not telling me that Maris was into this sooner,' he'd whispered to Karen after her spanking revelations.

He'd been ready to back off if she looked incensed, but she'd stared back at him challengingly: 'You could try.' Then she'd added: 'But you'll have to catch me first.' She'd set off half heartedly across the store and he'd caught her and carried her into the back, then pulled out a chair and got himself settled.

'Oh dear, I'm really going to have to discipline this wicked bottom now.' He'd edged up her A-line miniskirt and fondled her wriggling bum through the taut cream cotton for what felt like hours. 'Please don't punish me,' she'd whispered raggedly at last.

'I've no option,' he'd murmured, unveiling her small pert bottom. Then he'd lifted his spanking hand.

Not that that was the only part of his anatomy that had lifted, Richard acknowledged, as he nudged the Renault slowly into his drive. After brightening Karen's bum, he'd created a more thrusting vaginal-based friction. Indeed, he'd spanked then serviced her three glorious times.

Getting out of the car, he adjusted the testes inside his trews. They felt tight and fragile. He wanted a quick bath then a long sleep, arms platonically round his shapely wife.

'Only me,' he shouted, hobbling through the door. Maybe he'd skip the bath. He'd washed his cock at work after leaving the video store. He could shower in the morning. Shower this sweat-slicked adultery away. Both he and Karen had agreed that they'd loved the discipline-and-desire, but that they shouldn't have done it. They'd said all the things about loving their partners that they should have said before rather than after lust got underway.

Not that he felt he could *ever* fuck anyone again at the moment. Spanking a woman hard and talking her down before fucking her was much more demanding than a squeeze-one-breast-then-the-other traditional screw.

Richard flicked down the switch that operated all three of the lounge lights as he walked into the room. Only the subdued standard lamp came on. It illuminated his wife's bared bent-over bottom. She was lying across the coffee table with her black jeans and scarlet panties at her feet. 'I was bad,' she whispered, 'I brought myself off after watching your film, so I deserve to be punished.' She looked at his large palms, then indicated the table tennis bat and wooden spoon lying at her feet.

'That mannequin, Richard, the way you stroked its bum. I got so hot...'

Just his luck. 'If you've already come we can take a raincheck,' Richard muttered. His balls started to rise further up his body at the threat of further action. Each cell had been sated, longed for sleep.

'Master, no,' Maris had that look in her eye that said *take me, take me, take me*, 'It's your duty to whip and stroke and fuck your humble slave!'

‘I could just lick your clit for a moment...’ Dazed, he showed her his tongue.

‘Rich, I’m so horny, I need you inside me.’

‘Just a quick one then, dear?’ Richard half-sobbed.

‘No, my Lord - let’s make it an all night session,’ Maris whispered, getting up and pushing him into a chair, then lying obsequiously over his lap, her buttocks twitching, ‘I know the staying power you have once you get going. Let’s see if I can make you come three times.’

Rump Stake

At last the Parent-Teacher Evening was drawing to an end. Sherilee Patterson waved farewell to yet another trio of doting mums then she started to walk towards one of the dads whom she hadn't yet spoken to. He was tall and well-muscled, dressed in a black denim jacket, red T-shirt and jeans. Black leather gloves completed the ensemble, and he held a motor bike crash helmet beneath his stout right arm.

'I'm Sherilee Patterson, Class 5A's teacher. And you are...?' Sherilee started.

'You don't need to know that,' the dark-eyed stranger replied.

'A mystery man, huh?' Sherilee joked. It had been a month since she'd ditched her last lover, and her pelvis was aching with unmet need.

'You've heard of a contract killing?' asked the man, glancing suggestively at her skirt-clad hips, 'Well I'm here to deliver a contract *spanking*. I've to redden your bare backside for the next two hours.'

He'd to redden her bare backside. For a moment Sherilee forgot how to breathe, and all the oxygen seemed to rush from the spacious classroom. Dazedly she glanced at the three remaining adults in the corner. Had any of them heard what the man just said? A pulse started up in her crotch, then her nipples tingled. She felt a sense of personal shame.

'You can't just... do that,' the twenty-eight year old got out, 'It's ridiculous.'

The biker flexed one gloved palm then slapped it tellingly against the other: 'Ridiculous or not, I've been paid to carry out the contract,' he said.

Sherilee turned towards the door, half expecting to see one of her fellow teachers peeking laughingly round it. She'd been cock-teasing Mike from Maths and she'd recently two-timed the Deputy Sports Master, Bryan, so both had reason to pretend she needed a punished bum.

'Alright, the joke's over. Who set me up?' she murmured, forcing her lips to curve upwards.

The biker stared down at her impassively. 'Darling, I sure as hell ain't Jeremy Beadle. And I don't think you'll be grinning once I start to warm your arse.'

Again the air deserted the room. This time it was replaced by a blush which spread from Sherilee's feather-cut blonde fringe to her blouse-held mammaries. When the flush subsided, she drew herself up to her full five foot three.

'Right, I've had enough. You're being sexist. You're being rude. You're being...' Her vocabulary failed her for a moment then she went on to make her next point, 'And if you don't leave now I'll call the other parents over, and one of them will fetch the headmaster,' she said.

'The man who paid me mentioned that you might threaten that. He said that if you didn't go over my knee like a good girl that I was to show the headmaster some school's-out-for-summer photos,' the motor cyclist replied.

Sherilee felt her lips slacken with shock as his words hit her: 'You're... you're bluffing. I don't believe you. You wouldn't dare.'

In answer, the biker brought out a little black square wallet. From it he took six Polaroids. He held out photo after photo at arms length. The teacher stared at them for a frozen second then she glanced wildly around to make sure no one else had seen the tell tale snaps.

In the first picture Sherilee was wearing her school cloak, which was open down the front. Her bare tits and shaven pubes were completely visible. The background was the huge mahogany-panelled classroom they were now standing in. The second snap showed her sitting naked on her teaching chair, her legs as far apart as nature would stretch them. She was holding a stick of chalk suggestively next to her pinkly glistening quim.

The man seemed to know that her poor bum was in his power. 'You'll take your thrashing then, love? At the end of it, you get to tear the photos up.'

'I don't have much bloody option,' Sherilee said. To her chagrin her vulva tingled with anticipation, and her lower belly felt the familiar spread of lust.

The spanker waited till all of the parents had gone away before he closed the classroom door. He walked to the big teacher's chair and pulled it out to the front of the class, then sat down on it firmly. He looked over at Sherilee and expectantly patted his lap.

'Make me,' she whispered, knowing that she couldn't go voluntarily over his knee like some spineless slave girl.

'My boss said you'd need some taming,' the biker said. He stood up. Sherilee pretended to flee. She had to give the bastard a run for his money. This hired hand would be reporting back to one of her ex-boyfriends. She wanted her ex to know that she'd put up a bit of a fight.

The motor cyclist caught up with her as she reached the bookcases near the door. Sherilee felt two large hands span her waist. The feeling was sex-pulsingly pleasant. Then she felt herself being turned, picked up and put over his shoulder in a fireman's lift.

'You're a fuckin' gorilla!' she squealed, drumming her feet against his back in a gesture designed for effect rather than to cause anguish.

'Gorilla's have powerful arms,' said the man, 'Just right for doling out a hard spanking to a naughty girl.'

'I'm all woman!' Sherilee shot back snappishly.

'You're all cockteaser - that's what I've been told,' the biker said.

He put her feet on the ground, but kept his arms around her waist, holding her firmly. Then he manoeuvred her to one side of the chair, sat down and pulled her over his sturdy knees.

'Alright, so I haven't treated some of my boyfriends well, but I've been emotionally hurt before,' Sherilee rationalised.

'And now one of these boyfriends gets his own back when I spank your naughty bottom,' the stranger said.

Sherilee sucked in her breath and stared down at the floorboards. She wasn't conquering this debate so she had to search for another tactic that might win him over. Now that her punishment was imminent, she felt slightly afraid. She had to appeal to his sense of humour or lust or honour. The longer he was talking, the less time he had left to spank...

'Do I get to know who ordered the contract?' she gasped, as the biker hoisted her higher upon his lap, increasing her helplessness.

'Not at the moment you don't,' the man demurred in an insultingly blase voice. Sherilee sensed that he was gazing down at her haunches, still encased in their close black linen skirt. 'Darlin', this'll have to come off before I can tan your backside for you,' he continued, his fingers brushing her legs at the site of the skirt hem. Sherilee whimpered with desire and degradation as he edged the linen up.

'As we're getting so intimate, don't I get to know your name?' she murmured, twisting her head back with difficulty to look up at his impassive dark eyed features.

'We're not getting intimate, Missus. I'm about to turn your flesh crimson because someone paid me to,' the biker said. Sherilee cringed at his words. New lust surged through her loins as she felt him fold her skirt hem over her back, then unclip and unroll her stockings, 'But if you want to call me something you can refer to me as Master,' he said.

'Refer to you as *wanker*, you mean!' Sherilee retorted, determined not to be made easily sub. His sure fingers edged under the waistband of her panties and she didn't feel half as brave as she'd been acting. 'Couldn't I just keep my pants on for modesty?' she said.

'Don't start playing the demi-virgin,' her self-styled Master scoffed. He started to pull down her champagne silk pants and Sherilee knew he'd show no mercy, 'I've seen the photos, remember? Half of the male teachers at this school have seen your arse!'

But they hadn't *spanked* it, Sherilee thought, and she felt a queer deep thrill run through her. None of them had dared to stand up to her until now. Still, she couldn't show this go-between that the man who had paid him had won, had earned her curiosity and even a grudging respect.

'This ex of mine must be a real coward, sending a second along,' she said, forcing a sneer into her voice.

'Oh, he may put in an appearance to see you squirming over my lap yet,' the biker said. At the thought of an additional audience Sherilee pushed her shamed thighs together hard. 'Oh angel, this little pink button is the key to Open Sesame,' the man continued, fondling her swelling clit so that she moved her trembling legs apart.

He pulled her pants off and threw them over his shoulder to the ground.

'Don't you want to keep them as a souvenir?' Sherilee asked provocatively, trying to keep his attention from her newly-bared bottom.

'No, I just want to make these naughty nates beg for mercy,' the dispassionate tyrant said.

He started to spank her then, softly at first, but with an ever increasing harshness. It felt as if he had been practicing each whack for days. He roasted the centres of each globe. He warmed the sides. His palm licked her tender thigh backs.

The heat built as he slapped her helpless naked orbs from pink to red.

'Is that the best you can do?' Sherilee jeered, trying to appear unfazed by the growing torment.

'No, my palm never tires,' the man said, 'I've hardly started livening these small globes yet.'

The schoolteacher yelped as an especially well-angled spank warmed her bum's deep crevice, the heat radiating through each centimetre of blushing buttock flesh. 'How many?' she muttered, flexing her floor-based toes and fingers as the anguish continued, 'How many hard spanks do I have to take?'

She suspected from the movement the biker made that he was looking at his watch. 'I've been paid for two hours work. We wasted twenty minutes getting rid of the PTA crowd, which means I've got an hour and forty minutes to toast this backside and make it beg.'

'But you can't spank me for that length of time,' Sherilee said. She'd been curious about how his palm would feel. Now she knew that it hurt like blazes. If she could slide down upon his cock, this contractual punishment would quickly end.

'Can't spank you for a hundred minutes? Well I may stop and start for some question and answer sessions,' the seductive stranger replied, adding a few more spanks to her already sensitive areas. Then he fingered her hot sore rump until she quivered with pleasure and pain.

'You could just enter me,' she whispered, 'And thrust as hard as you wanted. I'd tighten my muscles so sweetly on your throbbing cock.'

'It's not part of my contract,' said the man. Sherilee tried to lift her head up in order to read his face, but the effort proved too much for her. Was he serious? Was he really turning down the offer of no-strings sex?

'But we mustn't let this naughty bum cool down,' the man continued. To her chagrin, he started to spank her again with renewed vigour, each smack re-awakening her bottom's previous fire.

'Ah, ow, oh!' Sherilee gasped.

The man continued to spank her bum. He grew ever more articulate. 'I'm going to enjoy giving out the longest spanking that I've ever administered,' he said. *Glad you've found job satisfaction,* Sherilee thought. But she daren't say it. If she was rude he'd doubtless tan her arse even more. 'Your bum's wriggling so prettily now,' continued the man. Sherilee knew that her clit was similarly twitching. But she wouldn't give him the satisfaction of knowing part of her was turned on. 'I notice you squirm extra hard when I spank the crease where arse meets thigh,' the biker continued. He smacked that tender area again, and Sherilee drummed her suede-shod feet against the classroom floor. 'Not that I'm going to neglect the other bits,' her spanker warned, turning his gloved palm's attentions in the direction of her upper buttocks. He smacked the glowing flesh in the centre till she writhed and groaned.

'Bet my ex boyfriend didn't say you could make me cry,' she muttered at last.

'He said,' the biker murmured, punctuating each second word with an additional spank, 'That I should tan your arse till it was the colour of my T-shirt.'

Sherilee knew that that particular garment had been the brightest red. 'And did he say,' she gasped on, brain trying hard to focus on anything other than her stinging arse, 'How you'd know when I was truly repentant, when I'd had enough?'

'He just said,' her tormentor answered, warming her helpless furrow four times in quick succession, 'That you were good at dishing out the hurt and the ignominy, and that this thrashing was your just desserts.'

'Used such cliches, did he?' Sherilee muttered sarcastically, then added 'Ouch, ah, sorry!' as her bare bum trembled under the force of another two punitive whacks.

'I'm going to make these red cheeks *very* sorry,' the biker said. He was as good as his word. He knew how to make a girl's bare cheeks sing for their supper. Sherilee endured twenty or thirty more spanks, then submission rushed through.

'I apologise for all the wrongs I've done,' she whispered, wriggling upon his knee, 'I won't treat my boyfriends badly again. I'll be a better person, Master. No more, I beg.'

To her relief, the biker stayed his hand. For a few moments he squeezed her scorched rear cheeks, whilst she squirmed with hot need and humiliation. Then she felt his fingers moving to her waist. It was a moment before the teacher realised that he was helping her to leave his lap, that her ordeal was presumably over. Flush-facedly she scrabbled backwards, then squatted at his feet. She looked over at her knickers then realised that her bum was too sore to be encased it them. Knowing that her close-fitting skirt would also pain her, she left it rucked up above her waist. As long as she stayed hunkered down like this facing him, her tormentor couldn't see her bare bottom - or spank it hard.

'Now all I've got to do is prove to your boyfriend that I carried out my orders,' the dark haired stranger said quietly.

Sherilee felt her body still into watchfulness: 'What do you mean, exactly?'

'Well, he'll be parked nearby by now with his mobile phone - so either I bring him in to see your bottom or I take a Polaroid he can view at home.'

'But if you take a Polaroid,' Sherilee said slowly, 'That means there'll be another X-rated photo of me available for the world to see.'

'Exactly, complete strangers might view snapshots of your hot bum and your pained expression. That's why I suggest that you go for the seeing-is-believing option,' the impassive spanker said.

The teacher hesitated. 'At least this way I'll get to know who ordered my thrashing,' she murmured curiously.

To her disappointment, the biker shook his head. 'No, you don't,' he explained, 'My client's anonymity is vital. You have to wear this.'

As he spoke, he drew a long black scarf from his inside jacket pocket. Sherilee let it run through her curious fingers. It was an opaque linen or cotton blend. Obediently she bent her head to let the biker tie it over her eyes and knot it behind her. At least it signalled that her punishment was almost at an end. Her ex-boyfriend would view her squirming haunches then she'd get to go home where she'd rush to her bedroom and... her mind pictured her recently-acquired vibrator and her wet loins throbbed.

It was strange having her eyes covered with the thick dark cloth. Sherilee became more and more aware of her own tiny movements. Her mind also focused further on her relentlessly well-disciplined little bum. Was the biker still staring at her naked thighs and groin? Should she try to tempt him into bringing her to climax? And what on earth would she say when her ex-boyfriend arrived?

The twenty-eight year old shivered with uncertainty and desire. She'd always been a bit of an exhibitionist. It was just that she'd never exhibited her chastened rear before. She listened intently to the biker's low voice on the phone. It said: 'There's a tenderised arse here for you to view, mate.' Sherilee blushed hugely and licked her lips.

She listened as the biker set his mobile down. 'Your ex will be here in five minutes,' he explained, 'We'd better display these sore cheeks to their full advantage for him.'

'You mean...?' Sherilee nervously shifted her position and a trickle of desire made its slow warm way down her leg.

Then she felt the biker's hands on her wrists. 'I'm going to help you to stand, then pick you up,' he clarified before doing just that, 'Then I'll carry you over to one of the front desks and lay you across it. Just let your head and feet hang down either side like you did when you were across my lap.'

'And if I don't?' Sherilee muttered, ashamed at the prospect of being this flagrantly displayed in front of two people.

'If you don't I'll take some very colourful photos,' the dark-haired stranger said.

The twenty-eight year old sparred with him verbally for a few minutes then decided to obey his commands. After all, in a moment of weakness she'd already called him Master. She shivered as she was lifted then lowered and shamefully displayed over a scratchy wooden desk.

'Is this what you want, Master?' she added gutturally, scissoring her thighs apart to show the back entrance to her vulva.

'No, I just want to see your well-warmed bottom, and know that you've felt contrition,' a second male voice said.

Sherilee stiffened. So the relevant ex-boyfriend had entered the room. She tried to analyse the quiet tone. Was it Geoff? Or John? Or Simon? Could it be that guy from the Italian cafe whom she'd stood up last week?

'Well, you've seen my rear,' she said icily, 'Is it red enough for you, you dirty bastard? Do I get to go home?'

'You could go home this second,' the man answered. She heard his footsteps growing closer to her exhibited bare bum,

'But when I tease this little bud with the gentlest of touches I think that you'll decide you want to stay for seconds.'

As his last word faded, she felt a finger brush her enlarged wet clit. 'Uh!' Sherilee gasped out, 'Ah! Oh yes. Jesus!' The pleasure was so intense that she almost shot over the desk. The teacher writhed desperately, trying to lift her hips and beg for further contact. Her pussy hungered for release. 'Please. I beg. Keep touching me like that,' she breathed, moving back against the unseen hand.

'Are you sure that a little wildcat deserves this much pleasure?' her ex-boyfriend queried.

'I do. I've been good. I...' She sounded like a four year old in a supermarket pleading for sweets.

'Did you take your spanking without complaint?' asked the man.

'Did she hell,' came the biker's voice, 'I had to put her over my shoulder and carry her to the spanking chair - then she wriggled and called me names and asked to be allowed to keep her pants on.'

'A request which you sensibly ignored,' said Sherilee's ex-boyfriend, and she quivered as he fondled her naked bum.

'I did. In fact I tanned her arse extra hard for even suggesting it,' the biker continued. Sherilee moaned with longing and shame, and tried to rub her mons against the stationary hand. Where were these all-knowing fingers? It was both wonderful and terrible being naked before two men with her well-disciplined small rump sticking high in the air.

'Please stroke my clit,' she begged again. The fingers obliged. The voice which accompanied them was less obliging. 'Keep asking real pretty,' it murmured gloatingly.

'Please,' Sherilee muttered, 'I'll do anything with my mouth, my hands, because I need this. Oh please, please, please, please, please.'

'Will you ask nicely for six of the cane?' her tormentor asked. The English teacher mutely shook her head. Her poor arse was already blazing. 'Well, if the bottom doesn't want a striping then the clit can't have an orgasm,' the man replied.

'My bottom wants cool ointment,' Sherilee begged.

'You could have that after the cane,' said one of her new Masters consideringly.

'But isn't the cane very painful?' the girl enquired.

'Six of the best on the bare? Put it this way - it's not meant to tickle, sweetheart,' added the biker's voice.

Sherilee groaned with hope as someone fingered her needy clit again. Then the finger was withdrawn, and she knew that she couldn't bear it.

'I beg for the cane, Master,' she whispered urgently.

'How many?' murmured the man.

'Six strokes, sir. I deserve six strokes, sir.' Just saying the words brought further heat to her eroticised triangle and thrill-led pussy lips.

But the cane's merciless focus took all thoughts of orgasm away.

'Aaaaaah!' Sherilee wailed, as the first brand made its way across her already reddened globes. She tried to get up, but one of the men sweetly fingered her pussy lips and she submitted to the rush of pleasure.

'Ask nicely for stroke two,' the clitoral teaser said.

'Please lay on stroke two, sir,' the English teacher forced out. At least this time she knew exactly what was coming. Still the line of pain momentarily took her breath away.

'Oh angel, you've got the hottest arse in Christendom,' her ex murmured, tracing the second weal, 'It's wriggling around like a roasted chestnut. It's the sorest backside I've ever seen.'

Sherilee felt the signals go off in her brain which told her she was nearing orgasm. How was it possible to get turned on by this man's contemptuous tone? 'It hurts so...' she whispered.

'Think of the climax, then beg nicely for stroke three,' the biker told her. Again he or the other man had to fondle her clit to persuade her to ask for more of the cane.

'Just get it over with,' she muttered, moving her small hips the little she could in her bent over position.

'Don't be impatient,' said the biker, 'We connoisseurs of bad bums like to take our time.'

They took their time lining up the cane for the third stripe. Sherilee tensed and untensed her glowing cheeks. She pushed her belly more firmly against the desk and tried to think about her ultimate orgasm. She moved her legs in an agony of anticipation, then tried to force her restless bum to stay in place. 'What a nervous arse: it must know that it deserves a thorough roasting,' laughed one of the two men. Then they laid the third stripe on and almost immediately followed it by stripe four.

'Can I rub my bum?' Sherilee pleaded, her hands clenching and unclenching on the legs of the desk.

'No, that isn't what we want,' came the biker's voice, 'You have to remember that this bottom belongs to us for the duration of your punishment. Until you've paid your penance that arse must do exactly what its told.'

'It's being good,' Sherilee muttered, wondering how she could convey with her sore globes that she was being obedient.

'If it was being good,' countered the man, 'It would have asked politely by now for stroke five.'

Sherilee asked and moaningly received the stroke midway down her well-chastened rump. One of the men applied the sixth stroke lower down, near her thigh tops. Then he turned his knowing light touch to her clit.

'Horny, sweetheart?' he asked.

'Uh, uh, uh!' Sherilee murmured.

'God, you're hot for it,' said the man, fondling her desperate bud with the lightest touch. 'Baby, your pussy's dripping,' he continued, increasing the gentle stimulus. And Sherilee stretched her mouth into a huge grimace of release and came and came.

She rode the waves of her climax for a very long time.

'I think that if I entered you now I could make you come again,' said her ex-boyfriend's voice when he finally removed his euphoria-inducing fingers.

'Do it,' Sherilee muttered, further spreading apart her already open legs.

'That was the old Sherilee speaking,' the voice shot back, 'The new Sherilee says please and thank you. She's very demure but asks nicely for some cock...'

Later her lover - or lovers - guided her to the school's gym showers. They soaped her, they rinsed her as she stood, blindfolded but trusting, every fibre of her being deliciously sated and thoroughly filled.

'Are we quits now?' she whispered as they dried her off. She already felt half in love with this masterful ex-boyfriend. But she couldn't say so - she had to maintain some pride.

'No, you're to come here again next week for your discipline and our pleasure,' her ex-boyfriend answered.

Sherilee turned her blindfolded face in the direction of the vaguely familiar tone: 'But I thought that you... why do I need further discipline?' she enquired.

'Well, as you were so difficult during *this* one,' the man explained, 'You've failed to fully wipe the slate clean. I've decided that you'll have to be further chastised.'

'I took a new Polaroid of your sore red cheeks tonight,' the biker chipped in, 'Talk about living colour. Those globes were just pleading for mercy whilst they were squirming over the desk.'

'And if I don't let you spank me, you'll...?'

'Yes, show a photo of your caned bare bum to the headmaster and tell him you agreed to it,' the biker said and Sherilee's clit started to swell again.

They finished dressing her. She strained to hear their words as the two men moved a little distance away. She stood there, trying and failing to peer through the doubled black cotton. She could just have untied the scarf of course, but that wouldn't have been entering into the spirit of the thing. What's more, it might have earned her an additional caning, and much as she'd loved the afterglow and the orgasm, she'd hated the latter sore stages of being striped.

The teacher craned her head as one set of footsteps faded away. 'Who just left?' she muttered.

'Your ex did so I can let you see now,' said the biker. She felt strong hands untying the blindfold, and she blinked until her eyes again welcomed the light.

'So, you... em... chastise me here again next week?' she asked.

'No, I don't. Familiarity breeds contempt,' the biker replied calmly. He started to walk with her towards the door.

'You mean...?'

'That's right. Your boyfriend will pay someone else to bare your bottom. And this time he'll use something other than the cane.' He winked as he added the words which made Sherilee quake with ongoing shame and new pelvic excitement, 'You're going to make the cutest little pony girl, sweetheart, as you wriggle under the springy riding crop.'

Wet, Wet, Wet

'Three hours till I declare *Waterbed World* officially open,' Katrina Mearns exclaimed. She waltzed round the glass-fronted structure, looking hungrily at each rippling King Size.

'Let's just rehearse your performance, Katrina,' Blake Lewison said.

'As you wish, Mr Lewison.' Katrina smiled at *Waterbed World's* manager for the four hundredth time, and wished he'd give her at least a token grin of appreciation. When she looked into his intent azure eyes she wanted to open much more than his bed store - she wanted to open her legs. But he seemed to be one of those business-orientated forty year olds who saw Beauty Queens as a necessary hazard or a total waste of space.

Well, she was really just a Beauty *Princess*, Katrina reminded herself. She'd won two local competitions. The prize money was helping to pay her way through College. A year from now she'd graduate in Retail Management and maybe land a job like Blake Lewison's for herself. He was *mentor* material, which was yet another reason to get close to him. Another reason to win his attention and preferably his respect.

She knew how to get the former, leastways. Katrina flexed her shapely calves as the manager checked the classical music cassette was in place. When he turned back to face her she was ready to give him a prick-perking performance. 'I know what to do. I just jump up and down on the biggest bed,' she said breathlessly, 'Making it look impromptu to get the punters attention. That way they'll associate our beds with fun and sex.'

'Just remember to...' Blake Lewison started, stepping quickly forward. But Katrina didn't hear his final words.

She'd already clambered on to the bed and was launching herself up from it, spreading her thighs apart in mid air as far as her short skirt allowed her to. She came down with both shoes together, grinned foxily and said 'There!'

'Ah,' Blake Lewison gasped out. Katrina stared at him hopefully. Had the sight of her black stockinged legs brought on an instant orgasm? As she smoothed her auburn hair back from her shoulders, something whizzed past her button-cute nose. She looked down. Water was spraying upwards. As she stared, dripping, the bed moved beneath her and another strong jet of water started from further back. 'You weren't supposed to jump on the bed till you were *barefoot with your swimsuit on*. You're still wearing your three inch stilettoes,' Blake Lewison said.

Now she'd torn it. Blushing, Katrina untangled her high heels from what remained of the mattress and squelched her way off of the King Size and on to the puddle-spreading floor.

'Either you lick it up with your tongue or you're going across my knee for a bloody hard thrashing,' the forty year old manager said grimly.

Katrina stopped in her tracks and gazed down at the spreading gallons of scented water. 'I can't lick all that up,' she said.

'A thrashing it is, then,' her mentor confirmed. He took hold of her upper right arm and marched her towards one of the beds that was out of sight of the windows. Then he sat down and pulled her firmly over his lap.

Was he serious? Katrina lay there stunned for a moment. Everything had happened so fast. One moment she'd been wishing she could get inside his boxer shorts, the next she was being restrained across his knee, both of her wrists imprisoned before her in his strong left hand. Would he really use his right hand to spank her? He seemed angry enough for anything, which was hardly surprising given that she'd just wrecked his precious thousand bed store.

'First I'm going to spank you hard over your pants. Then I'm going to pull them down and smack you on the bare until I grow tired of it. Finally, depending on how apologetic you've been in the interim period, I'll chastise you with an implement,' Blake Lewison said.

'And if I report you for sexual harassment?' Katrina muttered, closing her eyes as water from her fringe dripped into them.

'Believe me, my dear, that term doesn't apply.' He snorted angrily, 'After all, I won't touch your sexual centre. That is, not unless you ask me really nicely for a very long time.'

Katrina saw a way to avoid her punishment and have some satisfaction at the same time: 'I'd rather that you *caressed* my flesh instead of *correcting* it,' she murmured throatily, then winced as the man hoisted her bottom higher.

'Oh, the pudenda-based pleasure only happens *after* the posterior is thoroughly punished,' he murmured with a voice-held grin.

His words obviously helped him focus on the task in hand, for Katrina felt his fingers on the hem of her short black skirt, edging it upwards. She shivered as the air conditioning sent its currents over her rapidly-becoming-exposed stockinged legs. She was also wearing full length black crotchless panties. But Blake Lewison didn't seem to be interested in her crotch...

'Good,' he said when he'd finished rolling her skirt up to her waist, 'You're wearing nice clingy pants. Means I can see your bottom jiggling when I smack it.'

'I do aerobics and swim. It doesn't jiggle,' Katrina muttered indignantly. She realised that he was coolly assessing her small taut bottom, and felt her anal muscles self consciously contract. 'Just smack me if you're going to, for God's sake!' she continued gutturally, staring at the water-filled mattress beneath her limbs.

'Don't rush me, Miss Mearns. It's almost three hours till our Grand Opening,' Blake Lewison said.

'You can't correct me for that length of time,' Katrina gasped. She gasped again as his slapping palm made contact with her black-laced left cheek. Ouch, he'd put some force into that one. Then he toasted the right, then warmed the left again. Spank followed spank in a hot-fleshed merciless rhythm. Katrina's buttocks trembled. She tensed and untensed her finger-licked young thighs.

'It stings,' the twenty year old blurted out, her feet coming off of the bed of their own volition.

'A bum that's caused thousands of pounds worth of water damage deserves to do more than sting,' her tormentor said.

He slapped both hemispheres again. To Katrina's chagrin, she felt them jiggle. 'I'm going to thrash you until you never want to see another pair of stilettoes again,' he said.

'I never want to see another pair *now*,' Katrina muttered, wondering if that would save her fast-heating posterior.

'If only I could believe you,' the manager said sadly, squeezing both wriggling orbs. 'Problem is, I've studied young women like you. I understand the ways of the world. You spend half of your life wearing the kind of clothes and shoes that are designed to give any red blooded male a raging hard on - then you complain that these self same men are ogling you when you're half-dressed.'

'I've got a brain as well as a body,' Katrina muttered, then winced as the latter was subjected to another four hard spanks.

'I suspect that may be true,' Blake Lewison said, 'But so far I've only seen you use your thighs and breasts, dear.'

'I'll use my brain if you'll just stop spanking me,' Katrina got in quickly as her bottom's torment went on. She wondered how red her cheeks were under their sheer black covering. She wondered if they looked as hot as they felt.

'Oh, so your brain's come up with an idea to save our Grand Official Opening?' her spanker said, 'To mop up the carpets? To get the water back in the bed?'

'I... guess not,' the twenty year old muttered, tensing her curves in anticipation of its next lambasting. She didn't have long to wait.

Christ, this bastard knew how to spank. Her poor bum felt as if it had been baking in the sun for at least an hour. 'Time to pull down your pants and see how this vandalistic little arse is looking,' her employer said. It was a good bum, Katrina told herself, a shapely bum which looked great in a swimsuit. Still she felt ashamed that his first sighting of it was to be lying helplessly over his knee, all quivering and scared.

She started to pull her wrists free of his, intending to stop him taking off her pants. She'd kiss him, open mouthed, instead - she'd soon take his mind off her error.

'Naughty,' said the man, 'Bad girls must accept that they deserve a sore bum, and should thank their teacher nicely. Bad girls mustn't pull away.'

So much for her winning one over on him with her sexuality. Katrina squirmed in an agony of humiliation at his words and wriggled some more as she felt his arms moving. She twisted her head back to see him taking off his tie. 'I'm going to tie your misbehaving wrists in front of you,' he confirmed, 'So that you don't try to avoid the bare bottomed part of your spanking.'

'I wouldn't. You don't have to...' Katrina whispered, excited yet shamed by this deed. Part of her accepted that it was better to have her hands bound in front of her so that she couldn't push them back and get extra smacks for her trouble. And she'd read that it was easier to accept a chastisement if you knew you couldn't escape. The other part of her felt hugely aware of the increased vulnerability of her poor about-to-be-bared little bottom, felt a tiny bit afraid.

She flexed her wrists as Blake Lewison circled them firmly with his tie, watched numbly as he knotted the bonds in place. 'I've scissors in my inside pocket to cut you free if your arms start to cramp,' he said, as if that made all the difference to her ignominy.

'In the Boy Scouts, were you?' she shot back sourly, then trembled as he started to edge down her pants. These pants had so far hidden her backside, whilst the open crotch displayed her equally hot but as-yet-achingly-ignored cock-craving void. 'Please go easy,' she continued as he dragged her knickers down to just below her thigh backs. Her bare bottom was now helplessly displayed across his firm knees.

'Go easy on an arse which has lost me any chance of promotion? An arse which has ensured that we'll be the centre of all waterbed jokes for the next fifty two weeks?' He sighed low and long, 'Come to think of it, that seems a fitting second part of your punishment - fifty two bare bottomed spanks.'

Katrina sucked in her breath at the judicial sentence then let it out again in an impassioned wail as his palm smacked her exposed flesh for the first time. The spank echoed round *Waterbed World* and the mattress beneath them rippled in sympathy. Katrina tried to push her belly closer to his lap to protect her exposed bouncing globes.

'Count each spank out loud and thank me for it, Miss Mearns,' the man ordered evenly, 'If you get behind with your gratitude I'll have to start all over again.'

'Spank one - thank you, sir. Spank two, thank you sir,' Katrina managed, the words all rolling in to each other in her haste to get each acknowledgement out in time. She wondered if she could bear all fifty two without crying. She wondered if afterwards he'd let her come. The beauty queen whimpered with pleasure as she drove her pubis forward and it rubbed against his suit leg, whimpered with loss as her body arched back between spanks, taking the wonderful source of the clit-pleasing friction away.

By the time he'd gotten to spank forty-seven, Katrina had forgotten all about coming or going, had forgotten almost everything. She thought only of her cheeks and the spanks which were roasting them fast and hard. Her mind seemed to be floating somewhere above her body whilst her voice said number after number, then added 'Thank you, sir.' At last she gasped out 'Spank fifty two,' and muttered her gratitude, waited quiveringly for the next punitive slap.

'Right, Miss Mearns - that's your spanking completed. You may kneel by my feet apologetically,' Blake Lewison said.

Katrina stared numbly at the waterbed beneath her. *Kneel. Apologise.* She felt his hands under her armpits lifting her then depositing her on the carpet, saw the thick pole tenting his suit trousers. So he was as aroused and needful as she! Dazedly she crawled closer, pulled down the metal fastener, located the entrance to his briefs and carefully edged his manhood out. Its head was wet and pink and shiny. So was her tongue...

Katrina licked the first drop of salty stimulus away. A second one followed. She started to move her small palm up and down Blake Lewison's shaft as she tongued his tip. She put her free hand under his balls, weighing them appreciatively, knowing that their contents would soon rise in an ecstatic uncontrollable rush to meet her lips.

'I'm watching your crimson arse in the mirror over there,' Blake Lewison muttered, 'It's the hottest thing I've ever seen - and that's without the third part of your punishment.

Oh angel, by the time I've finished with that backside you're going to have the sorest little cheeks.' He pushed his groin closer as he said the words and Katrina tightened her grip on his hardness, watched as it shuddered and strained and came and came.

When the last squirt had shot upwards then followed gravity and come to lie between her T-shirted breasts, Blake Lewison helped her to her feet. 'You've got two hours till the champagne ceremony. Go into the staff room and have a coffee, something to eat, a shower. Then put on that swimsuit and get ready to cut the ribbon and smile and smile.'

'What about...?' Katrina indicated the ruined bed and soaking carpets.

He grimaced: 'I'm about to call some friends in the cleaning and floor covering business. I'll make clear that it's an emergency.'

'And what about...?' Katrina continued huskily, her hand straying towards her glistening sex leaves.

'You'll get to come after you've endured the third part of your punishment,' Blake Lewison said evenly, 'It'll have to wait till 5.30pm when we shut up shop.'

She'd run away. She'd tell someone. She'd stamp on his feet, the merciless bastard. Katrina planned her escape as she smiled at the cleaning crew. Next she smiled at the press and finally at *Waterbed World's* very first customers. She sashayed around in her swimsuit from corner to corner offering people green olives and red cherries and pale gold champagne. The beauty queen was glad that her costume was a dark purple silk - a white one would have been much more see through, would have shown that her buttocks were a tell-tale red.

By lunchtime her hot sore bum had cooled to a slight itch. A catering crew brought in assorted sandwiches, mineral water, Coronation Chicken and Assam tea. Katrina ate and drank as if it was going out of fashion. A hard spanking gave you a big appetite, she mused. She risked a glance at Blake, but he was talking to one of the sales girls about the conditioner they put in the water beds. 'Stress that they don't have to change the water very often,' he said.

He'd changed his underwear and suit since she'd fellated him. She wondered if he'd changed his mind about correcting her further. After all, the Grand Opening had eventually gone to plan, so all was well that ended well, wasn't it?

'Wouldn't mind getting wet on one of his beds,' the sales girl grinned lasciviously as she passed Katrina.

'Maybe he's all good looks and no action,' Katrina said. She was surprised that he hadn't attempted to unfasten her bra or touch her clitoris after her spanking. She felt... slighted, still felt heavy of loins as well.

And so she remained for the rest of the day. At 5.35pm Blake gently steered a loitering pensioner out. 'Do you want tea, coffee or more champagne, Katrina?' he murmured, locking the bedding emporium's thick glass door.

'Um - tea please.' Her mouth suddenly felt dry. She followed him into the staff room, watched as he filled the kettle, put tea bags into an earthenware pot, fetched the milk from the tiny refrigerator. When on earth was he going to take her in hand?

They talked shop, ate the rest of the sandwiches with some Brie and chased them down with two thick wedges of carrot cake. Katrina stared at Blake's hands, at his crotch, dared a quick glance at his features. He looked as if he'd forgotten the promise - well, the *threat* - he'd made earlier in the day.

Relief and disappointment creating a hard pull in her breastbone, Katrina got up to go. 'Well, I'll see you around sometime,' she said, striving for casualness.

'You can't leave until you've experienced the third part of your thrashing,' Blake Lewison said.

The beauty queen felt the sexual tremors start up in her Venusian Mount again: 'Wanna bet?' she muttered challengingly.

Blake Lewison shook his head: '*You* may have chosen a speculative career but *I'm* not the gambling type!'

It took the girl a moment or two to figure out what he meant. 'Oh, you mean the beauty queen business? I'm just doing that to help pay my way through College.' She stared at him defiantly across the staff room's pine wood table, 'I'm not a bimbo chasing some impossible dream.'

'No, but you behaved like a bimbo by almost wrecking our Grand Opening ceremony today, so your bottom still has to be disciplined,' the *Waterbed World* manager replied.

Katrina blushed and shifted awkwardly on that selfsame bum. The prospect of going over his knee again was just too awful. She'd feel so defenceless, so ashamed. At the same time she longed for some kind of physical contact, ached to come.

'If I agree to this will you... you know?' she muttered.

'I don't know. Tell me,' Blake Lewison said.

'Well, I pleased you with my mouth so...'

She watched the amusement light up his eyes and curve his mouth and his eyebrows: 'Ah, you want me to pay lip service back?'

'Whatever,' Katrina mumbled, toeing the ground with her bare feet. She wanted to climax under his tongue or his fingers or be impaled by his phallus. She wanted to come any which way she could. Her groin had stayed swollen, had quivered and pulsed since her earlier spanking. Her nipples had been hard with longing throughout the day.

'Oh, I'm sure that I can grant you some release after you've bucked under my belt for a while,' the manager said evenly, 'Or should I use that nice long ruler on my desk?'

He stood up and started to pace the room, picking up the everyday objects that lay scattered around. 'Should I use this big wooden spoon?' he asked, fingering the paddle-like ornament which graced the main wall. 'It was a present from the catering company across the street,' he continued, 'See the inscription? *A Gift From Grapevine Foods.*' He hesitated then put the spoon back, 'No, I suspect it's too light for the very sound thrashing that your bottom is clearly in need of. Have you any suggestions of your own, my accident prone little dear?'

Katrina had been busily contemplating the whorls in the carpet, but now she sucked in her breath and looked up. 'I suggest you stick your wooden spoon up your arse,' she said hotly. After all, she couldn't just submit to the chauvinistic pig. Even if he was sexually alluring and overwhelmingly attractive, even if one firm gaze from these blue eyes made her wet.

'Dear me, I'll have to bear your bad language in mind when I'm reddening that naked bum and making it squeal for mercy,' Blake Lewison replied.

He resumed his thoughtful walk around the room. 'There's the rope used to tie the curtains back, of course. I could double it into a makeshift whip, get you trotting around the room like a little pony girl.'

Katrina forced a sarcastic sneer to her voice and prayed that he couldn't see how ashamed and aroused and confused she was. 'Christ, with your imagination you're wasted as the manager of this poxy store!'

'Criticising my career now. You must be looking forward to a very sore arse indeed.' He contemplated her curves.

'I'm looking forward to going home,' Katrina parried, trying to make her flushed features look faintly bored.

'That may be true.' He walked over to her, reached down and pulled the leg of her swimsuit to one side so that her pubis was visible, then slid one deft finger inside her slicked entrance, 'But you're looking forward to coming even more.'

Katrina cried out at the exquisite contact and bore down upon his digit, but he pulled it smoothly away.

'Bastard,' she whispered.

'I'm surprised that you want a fatherless man fingering you, my sweet.'

'It's been a while, that's all,' she muttered, damned if she'd give him the satisfaction of knowing he was special.

'Oh, I see - you were saving yourself till you found a man that could warm your arse.'

There was only one answer to that, and Katrina said it with as much conviction as she could. 'Oh, fuck off.'

'Is that what you want? Wouldn't you rather have this?' He fingered her again and she moaned and closed her eyes tightly.

'Please let me come,' she muttered, 'Oh please!'

'Alright.' He sounded faintly amused, 'Take your punishment bravely and I'll let you frig your clit against my fingers for a little while.'

He looked casually round the staff room again. 'Now where was I? Ah yes, choosing the appropriate implement of correction for your naughty backside.'

Katrina followed his gaze, anxious to get the punishment over with so that the pleasure could follow. Her eyes alighted on the long thin rod that lay beneath the projector. He'd presumably use it for pointing to the screen during future staff training days.

'The cane,' she said tonelessly, 'I suppose I could take the cane.'

As she watched, he looked thoughtfully at the implement and then back at her. 'Have you felt the cane on your bare bottom before, Katrina?'

'No but...' They used it in private *schools*, so how sore could it be? Still she swallowed hard as Blake Lewison reached out for the pale slim wand and flexed it in his fingers before swishing it lightly through the air.

'And how many strokes do you deserve for flooding my premises and ruining a water bed and causing the company extra cleaning bills, Miss Mearns?'

Katrina winced as she remembered her list of crimes then opted for the traditional punitive aggregate: 'I deserve six.'

She waited for him to double or treble the number of strokes. Instead he studied her reflectively then said: 'Six it is. You're being extremely brave, my dear. I was just going to give you a half dozen swats with the spoon or with my belt or with a shoe.'

Did six swishes with the cane hurt more than those things? Surely not! 'No, I'll take the rod,' Katrina insisted, already looking forward to the moment when the last cane stroke ended and he began the first digital stroking of her clitoris, 'As long as we're quits on the water damage after I've had all six.'

'Oh, we'll be quits all right. In fact I'll happily give you a reference for having a sense of responsibility,' Blake Lewison replied. So she was figuring in his good books at last! Katrina treated him to a glowing smile, the kind of smile that had won her both previous beauty queen titles. 'Right, let's get that bum bared and bent over my desk,' her temporary boss continued, and the twenty year old's grin disappeared. Damn it, every time she thought she'd reached out to him or made an impression, he ruined her composure by talking her down.

Still, her spirits would rise after he'd made her clitoris crest. Desperate to reach that climactic moment, Katrina lowered herself across the smooth pine wood surface of the desk. She reached out and took hold of its smooth edge, and tensed, sucking in her breath.

She could hear the reproach in Blake Lewison's low deep voice: 'Sweetheart, you've forgotten to pull your swimsuit down. I want to see red stripes, not a purple silk covering. I want to watch you squirm as the rod singes your tender flesh.'

'I'll bet you do,' Katrina muttered. She searched for the most hurtful words she could find, 'You bastard, you're really getting off on this.'

'It passes the time,' the manager said nonchalantly, 'But hey, I'm not the one with a squirming wet pussy which is begging to be finger fucked.'

'Maybe I'm wet because I took one look at your ugly mug and pissed myself laughing,' Katrina spat out. She looked down at the desk beneath her face: she'd never been this crude before, or this hostile. There again, she'd never been spanked before today, far less caned.

'This ugly mug is ordering you to edge your swimsuit down,' Blake Lewison continued in an even tone. Katrina hesitated, then pushed the purple silk shoulder straps down her arms, edging the material over her breasts, waist and hips until it reached mid-thigh level. 'Leave it there,' the man instructed, 'It nicely accentuates the area I'm going to thrash.' At the mention of the word *thrash* Katrina's mouth winced nervously, but her female folds swelled and twitched.

'Good girl. Now grip the desk again.'

'I'm all woman,' Katrina shot back. A sudden streak of fire emblazoned its way across both naked orbs and she squealed like an injured pup. She pushed herself back from the desk and turned to face the manager, both hands desperately rubbing at her contours. 'You bastard! That was agony. That was...'

'That was what you requested,' the suited man reminded her, 'The first of six strokes of the cane.'

Katrina stared wildly at him: 'But it looks so thin. I had no idea that it would sting so much. I thought it would be milder than the belt or the ruler.'

Blake Lewison shook his impossibly handsome head and contemplated her calmly: 'Looks like your bare bottom's going to have to learn the hard way,' he said.

Katrina squeezed her hands even more firmly against her singly-striped bum. 'You mean you're going to make me endure the other five strokes?'

'That's what we agreed as payment for your wrongdoings.'

The girl demurred further. 'But that was before I knew how much it hurt.'

'You still did masses of water damage, my dear.' He cast a hand around the store: 'You've cost me time and worry, cost the firm a large amount of cash.' He sighed, 'Do you know how much it'll cost to replace heavy duty carpets like these? To have them fitted when the shop is shut, which means paying workmen for unsocial hours overtime?'

Katrina saw pound signs before her eyes: she realised that putting her wrongs to right would cost an awful lot. 'Couldn't I repay you in some other way?' she muttered, opening her thighs just a little and parting her lipsticked lips in what she hoped was a sexual take-me look.

'No, a deal's a deal,' Blake Lewison said, 'Let's have that bare bum facing me and asking nicely for its second scarlet stripe.'

Numbly Katrina looked at him and looked back at the desk. Grudgingly she took her hands away from her naked cheeks. She had no option: she'd either have to submit to the caning or end up owing *Waterbed World* a four or five figure sum. Even if their insurance covered it, this man would still see that her reputation in the Beauty Queen business and in retail management was no more. Katrina shifted from unshod foot to foot. In the last few moments the searing contact made by the hateful cane had mellowed to an insistent smarting. Maybe the second stroke wouldn't be so bad?

Taking a deep breath, she turned and lowered her torso over the wood, felt the hard pine under her soft exposed belly. Breathed in the scent of lemon furniture polish, then quivered at the hellish vulnerability of her waiting cheeks. The first stripe had been placed halfway down her arse: she could still feel its burning memory. She wondered where its successor would land.

'Raise that bum a bit higher, if you please,' Blake Lewison said.

'What if I don't please?' Katrina muttered, then cried out and jumped up as the rod left its second cruel taunt across her buttocks. 'Oh you bastard, you bastard,' she groaned, rubbing her sore rump and jumping up again. His mocking words had sent submissive pleasure rushing to her groin like a molten river, but the compassionless focus of the cane had momentarily robbed her of any depths of desire.

And yet... 'Only four more to go then your pussy gets to have fun,' Blake Lewison said.

'Four more like that and I'll need an ambulance,' Katrina muttered raggedly, still clutching her sore globes and facing her tormentor.

She heard the man's amused low snort: 'I know exactly what I'm doing. You won't need First Aid, my sweet.' He played the cane through his hands, 'I'm roasting the fleshier part of your arse. It hurts like hell, but won't do any permanent damage. The only long-term hurt is to your pride.'

'Gee, thanks,' Katrina got out. Part of her longed to triumph in this exchange, to shame this chauvinist. But the traitorous more obeisant side of her psyche wanted him to win!

'Assume the position for cane stroke number three,' the manager instructed. Making a supreme effort, Katrina again faced the desk and got in place over it. She wanted desperately to protect her flesh from a further tanning - but she wanted even more to protect her Beauty Queen reputation and her future retail career. 'Now I have to find a nice white space on that bad bottom and turn it scarlet,' the man said.

Katrina tensed in her poor bum as she sensed him lining up the rod with it. She taloned her fingers into the desk edge and pushed her thighs together, shoved her belly into the pine surface as the cane hit home again. By now she knew what to expect, but that didn't make the chastisement any easier. She'd never get used to this.

But she could get used to *that*! She whimpered with need as she felt Blake Lewison gently opening her sex lips and fingering her dripping rim. 'Only another three and you get to come, sweetheart. You're doing splendidly, taking it as well as a man.'

'You could cancel the other three.' She looked back at him over her shoulder, large eyes beseeching.

'I could.' He sounded thoughtful, 'But then you wouldn't register cause and effect so strongly, might make a similar vandalistic error again.'

Katrina shook her head: 'I wouldn't. I'll never jump on another waterbed. I'll never wear stilettoes.'

'I'm pleased to hear it,' said the manager with an enigmatic smile. He flexed the rod then pulled it back again, 'But as the damage has already been done...'

This time he pitched the cane against the area where buttock meets thigh. Katrina yelped sharply and drummed her bare feet against the floor. She rubbed quickly at her punished orbs then just as quickly took her palms away from them. She wanted to get the ultimate two strokes over and done with. She wanted to come.

'Angel, are you sure you haven't spent your entire life being punished?' her temporary boss murmured, 'You've bent that bare bum so prettily over my desk and across my lap.'

Katrina flushed and bit her lip. If she was rude to him again he'd probably just lay the rod on harder. And her tender crimson orbs couldn't take much more. 'I'm ready for cane stroke five, sir,' she said as obsequiously as possible, forcing the words out through slackening lips.

'I suspect a sore bum like yours is never really ready,' Blake Lewison said. Lust flooded her as he traced the cane across her flanks.

'Please,' she whispered, 'Oh sir, *please*.'

'Alright, I'll play with your pussy for a little while, and maybe make it sing for its supper,' the man answered, and Katrina sagged against the table with relief. 'Do exactly as I say and do it quickly,' he continued, 'Now get your bare belly across that adjustable padded stool.'

Katrina got up carefully from the desk and followed his pointing finger with her gaze, saw the tall thick wooden stool and shuffled stiff-leggedly towards it. Her swimsuit fell to her ankles and she kicked it off and made her naked way across the room.

'Turn round for a moment and show me your tits,' Blake Lewison said crudely and Katrina obeyed him. 'Now bend over the stool and beg me to enter you, my lustful dear.'

Beyond arguing, the twenty year old did as he wished: 'Please put your cock in me, sir,' she whispered hotly, 'Please fuck me hard.'

'How hard?' Blake Lewison prompted, coming up behind her and starting to slide a teasing finger down her feverish folds.

'As hard as you want to,' the desperate girl said.

She felt him push into her, every centimetre of her hollowness being exquisitely filled. She groaned as he moved half out and her clitoris rubbed against the wood.

'I can feel your hot arse against my belly,' he said, 'I'm looking down at it as I slide in and out of you. Christ, it's like a ruby apple. It twitched so helplessly under the cane.' She heard the growing urgency in his voice, 'It squirmed every time I stepped closer to it, and you puckered up your smooth thighs and your tight little anus. That poor bum was just begging for release.'

'But you caned it anyway,' Katrina muttered.

'I've postponed the last two for a while, love, haven't I?'

Desire rushed downwards to expand her peaking pubes: 'Only because you knew I couldn't bear it.'

His tone was smooth as syrup: 'Darling if I'd wanted to I could have played your hot pussy close to its orgasmic edge and you would have begged me to thrash you soundly for another hour.'

She came then, howling desire throughout the bed-filled rooms. He came moments afterwards. They lay there breathing hard for a long time then Blake Lewison gave her some lemon-soaked clean up tissues and a lift home and insisted on waiting by the outer door of her College Hall until she'd found her key. 'Can't be too careful nowadays,' he said calmly, 'There are some very strange people around.'

'Like men who cane their temporary staff?' she jibed sleepily, standing on the step.

'Like women who have multiple orgasms after being caned,' he shot back.

Katrina stared at him for a second, then looked uncertainly away. She'd hated the bite of the rod - but she'd loved the blissful orgasmic aftermath. Could she go through it all again?

'So, what happens now?' she asked, nodding as two of her fellow students hurried by.

'Well, I'm going home for a shower,' Blake said, reaching out to straighten her crumpled T-shirt.

'That's it?' Katrina asked hollowly, realising that she desperately wanted to see him and sleep with him again.

'Then you come back to *Waterbed World* at 5.30pm on Wednesday and take the last two strokes of the cane on your bare bottom,' the manager continued.

Katrina felt her nipples enlarge and her groin twitch. 'And what if I don't turn up?' she challenged, gazing into his eyes.

'I'll have to come here and cane you in front of your contemporaries,' Blake Lewison countered.

'You wouldn't.' She had a sudden image of him pulling down her jeans and panties in front of ogling students and lecturers.

'Want to put me to the test?' the manager said.

He left then. Katrina went to the shower and turned the temperature gauge on *cool* in deference to her chastened bottom. Languid with desire, the Beauty Queen washed her scented sex fluids away. The opening lines from her speech had already fled her mind, but they no longer mattered. She knew that the closing lines Blake Lewison intended to mark on her small bare buttocks would remain in her memory for a very long time indeed.

Cheryl's Game

Note to the reader: This story was written when a magazine asked me to produce a pastiche of an existing work. I opted to write an affectionate send up of a well-known horror novel which features a handcuffed woman and a feral dog in the same isolated house.

'I'm going to spank you very hard for forgetting to bring the massage oils,' Duncan murmured.

'That'll be right,' Cheryl scoffed, then shivered as he held her wrists behind her back and she heard the handcuffs click into place. The scrape of metal. That click. The start of pain that would hopefully lead to pleasure. The decision was his.

'It's my duty to pull your pants down,' her lover continued. He was a duty solicitor at the police cells much of the time so took such concepts very seriously.

'Might want to keep them on,' Cheryl muttered, pushing her belly harder against the bed. In the side wall mirror she could see herself lying on her tummy, her already-bared breasts squashed into the duvet cover, could see Duncan's concentrating gaze.

Her briefs elastic scraped against her bum and she felt the material tauten against her cleft for a second, before the cotton was pulled down, down, down. She could see both spherical buttocks being unveiled: small and pale and vulnerable. Duncan had vowed to punish them, so they wouldn't stay pale for long.

Cheryl licked her suddenly-dry lower lip as the solicitor finished pulling her pants over her ankles. Now she was completely naked, with her hands cuffed high up her back and he could do anything he liked.

'Such a bad bottom.' He started to stroke her newly-bared swell, 'So forgetful.'

'I could go out to the village shop and...'

'Good as that grocer is, I doubt if it sells exotic oils.' He continued to caress her rear, 'No, you've reduced my pleasure, so I'll have to take it out on your naked rear.'

'But...'

'You'll thank me one day,' he added, as she went sullen and silent. She would, Cheryl thought, but only when she'd enjoyed the orgasmic release that followed the wrigglingly-scorching pain.

'Ten minutes worth of spanks to teach you the error of your ways, I think,' Duncan finished. Cheryl closed her eyes and waited for his palm to land. Nothing happened. She opened her eyes again. 'Untense those buttocks now or you'll get double,' Duncan said. Marshalling her remaining resources, she stretched her back forward and her thighs downwards until her waiting arse was unpuckered and smooth.

'Keep it that way, or else,' said Duncan, then slapped down hard. Cheryl jerked then forced her rear end to relax again. She winced as he heated the other cheek. Then she drew in her breath as he repeated the twin spanking. Always, in her fantasies, it wasn't quite this fast and hot. But she was part of *Duncan's* fantasy, now, and he obviously fantasised about doling out some pretty severe thrashings. Especially to the bottom of a woman who'd promised - and failed to deliver - an oil slicked massage.

'Ouch - that really hurt.'

'I'm just getting started.'

Cheryl's bum was moving of its own accord now, tightening up and driving forward, straightening briefly between smacks as it tried to find a way to deal with the prolonged steadfast sting. She pushed her cuffed hands down towards her derriere, wishing she could get her palms low enough to ward off even a single slap of the spanking. Christ, he had aggressively accurate hands.

'Enough,' she muttered. They had a code word she had to shout when she'd really had enough, but once again she delayed using it. For if she stopped her own disciplining too early, Duncan teased her clit for the remainder of the session instead. He'd tongue her, then stop, lick some more then lapse into another discussion of how wicked she'd been until her female parts were frantic with unsated need.

Duncan spanked on, his palm roasting her arse from top to bottom, knowing palms slapping at the flinching tops of her thighs, at her furrow, at her jiggling underswell. 'I can't bear it,' she muttered, hips moving from side to side in a vain bid to avoid their correction, 'Duncan... Sir... Please!'

Sometimes if she begged sweetly enough he spontaneously squirted his pleasure over her back, then took her in his arms while he rested. 'I jerked off in the loo as soon as we reached the Cottage,' he said now, 'Sorry, Cheryl, I'm not going to spare your arse cheeks today.' He squeezed her burning spheres for a moment, 'In fact I'm going to thrash you harder and longer for being such a manipulative bitch.'

Cheryl peeked sideways at her bottom in the mirror, noting how the reddened flesh sported blurred deeper scarlet prints where Duncan's last few spanks had fallen. She flexed her shoulder muscles as best she could to keep her imprisoned arms from cramping. There was enough pain to be going on with in her poor backside.

'Oh baby, you're going to wriggle for me so much this weekend.' Duncan spanked on and on. Cheryl gritted her teeth and came close to yelling out the code that would end her chastisement. Then she broke through some inner barrier, and found herself half-wanting the fast-becoming-erotic punitive heat.

Which was when Duncan stopped, of course. He knew her so well, the beautiful bastard. 'I think you'd like to come, now,' he murmured, 'And I may let you eventually if you grovel ever so humbly for each long slow thrust of my cock.'

'Might do,' muttered Cheryl. She felt his swollen promise pushing at the entrance to her wetness and realised just how much she needed consummation, 'Duncan, please, slide it in!'

'How far in?'

'Right up me.' Her crevice was craving him now, reduced to a hollow ache that longed for fulfilling friction. She lay there on her belly, pushing her hips back in a silent beg.

'I suppose I could lend you an inch or so,' Duncan said thoughtfully, and she felt herself being widened as he started to nudge in.

She wanted more, more, more. Needed... Pushed back as best as she could - given that she couldn't use her cuffed arms for leverage - and heard him swear. 'Oh dear - you scratched me with your toenails. Haven't I told you to keep them short?'

'I didn't mean...' The handcuffs prevented her shrug. She lay there, helpless.

'I'll have to go to the village shop and buy some antiseptic now,' Duncan said.

Cheryl felt the head of his cock leave her sex. She never understood how he had the willpower to do this bit, to leave her body when it was so wet and welcoming.

'Please, Duncan, bring me off first,' she pleaded, rolling over onto her hot bum and cuffed hands and spreading her legs wide apart.

'I'm going to make you wait,' said Duncan, 'And you'd better not try anything yourself.'

'I've not got access to my hands,' Cheryl pointed out forlornly.

'Good,' said Duncan, 'I intend to keep it that way.'

He played idly with the tender nipple of her right breast as he put on his shoes. As usual, he'd stayed fully dressed throughout the session. 'I'm going to take the cuffs off and tie your hands in front of you to prevent cramp setting in,' he said, 'I'll leave the scissors on the dressing table in case there's an emergency. Stay exactly as you are if there's not.'

'Yes, sir,' Cheryl muttered, finding her spirit again.

'Call me *Master*.' She stuck her tongue out at him them shivered as he slid a hand under her body and squeezed her buttocks, 'You'll say it with feeling when I come back.'

He left. She heard the door banging back and forward. They really must fix that lock before they returned to the city. A chihuahua padded into the room and jumped up to lick the quarter of the duvet that was smeared with sex juice. Weren't they known as lap dogs? Cheryl wished she had a toffee she could put in a strategic place.

The canine midget left. Duncan would be gone for some time. Cheryl rolled over onto her side and pulled the bedside cabinet drawer open with her teeth. Now she could see the ten inch black ribbed multi-speed vibrator. Come to me, baby. She edged her tied hands forward. The free end of rope looped round the handle of the drawer by mistake.

Damn it. Carefully Cheryl edged her arms back, then up. The rope slid away from its impediment. Try again. She went in above the drawer at a right hand angle this time. Held her breath, then caught the end of the dildo between her fingers. Thank God he hadn't tied them or her thumbs. She had some movement in all ten digits which gave her leeway, used a swinging sideways throw to bring the sex toy onto the top of the bed. Then she pushed both pinkies upwards against the switch till it flicked to *on*, and the pleasure-promising buzz filled the room.

Now all she had to do was get it inside her. He'd bound her hands too high up for them to reach her labial lips. Cheryl trapped the toy under her belly then made rolling movements to push it down, down, down. Going, going... She caught her breath as the tip vibrated against her pubis. But she wanted it deep inside it, where Duncan's cock had so briefly been.

Left a bit. Up a bit. She half-raised onto her knees, looked under her body at the sweet sexual substitute prick. The dog trotted into the room again. Cheryl ignored it, realising it was just a diversion of the author's, who having cuffed his victim to a bed in a holiday cottage, doesn't know what to do with her for eighty thousand words.

'Damn you, Duncan,' she muttered, then added 'Didn't mean it.' God knows, the intrepid solicitor might well hear. Three weeks ago she'd brought a tape-recorder to the cottage, meaning to listen to *Wet Wet Wet* lyrics whilst she got the same way with her lover. He'd gone out to buy a replacement lightbulb leaving her chained to the settee. She'd struggled to bring herself off by squatting over a cushion and squeezing her thighs against it. 'Fuck you, Duncan,' she'd muttered, 'Screw you!' On his return he'd rewound the blank tape he'd sneaked into the machine and listened, mouth tightening, then he'd picked up the thick leather martinet...

She had to come. Like now. Like yesterday. Cheryl sat up again and grasped the vibrator between her ankles. She steadied it against her bound hands, then lowered herself slowly down. Almost, almost. The top of it opened her up. She wriggled until her body could take another inch, and another, only stopped when most of it was in.

Such pulsing promissory heat. Pleasure thrilled through her sex leaves to her belly. Even her anus felt more alive. And her clit! The area behind it and beneath it was a spreading network of near-bliss, thighs tensing as nirvana got nearer. Head pleading: yes, yes, yes, yes, yes.

Bound hands, a spanked bum, a vaginal vibrator and a lover who's forbidden you to... She moaned three times as the sweetness began to peak, hearing her own cries turning into something guttural and wolverine as she ground herself against the surging sensation and came and came.

'Oh dear, oh dear, oh dear.' She hadn't heard him come back, but then she'd been making lots of her own noises.

'You were gone so long,' she said, pleadingly, trying to wriggle free of the vibrator.

'Mmm. And do you know why? Because the village has now got a little gardening centre.' He unzipped his sports bag, 'And do you see what I bought there? That's right - a cane.'

'It's bamboo. Too thick. You're supposed to use a specially made rattan or...'

'I know. But in the circumstances your bum needs something severe.'

'I just...'

'You didn't wait for my seven inch cock, so that means seven of the best for starters.'

'So many?' Cheryl whimpered.

'Stop complaining girl, or I may make it ten.'

He untied her wrists. 'Right, let's get you over the breakfast bar stool, arse at the ready. No, bring it into the bedroom and place it in the centre of the floor.'

Cheryl did. Her face, her rump, her mons felt flushed: 'You'll fuck me till I come after my caning?'

'As long as you take every stroke without touching your sore rear end.'

Swallowing nervously, Cheryl bent over the piece of furniture until her bottom was raised high into the air. God, her cheeks felt vulnerable. Still, giving him an excuse to go to the shops had earned her time for self-pleasure before the next punishment began. She fancied that next weekend she'd forget to do the food shopping but would remember to leave that temptingly vibrating anal plug on top of the kitchen table. She knew that when it came to plotting out correction she was the real unrecognised King.

Three Colours Red

'So how long will you be away?' Debbie asked. She held her breath, aware that she wanted an encouragingly short answer.

'Oh, only two days,' Miles Johnstone murmured, setting his diary down on the pristine table top.

'That's not long,' Debbie said. She wanted to add *I'll miss you*, but she'd only been dating Miles for three weeks and he was still an unknown quantity who had yet to make her feel emotionally secure.

He made her feel excited, though - even if he hadn't yet made love to her. Oh, they'd kissed a few times, but at the end of each long lip contact he'd gently pushed her away.

'Problem is, I'm back for one night then away for a three day sales pitch in Paris,' Miles continued, stretching his legs out in the ample confines of the wine bar, 'The dry cleaners is closed by now, so I'll have to do my laundry tonight by hand if its to be ready for the second trip.'

Debbie grimaced inwardly. Every hour the manager of *Masculine Mode* menswear label spent laundering his suits was an hour that they couldn't be together. And she wanted them to be together soon in his bed. She cleared her throat and tried to make the offer sound casual: 'There's not much happening at College at the moment. Why don't I do your laundry while you're away?'

Miles quirked one eyebrow: 'Sweetheart, I couldn't presume. I'm quite capable.'

He looked more than capable. He looked born to be in charge. 'I have the time. You don't. It makes sense,' Debbie continued. She sucked in another breath. 'As a reward you can treat me to a candle-lit dinner on your first free evening back.'

'I will indeed,' Miles said. He produced a set of keys from his briefcase, 'Here's my spare set. I'll be away by 8am. Let yourself in any time thereafter.' He leaned forward, and Debbie breathed deeply of his *Pour Homme* scent, 'My shirts are in the Aladdin basket in the laundry room. You'll find that I don't have a washing machine or spin dryer. I like to wash and rinse each garment separately by hand.'

'I'll do the same, then,' Debbie murmured, hoping to get into his good books.

'It never occurred to me that you might do otherwise,' Miles replied. He covered her small hand with his larger one, 'I know some people think that an interest in clothes makes a man effete, and I want to assure you that's not the case here. It's just that I care about what I do, and I want to earn further promotion. I have to look immaculate so that I inspire the retail outlets to buy.'

'I understand,' Debbie said, smoothing down the black velour dress she'd bought with her recent birthday money. She suspected that if Miles saw some of her jeans and baggy jumpers he'd have an unfashionable fit.

Two days later he did indeed have a fit - but a fit connected with his clothes rather than hers, a fit that led to a thorough spanking. The kind of spanking that a girl doesn't forget...

Miles had driven to meet her straight from the airport, and had taken her out for the promised thank you meal. Then he invited her back for liqueurs and to see *Masculine Mode's* latest retail catalogues. 'You can give me a woman's opinion on what suits today's man in his thirties,' he said casually.

Anything that you wear looks ace, Debbie thought, undressing him with her eyes for the five hundredth time as she climbed the single flight of stairs to his deluxe apartment. She wondered if he'd take her own clothes off and make love to her tonight.

He let them both in. He poured her a Benedictine, then showered and changed.

'I like the way you've laundered my clothes and hung them all up,' he said when he returned to the lounge with a bottle of brandy, 'My French clients will love them.' He joined her on the long chintz sofa, 'Just one thing, Debbie - I couldn't find the cream raw silk grandad shirt.'

Debbie felt the first tremors of guilt spread through her breasts. 'Ah, I'd forgotten all about that one,' she said.

'You forgot to launder it? Damn! I'd better do it now. I need that shirt for my first meeting in Paris tomorrow. It's a specially made version of the new line we're hoping to sell there, and cost over three hundred quid.'

'Three hundred...?' Debbie felt her mouth drop open of its own volition. Miles Johnstone was going to hate her now, might even end the relationship. 'I meant I'd forgotten to tell you that it... got spoilt,' she continued hesitantly.

'What happened?' Miles asked. His features had gone sort of guarded, extra watchful.

The student felt her heart begin to speed faster. 'I... some dye came out of your scarlet gym shorts,' she said.

Miles stared at her as if he'd never seen her before. Then he patted his lap: 'You've obviously washed the garments together when I told you to wash them separately.'

Debbie cleared her throat: 'I thought it would save time, so I just...'

'Then you failed to admit to your crime when we met for dinner,' Miles Johnstone continued. Knowing that everything he said was true, the twenty year old stared at the floor. 'Such carelessness had cost me three hundred pounds, and will weaken my sales position tomorrow at the buyers meeting,' Miles finished, staring at her intently, 'You can give me the rest of the details lying over my knee.'

Debbie stilled with surprise. She felt the blush start somewhere in the centre of her cheeks. It spread warmly up and down her face then intensified further.

'You can't mean...?' She couldn't bear to say the words *"that you're going to spank me"* out loud.

'I mean that you've been negligent. That you have to be punished,' Miles Johnstone confirmed. As if to underline her fate, he took off his jacket and rolled up his shirt sleeves, 'There! Now I'm ready to teach a disobedient bum to behave.'

'But ruining your shirt was a mistake!' Debbie muttered. She wondered what a spanking would feel like, but she couldn't just throw herself across his knees like a sacrificial virgin. And being spanked like a naughty schoolgirl would be so embarrassing. She'd see if she could talk her way out.

'It would be a mistake if I didn't modify your bad behaviour by pulling down your pants and warming your rear,' the manager continued. Debbie stared at him with mixed curiosity and apprehension. Was he really going to do this or was he just trying to psyche her out, give her a scare?

'I'm stronger that I look. Bet you can't haul me across your knee,' she said challengingly. There was less shame in being bent across his knee if he put her there himself.

'I've spanked much bigger girls than you,' Miles said with a lazy grin. He reached for her arms and pulled her over in a single movement. Then he clasped both her wrists in one of his hands and placed the other in the small of her back. 'How many spanks should you get for not confessing you'd ruined my shirt in the first place?' he asked, stroking her wriggling bum.

'Eight?' Debbie muttered, beginning to feel vulnerably small. She'd half wanted this - but now she wasn't sure if she could bear it. What if he just pushed her away afterwards like he'd done when he'd kissed her before?

'Eight spanks for a three hundred pound shirt?' the manager murmured, continuing to trace her small buttocks through her tight velour dress, 'That hardly seems appropriate. I think thirty sounds fair - for starters, that is.'

'That's only the beginning?' Debbie muttered, then waited for confirmation. She was hugely aware of her pantied and skirted little bum.

'Here's what I have in mind,' Miles Johnstone said, 'First I give you thirty spanks over your dress as a punishment for disobeying my laundering instructions in the first place. Then I lift up your dress and give you another thirty for not telling me about the ruined shirt right away. Finally I bare your bottom and give you a final thrashing, the number of spanks depending on how good or bad you've been during the previous slaps.'

By then her buttocks would be the deepest vermilion shade, Debbie thought, and she shivered with shame and excitement.

'I plan,' Miles Johnstone continued, as if reading her thoughts, 'To turn your bum three colours red.'

Debbie sensed that he'd raised his right hand. She puckered up her bottom nervously, and closed her eyes. Then she opened them in surprise as the first spank lashed down on her taut left buttock. It felt surprisingly strong, though warming rather than sore. Miles treated the alternate buttock to the same firm treatment and it too began to feel more alive, started to tingle like her face did when she left the house and walked into the cold. The twenty year old pressed her tummy more firmly against the manager's knees as he repeated the full force spanks on her dress-and-panties-sheathed flesh.

'Been practicing, have you?' she muttered.

'I lift weights twice a week at the gym,' Miles said. He spanked hard at the tender underswell, 'Means I can really warm a naughty bum.'

'Congratulations!' the student sneered, squirming ashamedly against his knee. The repeated spanks were beginning to make her cheeks glow and burn a little, so she tensed her derriere, trying to turn it into a smaller target for the hateful hand.

'How many more?' she quavered.

'A few more over your dress,' Miles answered, 'I forgot to count so I'll just have to guess at the number you've yet to receive.' He continued to whack her wriggling bottom through the tight-stretched velour, 'Then we'll *really* begin to have some spanking fun.'

Because he'll be pulling up my dress. Debbie thought back to the panties she'd put on. Damn, they were fuchsia-coloured bikini style ones which matched the equally flimsy bra now moulding to her full hard nipples. Lingerie to inspire lustfulness, not lingerie to protect a punished bum. Miscreants in the past had put padding down their pants to protect their bottoms from the biting cane or the searing slipper. Her own poor buttocks would have no such padding at all. The student made little gasping sounds as Miles applied the final hard spanks to her clingy dress material. Then she awaited the next more shameful part of being taken to task.

For long moments the manager seemed content to just caress her tender curves through the black velour.

'It's getting nice and hot already, Debbie,' he whispered, 'Can you feel how tender it is?'

'Can't feel a thing!' Debbie muttered, wriggling on his lap like an eel out of water, and wincing at the outright lie. But she was dammed if she'd give this man the satisfaction of knowing that he was making an impact on her, even if he was making a very big impact. Being so close to him had obviously started off the familiar sexual signals, and now she was aware of a low insistent pulsing between her legs.

Miles squeezed her bum cheeks extra hard.

'Well, we'll have to change all that,' he murmured, 'After all, you *are* being punished.'

'You could just try sending me to Coventry!' Debbie said. She shivered as the man's large hands started to edge her dress up, and she realised that he was closer to baring her bottom.

'Rather than ordering you to keep silent,' he said with evident enjoyment, 'I'm hoping to make you squeal.'

'Sadist!' Debbie muttered. She whimpered with desire as Miles slid a finger inside the gusset of her panties and stroked her full wet labial lips.

'In that case you're a masochist,' he said sweetly, 'You've got the hottest little quim.'

He was right. She'd been climbing towards a climax from the moment he first suggested she bend over his knee. The twenty year old stared down at the carpet as he moved her dress hem up her back by merciless inches. She'd had submissive fantasies in the past - but now this was reality. And she had a feeling that it was going to hurt like hell. Debbie's pantied bum trembled. She knew that if someone had ruined three hundred pounds worth of *her* clothes she'd have been itching to get her own back. And, with her taut globes beneath his palms, Miles could do just that...

'Pink panties over an even pinker bum. How appropriate,' the *Masculine Mode* manager said. Debbie stiffened as she felt his fingers tracing the warmed flesh beneath her high-cut silken briefs. 'I can see the top half of each cheek. It's got a lovely glow,' Miles Johnstone continued, 'Looks really sore.'

'Into colour co-ordination now, are we?' Debbie sneered.

'No, I'm into rectifying a girl's mistakes,' Miles replied, raising his knees in order to hoist her bottom higher. Debbie quivered at her increased vulnerability and wished that she'd never ruined his designer shirt or tried to keep quiet about its demise.

'Maybe we could come to a deal about the spoilt clothes?' she muttered, trying to delay the next cruelly-sensitising slaps.

'The deal is that you get the hottest arse on the planet for being negligent and deceitful,' Miles replied.

Debbie felt the shameful lust rush through her. It was quickly followed by a new spread of nether orbs pain. 'Aah!' she gasped out as his palm slapped hard against one pantied cheek. 'Ow, that really hurt,' she added, as he toasted the other equally helpless rotundity. He was holding her down so firmly that she could only kick her ankles and writhe in place.

'Use the histrionics when I'm spanking your bare bum,' Miles murmured, 'Then you'll really have something to squeal about.'

'I... don't know if I'll be able to take it,' Debbie said gutturally, gasping the words between smacks.

'The option,' said the manager, 'Is that I give you a bill for three hundred quid.' He stopped spanking her, and just stroked her bum. He seemed to be waiting. 'Well, what's it to be?' he said at last.

'I...' Debbie was already behind with her rent and gas bills, 'I'll... alright, just keep doing it!' she said.

'Doing what?' Miles Johnstone countered, squeezing her hot sore spheres, 'Come on, sweetheart, don't be shy. What is it that you want me to keep doing?' he prompted, pulling at her waistband to tighten her fuchsia pants.

Debbie closed her eyes again. God, this was shameful!

'You know,' she got out.

'Articulate it,' Miles replied, 'My God, you're supposed to be majoring in English.'

'I... just continue the spanking,' Debbie said.

'That's what you want, is it, my dear?' the older man parried, 'A sore bottom for being a wicked little girl?'

Debbie clenched her teeth together. For a moment she wished that *she* was the one doling out the spanks. 'Yes, I... want you to keep spanking me,' she breathed.

'Tell me how your bottom feels now,' the manager went on.

More heat rushed to Debbie's groin. Her nipples hardened. But she couldn't say the kind of words he was insisting on. He was so new to her: she had to retain some dignity. Had to put up the vestige of a fight. Then Miles slid a thick knowing finger inside her rapturous recess, and all conscious thought fled. 'Please let me come,' she whispered, 'Sir - please!'

'Ask nicely for the rest of your spanking first,' her tormentor ordered, stirring the teasing finger deep inside her, 'You have to endure the main course before you can have dessert.'

He encircled her hungry clitoris. Then he stopped.

'Ask nicely,' he ordered again.

Debbie knew she'd say anything if her climax was the outcome. 'Please spank me hard, sir,' she said gutturally, blushing further, and dipping her head closer to the ground.

'Let's be more specific,' the manager continued, 'Say something like *please spank me over my panties then pull them down and really give me what for, sir.*'

In a shaky voice, Debbie began to repeat his instructions. Humiliation made her stumble over the phrase.

'No, I want it in your own words,' Miles Johnstone said when she'd finished. She sensed a smile enter his voice as he put a fingertip on her peaking-out clit and kept it there, 'I'll just touch this bud ever so lightly to remind you how kind I can be to you, sweetheart. If I feel that you're not being sufficiently humble I'll take my nice friendly finger away.'

'No - I beg. Keep touching me,' Debbie pleaded, closing her eyes in near-ecstasy and pushing her mons against the friction, 'I promise that I'll say...'

Each self-belittling word deserted her as Miles played with her pussy. Then he stopped the movement, and just held his finger teasingly in place. Debbie's clit made her do the talking.

'I want... I want you to finish spanking me over my pants,' she muttered shamefacedly, 'I want it really hard.' She searched for further shameful images, 'I... em... deserve to be made to squeal a lot and wriggle and beg.'

'Yes, you do, don't you?' the *Masculine Mode* manager said. He stroked each swollen labial lip. 'And what else do you deserve to happen to you, my naughty Miss?'

'To... have you take my pants down,' Debbie forced out.

The man was almost purring now as he cupped her pubis: 'You mean you know you deserve to be spanked very hard on the bare?'

'Yes, I... cause I've been a wicked girl, because I've been wilful.' Debbie squirmed with additional shame as she debased herself further. The urge to climax was colouring everything.

'And when your arse is the third shade of red, the hottest and sorest shade, what will you do to please me?' the spanker enquired softly.

'I'll take you in my mouth. I'll lick you from balls to shaft tip,' Debbie said. It was the most submissive image she could think of. To her surprise, Miles thought of an even more blatant one.

'I think I'd rather have you kneeling on the bed, with your head resting on your arms and your red rump sticking right up in the air,' he said thoughtfully, 'That way I could look at your hot bum as I fucked you, and could even spank it further if you continued to be bad.'

'Yes, sir - I'd push my arse right up for you. I'd beg for your cock. I'd ask really nicely for each thrust from it,' Debbie whispered, rubbing her engorged clit against his leg.

'I'm sure you will - but for now I'm not interested in your hungry little hole, only in your disobedient bum,' Miles said. He squeezed each pantied cheek, 'How many of the spanks with pants on are you still due, girl?'

'Ten, sir,' Debbie replied, recalling each focused and fiery whacking she'd already endured.

'Lucky for you that you remembered,' Miles said, 'Else I'd have had to start that particular chastisement all over again.'

'You wouldn't, would you?' Debbie whispered, appalled at the prospect.

'Let's hope for your poor bottom's sake that you never have to find out,' Miles said.

He pushed her dress further up her back, then once again pulled at the waistband to tighten her panties. 'Ten more over your knickers,' he repeated. Then he raised his right hand and doled out the entire number in an aching tattoo of spanks. Debbie tensed each buttock and jerked and shoved her belly forward in the hope of making her bum a smaller target, but she hardly had time to make a sound.

'Ah,' she said belatedly when he'd finished, 'Those hurt like hell.'

'I'm sure Hell is hot, but I like to make disobedient girls even hotter,' the manager responded lightly. Debbie heard another smile enter his voice, 'Especially now that you're about to have your panties pulled down to your ankles so that you can be chastened on the bare.' She felt his fingers moving against the waistband of her knickers as he continued, 'I do so love to remove a protective pair of panties.' Debbie winced as she felt the material being dragged over her glowing bum, 'It's just so nice, knowing how shamed she feels as I watch her small bum cheeks tremble. Knowing that I'm about to teach her true respect.'

'Oh, just get it over with,' Debbie muttered, pushing her pubis against his lap in a craving-for-a-climax gesture.

'You can't rush a sound thrashing,' Miles added sweetly, 'No, I plan to make this naked punishment last as long as possible. After all, my right hand's got all night.'

'Don't you want to save some of your energy for your second trip?' the twenty year old shot back, determined not to be totally cowed by her would-be lover.

'The trip is already at a disadvantage given that you've ruined its showpiece,' the *Masculine Mode* manager said.

The student quivered as he edged her panties over her thighs, calves and feet. With her dress pushed way up her back, she was hugely aware of her newly-stripped buttocks, of her legs in the ten denier hold ups. It was a bottom which already stung all over from the heat of the manager's large palm.

'How many did we say that this bare bottom would get?' Miles murmured.

'Thirty,' Debbie said quickly.

She heard Miles snort with amusement. 'So you want the full thirty, do you, my sweet?' He teased his fingers over her newly-bared bum, 'We originally said that the third part of your punishment was to be decided but if you think that your buttocks deserves another full thirty, then thirty it shall be.' Slowly he cupped his palm around her quim, making her moan with desire and bear down against his fingers, 'I hope you don't orgasm whilst I'm spanking you. I'd like you to wait until it's time to plead for my cock,' he said.

Debbie knew that she'd plead. She could feel the gelatinous strands of lust making their slow steady way out of her hot gaping entrance. Her wriggling had caused further sexual excitement to smear across her inner thighs.

But when the first spank enlivened her already sore flesh, she forgot about everything except her tender buttocks. She cried out, the sound following on from the heavy slapping noise which filled the room. 'Not so hard. Don't. Aaah!' she pleaded, trying to reach her hands back in order to place them over her squirming bottom. If she could just hold the burning flesh...

'Bad girls don't get to soothe their bums till the thrashing is completely finished,' Miles said.

'Have a history of girls ruining your shirts, do you?' Debbie muttered, flexing and re-flexing her sore buttock muscles.

'Let's just say that most of my girlfriends have digressed in some way at some time,' Miles replied.

'And you spanked each of their bums three colours red?' Debbie added sarcastically, trying to stall the remainder of her thrashing.

'No, sometimes I caned them mercilessly,' the irrepressible manager said.

The prospect of the cane sent further seductive signals to Debbie's sex, then Miles hand sent further cruel sensation to her arse. It was funny, Debbie thought, how she'd gotten wet by being threatened with a spanking. Yet the actual punishment took most lustful thoughts away.

'Not so hard,' she begged again, twisting her head round to stare at him pleadingly. But he just played with her clit till she agreed that he could spank her to his heart and hand's content.

'Twenty!' said Miles after what seemed an agonizingly long time, 'Twenty-one! Twenty-two! Twenty-three!'

Debbie felt his spanks land on the centre of each bare cheek. She felt his fingers mark her buttock sides. Other spanks strayed down near the tops of her thighs above her hold-ups. The ones over the full crevice between her globes hurt the most.

'It's only a spanking,' Miles said as she cried out, and Debbie wondered if he'd ever been spanked himself on his raised bare bottom. Surely not, for then he would have shown some compassion during these last few stinging whacks. If he'd felt the heat of a frequently applied palm, he wouldn't be saying 'Twenty-four! Twenty-five!' with quite so much zealousness. Only five more to go, she told herself bravely. Only four, three...

'Twenty-eight,' Miles continued, and Debbie winced as his large hand toasted the tender underswell. He added the twenty-ninth spank to the same susceptible region. Then he placed the thirtieth over the sensitive dividing crease. Not that it was really just thirty spanks, Debbie thought with bum-aching clarity - it was three sets of thirty, which made ninety in all.

'Permission to hold my bum, sir,' she whispered respectfully.

'Permission denied till I've examined it,' her punisher replied. He let go of her wrists, and she felt him take one hot buttock in each hand. He squeezed and stroked the tender rotundities till Debbie trembled. She was terrified that he'd start spanking them again.

'I'm sorry that I ruined your shirt,' she whispered contritely.

'I can tell that you're genuine about that,' a gentler-looking Miles said.

'It hurts so much,' Debbie added gutturally as he continued to mould and cup her scarlet posterior.

'You ruined hours of work done by tireless silkworms - its only right that you should be made to wriggle like they do,' Miles said.

She wanted to wriggle on his cock. She craved orgasmic satisfaction. Debbie waited for the man to order her to walk through to the bedroom. Instead he said 'Walk over to that mirror and look at your punished bum.'

'What if I don't?' Debbie muttered, feeling new shame spring through her.

'If you don't, then your clit doesn't get release. It's that simple,' her almost-lover replied.

'Alright - I'm walking. I'm walking,' Debbie shot back, her pubis begging to come.

All of the strength seemed to have drained from her arms, so that it took her a long time to lever herself up from his lap and from the low couch. Her legs, when she stood, felt equally languid. Another long string of lust started to wend its way from her wide-open vulva, and she hoped he couldn't see.

'What mirror?' she muttered, looking slowly round the room which now seemed brighter than she'd remembered.

'Turn round and walk straight ahead,' Miles said. 'No, leave your dress up over your waist,' he added as she moved to smooth it down over her exposed bare bottom, 'I want to see your bum cheeks jiggling about.'

Debbie turned quickly so that he didn't see the new blush which spread over her face and neck at his disparaging words. Then she realised that he was now staring at her sore rear - and that was even more shameful. She moved quickly towards the mirror, wincing every step of the way. She still wanted to cup her tender flesh and just hold it for a while till the fire subsided. But to do so might provoke further wrath.

'Now turn and bend over and look at your sore arse,' Miles instructed.

More lust flooding through her loins at his authoritative tone, Debbie hastened to obey. She stared back at the reflection of her rump: both small spherical cheeks were red from buttock top to thigh, especially in the centres. Each quivering globe seemed to radiate heat, to glow. 'You spanked me so hard,' she whispered, staring at her tormented derriere.

'And now I'm going to make you orgasm equally hard,' Miles promised, walking over to her and lifting her into his arms.

He carried her to his bed. She knelt then moved her head onto her bent elbows at his request, moaned with relief as he slid deep inside her. These moans intensified till she climaxed, the waves of pleasure rushing through her pubis again and again.

'I was so desperate for it,' she whispered, after he'd enjoyed his own rapture, 'My sex felt so hollow. I needed to come so bad.'

'And you needed to be spanked,' Miles said, putting his arm around her shoulders as they lay on the bed together. Debbie hid her face in his armpit. She wasn't so sure about that bit. 'Your bottom is already fading to crimson rather than it's original ruby shade,' Miles continued, looking down at her small taut buttocks, 'Red is the least stable colour in the wash cycle. Did you know?'

Debbie took her face from his armpit. 'I did after I washed your red cycling shorts with your white grandad shirt,' she said, 'You know, I put the shorts in first to test them for colour fastness, and no dye came out, so then I added your shirt to the soapy water. Two minutes later half of it had turned a mottled scarlet shade!'

'And you earned yourself a scarlet bum,' Miles concluded.

Debbie swallowed at his words, then tried to divert him from the subject by kissing his nipples. 'Well, I've learnt my lesson! I plan never to touch your laundry again.'

'And you think that will save those tender young cheeks?' Miles asked, 'My previous girlfriend had to be disciplined for turning up late, for flirting with other men, for being grumpily pre-menstrual.'

'I get pre-menstrual,' Debbie whispered anxiously, closing her eyes.

'Well, before you snap at me in the midst of some hormonal tantrum,' Miles replied sweetly, 'Just think about how it feels to go bare-arsed over my knee.'

'You mean you'd spank me for being bad tempered?' Debbie muttered. Already her breasts had started to gain weight, which signalled that her period was due within the next seven days or so. She usually snapped at boyfriends one minute and smiled at them the next.

'Oh, I might do more than spank you,' Miles parried, 'I might use this very effective long cane I keep in my wardrobe. Or I might just take off my belt.' He kissed her on the nose then pulled her closer and started to examine her round smooth contours, 'There are tawses and riding crops and paddles I can use on your bottom to turn it three colours red.'

Work Experience

He was being naughty. Very naughty. Vincent allowed himself a self-satisfied chuckle as he used the janitor's spare key to open Miss Kerr's office door. Any moment now he would be sitting in the big swivel chair that she worked from. He'd be as close to her warm flesh as he was ever likely to get.

Everyone bar the janitor who had lent him the key had gone home, so Vincent coolly put Miss Kerr's office light on. Then he walked over to the wire rack where she'd left a pair of her kitten-heeled shoes. Scarcely daring to breathe he picked up the well-formed footwear and traced its contours whilst breathing in her faint silk-stockinged scent. Now he must concentrate on reading Miss Kerr's work diary. He'd wanted to learn his unsettling supervisor's secrets for so very long...

An hour later the hairs on the back of his neck reared into sentry mode as he heard someone approaching. Vincent jerked his head from the second drawer of his superior's filing cabinet and whirled around to face the door. Alicia Kerr stood there in a belted black trouser suit and black velvet ankle boots. She was staring at him with obvious disapproval and rage.

'How dare you,' she said quietly.

Vincent felt the hot shame consume his features. 'I didn't mean to...' he said weakly.

'Tell it to the managing director,' the thirty year old goddess said.

'It wasn't... it's not work espionage or anything,' Vincent mumbled, running his hands through his short fair hair as if it could provide him with an escape route, 'I just wanted to know more about you - find those odd packages you sometimes carry about.'

For excruciatingly long moments Alicia Kerr stared into his eyes then she seemed to come to some inner decision.

'Alright,' she said slowly, 'Bare your bum for me and submit to a damn good thrashing. I'll introduce you to the contents of my packages tomorrow night.'

Vincent felt his mouth fall open like an unclasped case. Women simply didn't say such things - not to him, they didn't. He'd always led such a small but undaunting life.

'Bare... a thrashing?' he stuttered, focusing on her long trousered legs and cinched-in waistline. He waited for her to say that she'd spoken in jest.

'Strip from the waist down now or wave promotion goodbye,' his boss said matter of factly. She crossed to her desk and perched on the end of it to watch him. She looked as if she were enjoying herself.

'Okay, I'm stripping,' Vincent muttered, turning his back to her and fumbling with the buttons on his linen suit. One half of him wanted desperately to escape from this disparaging situation - but he knew that to flee could curtail his career path. The other half was curious to know what would happen next.

When he'd undressed the lower half of his body he was relieved to see that his shirt tail covered his small oval cheeks.

'Lift that right up - now tie it around your waist,' his raven-haired dominator ordered.

Vincent gripped the shirt's hemmed edge and then hesitated: 'Couldn't I take you out for a meal or... send round a crate of champagne?'

'You mean buy my silence?' She looked at his naked thighs until he shivered with uncertainty and degradation. 'No, I'd rather have my pound of flesh.' Then she smiled and pointed to the rosewood executive desk, 'Bend over that then stick out your bottom and await the strap.'

Slowly Vincent took his naked hemispheres over to the desk and presented them for the ensuing discipline. He'd never felt so vulnerable in his adult life.

As if to prolong his uncertainty, Miss Kerr seemed determined to take her time. With measured steps she walked to the other side of the desk and tilted his chin so that he was forced to gaze up at her. Then she moved her fingers to her own waistband. 'Watch closely, boy, as I take off my belt.' She pulled the leather strap through its stout silver buckle, 'See how firm yet supple this cruel contraption is?'

'Yes, Ma'am,' Vincent forced out apprehensively.

'Kiss it and ask nicely for your comeuppance,' his superior said.

Beyond rational thought, the twenty-three year old pressed his lips to the smooth thick punisher. He knew his pale cheeks weren't going to stay pale for very long.

'Not too hard, please, Miss,' he whispered as she prepared to discipline his helplessly-raised lower quarters.

'You should have imagined this thrashing before you gained illegal access to my office and went through my private papers,' the authoritative belt-holder said.

The air currents around Vincent's backside changed as she drew back her arm. He moaned as the leather strap lashed forward, driving into his soft buttocks.

'And again,' Miss Kerr said, subjecting his fearful haunches to another blow.

'How many, please?' he gasped out, squirming around as if polishing the desk top with his belly.

His enforcer snorted with amusement. 'That's for me to know and you to find out.'

Vincent looked back at her slightly flushed cheeks and sparkling large dark eyes, the sure way in which she doubled the leather punisher. Something told him that he and his bottom would be here for a very long time...

But after a mere ten lashes Miss Kerr ordered him to stand and pull his trousers up over his rosy arse.

'It's late. I'm tired. As I said before, I'll deal with you properly tomorrow after work, young man.'

'Here?' Vincent asked meekly, then winced as he pulled his Y-fronts over his tenderised flesh.

'No, report to my house.' Miss Kerr walked over to her desk drawer then handed him her personal address card, 'As I said, I'll show you what's in those packages that you're so curious about.'

'And you'll... chasten me further?' Vincent realised he might as well know what further trials awaited him.

'Yes, I'll teach you the sort of lesson you'll never forget.'

******

The next day at work passed very slowly for Vincent. He looked at the clock. He looked at his supervisor. He remembered how it had felt to be completely at her mercy. Was she remembering how he'd whimpered and squirmed across her desk? If he took his next punishment well would she allow him to prostrate himself before her? Let him use his eager tongue to sweetly serve?

At 6pm Miss Kerr put her project notes away. '8pm exactly,' she warned without looking back as she walked out of the office door, 'Don't dare be late.'

He was there. He was prepared to make his bottom bare. But again she totally out-guessed him.

'Strip,' she said as he entered her large warm lounge.

'What? Everything?' Vincent whispered, his heart beating faster.

'Yes, take off every last stitch so that you're naked for the duration of your training session,' Alicia Kerr explained. She watched as he clumsily undressed himself and removed his footwear. 'Naked except for this,' she said.

When he dared look up he saw that she was holding a studded dog collar and lead. Humiliation and desire surged for supremacy in his lower belly. Obediently he got down on all fours then crawled up to her in order that she could fasten the studded leather strap around his neck.

'The doggy has been sniffing around at work - so now we're going to show the doggy what's in the mysterious packages. Walk to heel, you bad puppy,' the disdainful beauty said.

She took a measured few steps forward until the collar tightened slightly at his throat. Vincent hastened to crawl after her like a good little canine. He stared at her black-stockinged calves as he lumbered across the room, then simply concentrated on his posture as he made his awkward hands-and-knees journey up the stairs.

At last they reached a cream-painted door. Alicia Kerr unlocked it and Vincent fearfully followed her into a massive square shaped bedroom. A King Size in the corner had four posts with ornate wooden bars connecting the top two posts and the bottom two posts. Three pillows had been placed in a pile on the centre of the bed, and Vincent had a horrible feeling he knew what they were for.

'I believe you were interested in the packages I sometimes carry with me?' Miss Kerr asked, coolly opening a walk-in cupboard, 'Well now you can try them out for yourself.' She stood back, still holding the lead, so that Vincent could see the contents of each of the dozen or so full shelves. They held box after box of erotic aids. 'See? I'm a Thrills-For-Girls party plan co-ordinator in my spare time,' his supervisor said softly, 'You know the saying, all work and no play...'

'Ah - so you were going on to the post office in your lunchbreak to send off the merchandise,' Vincent muttered, staring in awe at the arousing toys, 'Now I understand!'

'Well, the main orders are despatched straight from the suppliers,' said Miss Kerr, 'But I send out demonstration models to each party-plan girl who is hosting her first party. And I send them replacements when the originals break.'

She pulled on the leash until he looked beseechingly up at her. 'You still have to be punished fully for going into my office after hours, little pup, so lie on your belly on the bed.' As she gave the order she unclipped the short lead but left the demeaning thick studded collar around his neck.

The mattress creaked a little as he got into place but supported his eleven stone weight without difficulty. Without asking, Vincent adjusted his frame until his stomach was resting on the stockpile of extra-plump pillows. They pushed his oval cheeks defencelessly in the air.

'I'm going to stripe your backside and then I'm going to train you in the art of self control even if it takes me all evening to do so,' his supervisor said.

Vincent turned his head around to watch as she walked smartly across the room. Her breasts and buttocks were neatly hugged by her well-cut black sheath dress. A gold-hoop style metal belt glinted at her waist, emphasising her firm bone structure. He hoped she wouldn't use that same belt on his white buttock flesh.

Miss Kerr leaned into the built-in wardrobe and brought out a crook-handled cane. Then she walked to the side of the bed. 'Bring that arse nearer.'

Hastily Vincent moved himself and the pillows in a desperate last ditch attempt to please. Last night's leathering had brought grimace-making pain to his proffered bottom. He dreaded to think how the rod would lick into his flesh.

'Beg sweetly for the first stroke,' his supervisor said.

Vincent closed his eyes and tightened his inner thighs and eyelids. 'I beg to taste the cane, Mistress.' The word Mistress had escaped unbidden from his lips.

'Beg more humbly or I'll triple your thrashing - and I already intend to deal with you very severely,' his thirty year old superior said.

Vincent searched his awestruck mind for suitable words. He so wanted to get in and stay in her good books. If only she could look on him with affection if not with love.

'I've... been disobedient. I deserve to pay. I'd be very grateful if you caned me without mercy,' he whispered with hard won obsequiousness.

'Oh don't worry, you won't be disappointed,' Miss Kerr said.

She bounced the rod against his haunches a few times, the light sure touch sharpening his tactile senses. Then, just as he was letting his belly sink deeper into the pillows, she laid the rod on for real.

'Ah!' Vincent brought his hands out from under his chin and reared up, clutching frenziedly at his bottom. He chafed at the singed thin tram-line as if his fingers were erasers and the redness drawn in pen.

'Get back into position this instant, boy,' his disciplinarian instructed in her matter of fact tone.

'But it stings like blazes,' Vincent muttered, looking around.

'Just like it stung my sense of security to have you snooping through my office after hours,' Alicia Kerr retorted staring at him coldly. She pointed to the uneven heap of pillows. 'Straighten them and then bend over again.'

Reluctantly Vincent presented his buttocks anew. He prayed that this time she'd be more lenient. He cast a sorry look round at his singly-striped backside.

The second lash fell neatly below the first. He was in the process of rising up when Alicia laid on a third cane mark. Vincent cried out again and turned quickly around and sat on his hands.

'It's too much,' he whimpered, fingers kneading his blazing ovals.

Alicia laughed and squared her shoulders back so that her full breasts jutted through the clingy black. She stared down at him for thirty full seconds then pointed to the cupboard which contained the marital aids.

'Crawl over there and bring me back a battery operated vibrator, boy.'

Carefully Vincent skulked to the side of the King Size then lowered himself on to the carpet and crawled to the lowest shelf. His eyes searched the many boxes until he found a battery-operated oscillator that he thought might suit. Maybe she wanted him to run it across her silken folds for her ultimate delectation. He'd be happy - nay, ecstatic - to oblige.

Crawling whilst holding the package might have dented the glossy wet-look box so Vincent carefully opened it and put the hinged cardboard lid in his mouth.

'Good dog. Bring it here,' Alicia said more warmly.

Vincent's heart swelled with newborn pride. He parted his lips and she took the container from him and removed the oblong toy.

'Now bend over the foot of the bed - but keep your hands on the back of your head at all times or you'll be very sorry,' she said.

'Yes, Mistress,' the twenty-three year old mumbled, determined not to put her patience to the test. He stood up and quickly bent, aware of how the thick mahogany bar curved into his belly and pushed his bum out. The position immediately put a strong pull on his calves. 'I don't think I can hold this position for long,' he admitted, staring down at the duvet and wondering if he was dreaming.

'You won't have to - you'll soon be back on the bed begging for the rest of your caning,' Alicia Kerr said.

He was aware of a low buzzing sound. Ah, she'd obviously switched on the vibrator. Vincent's legs tightened further with apprehension and anticipation as the rich resonance filled the air. He'd read about such machines, of course, about how much pleasure they gave the ladies, but he'd never actually seen one, far less tried it out.

Something nudged against his inner right thigh. The vibrations spread up. The sensation was exquisite. He groaned and tried to push his body downwards to increase his contact with the pleasure-source.

'Bad boy,' Alicia Kerr said huskily, moving the implement a little away from him. The unyielding bed frame held him in place.

'I won't wriggle any more, I swear, Mistress!' Vincent gasped out, keeping his hands obediently where he'd been told to. He wished that he could grab hold of the wonderful sensation-bringer, but to do so would further brook his Mistress's displeasure and would lead to an increasingly severe training time.

Alicia continued to taunt his inner thighs. Vincent moaned more loudly at the almost-almost-almost sensation.

'Please show your bad slave mercy,' he whimpered, hearing the grovelling tone in his uneven voice tone, 'Oh I beg you, please!'

'Please cane me, Mistress - isn't that what you meant to say?' his superior queried, moving the vibrator to a much more exquisite place.

She'd left the cane lying on the bed. Vincent stared at its pitiless length with renewed trepidation.

'Couldn't you use your belt on me like you did at the office?' he gasped.

Alicia Kerr moved the erotic machine further down, stealing away his much-craved source of satisfaction.

'I'd much prefer to see you flinch and howl under my cane.'

The inference was clear - he had to taste the rod or she'd never grant him the ultimate bodily bliss. 'I've... been a naughty boy. Please whip my bare bottom soundly, Mistress,' he stammered.

Alicia immediately switched off the appliance and put it to one side. 'Let's bend you over the ottoman for variety,' she said archly. 'Come here so that I can affix your collar to your lead.'

Vincent pushed himself back from the bed's firm bar and flexed his limbs then got down on all fours again. He crawled meekly over to her feet. She led him next door to a large semi-circular dressing room. The ottoman was of the same mahogany as the bed. 'Go over it lengthways so that the lid supports your entire body,' ordered Alicia, 'That way the blood won't rush to your head.'

It wasn't his head he was worried about. Vincent felt very sorry for his manhood which was rapidly deflating. She'd taken him close to Nirvana a moment ago - if only she'd allowed him to reach his zenith with the machine. He shivered with sensuous suspense just imagining the possibility. If he pleased her would she take him to the very depths of his own wantonness?

'I'm obeying all of your orders, Mistress,' he mumbled shamefacedly as he lowered himself along the mahogany wood.

When his tummy and chest were safely supported he gripped the side of the ottoman. The position ensured that his legs were stretched out in the air at a downward angle with their weight resting on his inverted toes.

'Ask nicely for the cane, boy,' his work supervisor said, tapping the rattan against his oval cheeks.

Vincent told himself that he'd take his punishment like a man this time. 'Please redden me with the rod, Mistress, for illegally entering your premises.' He was congratulating himself on his obeisant tone when the rattan sliced into his naked flesh. 'Oh!' Vincent shouted the word and jerked his hips then realised that his position made protecting his rear very difficult. If he wanted to leave the ottoman he'd have to use all of his arm strength to lever himself up and back.

'But you told me that you wanted this, remember?' Alicia said smoothly and he felt her palm tracing the new sizzling line across his posterior.

'I want to...' Vincent gave himself up to the disinterested pleasure of her fingers then whimpered as she removed them, 'Yes, Mistress,' he said resignedly, 'Please cane my cowardly little arse again.'

Miss Kerr obliged. This time she laid the rod across the centre of his expanse. Heat seemed to radiate through him. Vincent writhed across the mahogany trunk, moving his buttocks from side to side in a vain bid to shake off the pain. When he at last settled down he heard her say 'I'm waiting, boy.'

'I need... need a further dose of correction, Mistress,' he gasped out.

'Oh you do, don't you?' the iron-willed Miss Kerr said. Vincent quivered with new pleasure as her hands encircled his waist, gripping his ribs with erotic firmness. Then he tensed as she rearranged his naked body till it was fully central on the ottoman again, 'Can't have you wriggling to one side without permission, slave,' she said coolly, and he heard her picking up the cane and flexing it, 'That bottom needs to know just who's in charge.'

Vincent quivered as he waited for the rod to land. When it did it seared a line across his apprehensive extremities.

'Is that what they mean by line dancing?' Alicia Kerr asked coolly as he did a little hot-bottomed dance. Vincent groaned at the ongoing humiliation but felt a new deep servility start to grow within himself.

'I'm listening,' his raven-haired dominatrix said.

How he longed to cover her hands and feet with his kisses. But he had to do and say only what *she* wanted - she was clearly in command. 'I'm due a hot sore bottom, Mistress,' he snivelled into the ottoman lid.

'Louder or I'll have you howling like a coyote.'

Vincent repeated his request and felt another unfamiliar low submissive thrill.

'Just one more - at least for now,' the thirty year old said as she traced his bands of scarlet, 'I do like a near-uniform glow on a male slave's arse.'

She enlivened the crease just above his hirsute thighs. Vincent flattened his belly to the wood and groaned softly at the impact. He did his by now familiar jitterbug then belatedly straightened and thanked her nicely for the lash.

'Now I'll take the good dog to the cloakroom. There's a nice high peg that we can tether you to,' she said.

She exerted a slight pressure on his lead and Vincent carefully lifted himself from the ottoman then hunkered down upon the carpet. The cloakroom was downstairs and she was kind enough to let him walk the single flight. 'Down boy,' she said again when they reached the bottom, pointing at the carpet. Vincent hastened to return to his hands and knees.

His muscles tightened as he crawled behind her into a rectangular room. Miss Kerr pointed to a peg which was set much further up in the wall than the others. 'Grip that whilst you take your pleasure. If you let go even for an instant I'll immediately stop.'

She slid a flesh-shaped ring around his private parts, then she switched on a small white control box. Vincent almost swooned with pleasure as the vibrations thrilled through his most intimate flesh.

'Oh thank you, Mistress, thank you,' he whispered.

'Just remember to control your responses until I give you permission,' his rigorous goddess said.

'I'll be a good boy,' Vincent promised raggedly, then yodelled anew.

She was kind enough to leave the current on. Soon he shouted his rapture to the rooftops. Then she bid him to let go of the high peg and he prostrated himself deliriously at her feet.

'I want so much to please you,' he whispered submissively, licking and kissing her glossy black shoes.

Alicia leaned forward and stroked his hair for a moment then tilted his chin so that he was looking adoringly up into her large dark eyes.

'Obedient slaves deserve a reward,' she murmured mischievously, beginning to slide her dress up past her stocking tops, 'We'll have to see what we can do.'

A Pony Tale

'Who'll give me a hundred pounds for this healthy young slave?' As the bid rose to this three figure sum the outdoor crowd fell silent. The couple who had gigglingly bid eighty quid ruefully shook their heads.

'Yeah - I'll offer a hundred,' muttered a small man with sparse sidecombed hair and a waxen complexion. Though she kept smiling, Magdalen nervously toed the wooden stage. She'd agreed to this charity stunt to raise money for Spain's many stray puppies. She didn't relish spending eight hours with this human stray!

'Going for a hundred pounds,' said the auctioneer. 'Going,' he continued steadfastly.

Magdalen parted her lips in mute appeal and stared pleadingly at the faces tilted towards her. She focused on a slightly-known sneer as Aaron Greaves, the owner of the Equestrian Club, stepped in front of the follically-challenged man. He held up a monogrammed cheque book cover in finest calfskin. 'I'll offer two hundred quid.'

Magdalen gasped. The auctioneer gasped. The crowd exclaimed and applauded and whistled. With funding like this, the Mediterranean Canine Rescue Depot would soon be underway.

The slave contract mock-solemnly signed and witnessed, Magdalen looked uncertainly into her new Master's assessing dark pupils. Aaron Greaves was thoughtfulness incarnate to horses and other animals, but she'd heard rumours that he soundly spanked his female staff.

'It's back to the stables with you, slave girl,' he said now, casting a thumb towards his sky-blue Daimler. Magdalen tugged at her tiny dress then tried to enter into the spirit of the game.

'Yes, sir. Whatever you say, sir,' she whispered, peeking up at him through long black lashes. 'It's wonderfully hot, sir, isn't it?' she offered after the older man had been driving wordlessly for an intolerable time.

'Speak only when spoken to, slave,' the wealthy landowner murmured. The naturalist shifted uncomfortably on the softly upholstered seat. Looking down at her bust, she could see both nipples straining through her bra like rubber bullets, as if seeking an exit through the thin dark dress.

At last they reached the vast acres of stables and grazing land that Aaron Greaves owned and he parked the Daimler. 'Have you eaten?' he asked neutrally. Magdalen nodded. 'In that case,' he continued, 'Let's set you straight to work.'

Thinking that she was to do household chores, Magdalen turned instinctively towards the large Edwardian mansion, but Aaron indicated she should walk through an arched doorway into a large gymkhana yard.

A lightweight chariot leaned against the nearest wall. Confused, Magdalen stared at the man who'd paid two hundred pounds for her. 'Let's get you bridled, sweetheart,' the Equestrian Club owner said casually.

'Bridled?' the twenty-three year old echoed, clasping her hands behind her back as if to keep them free of his clutches. Suddenly she felt even hotter than the strong August sun allowed.

Aaron Greaves looked at her till she awkwardly dropped her gaze. She sensed that his own stare continued. 'Just say "Yes, Master",' he replied.

Magdalen swayed and her vulva lengthened slightly with elation. His words both unnerved and aroused. 'I thought I'd just be doing your cooking and cleaning,' she muttered, pawing at the dust with her calfskin mules.

'Housework is a waste of time and energy compared to a sun-kissed canter,' her new Master said.

It was certainly a magnificent day to spend outdoors. Magdalen looked more fully at the waiting slave chariot and Aaron smiled encouragingly. 'The cart connects to a leather harness belt. You'll need the equestrian trappings.' He walked towards a side door in order to fetch them and Magdalen used the hiatus to discover how she felt. The sensible part of her being shrank from parading around this arena pulling her temporary Master. The darker less rational side felt hugely alive and inflamed. Aaron Greaves was attractive in a distant and demanding sort of a way, and it had been some time since she'd felt sexually shaken and stirred.

She stiffened as he reappeared in the doorway carrying thick black straps and what looked like studded shiny briefs and black stilettoes. The other garment he carried proved to be a studded open-nippled bra.

'Don't tell me - I put this cliched slut garb on then you order me to lie on my back and spread my legs,' Magdalen murmured cynically.

'I promise that I won't touch you sexually unless you beg for it,' Aaron Greaves said. He shrugged, 'I'm not forcing you into anything, angel. If you'd rather go home and forfeit the slave fee I've offered your pet charity then please just say.'

Magdalen thought of the Grecian and Spanish stray puppies that were completely relying on her. She thought of how disappointed the organisers would be if he cancelled his cheque. Then the naturalist imagined pulling her strict Master around in his chariot and felt another politically-incorrect but nevertheless powerful electric vulval thrill. 'Alright, but turn your back,' she murmured, 'Whilst I strip and put this tartish bra and panties on.'

Aaron Greaves stepped slightly closer and slapped his palm insinuatingly against his thigh. 'You'll be caned later for trying to give your superiors such crass instructions,' he told her, 'A pony girl should be seen and not heard.'

Magdalen's labial lips parted like a baby bird's beak at his words and she gasped with cowed humiliation and carnal hunger. She took the garments from the pony club owner then stared into the middle distance as she began to undress. His relentless stare psychically stroked her breasts and buttocks. Did he find her body too short, tall, fat or thin?

Slowly she stripped off her cotton crotch thong and mini dress, then squirmed into the black PVC studded panties. 'Good girl,' her Master murmured as she smoothed the glossy garment over her twitching bottom cheeks. Blushing, Magdalen unhooked her satin bra. *Think of the puppies,* she reminded herself as her soft breasts sprung free of their white lacy half cups. She picked up the peephole PVC bra and put it on, surprised and pleased by how decadent it made her normally coy pink nipples look. 'Satisfied?' she asked in what she hoped was a challenging tone. Inside she felt lusciously yielding and very passive indeed.

'Not quite - I have to attach these reins to your bra strap,' Aaron said mildly, and proceeded to do so. Then he handed her two further handles that were attached by another set of reins to the cart. Tentatively the naturalist stepped forward and the slave chariot obligingly lurched after her. The Equestrian Club owner quickly spanked first one pantied cheek then the other. 'Wait till I'm in the cart, girl, or you'll be bent over its side rather than pulling it, then you'll whimper under my whip for a very long time.'

Magdalen remembered the caning he'd said she was already due, and her spanked orbs trembled. They quivered some more as her Master climbed into the driving seat and produced a lightweight braided switch. 'This one's mainly for show, I'm afraid,' he said matter of factly, 'But even a light application reminds my pony girls to increase their pace.'

The chariot rocked slightly as he tugged on the reins. 'Canter round, love, and keep those pretty legs up high,' he warned, flicking the whip against her PVC-hugged buttocks. Magdalen stepped forward and was impressed at how lightly the chariot moved. She broke into a fast trot, her body teetering forward on the impossible high thin heels, her thigh muscles tightening. The sun highlighted her bare but PVC-ringed nipples and her pudenda pulsed inside the studded briefs.

Five times she trotted down the stretching yard then cantered briskly back again. Then she stopped and said 'Whew, I'm going to have to stop for a drink.'

Silence greeted her. She looked round. Aaron was pursing his lips and shaking his head. 'I'll have to increase your caning for this latest insolence. *Ask humbly* for water - don't *inform* your Master that you're going to stop pulling your cart,' he said.

'Right, well I'm asking now!' Magdalen muttered hollowly, worried by this further threat of being flogged.

She relaxed as her owner murmured 'So the little horse needs water,' before he disembarked and made his way to the enormous house.

He returned with a half-filled nose bag and held it up to Magdalen's gaping mouth. Feeling silly, she lapped clumsily at the brew, realising that it was carbonated mineral water. It trilled through her system like the finest champagne, wakening each cell of her body up, up, up. 'Now you're to be thrashed for insubordination,' the Equestrian Club owner continued. His eyes radiated both amusement and mischief but his mouth was set in a displeased firm line.

Wondering what her bum must look like in the clingy PVC briefs, Magdalen walked shakily before him to the house. 'The Punishment Room is that way,' he said, pointing to the fourth door along the hall.

'Flagellate your staff all the time, do you?' Magdalen asked with hard won temerity.

'Only when their lack of respect warrants a sore bum,' the affluent landowner replied. Magdalen wondered what a sore bum would feel like, and knew that each second took her closer to finding out. Her body now wished that she'd been more deferential whilst her mind longed to know how the cane felt as it flared against womanly flesh. After all, the females who worked here were reported to be addicted to this man's particular brand of punishment. Maybe these things called endorphins which made people feel all floaty would kick in...

Magdalen entered the chastisement area and stared at the disciplinary chairs and trestles, the leather tawses and polished wooden paddles.

'Bend your arse over that sloping punishment stool in the centre,' her Master said evenly, 'Then pull down those PVC pants.'

The twenty-three year old got awkwardly into position over the four-legged bolstered wood. 'Couldn't I just keep them on for the first stroke?' she murmured, holding on to her pants cajolingly.

Aaron's voice and words brooked no opposition. 'You've just earned another stroke for speaking out of turn, little slave girl. That's on top of your already allotted three,' he explained.

Four strokes didn't sound too bad. Magdalen reached back and pulled down the clingy black pants, wincing at the ignominy. Then she regripped the bar at the lower legs of the stool and awaited the first slender lash. She lay over the exhibiting rack with her bare bottom waiting. She waited and waited for a very long time. *Just do it,* she thought, as the anticipation built cruelly deep within her. Her entire being was now focused on her helpless backside. 'Don't wriggle,' said her Master's voice and she realised belatedly that she'd been tensing and untensing her smooth pale naked cheeks.

Magdalen forced her twin globes to relax - and immediately Aaron laid the first rattan stripe across her previously virgin hemispheres. The rod swished across their centre, and Magdalen yelled and swung her emblazoned hips from side to side.

'Shall I kiss it better?' a cool voice asked.

The twenty-three year old hesitated, torn between telling him to go to hell and wanting him quite badly. The needy part of her persona won. 'Yes please, sir,' she whispered huskily, 'Please lick and kiss my flesh.'

She quivered with loins-based lust as she felt his teasing lips trace the stinging stripe. How she longed for his firm tongue to move on to her juice-slicked pudenda. But after an enjoyable moment Aaron moved his knowing mouth away.

'You need stroke two,' he warned, 'You have to endure the pain before you can enjoy the pleasure.'

Magdalen obediently tried to hold her body in place. This stroke went lower than the first, and again she reared up in real protest for a moment and writhed and whimpered. 'Easy - those naughty cheeks are halfway there, sweetheart,' her Master said.

Magdalen felt the cane slide down her twin stripes as if deciding where to land next time. After an agonising wait it landed just above her taut young thigh backs. 'Aaargh,' she shouted and jumped up, both small hands rushing to her reddening bum. Shifting from foot to foot and snivelling reproachfully, she tried to rub the focused lines of heat from her aching curves.

'Were you given permission to rise?' Aaron asked softly.

'No, but...' Magdalen thought better of contradicting her Master and searched for a more obsequious phrase that would spare her buttocks, 'No, sir - I jumped up without permission. I'm sorry for being so naughty, sir,' she said.

Aaron jerked his thumb towards the punishment stool then shook his head. 'We have to make a naughty girl especially sorry. I'll have to push a pillow under your tummy to raise that runaway arse especially high.'

At his bidding, Magdalen got back over the stool then arched resignedly. She breathed hard as he slid the hill-shaped bolster into place then took his time adjusting it. It re-angled her belly and turned her bum into a much more obscenely displayed and vulnerable prey. The twenty-three year old squirmed about on the cushion as she awaited the last of her caning. Now she truly pitied her hot, sore, twitching nether cheeks.

'I'll have to apply the fourth stroke on top of the third,' Aaron said, 'I know it stings but it also beats a direct path to a submissive girl's clitoris and hungry hollow.' Magdalen knew by the wet threads spiralling from her sex lips that it already had.

'Please get it over with,' she muttered, opening and closing her fingers around the sturdy legs of the devilishly crafted punishment stool.

'No, a nice bare arse like this requires much gloating time,' Aaron said. He tapped the rattan against the crevice in her arse then laughed when she puckered up her bum cheeks in a body language plea for lenience, 'Now be a good slave and pony girl or I'll tell your seller that you weren't worth two hundred quid.'

'I swear I'll be worth it,' Magdalen shot back, opening her legs invitingly and trying to distract him from further whipping her bare bottom.

'Legs together girl, and ask nicely for the final rattan lash,' the Club Owner said.

'Please... uh... mercilessly warm me up for the last time today, sir,' Magdalen forced out through a haze of humiliation and desire.

At last her Master swished his cane into her writhing underswell. Magdalen's feet came up off of the floor and she bent back her legs as if to provide a belated barrier to shield her extremities. 'Now lie there without touching your bum cheeks and reflect on your crimes to date,' Aaron said. Magdalen lay over the stool - but all she could think about was her desperate clitoris and aching vulva. 'Please kiss it better again, sir,' she muttered wantonly, 'Oh Master, please!'

She lay there almost sobbing with need, then felt two cool hands palming her sore rotundities. They traced the blurred red lines causing hot bursts of spreading inner joy and fast-externalising love gel. 'Does the slave desire a teasing taste of her Master's cock?' Aaron's voice enquired.

'Yes, sir, the slave begs for even an inch of cock,' Magdalen groaned, excited beyond endurance. She sighed with relief as she heard his trouser zip go down and he drove in all the way. He slid his knowing right hand under her pubis and urged her to press against it. He thrust. She moaned then pressed. Thrust, moaned, pressed. Pleasure was building from within and without as his belly slapped against her scarlet buttocks. Her hard nipples rubbed against the correction stool as her mind and body soared closer to the edge. 'I'll roast your sore bare bottom again if you come too slowly. I'll look out the whip with the knotted multi-thongs,' Aaron whispered huskily as he thrust. And as she shrieked her orgasm, Magdalen understood why his staff accepted their bare bottom spankings and came back for many more.

Thereafter she showered and dressed and ate smoked salmon roulade with freshly-baked brown bread and lemon wedges. 'Shall I stay till dinner?' she asked sleepily as they sat in the circular dining hall.

The clock chimed 3pm. 'No need,' Aaron smiled, pushing aside his glass of claret, 'You've done more than enough, my bridled dear.' Magdalen checked that her house keys and ten pound note were in her slave dress pocket, then Aaron called for a taxi to take her home. 'You can borrow my housekeeper's coat,' he said solicitously, helping her button it so that it covered her bare young thighs and pouting mammaries. 'Great dress for a Slave Auction - but you don't want the cab driver making a pass.'

The next day Magdalen made a sun-kissed walk to Aaron's to return the coat. She thought with affection of their amorous antics. But as she reached the inner yard she heard two male voices, loud with glee and boastful pride.

'She did everything I wanted,' Aaron whooped.

'Expensive, though - I'd hoped to get her for a hundred,' said the second masculine timbre. Magdalen peaked around the gate to see that the second voice belonged to the balding man who'd made the penultimate bid.

'Thought I'd speed the process up. I wanted to get the video underway,' Aaron said archly. He handed over a black cassette, 'It's all yours, Eddie - watch our newest pony girl dress down and up, trot, get caned and finally climax. Her face doesn't appear on the film, needless to say.'

'The punters don't care about her face,' the greasy man laughed. Magdalen could only see him in profile but she was sure that he was winking. 'They just want to view a well-caned female arse.'

'And they will, they will,' Aaron shot back. His voice sounded uneven from either desire or desperation, 'Those previously untouched striped cheeks will bring in loadsa money for you both here and in The States.' He patted the other man's shoulder ingratiatingly, 'It'll give your regulars a change from my usual staff.'

Magdalen watched as Eddie pulled out a wad of notes and handed it to the equestrian man. Aaron counted it studiously but fast. The smaller man laughed knowingly, 'That should keep you betting on the ponies for a while.'

She was one pony who had definitely had enough. The naturalist hid behind the fuchsias till the greasy toad had gone then she walked determinedly up to Aaron who suddenly looked very nervous. 'I'll tell the police and press how you've been conning women,' she murmured, 'Unless...'

Moments later she cracked the whip over the buttocks of her very own male steer as she rode him bareback. 'Are you going to run faster, my naughty pony boy,' she murmured contentedly, 'Or do I have to motivate your flanks by fetching the spurs?'

The Tutorial

Nervously Bertha Morton entered her new employer's redbrick mansion house.

'Here are my references, Ma'am,' she murmured, holding out her floor length calico skirts in a deep low curtsey.

Mistress Randolph accepted the proffered character and unsmilingly studied it. 'Your last employer tells me that you are a very good girl. I hope so, for I expect total obedience from my staff.' Her dark hair was pulled back in a top knot, a severe style which brooked no opposition. Her full navy skirts were expensive, but equally drab.

'I'll always do your bidding, Ma'am,' the eighteen year old governess said, dipping her full-figured young body still further towards the floor.

'I trust you will,' the plain-faced older woman said archly, 'For infractions in this household are strictly punished by the rod.'

Bertha blushed but nodded her head. Servants were regularly whipped and caned and birched in this, the reign of Queen Victoria. She'd be all-seeing and all-knowing as she'd been in her last household where she'd never had to endure the severe kiss of the cane.

For the first few weeks of her indenture Bertha listened and looked and managed to please the Randolphs. She instructed Lucy, four and Charles, six, during daylight. Sometimes she went downstairs to the kitchen at night to talk to the other maids. One day the children wanted to avail themselves of the beach, but it was raining heavily. 'I shall fetch the sea indoors,' the innovative Bertha said.

She drew buckets of water from downstairs and brought them up and filled the large tin bath in the corner. 'See? We can study how objects float and how they behave when they're submerged.'

'Mistress wants to see you now,' one of the servant girls said breathlessly, hurrying in. 'Don't tarry, Miss, or you'll make her angry.' Picking up her skirts, Bertha hurried to Mrs Randolph's rooms.

The older woman sat on the brocade chaise longue in her sun lounge looking slightly displeased. 'My husband gave young Charles a simple math test yesterday. He hadn't improved since his nanny left,' she said.

Bertha licked lips that were suddenly dry. 'Begging your pardon, Ma'am. I thought I'd get to know their dispositions better before taxing their young minds too thoroughly. Plenty of time for book learning when...'

'As I said when you came into service, I expect obedience, Miss Morton,' Mistress Randolph interrupted, 'I want well-schooled children - not ones who idle their formative years away.'

'I intend to see that...' Bertha started humbly. She grimaced as a drop of water landed on the end of her nose. It was followed by another drop and another. Both women looked up to see a cascade starting to pour through the ornately-corniced roof.

'Fetch the housekeeper - tell her that there must have been a cloudburst above,' Mrs Randolph spluttered.

Bertha felt her face glowing. 'I... suspect that it's my fault, Mistress,' she said.

The next few moments were filled with commotion and distress. Every servant in the household mopped at the ruined rugs and sodden curtain ends and water-stained carpets. A maid righted the bath that the children had turned over then took them away to change them into new dry clothes. Mistress Randolph listened grimly to how Bertha had left the children unattended then pointed to her husband's study at the end of the ground floor hall.

'Bend over my husband's desk, Miss Morton, and await your caning. I'll be in to thrash you soundly when I've taken tea.'

Bertha's full breasts heaved at this new belittlement. 'Mistress, perhaps you could dock my stipend or... or withhold my lunch for a few days instead?'

'No, as I said before, a broken rule earns the culprit a badly beaten bottom,' the older woman said.

'Perhaps you could cane my hands, then?' Bertha whispered, holding out both palms in a pleading gesture.

'I'd rather turn your arse the colour of those glowing crimson curtains,' her employer explained.

Bertha coloured still more at the use of the word *arse* - a word that Mistress Randolph would never use when taking tea with her genteel lady friends. She'd only debase a helpless servant in so crude a way. Realising that a partial stripping was inevitable, the helpless governess curtseyed. 'Yes, Ma'am. As you wish, Ma'am. I'll go to your husband's study now and await the rod.'

Slowly she left the nursery and walked to the oak-doored room then tremulously entered it. She'd seen and heard servants being whipped on their raised posteriors, but had never had her own buttocks soundly thrashed. Now she stared at Mr Randolph's large mahogany desk with its leather-bound blotter and equestrian paperweights. Moving with the greatest care, she put each object on the nearby fireplace then she took a deep breath and bent her belly over the smooth hard wood.

For five minutes or ten Bertha lay there, feeling ever more fearful about the fate of her virgin buttocks. At last she heard the clip clop clip of her Mistress's high-heeled shoes.

'I've no choice but to discipline you severely for that dangerous escapade,' the older woman said softly. 'Keep your bottom bent over but lift your skirts.'

Bertha quivered but obediently pulled her floor-length dress up and folded it over her back. She then did the same with her layers of lace-trimmed petticoats.

'Show me your bottom,' her employer ordered from her stance behind Bertha's quivering rear.

Bertha reached for the slit in her drawers, then she hesitated, overcome with her usual shy modesty. 'I beg of you - beat me over my bloomers, Mistress,' she said. Then she writhed in an agony of anticipation as the older woman pushed her skirts even further up her camisole-clad back.

'No, I always birch my servants for the longest time with their little rumps quite naked,' the Victorian matriarch said.

'Yes, Ma'am. I'll bare my bottom for you now, Ma'am,' Bertha forced out. She swallowed hard then bade her nervous fingers to pull her bloomers slit apart to their fullest. The opening now showed off her plump but firm projections and deep dark crease.

'I'm afraid that won't do either. Please take your drawers down fully so that I can examine every inch of the parts to be attended to,' Mrs Randolph said.

Bertha breathed fast with humiliation as she unbuttoned her lavender-embroidered pantaloons. She let the loose material slip down to her knees and felt them caress her slender ankles. Now she was bare from her back downwards - and hugely aware of her exposed and vulnerable nether cheeks.

'In a moment I'm going to fetch the rod - and I certainly shan't spare you,' Mistress Randolph murmured, 'But first I'll just pin your petticoats back to keep them out of the way.' She moved closer, and Bertha felt her fumbling with the layered garments. Then she walked across to the other side of the room and selected an implement from a large pottery urn.

Bertha looked sideways at the pale yellow cane. It was long and thick, a wooden streak of cruelty. She wished that she'd been a more careful governess who hadn't left her juvenile charges alone.

'I apologise again for any water damage to your carpets and danger to your little ones, Ma'am,' she whispered humbly.

'I'll content myself with seeing your striped flesh look equally apologetic,' her employer said.

She raised the rod, and Bertha's fingers flew back to cover her silken bum in a frightened reflex gesture.

'Grip the edge of the desk, Miss Morton,' the forty year old woman ordered, 'If your hands come back again I'll cane them too.'

Bertha did as she was told, anxious to spare her palms if not her posterior. She'd seen the scullery maid flogged on her twin rotundities and then on her overly-protective fingers just the other day.

'I'm truly repentant, Mistress Randolph,' she whispered, knowing that she'd never forget this salient lesson. Then she took hold of the desk edge and tautened her soft cheeks in readiness for the first searing stroke.

Prepared as she thought she was, the sheer biting nature of the cane still caused her to howl like a she-wolf. Bertha jumped up, fingers clasping the burning brand.

'Bend over,' the woman said coldly, staring at her tear-filled eyes and trembling lower lip. 'Present your backside for the rod this instant or leave this house.'

Where would she go? What would she do? The streets were full of young women who were destitute. Bertha gave a last surreptitious rub of the sizzling tram-line then steeled herself to go over the desk again. She wriggled with further shame as her employer traced the scarlet stripe with her fingers then slightly parted Bertha's quivering upper legs.

'That stroke doesn't count because you disobeyed me,' the lady of the house said calmly, 'You'll have to endure it all over again.'

'Yes, Mistress. I understand, Mistress.' Bertha tried to sound resigned to the woman's merciless pronouncement but her voice quavered. She sensed that her employer had picked up the cane again so scrunched her buttocks into terrified fleshy knots. For long moments she squirmed against the desk on her naked tummy. Soon the lactose flooded her buttock muscles and she had to let her protective stance relax. Her Mistress had obviously been watching that selfsame bum carefully for she chose this crucial moment to lash it hard again.

'Oh please,' Bertha gasped out, half rearing up then obediently flattening her belly across the table, 'I don't think I can bear much more of the cane!'

'You should have thought of that before you almost drowned my children,' the older woman retorted.

Bertha quivered as she felt the rod's blunt tip being tapped against the central portion of her buttocks. She let out a nervous little groan.

'Raise that arse higher for me, if you please.'

With effort, Bertha flexed and straightened her calves and moved her back until her bare bottom stuck out further, then she strained to hold the pose.

Again the cane lashed down. Again she bucked and yelled, her lower legs bending up as if to cover her disarmed hindquarters. She felt so silly with the older woman staring at her exposed and heated squirming bum.

'Prithee Mistress, how many more?' she mumbled, keeping her hands to the front with almost uncontrollable effort.

'I've never gone in for numbers. I just thrash a girl until she's as subservient as a maiden ought to be,' the Lady of the House said matter of factly, 'I'll probably thrash you until your backside's the colour of ruby wine.'

She raised the rod and scourged the maiden's flesh again. Bertha began to cry openly.

'Oh it hurts,' she sobbed, 'It hurts so much.'

'This one will hurt a lot more because you're making such a fuss, girl,' the Victorian matriarch said coolly. She caned the lower portion of Bertha's globes and the eighteen year old could take no more.

With a loud wail she jumped up and raced for the door - only to find Cook standing behind it.

'Take your punishment, dear, then tomorrow all will be forgotten,' she counselled softly, 'Better that than join the hordes down at the Embankment every night.'

'But it pains and shames me so,' Bertha said in a little choked voice, tugging hopelessly at her pinned-up petticoats.

'Get back here this instant or I'll be searching for a new governess,' Mrs Randolph said.

'A sore bum or a starving belly,' the Cook continued cajolingly, 'Go back in, my dear - you can take it.'

With a last beseeching look at her kindly benefactor, Bertha obsequiously closed the door. 'Forgive me, Mistress,' she begged as she stumbled back towards the wooden table.

'You obviously can't keep your hands off your bare bottom when you're bent over my husband's desk,' said the forty year old, 'So let's try a much more demanding position instead.'

She pointed to a large brocade armchair in the corner of the room.

'Bring it into the centre of the study this instant.'

'Yes, Ma'am,' Bertha murmured, starting to curtsey then realising that her skirts were still pinned up above her bare backside. Dipping her head at the continued ignominy, she walked over to the plush black chair.

When she'd pulled it into the required place she looked fearfully at her cane-wielding Mistress.

'Bend over it sideways,' the woman ordered, 'So that your head is cradled in your hands on the chair's furthest arm.'

Slowly Bertha got into place. Once she was there she realised the innate vulnerability of her position. Now if she tried to reach her hands back her breasts and belly would curve down into the chair seat and the position would put a hellish strain on her back. All that she could do was lift her legs back, and she already knew that she couldn't lift them high enough to protect her nakedness.

'Perfect. Now take this cane back and get me another implement instead,' Mrs Randolph murmured, 'Something that'll bring the colour to those soft full globes you seem so hellbent on protecting. I've no option but to punish you for starting to leave the room.'

'It stung so much, Mistress,' Bertha whispered standing up and taking the pitiless rod from her employer.

'It's going to sting a lot more now, I can assure you,' the Victorian matriarch said.

Snivelling, Bertha walked towards the urn. She slid the cane back into place amongst the other implements, glad to be free of its compassionless long-lasting bite.

'Now, what shall I torment that disobedient little arse with?' the older woman murmured. She smiled coolly at Bertha, 'Hold out the tawse. No, on second thoughts it'll go all over the place and may sting your upper thighs too much. And we want you to be able to walk without stiffness tomorrow when you're back at your governing tasks.' Bertha nodded then stared tremulously at the dressage whips and crops and studded tawses protruding from the handpainted urn. 'Bring me the razor strop.'

'Which...?' Bertha stammered, fingers skimming over the handles as she wondered which implement would roast her defenceless hemispheres.

'The one with the wooden handle,' Mistress Randolph clarified.

Bertha picked up the punisher. The part designed to redden a naughty girl's bum was at least two feet long and made of heavy leather. It was approximately two inches across. The punitive strop was set in a short black wooden handle upon which the punisher could maintain a steady if merciless grip. Bertha fingered its stern contours and imagined what they'd feel like as they whipped into her upturned nether cheeks. 'The armchair awaits, Miss Morton,' Mrs Randolph said.

Bertha attempted another skirt-free curtsey then walked stiltedly towards the waiting furniture. With an enormous effort of will she forced herself to bend sideways over it, resting her head on her folded arms. Now her bottom was fully served up for the ensuing correction and she couldn't protect it with her pleading hands.

'There, that's better,' her employer said with obvious satisfaction, 'Much more accessible and nicely raised.'

Bertha whimpered. Then she cried out as the thick leather razor strop drove into her already-striped posterior. She threw her haunches from side to side as if attempting to shake off the fire lodged in her bare buttocks, but there was no escape.

'Calm,' her Mistress said. A cool but completely dispassionate hand fondled her sore extremities. Bertha groaned loudly but tried to slow her tormented writhing down.

'I'm so sorry that I failed you, Mistress,' she said with feeling.

'Save me the impassioned speeches,' the older woman muttered, again palpating the younger girl's exposed hot bottom, 'Tell me what a naughty girl you've been.'

Bertha groaned again. She so wanted to be treated as the older woman's intellectual equal. How could her employer treat her as if she were a little child?

'Oh dear, you've gone strangely silent. Perhaps this nice thick strop will elicit a response from you.' Bertha squirmed as she was subjected to another taste of the strop.

'I've been a naughty girl, Mistress,' she half sobbed, tensing and untensing her fevered hemispheres, 'I deserve a hot sore bum.'

'Very hot and sore and extremely tender,' her Mistress confirmed before toasting the girl's tenderised tissues. 'I'm waiting,' she said when Bertha's quivering bottom at last slowed down.

Bertha realised that she must debase herself still more.

'Please leather my arse cheeks further,' she said in a low shamed whisper.

'Speak up, girl,' Mistress Randolph said, 'Or the razor strop will wring further pleas from you.' She thrashed three times at the underside of both soft cheeks.

Bertha moaned loudly then put one anguished hand to her mouth to stifle her cries. She hated giving the woman this satisfaction. Then the razor strop tanned her writhing haunches again and she knew that she had to speak.

'My... my backside wants to plead for mercy, Mistress,' she choked out, 'But it knows that it must writhe under your lash for as long as it's bidden.'

'At least it's learning,' her employer said, and laid on the strop more lightly across the centre of Bertha's crimson spheres.

'It wants to learn, wants to please its Mistress,' Bertha humbly gasped.

'Spread your legs a little further apart for me for the final two,' the older woman murmured, slapping lightly at the naked thighs before her, 'It'll help open up that furrow, your most secret place.'

Closing her eyes with renewed shame, Bertha obeyed her. She could feel the woman's eyes feasting on her most intimate female parts. 'Last but not least,' Mistress Randolph warned. Again she took her time, squeezing and stroking at the girl's naked cheeks as if to increase their shameful scorching. Bertha wriggled with humiliation as the woman fingered her bum crease and the virgin entrance to her sex. 'Part of me thinks you've had enough, but the other part of me enjoys watching your sore buttocks dance,' her tormentor said.

'They're very hot, Mistress,' Bertha confirmed in a shamed low whisper, 'They know that they've been bad but they beg very sweetly for clemency.'

'Do they indeed?' the older woman murmured, picking up the strop again, 'Well let's make this last but not least.' She drove the leather length smartly into the crease above the governess's thigh backs then told her to stay, wriggling and whimpering, over the side of the chair.

Twenty minutes later Bertha was allowed to put on her bloomers and unpin her petticoats from her waist. With glassy eyes she made her tremulous way to her tiny bedroom. There she sobbed for a while before coming up with a fetching plan. Yes, she'd looked and listened for the weeks that she'd been in this supposedly straight-laced household, had seen and heard all manner of unseemly things.

Late that afternoon when Mistress Randolph retired to the chaise longue for her usual nap. Bertha sneaked back into her employer's study. Then she slipped a love letter from Mistress Randolph to her secret lover into Mr Randolph's top desk. Bertha smiled to herself. She'd already heard how the man dealt with any dispute. After a second's contemplation she put a birch on the top of the desk. It was a long thick chastiser made of twelve thick rods of willow. She only hoped she'd be in earshot when it came down on Mistress Randolph's adulterous plump cheeks.

The Bottom Drawer

Ryka smiled as she selected the nightgown she would wear on her impending honeymoon. It was three long days till she married Thomas. Three days until her traditional English wedding took place! Again the Russian girl looked at the book on marriage customs which she'd bought, and read of lucky horseshoes and rice and confetti. It was all very different to the Russian village where she'd been raised.

'What are you thinking, dear?' Thomas asked her now. He was a mature intelligent man, who, at thirty-five was fifteen years her senior. He'd been her boss at the translations publisher where she'd worked since coming to Britain two years before. Now she hoped he'd also be her boss in the master bedroom, for that was what she suspected she would most enjoy. Her mother had told her little of such intimate matters. So far Thomas had kissed and caressed her but he hadn't presumed...

'I'm wondering which of your English customs you'll want to adopt on Saturday, and thinking of Russian wedding customs,' she said, loving the strict smart lines of his formal suit. She so wanted to please.

'I've heard of one old Russian custom,' Thomas said slowly. His gaze seemed to become more assessing, 'On her wedding night, the Russian bride would be told to choose from a pair of shoes which her bridegroom had left peeking out from under the marital bed. One of them was empty, the other contained a coiled whip.' He smiled then kissed the top of her head in an avuncular gesture, 'If she chose the shoe with the whip she got a taste of it right away.'

'And have you bought the shoes?' Ryka murmured, aware of a slight blush colouring her usually pale strong features.

'I have,' her fiance murmured, 'So now you must buy the whip.'

The next day Ryka shyly set off with a very special shopping list. Thomas had written down all the details. He walked determinedly by her side.

'I will blush all the time that I'm doing this,' she said.

'But it will also excite you,' Thomas answered. He took her hand and pressed it lightly. 'I'll consider it an act of pure love.'

The first two words on the list read *Riding Shop*. Thomas drove Ryka there and they entered the premises.

'My mare's being skittish. I need a whip to calm her down,' he said.

The man behind the counter raised an eye. 'Obviously we're not in favour of excessive punishment.'

'Nor am I, sir,' Thomas replied.

The man brought a selection of whips and placed them in turn in Thomas's hands. He flicked each through the air, then handed them to Ryka. She fingered the knotted cords of nylon braid and new cut leather. Finally she chose a fibreglass dressage whip.

'Shall I wrap it?' the assistant asked softly.

Thomas ran the riding crop through his fingers. 'No, I'll be using it very soon,' he said with an anticipatory wink.

The next item on the list read *Cook's Store*.

'At least they'll just think I'm going to be baking!' Ryka murmured.

'Your bum will be baking if you're naughty,' Thomas replied.

Ryka blushed and dipped her head for a moment, then gave him a loving little kiss. She knew that men sometimes lovingly chastened their women as part of a consensual erotic arrangement. But hearing him talk like that - and imagining such discipline - still made her go red.

The Cook's Store held everything an amateur chef might need. It also contained the implements which Ryka had been ordered to buy for her own small bottom. Nervously she selected a long wooden spatula and a paddle-sized wooden spoon. Again, Thomas said that there was no need to wrap the thick smooth punishers. 'This gives a whole new meaning,' he said, 'To a girl setting up her bottom drawer!'

Thirdly Thomas took her to the maths department of a large scholastic store. There Ryka examined wooden and plastic rulers. When no one was watching, Thomas swished first the plastic and then the wooden one against her skirt clad cheeks.

'Which hurt the most, love?' he asked consideringly.

'The second one, I think!' Ryka stammered, thrown by the public nature of the lash. Her soft high bottom tingled and the curve between her legs gave an answering lurch. She put the plastic measurer back on the shelf then turned towards the counter.

'Remember,' he added, 'That when you next feel the ruler you won't be wearing a skirt or underslip or pants.'

Finally they made their way to a very adult shop. The two men serving there obviously recognised Thomas.

'Not got Liz with you?' one of them asked.

'We broke up last year,' Thomas said.

'So what can we do for you?' the man continued.

'Liz took all our equipment with her. Ryka's here to buy new stuff,' Ryka's fiance replied.

And buy new stuff she did! Ryka dipped her head prettily as the men brought out long whippy canes and Scottish tawses and razor strops and laid them out on the long glass counter. The assistants whisked the thin rattans through the air to show her how they'd sound before they made contact with her completely bare bum. 'This one leaves a thin red line, whereas this type creates a wide pink band which glows for longer,' the oldest man said with relish. No wonder they called discipline the English vice!

'I think we'd like this rattan,' Ryka said nervously at last. She noticed Thomas looking longingly at the leather instruments. 'And a four tailed tawse,' she added haltingly, glad to see lust and gratitude entering his eyes.

Thomas put his arms around her waist and pulled her back against him. 'I'll be firm with you,' he whispered, 'But I'll also be scrupulously fair.'

The wedding went well, and at last Ryka's honeymoon night began in earnest. She walked to the hotel's large bridal suite, wondering what awaited her therein. She'd never had full intimacy or even undressed before the opposite gender! And she'd no idea if she could bear the whip or ruler or the tawse.

Thomas was already in the room, putting his suit jacket on a hanger. He rolled up his sleeves then smiled at her expectantly. 'Ryka, would you like to choose a shoe?' he asked, indicating his new bride's side of the bed. Ryka looked down. Two black glossy toes peeped out at her. There was no way of telling which was empty and which was full.

'I'll take the right one,' she murmured, drawing it out.

She saw immediately that it contained a small coiled whip, a sort of lightweight riding crop. Taking it from its lair, she handed it to Thomas then stepped back.

'You can taste the whip or choose whichever implement you prefer,' he offered.

Remembering how he'd obviously liked the leather goods, Ryka opted for the four tailed tawse.

'Fetch it from the suitcase now, and bring it to me,' Thomas ordered. He smiled more gently, 'When we get home we'll keep such implements in your bottom drawer.'

‘And will we use them often?’ Ryka whispered, her trepidation increasing as the moment of her punishment drew nearer.

‘We’ll use them whenever the situation warrants it,’ Thomas said.

Then he smiled. ‘For now you’re to be disciplined to maintain the old Russian custom. That is, because you chose the shoe with the disciplinary implement in it you’ll get a taste of the tawse.’ He looked thoughtful, as if remembering her transgressions, ‘And I’m also going to chasten you for hesitating when it came to buying these self same punishment tools.’

‘I was shy about approaching the shopkeepers,’ Ryka murmured, with an apologetic wince ‘I was uncertain.’

‘Perhaps you’ll be more certain when you’ve a hot sore bottom to sit on,’ her new husband said.

Ryka looked nervously at him. Next, she looked down at the leather tawse she was still holding. ‘Hand me the implement and then lie on your tummy on the bed,’ Thomas bade.

The Russian bride did so, her movements jerky. She wondered how she’d feel about what came next.

‘Lift your dress up above your waist,’ her spouse continued.

Ryka reached her small ringed hands back and pulled at her hem until the ankle-length brocade skirt moved away from her haunches. She knew that her equally long petticoat still remained in place.

‘Now raise your underskirt,’ Thomas said. Ryka did so, then felt her husband adjusting the material so that it would stay folded over her back. ‘Which garment do you think comes off now, Ryka?’ he murmured exultantly.

‘My panties, sir,’ Ryka said.

There was a pause. Ryka reminded herself that she was married now, that such acts were allowable. Still she felt very vulnerable and a little scared.

'Oh dear, I requested a bare bum and I'm still looking at a fully clothed bum,' Thomas said softly, 'I'll have to redden it more fully for failing to obey.'

'Please don't! It's not that I don't want to... It's just...' After a few more moments of internal struggle, Ryka slowly pulled down her lace-trimmed pants. She lay there on her tummy, knowing that her new husband was staring down at her newly-bared bottom. A bottom that had never before been tawsed or paddled or whipped.

'Good girl,' Thomas murmured. She felt the mattress give as he knelt on one side of the bed and pulled back one arm. Ryka knew without looking that that arm contained the tawse. 'Would you like to count each stroke out loud and thank me for it?' he asked softly. Ryka nodded into the pillow, but didn't speak. 'I'll have a verbal answer, if you please,' her new spouse continued, 'Good communication is vital between husband and wife.'

'Yes, sir,' Ryka answered, her feelings of desire and degradation increasing. She pushed her legs more tightly together and waited for the lash to fall.

Suddenly heat sizzled across both twitching buttocks. This was a veritable brand! This was lightening in the form of leather! Ryka gasped loudly and started to scramble up from the bed.

'Going someplace?' Thomas asked.

She looked at his face. It showed both sadness and disappointment. 'N... no sir,' she gasped out.

Slowly the girl flattened herself to the mattress again. Her hands fluttered by her waist, half-wanting to cover her bare bottom.

'Perhaps it would be easier if you gripped the lower rung of the headrest,' her thoughtful spouse said.

The Russian bride did. The tactile certainty of the wood somehow helped her to control herself. Still, she sucked in her breath as she waited for the second searing stroke.

When it fell, it went lower than lash one. It licked the tender crease at the top of her thighs, and seemed to reverberate through to her belly. Ryka groaned and shook her hips from side to side. 'Only four more to go,' Thomas said, 'Then we'll move on to the second stage of your punishment.'

Registering his words, Ryka groaned again. She tried to avoid her next sore taste of the tawse. 'I've accepted the tawse to please you, sir. Can't we go on to the Russian whipping custom?' She hoped that the whip would sting much less.

'We probably could have,' Thomas replied, 'If you hadn't failed to obey me when I told you to take down your panties. That's why you're due six hard strokes of the tawse.'

Ryka nodded into the pillows. She knew that this thrashing would ultimately make her less coy, would help bring her womanly urges to the surface. Her fantasies had always been of dominant older men. That said, it still took lots of willpower for her to ask her spouse nicely for the third tawse lash. When it came, it scorched across the centre of her naked globes. All four leather tongues seemed to flicker out their smarting impact. 'Aaah! Aaah! Aaah!' the Russian girl whimpered. She rolled wildly onto her back, both palms cupping her reddened bum.

After rubbing her tender flesh for a few moments, she recovered herself and peaked curiously over at her man. He was still holding the tawse and was looking down at her impassively.

'It hurts,' Ryka said in a plaintive little voice.

'Of course it hurts. It's punishment,' her beloved answered.

'But it's our wedding night. We should have... we should have pleasure,' Ryka cut in.

'And the pleasure will be all the more strong due to this bum-based stimulus,' Thomas replied knowingly. He touched her in her most intimate place till she almost swooned with yearning. Desperate once more to please him she rolled back onto her tummy, presenting him with her hot red arse.

Her husband fondled that same arse for a moan-making moment whilst she forced herself to grip onto the bed's wooden headboard. Then he picked up the tawse and brought it down across her tenderised underswell. Before Ryka could cry out, he'd raised the punisher again and whacked it further up her jerking bottom. Then he placed the final stroke nearer the top of her heated bum.

'Aaah!' Ryka gasped out. Her hands flew back to massage her rump cheeks, but her husband caught her wrists and held them away.

'No, no, my dear. I want you to contemplate how vulnerable your bum is after it's felt the lash. You mustn't protect it.'

'Couldn't I just hold it for a second, sir?' Ryka whispered throatily.

'No, but you can come and look at it in the mirror before it receives its whipping,' Thomas said.

Curious, Ryka started to rise up from the bed, obediently keeping her hands away from her bare buttocks. As she moved, her skirt and petticoats started to fall down. Helpfully Thomas took hold of the hems and put it between her nervous fingers. 'Keep them up above your waist, sweetheart. We want to be able to see the bottom that we're still chastising,' he said.

'Yes, sir,' Ryka murmured hesitantly. Part of her wanted to see how crimson her virgin haunches were, to admire her own courage. The other part felt flustered and ashamed.

With Thomas's hand on her upper arm, she marched towards the full length mirror. There she turned so that her bare bottom faced the glass. Then Ryka took a deep breath and peeked over her shoulder at the chastened orbs.

'They're really red, aren't they?' she whispered, feeling a sense of pride and self discovery as she surveyed both scarlet hemispheres.

'These little cheeks are about to get even redder,' Thomas said.

He walked over to where the whip lay coiled on the floor. Its clean dark lines looked sleek and almost pretty. 'Would you like to kiss it, my dear?'

Ryka nodded and pressed her lips slackly against the slender braid. 'Shall I hold onto the bed rail again?' she muttered huskily.

'I think so. But we'll put a pillow under your tummy first to make your bottom a more obvious target,' her husband said.

Ryka held her breath as he pushed a pillow in place. It tilted her body slightly so that her bum felt even more vulnerable. 'Let's see how this works out,' Thomas said.

The Russian girl felt the bed move and the air currents change and knew that the first whip stroke was imminent. She wondered how it would feel on already sensitized buttock flesh. A moment later she knew that it felt incisively sore! She yelled and rubbed at her cheeks and shoved her belly into the bolster.

'Oh dear. You touched your sore bum without permission. Now I'll have to use another pillow,' Thomas told her, voice holding a frown. Again the mattress moved, then the girl felt a second pillow being added to the first, raising her globes still further. A moment later she felt the whip connect with her tenderised rump again.

'Aah! How many more?' she gasped out plaintively.

'You mean "How many more, sir?",' Thomas corrected, 'Respect goes so quickly from a marriage nowadays!'

As if in answer, he applied the whip for the third sore time. Ryka howled and drummed her feet against the bed and puckered up main muscles in her bottom. 'Untense that bare arse! I like to whip a nice smooth canvas,' her husband said.

Pleasing him would ultimately mean more pleasure for herself so, with difficulty, Ryka obeyed him. She forced her bum to lie still, if not exactly relaxed. God, it was hot! She wanted to smooth cool body lotion into her twin rotundities. She wanted her man to kiss the pain away.

But the kisses would come after the olde worlde Russian whipping. Ryka reminded herself that she'd agreed to this chastisement for their marriage's greater good.

'Please use the whip on my haunches again, sir,' she said raggedly.

'Haunches is too coy a word for a married woman,' Thomas said.

Ryka twisted her head back to look at him. 'I don't understand. What words do you... which words are proper?'

'Say "I've been a disobedient young wench, sir, and I deserve to get a red hot arse for causing trouble",' Thomas bade.

Eyes downcast, Ryka repeated the words. They set up a fluttering in the secret core below her belly. She so wanted the initiation into womanhood to begin! 'Yes, you're a naughty girl who won't escape whipping,' Thomas continued, raising the riding crop. He flicked it against the crease where bum meets thigh. 'Where do you think you should get the next lash?' he continued in a conversational voice.

'Anywhere but there, sir!' Ryka replied fervently, still feeling the newest line of erotic anguish. Obligingly, Thomas applied the lash further up.

At last he set down the whip and fondled her glowing small buttocks. 'What should I use on you,' he whispered, 'The next time that you fail to please?'

Ryka thought of the implements they'd bought so far and imagined their effect on her bare bottom. 'The wooden spoon which doubles as a paddle, sir,' she said excitedly.

'And how will you be displayed for your punishment?' Thomas continued.

'With a...' Ryka writhed about on her tummy, still loathe to say the words, 'With a completely bare arse.'

She felt Thomas's lips brush her hair. 'That's not what I meant,' he said, 'I meant will you lie on the bed or bend over the dressing table or...?'

Ryka envisaged various punitive options which all involved pulling down her pants. 'Over the kitchen stool, sir,' she said raggedly, remembering the whipping stools that they'd seen in the adult shop.

'And will you count each swish of the paddle out loud after you've received it?' her man continued.

'Yes sir, and I'll ask nicely for the next!' Ryka said.

'Good girl,' Thomas murmured. He turned her over and took her into his arms, his fingers caressing. And Ryka knew that she wouldn't have to ask for anything else.

Raising Awareness

Was she ever going to grab Gordon Wesley's attention? Jo-Anne simmered with frustration as she crossed the Petroleum Refining Plant. Once again she'd flirted with her employer. Once again she'd been subtly rebuffed. She knew that she was alluring and alert, with a reasonably curvaceous figure. Had heard that he was single but had dated other employees in the past. Yet the most intense dialogue she'd extracted from the man was 'Memorised the Fire Hazards Manual yet, Ms Kern?' and 'Don't forget to wear your safety hat.'

He was obviously a stickler for protocol, Jo-Anne mused - and suddenly a dare-devil thought raced through her. She could arouse his wrath then burst into tears when reprimanded and seek solace in his arms...

Ten minutes later the twenty-two year old deliberately hopped over the ground-painted red line. It signalled an area where all staff were supposed to wear goggles. Gordon walked past at his usual time, then stopped and stared.

'Ms Kern - you're infringing the rules. Put those protective glasses on this minute.'

'What if I don't?' Jo-Anne parried, with a please-make-me smile.

'You'll get a black mark on your record.'

Her belly tingled as she envisaged a red mark on her bum. What on earth had made her think of such a flagrant image? It wasn't as if she'd ever been spanked...

The next morning the trainee manager flagrantly crossed a blue line without donning her ear muffs.

'Good grief, woman - have you taken leave of your senses?' Gordon Wesley asked.

'My senses are sound - they can handle 90 decibels,' Jo-Anne replied.

Angrily, the forty year old man shook his head. 'You're demonstrating unsafe working practices to our newer staff, and you could get us into all sorts of trouble with our insurance.' He told her to follow him through the Control Room into his adjoining office space.

'I'm going to have to make an example of you, Ms Kern,' he said coolly, picking up the Employee Records book.

'Oh no! Surely you aren't going to spank me, sir?' the twenty-two year old said.

There was an eerily long silence after the words *'spank me, sir'* had faded away. Jo-Anne closed her eyes and wished that she'd kept her mouth shut likewise. What on earth had made her issue such a provocative dare? Would he ignore her challenge or stroll over and aim a few slaps at her fully-clothed backside?

'A sound thrashing does indeed seem called for,' the older man said pensively before marching her across to the long low couch.

He sat down then hauled Jo-Anne imperiously over his lap. His knees supported her tummy. The twenty-two year old wriggled about like a caught fish then reached both hands forward to steady herself. As she did so, Gordon caught and imprisoned her wrists in one of his hands and held them in front of her. 'As you seem incapable of obeying instructions, I won't ask you to keep your palms away from your reddening backside.'

Without further ado, he began to whack hard at her boiler suited bum. The padding absorbed virtually all of the impact. *At least he was touching her,* Jo-Anne exulted, *and it didn't hurt a bit!* Deep down she felt just a little disappointed: she'd wondered what a genuine adult spanking would be like.

Seconds later she realised she was about to find out.

'This boiler suit will have to come off,' her employer instructed, lifting her up and depositing her gently on her steel-capped safety shoes, 'Unbutton it now,' he continued, 'And push it down to your knees.'

Telling herself that hugs and kisses would soon follow, Jo-Anne tremulously obeyed him. The yellow material bulked at her ankles and she took off her footwear and kicked the suit out of the way. Now the only garments which clung to her five foot five frame were a plain white cotton T-shirt and white cotton pants.

'Good girl. Now get those girlish globes over my knee again,' the dark-haired man said impersonally.

Her loins turned to warm syrup at his words. Nevertheless, she had to use up most of her courage to bend over his lap, especially now that she knew he'd be contemplating her knicker-clad bottom. Would he lust after her audaciously oval-shaped cheeks? Jo-Anne was glad that she'd worn her newest and most buttock-hugging panties as she arched her small rump over Gordon Wesley's knee.

'A girl who's been disobedient doesn't get to keep her panties on,' the man explained. Jo-Anne tensed as she felt him drag the cotton down her soft pale buttocks.

'You can't pull my pants off!' she whispered, both excited and afraid.

'I prefer to spank bare bottoms,' Gordon Wesley replied, immediately letting go of her knicker elastic, 'But if you'd rather return to work...?'

If she returned to work he'd return to being distant, and she really and truly fancied him.

'I give you permission to bare my buttocks, sir,' Jo-Anne whispered, hoping that the chastisement would lead to affection and at least one date. At the moment he simply saw her as a trainee manager who organised the lube oil unloading. After this, he would appreciate her own inner oil...

Her belly rubbed against his dark grey suit as he pushed her panties down to her mid-thighs and unveiled her peachy bottom.

'Right, let's get this backside nice and naked, and give it the spanking of its life.'

'No one's ever spanked it before, sir,' Jo-Anne muttered, hoping for leniency.

'In that case,' Gordon Wesley said, 'It's well overdue.'

The first spank on her bare bum was exploratory rather than reproving, as were the next eleven or so. Thereafter, her boss started to put more ire into his arm.

'You must obey all safety instructions! Show due deference to your superiors!' he instructed, punctuating alternate words with a hard buttock-slap.

Jo-Anne grimaced at the heat radiating through her bare bum, squealed as handprint followed handprint. 'I'll wear the goggles and earmuffs from now on, sir!' she gasped.

The senior manager stayed his hand, and for a moment Jo-Anne thought that her spanking was over.

'I'm truly sorry,' she whispered, twisting her head round to look up at his face. Surely now he'd comfort her with kisses and the relationship would swiftly and erotically progress?

'I have to *make* you truly sorry,' the man said, beginning to trace the hot marks left by his lashing fingers. Erotic arrows winged their way to her pubis, and Jo-Anne flopped down again with languid need. 'It would be easy for me to leave this at a few token smacks,' the forty year old continued, 'But as your employer I should impart a prolonged and painful lesson to those upturned cheeks.' He fondled those same squirming spheres again, kneading firmly at the redness, 'When you think of your soft sore bum you'll remember to wear your hard safety hat.'

'It was my goggles and ear muffs I forgot to wear!' Jo-Anne shot back, her spirit reasserting itself.

'And now you're forgetting your manners,' Gordon countered, doling out eight full-force whacks.

Jo-Anne yelled from the first to the last and moved her bare bum from side to side in a futile attempt to avoid each buttock-based smacking. Her haunches felt slightly swollen, had an all-over glow. She looked around reproachfully at her writhingly vulnerable little hemispheres and pitied their scarlet shading. God, he knew how to make a girl's buttocks dance! At the same time Jo-Anne felt a grudging new respect for her employer. After all, she could have gotten him into trouble with her acting-out.

'How many more spanks am I due, sir?' she gasped out between stern whackings.

'Oh, I'll know by the colour of your arse when you've had enough,' Gordon Wesley said. The conversation obviously over, he began to spank her again with easy vigour. He spanked the top of the right orb, then the top of the left. His palm connected with the centre of the right sphere before landing with similar impact on its twitching twin.

'Ah! Ow! Oh!' Jo-Anne squealed as the heat in her naked red rotundities intensified. She'd wanted to gain her boss's attention, but hadn't quite bargained on this!

'Let's stop for another little break,' the forty year old said after a few more resounding smackings.

Jo-Anne nodded, glad of the opportunity to catch her breath.

'I'm being a good girl now, sir,' she said submissively as the telephone to one side of them began to ring. Gordon let go of her wrists to flick on the answering machine, and she used the moment to lever herself up and sit, kitten-like, on his lap, looking sweetly sexual. Beginning to feel in control again, she kissed the side of his neck.

'What are you doing, Ms Kern?' His voice was neutral, unreadable.

Jo-Anne faltered. 'I was... just being friendly, sir.'

'Well, I'm in the midst of disciplining your ill-behaved bare bottom. Save your offers of friendship until I've finished tanning your naughty cheeks.'

Jo-Anne blushed with new shame. 'I thought that you *were* finished, sir,' she muttered, shifting about on her radiant extremities.

'No, failure to obey the plant safety rules requires a much more severe spanking,' her employer said. He slid both palms underneath to cup her rosy hemispheres, 'Of course, if you prefer, you could have an official warning instead?'

Jo-Anne bristled at the thought. 'God, no - I want promotion one day,' she muttered. She shivered with delight as he continued to caress her hot bare bum. Maybe there was a way to make him keep touching her which would also ensure that today's hard spanking stopped?

'I've a confession to make,' she whispered, nibbling briefly at his nearest earlobe, 'I ignored the safety measures deliberately in the hope that you'd notice me.' She grazed again at his ear then sat back on her haunches and looked fully at him, expecting to see the self-satisfied smirk of bolstered male ego. Instead her boss looked even more grim.

'Are you really trying to tell me that you deliberately risked your own health and the reputation of this company in order to flirt during working time?'

Put like that, it sounded reprehensible. For once lost for words, Jo-Anne nodded her head.

Gordon Wesley helped her to her feet. 'A sound spanking obviously isn't going to be enough,' he sighed, running his fingers through his hair in a distracted gesture.

Jo-Anne caught her full lower lip in her small white teeth. 'What... what do you mean?'

'Lucky that I keep a pair of slippers here for when I'm working the late shift. They'll connect nicely with a flirtatious female arse.' So saying, he marched her across the office to a four-legged square stool. 'Let's call this staff training session *Raising Awareness*,' he said with a half laugh as he helped her bend her body over the seat.

Her buttocks were indeed vulnerably raised - and it was a vulnerability which increased as Gordon Wesley brought a cushion over.

'Just to stop your belly from rubbing against the wood as you squirm,' he said evenly, pushing the bolster into place.

'Very thoughtful, I'm sure, sir,' Jo-Anne replied with as much sarcasm as she could muster. She'd wanted to make him notice her good points - not redden her badly-behaved arse! Still, he'd made it clear that she could walk away at any moment. It must be the more brave and curious part of her psyche that was making her stay.

The brave part faltered as Gordon Wesley laid on the slipper for the very first time. The smooth rubber size nine lashed her upturned buttocks.

'How many, sir?' the trainee manager yelped out, holding on tremulously to the rungs of the stool.

'Mm? Oh a slippering is like a spanking - one tends not to decide a specific number of whacks in advance,' the older man said.

'You mean I'm getting more than six of the best, then?' Jo-Anne whispered.

Gordon applied his slipper to her elevated rump again. 'That depends on your attitude, doesn't it, my dear?'

'Yes, sir. I'm a reformed character, sir. I'll be the best employee in the whole world from now on!' Jo-Anne promised as she sensed him raising the slipper in the air.

'Let's prove that,' her boss murmured after a moment's gloating reflection, 'Let's have a little test.' He set the slipper down on Jo-Anne's back, and her bottom gave a little twitch of trepidation. She could feel the rubber resting against her skin and knew how it felt as it whipped her bare backside.

'A test, sir?' she muttered warily.

'Mm,' said Gordon, 'An impromptu safety quiz.' He stroked her raised sore bum and Jo-Anne moaned with lust and pubes-based wanting, 'Obviously a girl has to be able to think quickly in a hazardous situation,' he continued in a merciless voice.

'Yes, sir,' a baffled Jo-Anne whispered.

'So I'll expect an immediate answer to my questions, or that arse will pay a punitive penalty.'

'I'll answer right away! I promise, sir!' Jo-Anne gasped out. She reckoned that she knew all that there was to know about the plant's security measures. She knew where every safety station and outdoor shower had been built.

'What does the sign by the lined tank say?' Gordon asked. As he spoke, he ran a finger down Jo-Anne's bum cleft and all non-sexual knowledge went out of her memory. Moaning, she opening her thighs in a gesture of need. If only he'd slide a finger up and down her feminine opening. It was so hollow that it hurt.

'No answer equals another application of my slipper,' Gordon said. He picked up the footwear and brought its sole smartly down on her upturned bare cheeks.

'Ah! Ouch! Ask me another question,' Jo-Anne muttered, tensing and untensing her bottom in a centuries-old cadence.

'How many burners are in each furnace?' her employer quizzed. Again he stroked his way down that most sensitive secret crease and the girl almost swooned with wanting.

'Please, sir,' she whispered huskily, 'Oh, please!'

'No, please wasn't the correct answer. Forty-eight was,' the man said matter-of-factly, 'That raised rump simply isn't trying, is it, my sweet?'

'It means to try, it just...' Jo-Anne's focus again shifted to her hot hindquarters.

'It doesn't know the safety drill,' her employer murmured, 'So it'll have to taste the nasty hard slipper again.'

Jo-Anne could sense him moving about, doubtless lining the footwear up with her tenderised buttocks. She trembled with uncertainty and anticipation as he got into place. She couldn't decide which was worse - the aching glow in her upturned hemispheres or the unquenched heat between her parted legs.

'Can't we just negotiate?' she muttered raggedly. The rubber sole smarted its try-harder message into her posterior and she bucked and yelled.

'Safety measures aren't negotiable. Protective rules are there to be obeyed,' Gordon said.

He, too, was here to be obeyed. She was getting the message. And she wanted to obey him, Jo-Anne thought lustfully - she really did!

'Let's try again, shall we?' Gordon continued in a conversational tone.

Jo-Anne felt a sudden streak of irritation at his complacency. 'Oh, let's!' she muttered in a challenging voice.

'A bum can earn extra marks for insubordination,' her employer continued.

'It'll be a good bum from now on!' a contrite Jo-Anne said. She wasn't so sure that her clitoris would be good for much longer. If he fondled her furrow again she might spontaneously disobey...

Gordon Wesley seemed to sense the sexed-up state she was in. 'Lewd wriggling and wrong answers will result in a more disciplined derriere,' he said matter-of-factly.

'Going on to the French test, are you?' Jo-Anne sparred, then gasped as he clapped the slipper across both elevated cheeks. A percentage of her being wanted to mock him so that he chastened her arse to its absolute limit. Another percentage wanted to cup both well-punished globes in her small silken hands.

'Back to the safety exam, Ms Kern. What does PH stand for?' Gordon Wesley queried.

'Potential Hazard!' the trainee manager gasped out as he fondled her secret gully from start to end.

'Good girl. You got that one right.' She felt a small surge of disappointment as he put the slipper down.

'Now for a question about the pressure control valves...' Gordon Wesley continued. He rimmed her anal ring with a knowing finger as he completed the question and she moaned and squirmed and her answer didn't make sense. 'At this rate your grievance procedure will go on all day,' the older man warned, fingering the eroticised groove between her upturned buttocks again.

Jo-Anne groaned wildly and pushed her haunches back, unable to bear his teasing.

'Slipper me as much as you like later,' she half-sobbed, 'But for God's sake let me come!'

'You're forgetting who's in charge here,' Gordon Wesley murmured, slippering her scarlet spheres for another thirty seconds. 'Is this what you've been begging for?' he continued, gliding a hand between her legs...

Exactly six months later Jo-Anne was in reminiscent mood as she wandered around the plant's outdoor section. She and Gordon had had a good half year, but their relationship had recently reached its natural end.

But their beginnings in bed had been great! She smiled contentedly as she looked at the factory's feedstock, then shivered with delight as she contemplated the splitter and control valves. She must be yearning for a new lover: leastways everything today was reminding her of sex! Jo-

Anne gazed at the steam which rose from the fireman's lake and identified with its churning heat.

Lost in thought, she turned towards the methanol unloading area. Belatedly she realised that one of her superiors was watching each unprofessional move.

He stared coolly: 'You were daydreaming on duty, Ms Kern.'

'I didn't mean to, but... well, yes, Mr Andrews.'

'You've also gone missing from your post most weeks for at least an hour.'

'I know, but...' She could hardly admit that she was often in Gordon Wesley's office getting a sound spanking! 'I'm very sorry, sir,' she said.

The grey-haired director sighed. 'But saying sorry isn't enough, is it, my dear young woman? You'll still have to be disciplined for going absent without leave.'

So the rumours about him had been true! Jo-Anne felt a new rush of lust at his use of the word *disciplined.* She peeked up through her lashes at his challenging grey eyes.

'I deserve the most stringent correction. How exactly will you do that, sir?' she whispered, then stared hopefully at his heavy leather belt.

Motion Pictures

Lights. Cameras. Action! The sound man and the leading actor got into position behind the punishment trestle, but where was Leanne?

'Has she sneaked away to do her makeup again?' Dave the video producer asked the rest of the production team. He tried to keep his tone light hearted, but the irritation he was feeling showed through.

'Christ knows why she bothers,' the camera man added, 'I mean, the viewers are only going to see her arse.'

But what an arse! The flawless suntanned hemispheres were divided by a slim deep crease. The twin rotundities were taut yet softly smooth against a man's eager fingers. Dave knew just how good they felt - he'd moved her bottom into various angles whilst helping her to pose for his CP videos. It was a bum that deserved to be caressed and squeezed and held and gently bitten, a bum which visually cried out to be spanked.

But Leanne wasn't into spanking, unlike the other CP models he used in his film work. She was in it for the fame and the short working hours and the modest fortune: it was as simple as that. Not that she made his life simple with her frequent makeup breaks and increasingly unpunctual hours.

'Take six!' she grinned now, strolling back in wearing only a triangle of white cotton panties and a cobalt blue dress which skimmed the tops of her thighs and just begged to be lifted.

'You'll get six of the cane for real if you cause any more delays today!' Dave muttered, and was gratified when she blushed. Maybe there was an ounce of submissiveness in there after all, a desire to be dominated? He'd taken her word for it that she wasn't sub...

'I'll stick with the padded paddle,' Leanne answered, lowering her belly over the high punishment trestle and pulling down her pants for the camera's benefit. Her taut posterior was now beautifully bared.

The leading actor bent to tie her wrists and ankles to the furniture's legs, then stood back to admire his handiwork. 'You're going to stay like that for the next hour, slave,' he murmured, 'Whilst I tan that pretty arse.' The camera zoomed in on the girl's helpless backside as the actor playing her Master lifted her dress up and drew the paddle back.

And brought it down across both tethered cheeks with an echoing whack. Dave smiled as he watched and heard: the soundtrack would reverberate nicely. It was a pity that Leanne insisted on this special softly upholstered paddle which dealt her almost painless slaps.

He felt his groin tauten as the mock discipline went on and on. All the other video models really took the cane, the belt, the whip across their naked arses. Their bums got red and their sexual centres got wet. 'Want to finish me off?' they often groaned at the end of a long day's punishment filming. And he used his fingers on their clits, knowing that in a few moments they'd turn their own slim fingers in the direction of his cock.

Leanne literally did nothing for him - but she did everything for his video's circulation figures. She was the girl who got the most fan mail because she had the best backside. It was a pert and cheeky screw-you kind of an arse, one that tilted up as if to say that it was better than other arses. One that men fantasized about taming with their hard-slapping hands.

'Cut!' someone said as the action came to its scripted end. The crew started to gather their gear together and drifted towards the doorway.

'Can someone untie me?' Leanne asked.

Dave looked over: 'In a minute, love.'

'You'd better see this first,' gasped Pam their Public Relations Officer, hurrying in.

She handed him the latest issue of *Hot Bum* magazine which was published by a firm who produced rival spanking videos. *Leanne Just Has Her Bottom Rouged For Photos And Films* read the front cover line. Dave's heart started to beat faster and he took a very deep breath before he looked at the article inside. My God, she'd betrayed him to the enemy. She'd shown that his company rouged her bottom thus resorting to artifice.

The video-maker flexed his spanking palm and looked towards Leanne's still-bared bum. The makeup girl had wiped the scarlet blusher from it as soon as filming ended. He suddenly realised he could redden those globes for real.

'Leanne, want something to read while you're tied up?' Walking over to her face he crouched down and held up the tell-tale magazine. Then he watched her eyes widen with embarrassment and surprise.

'God! They promised this wouldn't hit the stands until I'd finished your video, the lying pigs!'

'You're planning to work for them exclusively from now on, then, I assume?' After all, she'd queered her pitch with him by selling her confessions.

'Well, yeah.' She tugged at the thick ropes that held her wrists and ankles in place, 'They promised much more cash.'

'What about loyalty?' Dave said. He got up and moved round to her rear, stroked the smooth bondaged orbs till she wriggled and drew in her breath sharply, 'Doesn't this bum have any allegiance to me, my dear?' He took his time, fondling and gently palpating each cheek, 'After all, I took you on despite the fact that you weren't willing to be genuinely spanked like the other girls. Gave you a start in the film industry when you were a complete unknown.'

'I guess! I just wanted to get to the top. They've a bigger publicity budget and offered royalties. I figured...'

Dave squeezed just a little bit harder: 'Figured you'd just sell me out.'

He let go of her cheeks and watched the marks of his squeezing fingers fade.

'If you'd just untie me please,' Leanne muttered.

Dave ran his middle finger down the cleft between her upended buttocks, 'No sweetheart, I've paid you to work here for another couple of hours so you can stay in the position you're paid for till we finish our little chat.'

He opened the magazine and scanned the centre page. 'Let's have a read... *Leanne Bares Her Soul.* Oh darling I've got more than your soul bared here, haven't I?'

'Meaning?' the CP model squeaked.

'Meaning that raised cheeks can't avoid a bloody good spanking.'

'Spanking me's an assault!' the model squeaked, tensing then untensing her naked globes.

'It won't be an assault because you're going to ask me nicely to punish you,' Dave continued.

'In your dreams!'

'Uh uh. In your *reality*, darling. You see you've made a mistake with this article - a very big mistake.' He read out the salient paragraphs, 'You've given the impression that we put rouge on *all* our girls bums instead of smacking them. That simply isn't true, as you very well know, which makes it libel - and libel that'll be read by our customers worldwide.'

'Well, you put rouge on *my* rear end!'

'Only because you've always insisted that we do.' He felt her cool flesh some more. 'And therein lies your second mistake. You've given loads of interviews where you pretended you were into CP, where you've lied to your video audience. Yet we have masses of makeup footage showing that you would only accept the softly-padded paddle when the other models were really being whipped or caned.'

He slapped lightly at her left cheek. 'If we release such proof of your deception you'll never work for our rivals or for anyone else in the industry. You might as well join the very lengthy dole queue now.'

'You wouldn't.' Leanne's shoulders seemed to slump a little over the punishment bench, 'I've worked hard to tone up my bottom, improve my voice for my film work. I'm not good at anything else, Dave. I...'

'Then submit to whatever punishment I deem appropriate,' Dave said, 'And I'll keep the makeup footage to myself.'

'Couldn't I give you a few quid?'

'No, you can pay me in kind by submitting to a thrashing.'

'I could do some free promotional work?'

'I'm only interested in promoting the colour of your arse.'

There was a silence - a silence in which the bum before him obviously realised that it was going to have to submit to a painful and lengthy whacking. It puckered up, smoothed out, middle muscles twitching. 'Alright, you can do whatever you want to me,' Leanne sighed.

'To your bare bottom, you mean? That's the only part of you that I'm interested in,' Dave said, spreading his fingers over the unblemished cheeks that had clearly cost him in terms of lost sales to would-be customers, 'I'm just taking your rump's temperature,' he added, 'Enjoy the coolness whilst you can because it'll be days before it gets this cool again!'

He smiled and walked over to the row of punishers on the wall. 'What will it be? I think we'll build up to the cane. Mmm, let's liven you up with the paddle for starters.' He winked at her, grinned as she shut her eyes and dipped her head. Walked back and lined the implement up with her helplessly captive bottom, 'Obviously I'm using the nice hard polished wooden one.'

'Please, go easy,' Leanne whispered.

'After the damage you've done to me, honey? No, you've hurt me both professionally and financially, so it's only fitting that I apply an equally painful chastisement to those libellous little cheeks.'

Warning over, he brought the paddle smartly down on her left buttock, smack in the centre. Roasted the other cheek in the exact same place.

'You don't thrash the other models this hard!' Leanne squealed, making little shoulder movements as she obviously tried hard to tug her arms from their bondage.

'That's business, but this is personal,' Dave said.

He lashed strokes three and four on the more sensitive underswell. Leanne howled and jerked her tied-apart feet. Her buttocks moved the little they could in their stretched out position. The pink marks caused by the paddle stayed.

'Now for five and six... I think a little higher up.' He knew where to safely land the punisher, keeping well away from the base of her spine and her sensitive backs of thighs. He'd take his time doling out this discipline that she'd so reluctantly acquiesced to. He was going to teach her a measured lesson she would never forget.

He warmed the implement against the upper parts of her gorgeous cheeks, enjoying the way the flesh momentarily flattened. Then he dealt her another two wallops at the suntanned tops of her firm thighs.

'Now the bad girl's going to lie over Dave's knee while Dave tells her about the next stage of her punishment.' He swiftly unbound the model from the leather straps that held her in place over the punishment trestle, and she pushed herself back and scrabbled off of the padded restrainer with obvious relief.

She turned slowly to face Dave, her hands over her toasted bum.

'Take your hands away from your bottom, angel. I didn't give you permission to hold your sore cheeks.'

'But it glows so!' Her proud head looked a little less defiant than usual.

'Does it? What a pity. It's going to do a lot more glowing. We've hardly started yet!'

'How many more strokes?' She shifted from one bare foot to the other as she stood before him.

'Till I decide your backside's had enough.'

'I could make amends another way, Dave.' Moving closer, Leanne sank to her knees.

He shut his eyes as she edged down his zip. Felt her small hands scooping out his rising cock, her lips cloaking it. Came at the fourteenth or sixteenth insistent suck of her mouth.

He opened his eyes to see her licking away the last of his juices from his lower shirt.

'Good girl - now get that pink arse over my knee till I decide how to redden it.'

'But I thought...'

He looked down at her dispassionately: 'Yes?'

'Oh, nothing.' She ran her tongue over her lower lip and continued to gaze up at him, 'Couldn't I just go to *Hot Bum* magazine and say that I made the story up or something?'

Dave shook his head: 'It's too late for that, sweetheart. You just have to take a hot bum of your own.'

A *very* hot bum. A scorching bum. Leaning forward, he put his hands under her arms and pulled her up and laid her firmly across his lap. She seemed too unsure to put up much resistance. Or was some shameful part of her languid with desire? He brushed his right hand over her labial lips and his finger tips came back wettened. He knew it would be a long time before he brought her off - if ever. She was here to be fairly corrected and made to see the error of her ways.

He held her over his ungiving knee. 'Let's have a look at that little bum, see how the paddle's kissed it.' He edged her dress hem up inch by tantalising inch. Her cheeks were nicely pinkened where the smooth wooden surface had hit home and they felt attractively warm when he touched them. But they'd get much hotter yet.

He fondled both cheeks. 'I'm going to cane you next. It hurts like hell. Even girls who really enjoy a reddened bum sometimes beg not to take the rod on their bare bottoms.'

'How... how many?' Leanne muttered, writhing.

'At least six.'

'And if I can't bear it?'

'Then you'll take twice as many of the riding crop instead.'

He pushed the girl's warm weight from his knees. 'Fetch the rattan from the third hook on the wall and bring it back to me, honey.'

Leanne got up slowly and started to walk towards the wall.

'No, get down on your hands and knees and crawl, girl.' Watched as she turned, stared at him, shook her head and continued walking towards the slender cane.

She brought it back, kept standing upright. Moving swiftly, Dave took hold of her nearest shoulder to hold her in place and quickly lashed the cane four times across her dress-sheathed backside.

'These four were for insubordination. You've six still due.' He stared into her eyes. 'It's a nice swishy cane, isn't it? Aren't you just a little curious about how this is going to feel on your naked backside?'

Mutely Leanne shook her head, but her eyes were trained on the long yellow-brown rod. Her fingers strayed towards her bottom.

'Don't touch, remember, angel?' She'd touched his bank balance with her stupidity and now she deserved to pay for it, 'You'll get extra helpings if you do.'

'I'll be good,' Leanne muttered, putting her hands in front of her.

'Then start by putting your sweet soft belly over the side of that chair.' He indicated the overstuffed wingback in the corner, 'Let your head hang down and put your palms flat on the floor.'

Dave watched as his best-selling model walked swiftly to obey, her short dress flapping slightly to expose the pinkened underswell of her silk-to-touch bottom. He wondered how she'd cope with a caning on the bare.

The chair was wide. To stretch over it and place her palms on the other side she had to rise up on tiptoe. The movement further tautened her haunches, thighs and calves.

'Make sure you maintain the position,' Dave said evenly, walking over to her dress-clad bum and lifting the material. He folded the hem until it lay high up her slender back.

Now her bottom was bared for the thick hard rod. He moved his hand back in a strong sure gesture, whacked the implement neatly across the middle of her bottom so that the crack of her arse and the red weal crossed to mark her buttocks into quartets.

'Uh!' Leanne drove her belly forward against the chair and seemed to expel every ounce of air within her perfectly-formed being. Then she inhaled sharply and wailed.

'Save the histrionics for the libel suit,' Dave warned, swiftly reminding her of her wrongdoing, 'There are worse things in life than a caned derriere.'

Leanne twisted her flushed pouting head back, 'But it really hurts!'

'Of course it does.' He traced the painful raised line that his cane had made, 'But being unemployed and broke and sent to Coventry by your own colleagues would hurt much more.'

The girl seemed to see the sense in what he said. She let her head hang down: 'I'll take the second stroke whenever you're ready, sir.'

Dave stared at her suddenly-obsequious bottom and decided to make it wait. Let her squirm for a while, wondering when the next stinging stroke was coming. Let her tense and untense these naughty cheeks.

At last he again lined up the rod with the lower portion of her bum, the portion that was most sensitive. He drove the cane in with a sure short wrist movement that made her cry out and get half up from the chair. Putting his palms gently to her waist he coaxed her back over. 'Come on, sweetheart. You're a big girl now. Big enough to go to a rival publication and kiss and tell.'

Leanne groaned low in her throat as he reminded her of her crimes. Her bared bum obviously knew that it deserved the most painful punishment. It writhed and twitched and generally took on a life of its own.

'Keep that pretty bottom still, darling,' he murmured, enjoying her ignominy, 'We're not making a motion picture here.'

'I'm trying not to move. Just the thought...' Leanne whimpered, wriggling on her softly curved belly.

'I know, dearest. I can tell that all you can think about is your helpless little rump.'

He traced the merciless bamboo rod over that selfsame exposed backside and its owner trembled. 'Stroke three coming up,' he said and laid the stripe on just above its predecessor, creating a wider two-tone band.

It was too much for Leanne. Howling, she jumped up, rubbing her disciplined flesh, her face hectic. Dave gloated as he saw a chance to punish her further. 'What did I tell you about not touching your arse?' he said.

'I... It's too much!'

'Six strokes of the cane for trying to ruin my career? I think you're getting off lightly.'

'If I could even keep on my pants...'

'I want to see your bottom being tanned, know that it's repentant,' Dave said evenly.

'It is!' the girl said. She choked back a sob.

'Not repentant enough to realise that it ought to submit fully to this correction. Not repentant enough to begin to do what it's told.'

He shook his head at her. 'It's up to you, of course. If you'd rather go and face the hurts of the outside world rather than take a thorough thrashing.' The girl licked her lips and stared mutely at the ground. Dave nodded. 'Very well. I'll assume by your silence that you've decided to sign on the dole queue rather than have a sore bum.' He turned and began to walk away.

'No, please,' Leanne muttered, hurrying forward and taking hold of his arm to hold him in place. 'I'll take the cane.' She started to pull him back towards the armchair as if eager to get it over with.

'It's not that simple now,' Dave said regretfully, 'I mean, you touched your posterior without permission and jumped up from the chair.' He looked at her appraisingly, 'What is your bad bum going to do to make amends?'

Leanne licked her lips. 'Please, not extra with the cane.'

'You've three strokes to go - they're not negotiable. But you can have a different implement for your additional punishment.' He smiled into her eyes, 'A hand spanking or a session with the hairbrush? I'll let you choose.'

He saw the relief and hope in her large brown eyes: 'A hand spanking, please, sir,' she said.

'So be it.' She'd find out in a moment that he had a very hard hand, 'Now let's get back to your caning.'

'Please cane me, sir,' she muttered, obviously hoping to please him by sounding submissive.

Dave stared at her still-defiant eyes: 'You can ask more nicely than that.' He put his right hand on her nearest arm, led her gently back to the furniture's side, helped her over, 'Ask with some humility as befits a traitorous girl.' He fondled her hot sore cheeks, 'Tell me how much you deserve having your panties pulled down then thank me for each lash.'

The girl's slender shoulders slumped. 'I... I'm due a hard caning on my bare bottom, sir.'

'*Very* hard,' Dave corrected. He stroked her exposed posterior, voice fiendishly light, 'If I feel that you're truly humble I may not lay the rod on with quite as much severity, may make you wriggle less.'

'Thank you, sir. I... I've been a wicked girl.'

'Extremely wicked.' He ran the pad of his thumb down her crevice, 'And what do we do with extremely wicked girls?'

'We... take the rod to their bottoms, sir.'

'To their *bare* bottoms,' he corrected.

'Y... yes!'

The bottom in question twitched apprehensively. Dave pushed her dress further back to denude it completely. The earlier cane marks had already receded so he laid on the fourth one higher up, taking care to keep the rod well away from her spine. Leanne whimpered, but kept her position. She jerked as he dealt out the fifth lash to the top of her thighs. Determined to make her remember this thrashing he repeated the sixth in that same tender place.

'I'm sorry, sir. I'm sorry. I'm so sorry!' Leanne whimpered.

'Then come and lie across my knee and tell me how good you're going to be from now on,' Dave said.

The girl crawled over to him on her hands and knees then let herself flop over his lap. He skimmed his right hand over her reddened bottom. She was his now, was being suitably slavish. Deserved the pleasure after pain. 'Now my fingers are going to search for an area to spank,' he teased, running his middle finger along both inner thighs. The girl parted them eagerly. 'Does this bit need a thrashing? Or this bit? Or this bit?' He stroked each labial leaf in turn, then moved his soft caresses to her clit.

Leanne made a guttural sound and pushed down against his fingers. 'Stay in place, girl, or I'll toast my hand against your hindquarters. Don't be greedy.' He used his left hand to hold her immobile whilst he played his right fingers over the sex-slicked bud. Jesus, she was wet! On some level she must always have been submissive. Her poor bottom had shrank from the lash even as her vulva welcomed it.

'Don't move. Don't you dare.' He touched her nub lightly round, round, round, and she gave ten hoarse little half-barks and moved her loins frantically against his fingers. When her climax faded he slid two curious fingers inside her and felt the post-orgasmic contractions gripping each tip.

'Bad girl!' he laughed. She'd had enough for today - but there would be other days. He touched her flaming red posterior, 'You'll have to come back here next week to take that spanking you're still due.'

'Yes, sir. Permission to sit up, sir,' Leanne muttered.

'Permission granted, girl.'

He groaned silently as she moved to straddle his lap and her pussy rubbed against his throbbing manhood.

'Permission to fuck the video director,' she continued, pulling down his zip and sliding onto his phallus in double quick time. She hadn't waited for an answer, Dave realised exultantly as he thrust inside. He smiled coldly as he cupped the girl's hot sore bum, pulling her harder against him. He'd have to punish her for that at a later date.

The Hired Hand

Shari smiled encouragingly at the stranger as they waltzed around the room. This was turning out to be some party! She hardly knew the girl from work who'd invited her here - but she was getting to know all the girl's male friends.

'Maybe we can go on to a bar for a quiet drink?' the stranger murmured, his lips brushing her earlobe and sending sweet frissons to her nipples.

'Can't - I'm here with my husband,' Shari explained.

The stranger stiffened in her arms and a grimace darkened his beguiling face. Then he smiled wryly. 'We could sneak out the back door,' he said.

Shari shook her fair fringe from her eyes. He was making her pulse race and she was very tempted. 'Sorry, I don't play away from home,' she smiled.

'In that case,' the man said gently, 'I must leave you without loving you. But how about a farewell kiss?'

Shari cast a quick glance around. Just touching her lips to his would be exciting, would fuel her fantasies. Impulsively she stood on tiptoe and he bent his head. Their lips met and she didn't pull away when his became more demanding. When she looked up her husband, Jules, was staring over at them.

Muttering her goodbyes to the stranger, Shari hurried to her husband's side. 'You seemed to be enjoying yourself,' he said drily.

Shari's heart beat faster. 'It was just a kiss!'

'From where I stood it looked more like tonsil hockey.'

'Well, we were just flirting and...'

'And you forgot your wedding vows about forsaking all others, eh?'

Shari moved her guilty gaze from his face. It then focused on his hands and she winced at the prospect of a long hard spanking. 'Alright! I've been caught in the act!' she muttered, 'When we get home you can put me over your knee.'

Jules ran his fingers over his mouth. It was a gesture he used when he was going to increase her punishment. 'Unfortunately just being spanked by your husband doesn't seem to be enough any more,' he said.

Shari glanced quickly around, but thankfully no one was in earshot. She cleared her throat: 'Jules - what do you mean?'

'Well, I send my laundry out to an ironing service. I have my lawn mowed by a landscape gardener. It seems clear that I also need a professional to discipline my wife.'

'And you know someone like that?' Shari told herself that he was bluffing, that he'd personally spank her.

'That's for me to know,' Jules said smoothly, 'And for you to find out.'

For the next three days Shari jumped whenever the phone or the doorbell rang. It would be so shameful having a stranger correct her pert bottom. She'd gotten used to pulling down her pants for Jules and the unveiling no longer made her blush. But to strip before someone she'd never met would take real courage, would make her squirm...

On the fourth night she was relaxing with a drink when Jules came into the lounge. 'You're to visit your new Master in an hour. I suggest you bathe and change,' he said quietly.

'You're bluffing!' Shari gasped, but her spouse refused to be drawn further. Eventually she gulped down her vodka then hurried to the shower. When she re-emerged she was scented with tangerine bathing gel and sheathed in a sandwashed silk dress.

'How do I look?' she muttered, adjusting her thigh-gripping hold-ups and seeking Jules approval.

'You're not giving him a fashion demo. He just wants to redden your rump,' her husband said.

They got in the car and he drove to a large Mews House. On the way Shari tried to ask more questions but Jules steadfastly refused to answer. 'You'll find out all about him - and his implements - soon enough,' he said.

'Couldn't you punish me whilst he watched?' Shari whispered, 'That would still be humbling.'

'No, if you're going to kiss a stranger then you can have your arse roasted by another stranger,' her determined spouse replied.

Shari hoped that he'd leave her at the door but instead he shook hands with her new Master and followed the two of them into the hall. 'I've got the punishment equipment ready,' the fortyish disciplinarian murmured. He had the kind of poise that made twenty-four year old Shari feel like a gauche girl.

'This is the bit that needs correcting,' Jules said, pointing at his wife's quivering dress-covered bottom.

Shari blushed the colour of a robin and stared miserably at the floor.

'My Correction Suite is through this way,' the dark-haired man continued. He ushered them through. Shari stared around the rectangular room with its thick punishment stools and disciplinary trestles. Martinets and paddles lined the walls. 'I thought the cane would improve her behaviour most,' the stranger said, looking at Jules for confirmation.

'Indeed! I've found it to be very effective,' Jules said.

Shari stood staring at the whips, acknowledging the familiar rush of low dark pleasure. She knew that when the cane swished down that pleasure would quickly abate. Afterwards Jules always brought her to orgasm and she half-swooned with rapture. That - and the fact that she knew that she'd been wrong to kiss her dance partner - would help her endure the cane.

Jules took a seat by the wall. Their host strolled over to Shari, then walked reflectively around. 'Right, raise your skirt, girl,' he ordered. Reaching for her dress hem, Shari fumblingly obeyed. 'Now leave your hold-ups on but pull down your pants,' the man continued, walking round to her rear. God, was he really going to cane her on the bare? Shari hesitated then stared supplicatingly at her seated husband. To her chagrin, Jules smiled encouragingly. 'I've just doubled your punishment for insubordination,' her new buttock-teacher said.

'Please sir - not double!' Shari whispered. Swallowing hard, she removed her white silk panties. For humblingly long moments she stood there displaying her small bare bottom. All that she wore now was a waist-skimming Chinese blouse. 'Get your belly across that whipping stool,' said the man at last, dragging a chunky four-legged contraption into the floor's centre. Shari walked gingerly forward on the high heels Jules had insisted that she wear.

When she reached the device she took a deep breath then let her weight carry her down. The stool's construction was such that her bottom was left sticking up high in the air like a pale soft beacon. How she wished that she was just prostrate across her husband's knee! She sensed that this forty year old man was very experienced, that he truly understood how to dominate and discipline a recalcitrant girl's arse.

Shari tensed up her bum cheeks as she heard him approach. 'Whilst you are here,' he said quietly, 'You will refer to me as Master.'

'Yes Master,' Shari murmured compliantly, hoping that he'd go easier on her cheeks.

'I'll give you eight strokes of the cane. It was initially going to be four but you were too slow in baring your bottom. You can have a moment between each lash to recover your poise.' He paused and walked round her submissively bent body again, 'Recovering means that you can wriggle about a little on the punishment stool but on no account must you touch your chastened rear.'

'What if I can't help myself?' Shari muttered nervously. She knew that even when Jules was spanking her she often reached her hands back to protect her sore posterior.

'If you disobey your Master your rump will be reddened further,' the dark-haired dominator said.

He walked in front of her: 'Kiss the cane.'

Shari stared at the long thin bendy rattan then pressed her lips to its hard smooth promise. 'I really am sorry that I flirted with a stranger,' she whispered, giving the man a cutely pleading look.

'You'll be even more sorry when you've got an arse as striped as your favourite T-shirt,' Jules murmured from his seat somewhere behind her, 'I think you'll take your marriage vows more seriously when you're nursing a sizzling arse.'

Shari sensed that the stranger had stepped back. Seconds later a long line of fire crackled its way across her lower bum cheeks. Shari lifted her hands a little way from the stool's legs and flexed her ankles and yelled. She was aware of her belly writhing against the smooth wood, of her main buttock muscles tensing and untensing as they tried to come to terms with the scorching stripe. 'That's right, you wriggle it out of your system, darling,' the disciplinarian murmured softly, 'Then get that adulterous arse ready for cane stroke two.'

'It wasn't adultery. It was just a kiss!' Shari said defensively, twitching her bum some more then staring down at the carpet.

'It might have become more than a kiss if I hadn't interrupted,' Jules murmured from his seat somewhere behind her naked orbs.

Shari knew that her husband was right, that his guidance helped keep her on the straight and narrow. She cleared her throat and said 'Master, I'm ready for cane stroke two.'

'Are you indeed?' the stranger murmured, and his voice held a note of mingled power and amusement. Shari gripped the lower legs of the whipping stool as she waited for the rod to strike home. She wished that the sloping wood didn't make her bare bum jut up quite so keenly. She wished she'd been allowed the dignity of retaining her pants.

When the cane fell it struck low, searing just above the tops of her thighs and accentuating the rest of her uncovered bottom. 'Aaah!' Shari gasped, jerking and wriggling, and using all her willpower to keep her belly on the stool. 'Easy,' her Master murmured as she took her hands from the wooden legs, 'Remember that you're not to cup your punished arse cheeks. If you do you'll end up with an even sorer rump.'

Shari nodded then belatedly whispered 'Yes, Master' in an attempt to get on his better side. She wondered if the bastard had one. All he seemed to care about was striping her raised small buttocks with his cane. Jules was much more kind. He sometimes kissed her flaming cheeks when she was mid way through a spanking. And he ended a caning early if she put on an Oscar-winning performance and made a lot of noise.

'The disobedient bottom will now receive stroke three,' came the stranger's voice.

Shari closed her eyes and curled her fingers around the stool again. She didn't feel at all ready. When the rod whacked into the centre of her bent bum she quivered all over and gasped and wailed. 'It's too much!' she whispered huskily, 'I can't bear it!'

'You were ready to bare it for some stranger on the dance floor,' her husband said.

Shari knew that she'd done wrong. She forced her body to stay in place, trying to find the courage to accept the rest of her chastisement. If only the cane didn't sting so hard and sear so deep. 'I know that I've been bad, and I... ask nicely for the fourth stripe,' she forced out reluctantly. The hired hand immediately obliged.

Shari shoved her bum to one side in a reflex action as she sensed the rod sizzling down. As a result, the tip of it bit into her tender buttock crevice. Wailing, she pushed herself off of the whipping stool, turned, and rushed up to her husband, flinging herself at his feet. 'It hurts,' she whispered, wrapping her arms around his calves and holding on tightly, 'I really can't take another four!'

She'd expected Jules to cuddle her and say that she'd had enough, but instead he lifted her so that she was lying over his lap, her slim thighs parted. Slowly he slid one hand under her belly, and Shari realised that she was very wet. Her husband spread apart her sexual lips then traced her vulval rim, causing intense circles of pleasure. Shari groaned lustfully and pushed down against his palm.

'Ask your Master nicely for the other four cane strokes,' Jules said.

Shari opened her eyes. The stranger was standing before her, staring down at her glowing hemispheres. She wriggled with embarrassment, knowing that he'd seen her writhing against Jules palm. The squirming caused her labial lips to brush against her husband's fingers and she pushed down again and moaned with renewed desire. 'Bad girl,' Jules whispered, taking his hand away. It was clear that she wouldn't receive satiation until she'd endured her full caning. 'Please Master,' Shari whispered, 'Teach my bottom obedience with your long rattan cane.'

'You'll have to be spanked first for leaving the whipping stool,' her chastiser said in a very offhand way. He took a seat a few feet away then said 'Wriggle over to me on your belly, sweetheart so I can smack your bum.'

Humiliated yet strangely excited, Shari clambered off of Jules lap and prostrated herself on the ground. The carpet was thick and warm beneath her flesh, though her hold-ups snagged slightly as she wriggled. When she reached her Master she kissed his leather-shod feet.

'Now bend that arse across my knee,' the stranger said. Shari swallowed hard as she stood up then arched carefully and totally over. Her bare buttocks felt hugely exposed by being prostrate like this in the man's firm lap.

'I'm sorry that I left the whipping stool,' she whispered contritely, breathing in faint pine aftershave and an underlying muskier aroma. She trembled as she felt the stranger start to fondle her red-and-beige bum.

'Why are these globes so bad?' he asked, caressing both fleshy contours.

'I promise they're going to be better!' Shari said.

The stranger continued to palpate her tenderised orbs. 'This arse only gets better after a roasting,' he said regretfully, 'I hope that it won't wriggle too much as it begs for the final four.'

'I'll beg so sweetly, Master,' Shari gasped out, knowing that the sooner she got caned the sooner she would get to orgasm with her husband.

'I want you to really humble yourself so that you remember the consequences of kissing a stranger,' her chastiser said.

He began to spank her bare bottom then, the slaps slow and somehow thoughtful. Shari whimpered as he toasted every centimetre of her buttock flesh. 'I've found that if you spank her lower cheeks the most she gets quite excited,'

Jules said mildly from somewhere in the middle distance, 'Let her get all hot then make her wait.'

Shari skulked some more across her dominator's knee. It was awful being spoken about like this as if she was a sexed-up mongrel. But her spouse's words were degradingly true.

Soon she felt her body moving on to another plain, the plain of pleasure. She arched her bum up to meet the next spank - and her Master stopped. 'There! I've made a glowing red canvas on which to imprint the last four cane strokes,' he murmured contentedly. He set her on her knees on the floor. 'Go over to the whipping stool again and position your flirtatious arse upon it,' he ordered mildly. Hoping to please him by crawling rather than walking, Shari wriggled on her belly all the way.

She reached the stool and touched its smooth top, knowing that she had to slide her belly onto it. 'I'm waiting,' her disciplinarian told her. Shari risked a quick glance back. Both the stranger and Jules were gazing over at her, staring at her hot striped haunches. Shari arched her half-bared body across the wood.

This time her bottom felt even more exposed than before for the growing heat made it feel larger. She could think of nothing except her raised backside. 'I don't hear you,' her Master called. She heard him walking close then closer. Steeled herself to ask for the fifth cut of the cane. 'My derriere was bad to run away from the rod,' she muttered, tensing and untensing her buttock muscles, 'It deserves to be soundly thrashed.'

'Your *derriere*?' the dark-haired man mocked. She felt his hands palpating her cheeks, 'This here is an *arse* - a British arse. Save the French for when you go abroad.'

Shari quivered as she used the more vulgar word 'My... *arse* needs to be taught a lesson. Needs soundly caned.' She sucked in her breath then let it out as the rod connected with the centre of her rosy hemispheres. She scrunched and unscrunched her hot rotundities in an effort to dislodge the pain. 'It's so hot,' she whispered to no one in particular, 'So very sore.'

'You should have thought of that before you cuckolded your husband,' her new Master said.

'I know,' Shari muttered, wishing again and again that she hadn't lifted her lips to the stranger's.

'Tell me how naughty you've been,' her dominator urged.

Submission thrilled through her belly even as arrogance flooded her brain. 'I just flirted on a night out,' Shari mumbled. The man traced the rod down her naked cheeks again and again. 'I don't think that the word *just* applies to throwing yourself at other men,' he said smoothly, 'This rod is very strict about such matters and comes down very hard on bottoms that play away.'

Shari shrugged. Some little devil had taken hold of her mind when he tried to make her sound immature by calling her naughty. Hell, she was a twenty-four year old woman, and deserved a measure of respect! 'Jules, perhaps you'd like to give her a quick spank to teach her manners?' the man asked softly. Shari heard her husband's footsteps approach. In seconds he'd pushed one finger inside her, and was using the other hand to spank her soundly. Shari slithered whimperingly about as the mingled ecstasy and affliction brought her close to climax again.

Then Jules stopped and moved away, leaving her desperate for relief. 'I've been a very bad girl,' she whispered raggedly, 'A girl who needs the hottest and sorest arse.'

'Yes you do, don't you?' the stranger murmured.

Shari heard him flex the rod. He seemed to be waiting. She searched for yet more demeaning words. 'I'm... glad that you made me raise my skirts and pull down my panties,' she whispered humbly.

'And?' the man prompted.

'And you were right to spank me for clambering off the whipping stool,' she replied.

'Tell me that you also deserve the rod,' the man said, swishing it through the air until her bottom trembled.

Shari cleared her throat: 'And now you're equally right to thrash me with the cane.'

As she finished saying the word *cane* the implement itself bit soundly into her flesh, midway across her bare bottom. Shari moved her hips so violently that they almost fell off one side of the stool.

'Oh dear,' murmured the man, 'We do seem to be jumping about a lot. It's most unseemly.'

Shari squirmed about some more then tried to make her bum cheeks stay in place. 'I'll try not to wriggle so much,' she promised, forcing her bum to stay prostrate.

'If only I could trust you,' the man said. He strolled calmly to the front of her then tilted her chin and stared into her eyes, his own gaze assessing. 'No, I can see that your bum can't help itself.'

He walked around to her posterior and softly palmed it from lower back to thigh. 'The problem is that if I let you jerk so much you may hurt yourself. And as you know, a Master is only interested in hurting his slave's insolent arse.' He palmed gently at that same arse, 'No, I'm afraid that I'll have to adjust the contours of the whipping stool so that you can't fall off of one side.'

Shari started to obligingly slide from the contraption but he softly told her to stay in place. 'All that I have to do is turn this handle and it'll change the alignment of the wood,' he said impassively. He obviously did so, for Shari felt the front legs of the stool contracting and the back legs lengthening so that her buttocks were pushed even more obscenely into the air. She felt excited yet debased, aware that both her Master and her husband would now be able to see her crack and anal hole more clearly. She was completely open to their gaze.

'You were about to ask nicely for stroke seven,' the stranger said.

Shari cleared her suddenly clogged throat. 'I deserve...' she started to mumble.

'Let's get creative. Describe your punished arse to me,' her Master murmured, his voice containing a smile.

'It's... very exposed and... um... tender all over where it's been spanked,' Shari mumbled, closing her eyes against this new degradation, 'And I can feel the cane's separate weals.'

'I can *see* them, and very pretty they look too,' her husband murmured from his seat in the background. Reminded that there were two men staring at her red rotundities, Shari groaned.

'I think I'll lay the seventh stroke a little further up. They say that seven is lucky for some, but not for your twitching cheeks,' the stranger said softly. Shari felt the rod smack into her newly-raised bare bottom and she squealed again.

'Please put the eighth stroke further down,' she whispered beseechingly, 'Oh sir, please!'

'I usually let her off when she begs so prettily,' came Jules voice, his tone thoughtful, 'But being merciful obviously hasn't done our marriage any good.'

Shari whimpered as her submissively bent bare bottom awaited the final stroke. Her Master teased her with the rod, tracing it across the seven existing lines and keeping her in an agony of anticipation. 'I favour that nice tender line where your thigh backs meet your bottom,' he said at last. Shari tried to push her belly more firmly into the stool but the wood held her buttocks fully raised. Other than letting herself slide over the top of the stool, she couldn't escape her thrashing. And anyway she'd agreed to this caning as a way of absolving her earlier sin. She wanted to show her husband that she valued their relationship, that she was truly sorry for that snatched illicit kiss.

'I've got the reddest arse in the world, but I'm accepting the eighth stroke to show that I love you, Jules,' she said into the Punishment Room. Then she twitched that same sore arse and asked nicely for the cane.

Her Master mercifully applied the final stroke where she'd asked him too - but it was still low and long and swishy. Shari moaned loudly and writhed the little she could upon the cruelly-raised corrective seat. 'Can I get down and kiss your feet now, Master?' she asked humbly when her wriggling had subsided. She wanted to hug the man's knees and plant little kisses on his shoes. Then she wanted to crawl to Jules and please him with her hands and lips.

'No, stay where you are and try not to twitch your chastened bum,' her dominator ordered, 'I like a slave's arse to remain in situ for ten minutes after it's been thrashed.'

'But I feel so exposed,' Shari whispered, opening her eyes to stare ahead of her at the martinets and paddles.

'Use the time to reflect on your wrongdoings,' the disciplinarian replied.

Shari lay there, contemplating her smarting scarlet globes. After an unspecified time she heard footsteps approach them. She tensed as an exploratory finger was teased down her sensitive buttock crack. 'Relax. It's me,' Jules whispered, his knowing hands sliding under her tum to seek out her rosebud of pleasure. Shari groaned with excitement at the prospect of relief. Then she heard her Master's voice. 'Show control, dear. I don't want you to come for at least twenty minutes. If you disobey me you'll be back here for a tawsing next week.'

Playing The Game

Coming here had been a mistake. Becky stared sullenly around the amusement arcade. Thanks to Paul she'd seen most of the arcades in Scotland during the past few days. She'd only gone on this touring holiday with the people from her work because she secretly fancied him. She'd thought that the feeling was mutual when he'd suggested they separate from the rest...

But he'd merely driven her to town after town to sample the gaming parlours. Now Becky tugged at his elbow. 'I'm going mad with boredom here. Can we leave?'

'But I've got a hold,' Paul muttered, not taking his eyes from the flashing symbols before him.

'Bloody machine!' Enraged beyond endurance, Becky pulled her foot back and kicked it hard. Paul kept playing. Her anger growing, she aimed her ankle boot at the next machine and the next.

She was throwing herself on the fourth flashing box when strong arms wrapped themselves around her waist and lifted her away from the slot-based devices. At last Paul had noticed her. Becky let her body relax against his chest. Then she stiffened as an unfamiliar male voice spoke slowly but assuredly in her ear.

'We don't tolerate vandalism in this town,' it said. Becky felt herself being set down, being held in situ. Then the man turned her around to face him, still keeping his fingers on her upper arms.

'I... it was just a moment's anger,' Becky stammered, daring a quick glance at the guy. He looked to be about ten years her senior.

'A moment's anger can have lasting repercussions,' her captor said.

Becky looked at his hands, at the way they were wrapped around her flesh. She was beginning to feel trapped and a little bit frightened. 'I'm truly sorry,' she muttered, 'I'll pay.'

'Oh you'll pay all right,' said the man.

Becky looked wildly around for Paul. He was standing about three feet away, his mouth half-open. 'I'm with my friend Paul,' Becky said. She waited for her colleague to step closer, to defend her.

'Nothing to do with me. She and I just work together,' Paul offered with a sheepish grin. He looked back at the machine he'd been playing, 'I just need one more nudge to make this baby sing for its supper. Can you give me another quid's worth of ten pence pieces, mate?'

'Sorry, I'm closing the arcade to deal with this little vandal,' the man replied in a calm but no-nonsense kind of voice. He looked at his watch, 'You can come back for her in three hours if you want to. By then she should have learned her lesson properly.'

'If she needs bail, don't look at me. I'm down to my last tenner,' Paul added in what Becky thought was an appallingly casual voice.

'It's certainly going to cost your friend dear,' the older man said.

Paul left. Becky watched him go. The arcade manager kept holding her lightly.

'Is there any way that I can make amends?' she murmured, parting her lips and looking up into his inscrutable brown eyes.

The man smiled a long slow smile which gave her ample time to scan his lightly-stubbled features. 'Certainly. You can rectify the situation by going over my knee,' he explained, striding over to lock the arcade doors.

'But that's not right!' Becky gasped. Inside her white satin bra her nipples tingled.

‘Nor is sabotaging my property,’ her new dominator said.

So he *owned* this place! That meant he’d seriously care about the arcade and its contents. That meant he had even more reason to tan her hide. ‘Can’t I just give you my holiday spending money?’ the twenty-one year old parried, looking insinuatingly at her cash-filled shoulder bag.

‘No, you can give me your naked bottom across my lap right this minute - or get ready to appear in court,’ the man replied.

He seemed to take her nervous silence for an affirmative. Leastways, he marched her towards the long couch which ran along the arcade’s entire back wall, and settled himself upon it. Then he pulled her over his knee.

‘What if someone peers in?’ Becky muttered, not sure how much they’d see of her imminent chastisement.

‘Then they’ll see me turn a disobedient white bum to a supplicating scarlet,’ the manager said.

‘Shouldn’t we be formally introduced?’ Becky quipped, trying to take his thoughts and words away from her helpless buttocks.

‘I’m Ged Alcott, but just call me sir,’ her tormentor said. Becky murmured her own name, but he didn’t seem to be listening. Instead she felt his hands patiently edging up her leather skirt and then equally slowly pulling down her silken pants. ‘What a pretty little arse,’ he mused, ‘I’m going to enjoy thrashing it soundly. I’m going to make it very sore indeed.’

‘Screw you,’ Becky muttered, squirming about at his mocking and shameful words.

‘Well, I don’t know about that, but I may relieve your hungry little clit in an hour or two,’ the arcade owner continued, hoisting her higher upon his knee. He yanked her little panties down even further so that they settled at her mid-calves, 'But for now I want to concentrate on tenderising this defenceless flesh.'

Becky sensed that he'd raised his palm. She shut her eyes. Then she opened them wide and gasped as he slapped strenuously at her right buttock. Before she could protest, he'd doled out an equally harsh spank to the left.

'Ouch!' she muttered, realising that no one had ever spanked her on the bare before, 'You pig! That stings like hell!'

'It's meant to - it's reparation for trying to wreck my business,' Ged said.

He toasted both disarmed buttocks again then repeated the smarting gesture. He slapped hard at the creamy white flesh from just below her waist to the sensitive silky underswell.

'Ah,' Becky muttered, 'Oh. Ow! Aargh! Uh! Jesus!'

'Spare me the soundtrack,' her determined disciplinarian said.

'But it really stings,' Becky whispered, lifting and turning her head with effort to look back at him.

'Would you rather have a police record and be sentenced to community service?' Ged asked.

'Well, no, I...' A record could affect her future career prospects.

'Then take your spanking and caning without complaint,' the arcade owner said.

Becky exhaled hard and long against the leather settee at the mention of this further chastisement. 'A caning?' she whispered, the chagrined heat rushing to the hirsute curve between her legs.

'Yes, six strict strokes of the cane with you bent over the snooker table,' Ged Alcott explained, stroking her bare bottom.

'Could I at least... you know... smooth my skirt down again?' Becky mumbled, wriggling about even more nervously upon his knee.

'No - I like a girl to taste the rod on her nude buttocks,' the disciplinarian parried.

Becky gulped again. 'But isn't six strokes a lot to bear?'

'Undoubtedly,' Ged confirmed. He caressed her quivering extremities. 'I had to use it just recently when a female customer with an account here ran up significant debts. She didn't want to go to prison so I offered her the option of a caning. She howled from the first stroke to the last.' He added two more echoing spanks to Becky's rump, 'She put her hands back to protect her arse so I had to give her an extra stripe with the larger reformatory rod. I hope you won't make a similar mistake.'

'Couldn't I just have a longer spanking?' Becky murmured beseechingly.

'You could, but it wouldn't be sufficiently daunting. And anyway I like to see a bad girl writhe beneath the cane.'

Slowly he helped the twenty-one year old to her feet. She leaned against him, thighs weak with humiliation. 'There are other alternatives,' she whispered, brushing a hand against his groin.

'You'll feel the rod bite more deeply now because you tried to distract me,' said the arcade owner coolly, marching her towards the green baize table. Becky wished yet again that she hadn't vandalised his machines.

'I've already been punished by the spanking and by being half undressed by you,' she muttered, her buttocks trembling at the prospect of this further shaming.

'I'll know when you've been truly punished because that hot little arse will beg for forgiveness,' the man said.

Christ, he was crude! But the girl forgot all about his words as he started to encourage her gently over the snooker table. As her tummy brushed the bulk cushion she hesitated then glanced over her shoulder at Ged.

'Remember how cathartic this will be for you, how it'll cleanse you of your bad temper and mood swings,' he said.

'Well, go easy on me,' she whispered, lowering herself over the green baize so that her bum was a reluctant naked sacrifice.

'I'll be strict without being merciless,' the arcade owner explained.

Becky let her lids flutter down so that she couldn't watch her tormentor fetch the slender stick. Then she opened her eyes again for not seeing was a form of sensory deprivation. All she could think about was the exposed soft target of her haunches, of the cane that Ged Alcott was approaching with.

'What if it's too much for me?' she mumbled nervously.

'You can cover your bottom with your hands at any moment and ask me to call the police and report you for vandalism instead,' the man responded, flexing the rod between his hands. He walked behind her and then seemed to stand in situ. Becky shivered, knowing that he was studying her proffered curves.

Then a stinging line emblazoned its way across her flesh and she forgot about what she looked like. Forgot about everything except that one red stripe which heated her sensitive sphere.

'Uh,' she groaned, half getting up from the snooker table.

'Five more to go until you leave here, honey,' Ged Alcott said.

Becky thought about taking the option of a court appearance. Then he put his hand on her back to help her down again and as his fingers brushed her spine she shivered with unexpected desire. 'Wouldn't you rather give me a kiss?' she whispered, peeking round at him and licking her lips invitingly.

'I'd rather give you the hottest arse in the universe,' her dominator said.

Becky cried out again as he laid on the second stripe. She could tell from the air currents that he wasn't drawing the cane back far, was merely bouncing it against her haunches. But the focused thinness of the cane and the tenderness caused by the earlier spanking meant that her soft globes were both susceptibly aglow. *Four to go,* she told herself. *Just four more painful swishes. Then I get the pardon which I crave.*

Ged Alcott seemed to crave turning her into a girl who wouldn't sit down for a week. 'You're squirming so nicely,' he said, 'Your bottom's all fiery and red. And it wriggles every time I move my arm back because it knows what's coming next.'

'Full marks for observation!' Becky snapped. She sucked in her breath and wondered if he'd cane her more firmly for insubordination. Howled when he laid on the third stripe extra hard.

'Only three more strokes till you get to look at your sore cheeks in the mirror,' the arcade owner said matter-of-factly, 'Most women feel proud at that bit.'

Did they, now? The twenty-one year old shivered with degradation and mild desire at the very prospect. Then she flinched, gasped and swung her body from side to side as Ged Alcott laid on stroke four.

'Oh it hurts, it hurts,' she wailed, jumping up and clutching her crimson cheeks, trying to rub away the soreness.

'Of course it hurts. It's punishment,' her dominator said. He looked at her sternly. 'I warned you what would happen if you didn't obediently hold the position. Now I'm going to have to display your haunches more fully and more vulnerably. And after the sixth stroke you'll have to endure a seventh with the stricter reformatory cane.'

'Yes sir,' Becky whispered. She realised that for some strange reason she no longer wanted to fight him. She would try to endure the rest of her flogging stoically.

Nevertheless, she whimpered as the arcade owner returned with two plump cushions which he set on the snooker table.

'Where do you think these are going, my disobedient young miss?'

'Under my belly, sir,' Becky said with guttural submission.

'Why?'

'Because...' She toed the ground with one bare foot, 'Oh hell!'

'Say it,' said the man, 'Or it'll not go well for your haunches.'

'You use... you use the cushions to push my bottom up higher into the air.'

'Your *bare* bottom,' the man instructed.

'My bare bottom, sir,' Becky said.

'Good girl,' he murmured as she arched her body to let him place the pillows above her mons. She pushed her thighs apart and felt hugely wanton. 'Such a pretty little bum,' Ged continued. He traced the cane lines as he spoke and Becky thought that she'd faint with the rush of carnal craving which enveloped her lower flesh. Her mind shrank from this subordinate situation but her body was excited at being half stripped and exhibited like this.

Now that the bolsters were in situ her buttocks were even more obscenely displayed. Becky closed her eyes and tried to think of Paul whom she'd so recently fancied but she could hardly remember what he looked like. She tried to think of work, of her friends, of home. Instead her mind came back again and again to the ignominy of her raised naked hemispheres, to their imminent fate.

'Just do it - just lay the cane on,' she whispered raggedly.

'Oh, I'm admiring the view too much to rush things,' her newfound tutor said. She heard a smile enter his voice. 'I want you to think about this the next time that you're tempted to take your bad mood out on some innocent victim. Think about how it feels being stripped and exhibited like this.'

Becky was thinking about just that when he laid on lash number four. Thereafter all she could concentrate on was her smarting tissues. She rubbed them quickly and skulked around on her belly but otherwise stayed obediently in place.

'Now for the fifth one,' said Ged, 'I think you'll have to take it slightly further down. That particular section of those naughty globes doesn't look quite as red.'

'Even it up, why don't you?' Becky muttered then snivelled as he did just that.

Time for the last one, she told herself, gripping the table's end. Her body was puckering and unpuckering of its own volition. She could imagine how it looked to Ged's coolly assessing gaze.

'Like what you see?' she whispered throatily.

'I like it even better at the moment of impact,' her disciplinarian said. He ran the rod down her tremulous orbs in a warning gesture. 'The arse drives forward as the cane bites into it then it comes all the way out again as if mutely begging for the next stern stroke.'

'You're a pig!' Becky muttered.

'No, I'm a civilised man who doesn't appreciate having his business destroyed by a bad tempered wretch.'

He had a point. She'd started this whole painful business. 'Okay, I'm sorry,' the twenty-one year old forced out, 'Please lay on stroke six.'

The man traced the cane along her haunches some more whilst she squirmed in anticipation on the cushions. Then he obliged.

'Now put your hands on your head and walk to the mirror,' he said. Becky stood up and followed his pointing finger. Her panties bunched at her ankles making her punishment walk restrained and mortified.

'Impressed by my handiwork?' Ged asked.

Becky looked in the silvery surface and saw her small round cheeks reflected back at her. There were dark crimson tramlines on a background of well-spanked red.

'Very colourful,' she said dutifully.

'A nice canvas on which to lay the reformatory rod,' the man explained.

'But...' Too late Becky remembered that she'd jumped up without permission and earned herself an extra punishment.

'That's butt with two t's - and I'll have you touching your toes for a change,' the man said.

With a last anguished glance at him, Becky obeyed. Her buttocks lifted as she awkwardly assumed the position. Her cheeks seemed to part a little as if allowing him access to their central core.

'Kiss the rod and ask nicely for forgiveness,' he said, bringing over the lengthier new cane.

As Becky did so some new level of submission rushed through her and she dropped to her knees and subserviently kissed his feet.

'I think those chastened cheeks have had enough for now,' he murmured, putting aside the unused rod then gently caressing her. Overcome with desire, she swayed.

And so to bed. Two hours later they relaxed by the fire in his upstairs flat.

'Now what?' Becky asked happily.

'Now we go downstairs to the amusement arcade again.'

'Can't I amuse you up here?' She ran a hand inside his shirt which was still unbuttoned.

'No, I want you to stand gripping the coathooks on the back wall whilst you taste the reformatory cane.'

The reformatory cane. Becky stilled into watchfulness. 'But I thought...'

'The pleasure we've just had doesn't cancel out your punishment.'

'It's just one stroke. Hardly worth it.'

'It's two now because you've just been so presumptuous,' the older man said.

'And if I can't be bothered going downstairs?'

'I'll have to carry you.'

'And if I refuse to hold onto the coathook?'

'I'll have to tie your wrists to it instead.'

She'd met her match. Carefully Becky stood up. She felt a new low rush of lust as he pulled down her so recently pulled up panties. Then she felt another thrill of trepidation as he picked up the big cane and led her downstairs.

Sitting Uncomfortably

Model Tenants Incorporated had few rules, but the rules which it did have were strictly adhered to. Linda was told this when she applied for evening work there.

'Are you always punctual?' the interviewer asked.

Linda hesitated, then reminded herself that people invariably lied at interviews. 'Oh yes, Miss Breeson. I detest lateness in others,' she replied, forcing her lightly-glossed lips into an amenable grin.

There was a silence. The interviewer seemed to be not so much looking *at* her as looking *through* her. Linda glanced at the desk and squirmed in her seat. 'In fact if anything I'm usually too early,' she babbled on, 'Sometimes I'm so punctual for my night class that I end up helping the tutor to arrange the chairs.'

'At least you talk a lot,' the older woman said drily, 'That helps show potential burglars that the property is occupied. You can talk to yourself as much as you like while you work.'

She went on to explain exactly what the *Model Tenants* agency did. 'Basically you house-sit when a property's owners are away for a week or two. You only work for a few hours at a time so it's not too restricting, but you don't leave till another employee comes along to relieve you of your shift.'

'And I just *sit* there?' Linda queried, unable to believe that she was to be paid so handsomely for so little output.

'Well, you switch lights on and off at irregular intervals. You put on the TV and radio in various parts of the house.'

'Sounds like a home from home,' the blonde girl joked. Again she saw that the vaguely masculine-looking interviewer wasn't smiling. Miss Breeson's demeanour spoke business, from the unadorned cut of her navy skirt suit to her feather cut dark hair.

One week later Linda began her new evening job. It sounded foolproof. By day she worked her usual hours as a market researcher. By 6pm she was ensconced in the otherwise unoccupied hotel or sprawling house. There she played music and switched on and off the conversational tapes and watched television. At midnight she went to bed. By 8am the next day one of the other guards arrived to start the day shift, and Linda left the house in his or her capable hands.

But excitement soon turns to apathy. Newness dulls into routine. After a few nights Linda was bored with looking at the oil paintings and Chinese statues she was supposed to be guarding. She wanted dancing, drinking, life. She could sneak out of the back door and hurry along to the Mon Ami Club for an hour, she told herself, brightening. Her best friend worked in the Cocktail Lounge there. If she kept the lights on in the house and left her car outside then potential burglars would never know she'd sneaked away.

She went. The music was soft but the drink was harder. The hour stretched into two hours, as it usually does when you're having fun. Half-laughing to herself as she remembered her friend's gossip, Linda eventually returned to the Tudor-style house. Quietly she let herself in the triple-locked front door and strolled nonchalantly into the living room - then she screamed.

Miss Breeson sat there on the long leather couch. She was staring off into the middle distance. 'You've let the firm down badly, my dear. You'll have to be punished,' she said.

'Miss Breeson! I didn't mean to... I... em... had a headache so went for a walk,' Linda muttered faintly.

'If a guard needs to leave the house there's a procedure to follow, as you well know,' her boss replied.

The drill involved phoning Head Office to ask for a replacement guard to be sent. Linda cleared her throat. 'I... uh... didn't think about the rules for a few moments.'

'And *Model Tenants* doesn't employ unthinking people. I'll have your P45 ready by next weekend.'

Linda stood, dismayed, in the centre of the room. She stared at her boss's somewhat Teutonic features. She'd heard rumours that the woman was attracted to slim fair-haired girls like herself. Now she wondered if a little flirtation would make all the difference. She had to keep this job.

Slowly she sidled over to the elongated couch, shrugged her jacket and shoes off, then sat next to the older woman, thigh side to thigh side. Her sand-washed silk dress looked very girlish beside Miss Breeson's black denim suit.

'I'd love to make amends,' Linda whispered ambiguously.

'In that case,' the older woman retorted, 'Get that disobedient young arse over my knee.'

There was a pause, an even more awkward pause than Linda remembered from her interview. The woman had unnerved her then - but she was positively shaming her now!

'You mean you're going to...?' she started, but couldn't bring herself to add the words spank me.

'I'm going to turn your arse the colour of a Macintosh Red apple,' Miss Breeson replied.

Linda stared at the carpeted ground. She tried to think of some clever word play about fruit but her imagination failed her. Instead, she began playing desperately for time. 'How about if you give me extra unpaid shifts?' she asked.

'You're incapable of meeting your current work tasks so I hardly want to entrust you with extra hours,' her employer answered.

'Dock my wages, then, Miss?'

'Either you accept that this is your *last* wage or you bare your bum.'

Another laboured silence ensued. Linda looked at her boss's firm hands. She looked at the hem of her own silk dress and imagined it being lifted. She tried to remember which panties she had on.

'Just a... a few smacks and I keep my job?' she queried breathlessly, trying not to picture such a scenario.

'Just two well-thrashed cheeks and you get to continue working for me,' Miss Breeson confirmed.

Linda knew that she really needed this evening job. It had lifted her out of debt and was indeed now providing luxuries. And how many people got paid to live in wonderful Tudor-style houses filled with intricate antiques?

'Alright,' she said in a dazed small voice. Then she quivered as the stronger woman rolled both her sleeves up and pulled Linda over her dauntingly muscular knee.

For a few moments she lay there breathing heavily as her employer told her how bad she'd been and stroked her dress-sheathed buttocks.

'I'd like you to answer "Yes Ma'am" when appropriate,' Miss Breeson added sternly.

'Yes, Ma'am,' Linda muttered, gritting her teeth with humiliation. Her face burned at the thought of the spanking which was to ensue.

Miss Breeson was obviously thinking of the spanking too. Leastways she said 'Let's lift this skirt up.' Linda closed her eyes more tightly as she felt the lower half of her dress being lifted away from her bottom and thighs. It was a warm August night so she wasn't wearing any stockings. Now all that there was between this woman's hard palm and her own soft bum was her lace-edged flimsy pants. 'After the skirt goes up, the pants come down,' the older woman continued matter of factly. The twenty-five year old skulked ashamedly on her tummy as she felt her briefs being dragged down her thighs.

'Mmm, quite a spankable looking spread,' Miss Breeson continued, hoisting Linda's backside more firmly onto her lap. 'It's small, but those little round cheeks are nicely fleshy in the centre.' She fondled both spheres as she spoke, and Linda groaned. 'Ask me to spank this bum hard if you value your employment,' the forty-something woman continued. Linda forced out the words then moaned some more. An hour ago she'd been laughing and dancing at a club - now she was across this woman's lap with a totally bare bottom. Her only consolation was that no one else could see.

But she herself could certainly feel. She gasped as a heavy palm lashed down on one fair cheek. She was just recovering her breath when the woman smacked her other pale round buttock. Linda automatically reached her hands back to protect herself as the woman started up a veritable tattoo.

'Ah, ow, that hurts!' she muttered, trying to pull her employer's hands away. Those same hands caught her wrists and brought them together behind her back.

'I'd hoped that you'd be obedient,' Miss Breeson said softly, 'But as you're not I'll have to tie your naughty hands out of the way.'

'But that hurts my shoulders!' Linda protested as the woman started to wind something round both wrists, thus imprisoning her hands above her buttocks.

'I'll tie your hands in front then,' the older woman said conversationally, 'The only thing I want to hurt is your bum.'

She half-lifted Linda and set her on the floor, then took hold of her arms and tied them loosely before her. 'That's better,' she said with obvious satisfaction, 'Now we won't have any little fingers trying to shield those naughty globes.'

'Please don't make the other spanks so hard,' Linda pleaded piteously as her boss hauled her over her firm knee again. Her rotundities trembled.

'When you've failed in your work duties and potentially brought my firm into disrepute? I have to make the remaining spanks very harsh indeed.'

Miss Breeson raised her palm. Linda buried her face in the leather couch. She wished that her bum wasn't such a vulnerable target. She howled as her employer began to whack alternate buttocks again. 'Oh please,' she spluttered, writhing helplessly on her silken belly. She kicked the little she could with her equally bare slim legs. Why didn't Miss Breeson fondle her breasts or peak at her blonde-haired pudenda? Why was she so obsessed with heating her disarmed writhing bum? Linda moved her hips from side to side. She pressed her belly into the ungiving lap beneath her. She tried to pull in her buttock muscles to make each cheek a smaller target, but to no avail.

Then suddenly Miss Breeson stopped. 'I think this arse and I should have a little chat,' she said coolly.

Linda nodded, then uttered a belated 'Whatever you want.'

'Is the arse sorry that it left its post without permission?' the older woman murmured.

'Oh yes, Ma'am,' Linda said. She searched for the words which would grant her release from her supine state, 'This bad bum is truly humbled and will never again leave a house it's supposed to guard.'

'I'm glad to hear it,' Miss Breeson said matter of factly, 'Now we just have to punish it for its earlier lies.'

Linda felt her heart sink. Her reddened hemispheres jerked of their own volition. They were already invested with a rosy glow.

'What lies did I tell, Ma'am?' she whispered raggedly.

'That arse lied about having a headache,' her employer retorted, 'When in truth it went to a nearby club.'

'You watched me?' Linda asked weakly, knowing that her bottom was in for a further warming.

‘Of course I did. We at *Model Tenants* have to keep a firm eye on our trainees,’ the dominant woman replied. She reached for a plump cushion and pushed it under the younger girl’s lower tum. ‘Let’s get that backside raised to its very utmost.’

‘Please have mercy,’ Linda whispered, puckering up her anguished flesh.

But her boss seemed to have a pre-determined number of spanks in mind. Leastways she whacked at Linda’s lower curves and at her middle cheeks, ignoring her gasped-out promises that she would do better. She spanked the dark divide of the girl’s posterior. She smacked the delicate fold at her nether thighs.

‘I’ll do anything, Ma’am,’ the failed house sitter whimpered, tensing and untensing her smarting bare bottom.

‘Do you mean that, girl?’ the older woman replied.

She stayed her hand. Linda’s brain raced with scenes. If she pleasured her boss she might get extra weekend shifts and become her favourite. And it was probably as easy to rub another women to orgasm as it was a man.

‘Yes, Ma’am, I long to please you,’ she said gutturally. Then she whimpered with relief as she was hoisted from her boss’s imprisoning lap.

Linda stayed crouched on the floor waiting for her employer to untie her hands. Instead, Miss Breeson just pulled off her own jeans and briefs then opened her strong legs widely.

‘Lick thoroughly, dear,’ she said.

Linda stared at the pinkish-brown folds of skin. The woman’s labia was darker than her own, the lips longer. Her clitoris was peeking from its hood. ‘I’ve never...’ she admitted faintly, rocking back on her heels.

‘I hope that you’re not reneging on your word? You said that you wanted to please me,’ the forty-something woman murmured. She reached forward and squeezed the younger girl's tenderised spheres. Linda gasped at the pain and jiggled about on the carpet, then she put her open wet mouth to her employer's oiled flesh...

For the next few weeks the *Model Tenants* agency had a model house sitter who turned up for work early and who never went out. She earned herself extra shifts until she was house-sitting every spare moment. It was lucrative. It was uncomplex. Until she met Nick.

Nick looked and smelt like one of those tanned muscular men in an aftershave ad. He sat next to Linda at the bar and desire traced its paths through her wanton flesh. After a double gin she made it clear that she was a single girl in search of communal pleasure. They danced and flirted all night.

'Let me take you to dinner on Saturday,' he suggested at the end of the evening as he called her a cab.

'I'd love to, but I'm house sitting,' Linda murmured.

'Next week then, please?' he pressed. She loved the fact that he cared enough to pursue her - but she was housesitting the next week and the next. 'In that case,' Nick continued, 'Why don't I come to you? I'll order from that *Home Comforts* place in the high street. They supply the champagne, the crockery and the meals.'

'Sounds idyllic,' Linda said. In truth house sitters weren't supposed to have guests on the premises. But no one would ever know.

He came. He stayed. She was deliciously conquered. She could still feel the memory of his manhood inside her when she opened the door to Miss Breeson the next day.

'You broke the rules by entertaining here,' the older woman said.

Linda swallowed hard, but knew better than to deny it. 'I've known him for years,' she lied, 'He brought us both a meal.'

'He also took a Victorian jewellery box belonging to the lady of the house,' Miss Breeson informed her.

'He wouldn't do that. He was so nice,' Linda said, her voice rising to something resembling a wail. She realised belatedly that con men *had* to be nice in order to fool people. Maybe he'd even known that she was a housesitter and had followed her to the club?

She was still musing over the situation when Miss Breeson marched into the lounge and turned on the security tape. The film showed Nick sneaking into the house's dressing room at 3am and taking the jewellery box.

'I assume that he was gone when you got up?' Miss Breeson asked.

'Well, yes,' Linda muttered, still unable to believe that she'd been duped so easily, 'But he left a note saying that he would phone me tonight.'

'The police picked him up as he left here. The only phone call he'll be making is to his solicitor,' the older woman said abruptly. She sighed. 'It's lucky that the guard in Head Office was reviewing all the in-progress tapes and saw Nick actually stealing the valuables. Otherwise he'd have gotten well away.'

Linda knew when she was beaten - or when she was about to be. 'Are you going to spank me again, Ma'am?' she asked in what she hoped was a seductive little voice.

Her boss shook her head. 'The spanking obviously wasn't severe enough so I'm going to have to cane you. Be at the training hall for 8pm.'

At 6pm Linda had a bath. By 7pm she'd eaten a light meal and put on her tightest blue jeans and a classic white polo shirt. She wanted to look neat yet casual. She wanted the thick denim to protect her bottom if her boss chose to cane her over her jeans. The younger girl feared the prospect of the rod lashing down on her helpless buttocks, but she was endlessly grateful that Miss Breeson hadn't handed her over to the police. After all, she'd let a virtual stranger into a house filled with near-priceless belongings. They might consider her an accessory to the crime.

Crime led to punishment. So be it. Determined to accept her caning with good grace, Linda drove nervously to the spacious training hall where *Model Tenants Incorporated* trained its employees. She was very aware of her small hips pushing into the car's driving seat. Would she soon need a cushion under these same haunches? An ex-boyfriend had been caned at public school, and he'd said that it cut like hell...

Cut it out, she told herself, parking outside the *Model Tenants Incorporated* facility. She walked slowly along the corridors till she reached the training hall. After taking a deep breath, she walked through the door - and abruptly stopped. Miss Breeson stood just inside the hall, but there were twenty men and women sitting in the seats around the arena. Peering closer, Linda recognised three. 'Meet your contemporaries,' her boss said, 'They are all here because they've broken the rules, like you.'

Linda licked her lips. 'You mean we're going to watch each other being... You'll chastise me in front of them?'

'I've found it helps to drive the message home,' her employer said. She swished something lightly against her military-style khaki trousers and for the first time Linda saw that she was holding a rattan cane.

Lost for words, the twenty-five year old looked around the well-lit room. There was a piece of wooden apparatus in the centre.

'Meet your punishment rack,' said the older woman, following her gaze.

'You mean we... get strapped in there?'

'Well, *you* do.'

'And get caned in front of everyone?'

'Only everyone who is here,' her boss confirmed. She paused, 'Remember, your audience is comprised of fellow wrongdoers, so they're unlikely to tease you. My other eighty employees have an exemplary record and will never hear of this day.'

Linda looked at the rod again. It was wickedly long and thin with a thicker curved handle.

'Couldn't you cane me in private, then I could please you with my tongue again?' she asked in a soft low voice.

'Private humiliation obviously wasn't enough. I need to set an example,' the forty-something woman answered, 'Go to the punishment rack now and take down your jeans.'

'And if I don't?' Linda muttered, her cheeks flaming.

'If you don't I'll inform the police that you aren't fit to be a housesitter, and you can leave my employ right away.'

She loved the job. She liked the evening hours. She adored the money. Resignedly Linda walked towards the wooden contraption, Miss Breeson in her wake. Every one of the watchers leaned forward. Linda realised that when she got onto the rack they would all be facing her helplessly raised small rear. She couldn't let them see it being exposed or let them stare at its naked trembling. She couldn't bear them watching it take on the sizzling red lines of the cane.

'Just one thing - I get to keep my jeans and pants on,' she said fiercely.

Miss Breeson put her head to one side: 'Well, for now you can keep your pants on.' She looked at the punishment rack then back at the girl, 'That is, as long as you don't try to touch your punished arse.'

'And if I do?' Linda muttered, fearing that she already knew the answer.

'If you do I'll have to cane you harder on the bare.'

Linda nodded. She'd show the woman that she was made of sterner stuff. She'd take her thrashing without a whimper. Marshalling her courage, she stepped forward and clambered awkwardly onto the unpolished long oak rack. 'There are straps for the miscreant's ankles and wrists, but we'll only use the ankle ones seeing as you've promised to control yourself,' her boss said evenly. Moments later Linda felt soft thongs pinioning her lower legs. She put her face down in the velvet-lined hollow that was obviously custom built for just this purpose. Miss Breeson adjusted the machine and a bolster pushed up Linda's tummy to its fullest extent. She closed her eyes with shame and a low spread of desire as she felt the woman tugging her jeans to below her knees.

Miss Breeson walked around the rack and stroked Linda's blonde hair for a moment. Next she turned towards the back of the room, obviously addressing the rest of her staff.

'Linda failed to protect one of the properties she was housesitting. Then she let a stranger into another house,' she said. 'She's opted for corporal punishment rather than for dismissal. Be aware that you may meet the same fate.'

'What do you mean that they *may*?' Linda muttered, twisting her head round to stare at her boss in panic, 'I thought that I was just the first wrongdoer? I thought we were all to be caned?'

'No, they are all on their first warnings. They're only here to witness your own bum turning scarlet,' Miss Breeson said.

God, the shame! Linda closed her eyes and mouth, and tried to close her mind to her increasing indignity. Then she sensed that Miss Breeson had pulled her arm back, and automatically tensed her bum in readiness for the first smarting stripe. She lay there in an agony of anticipation. Behind her one man whistled and a second man laughed.

'How many do you think you deserve?' her employer queried.

'Six?' Linda asked nervously.

'Let's make it twelve, seeing as you're getting to keep your knickers on,' the older woman parried, 'That is, unless you touch your arse.'

She wouldn't touch her rump no matter how much this hurt. She just wouldn't. Linda summoned up all her willpower and clutched the front of the rack. Then she yelled, her voice tone trembling, as the first stroke made contact somewhere near the centre of her pantied orbs. Linda cried out and her bottom jerked almost of its own volition. Then Miss Breeson announced that it was time for stroke two.

This stroke went lower than the first, though it felt as if it were parallel to it. Again, there was little protection in her cotton briefs. Forgetting that she'd promised to stay in control, Linda writhed upon the bolster. This time her fingers began to leave the front of the rack. Remembering just in time that she mustn't protect herself, she put her hands back in situ and waited breathlessly for the third corrective lash.

'Now where shall we put this one?' her merciless boss asked. Linda had some suggestions, but they were too rude to mention. Instead she lay there trying to psyche herself up for the next taste of the cane. It soon fell further up her spheres, and seemed to go slightly diagonal. 'Stop wriggling, girl, I like a nice still canvas,' Miss Breeson said.

'But it hurts,' Linda moaned, twisting back her head to look at her employer.

'Of course it hurts. It's meant to ensure that you become a better employee,' the woman said.

'Couldn't I just go on a course?' Linda murmured. Then she howled as her boss swished the rod twice in quick succession across her curved expanse. Beyond thought, she reached back her hands, spreading her fingers out and rubbing desperately at her punished buttocks. 'Oooooh!' she moaned.

A few seconds later she realised what she'd done and quickly moved her palms back to the front again. Miss Breeson marched around and lightly bound her wrists in place. 'What a pity that you disobeyed me,' she said softly, 'Now I'm going to have to pull down those pretty pants.'

Bent over the ungiving punishment rack, Linda bit her lip. Her twin globes tried to cringe away from the humiliation to follow. Her colleagues were about to see her naked cheeks.

Miss Breeson seemed to be savouring the moment to the full. She walked slowly towards Linda's knicker-clad orbs, which were raised like a sacrifice upon the bolster. She traced the sore cane marks through the taut white cotton, then she repeated the taunting touch again and again. 'What a wonderful heat,' she murmured with obvious relish, 'I hope they look as adorably red as they feel.'

She seemed to take her time pulling the blonde girl's panties down. Linda groaned with shame and wriggled her sore hindquarters. 'Easy,' Miss Breeson murmured, 'You aren't going anyplace till you've had seven more of the cane.'

'I don't know if I can bear it,' the twenty-five year old murmured plaintively, trying to suck her nether cheeks in closer to the bolster.

'I've already bared it for you, sweetheart,' her employer said.

Linda quaked as she felt the older woman pulling her briefs to below her knees. She quivered as her glowing pained stripes were fondled. 'They're a lovely scarlet shade, my dear. It's just a pity that some of the bands have merged into others. I wish that I could create separate parallel lines.'

She palpated the sore globes some more, 'Oh well, I suppose that all I need is practice. Maybe next time you're bad?'

Linda promised herself inwardly that she'd never be disobedient again. This caning would be her first one and her last one. It was hellish being displayed like this, her red haunches exposed for all to see. She wanted so much to put her jeans back on or at least hold her helpless chastened cheeks.

But these same soft cheeks still had to endure seven more strokes of the rod. Miss Breeson ordered her to count them. 'Thank you for stroke six,' she gasped belatedly as the first of the thrashings on the bare whacked down. Her poor bottom puckered up then relaxed then puckered again as it tried to anticipate when the next stroke was due.

The strong-armed Miss Breeson took her time. She seemed to know exactly how to keep a nervous backside waiting. Linda sensed that she'd raised her muscular arm. In turn, the younger girl tensed her bottom. Eventually her buttock muscles tired and she had to let them relax again. The second that her bum returned to smooth-bottomed splendour she felt the cane bite harshly into both lower cheeks. She made a sort of yodelling sound, shoving her belly into the bolster as far as she was able.

'I don't hear you counting the stroke and thanking me for it,' her employer said.

'Thank you for the seventh stroke, Miss,' Linda muttered into the velvet hollow. She shivered with shame and a low deep pleasure as the older woman fondled her upturned bum.

'Ask prettily for the eighth,' the woman prompted.

Linda hesitated and sucked in her breath.

'Can I be the one to lay it on?' a hoarse man shouted.

Reminded of her audience, the blonde girl skulked upon the punishment rack with additional shame. Just five more strokes, she reminded herself. Five more and it would be over - hell, schoolboys took more than this. She'd get to keep this job with its attractive wage.

'Ma'am, I'd appreciate receiving stroke eight,' she whispered, anxious that the man who'd spoken wouldn't lay the rod on. The thought of a male colleague whipping her bum was even more hateful than the thrashing which was already taking place. 'Ma'am, please apply stroke eight to my rear end,' she repeated as the worrying silence stretched and stretched.

'Oh you can plead for it more nicely than that,' her employer said. Linda hesitated, not wishing to degrade herself further. 'Perhaps Thomas will change your mind?' Miss Breeson asked.

'No - don't let him. I'll ask really sweetly,' Linda forced out. She squirmed as she thought up the words, 'I... I've been a reckless little girl, Ma'am. I've got a naughty bottom. It deserves to...' She choked back a sob, 'Deserves to feel the cane on the bare.'

'It does, doesn't it?' the forty something woman said, 'It really needs it.'

Linda howled as she tasted the thin hard rod again. The blonde girl asked equally obsequiously for the ninth stroke, but her imagination and courage faltered when it came to asking for the tenth. 'I'll have to give *two* swishes of the cane in the same place if you fail to please me,' her employer murmured, stroking her flesh.

Linda moaned at her words and actions. 'Please no! I want... My backside's really red.'

'Tch, tch,' the woman said, 'You're not sounding servile enough. You're really not trying.' She laid on two gentler strokes above Linda's thighs.

They still stung and Linda moved her bum powerlessly about for what felt like hours. Finally she settled down.

'One to go,' the woman said, 'Now, I can cane you further up where the flesh is relatively unscathed, or I can make you taste the rod in that hugely sensitive place you've just experienced.'

'Oh please, Ma'am, do it further up,' Linda said.

'I don't hear you asking nicely,' her employer prompted. She traced the cane along the twice-caned area until Linda begged.

'I... I've got the sorest arse in Christendom,' she said thickly, 'It's so hot and red that I can hardly bear it.' She sniffed loudly, then made herself continue, 'But I know it needs to take one more swishy stroke so that I never lie to my employer again.'

'And should that stroke be hard?' Miss Breeson teased.

'Very hard,' Linda forced out piteously.

'You're pleading nicely now,' the older woman said thoughtfully, 'But I'd like to hear you beg.'

There was a pause. 'I beg to taste the cane,' Linda said.

'Then lift your bum further up for me,' her employer countered. Snivelling with shame, Linda pushed her lower body up the little she could.

'I beg you to cane me hard, Ma'am,' she repeated tearfully.

Her boss drew back her arm and obliged. This time the rod fell further up the blonde girl's tethered bottom. Linda let her body sag against the bolster with long-awaited relief.

An hour later Miss Breeson sent Linda home, having promised that she could keep working for *Model Tenants*. When Miss Breeson herself got home she saw that her younger brother was there.

'Have fun?' he asked.

'Lots of fun,' Miss Breeson answered. Her labia was still tingling from her employee's obsequious tongue.

'Linda's got a great arse, doesn't she?' the younger man continued. 'I kept looking at it the whole time I was making love to her,' he added with a knowing grin.

Miss Breeson smiled brightly at her ever-helpful brother. 'She does indeed, Nick,' she said. She paused, 'I'm through with Linda for now, but maybe next week you can start checking up on young Mandy. She's supposed to be guarding the Riverside Hotel but I'm sure she'd break her curfew if you asked her for a date.'

Also available from Palmprint Publications

Subculture by Sarah Veitch

ISBN 0953795306 A-format paperback, 252 pages, £9.95

Lisa's work takes her to Malta - where she finds that her new employer, Dr Landers, is a strict disciplinarian. He soundly canes and tawses the girls who work at his deluxe Health Clinic and lets his senior receptionist spank the younger staff. The doctor is intriguing and Lisa is hugely drawn to him. If only he didn't resolve every dispute by pulling down her pants...
Will she reluctantly submit to the rod and reach new vistas of shame and ecstasy? Or will the obstacles she faces send her fleeing into a more conventional lover's arms?

'*An entertaining tale from someone who knows and respects the genre*' - Forum
'*Scores 8 out of 10 on the wank-o-meter*' - Desire
'*Subculture starts, continues and ends with lots of authentic scenes, many of which are almost painfully arousing*' - Kane

Subculture can be ordered from any good bookshop, from amazon.co.uk, or buy it mail order at the publisher direct price of £7.95, inclusive of postage & packing to UK addresses, by completing the form overleaf.
For delivery outwith the UK add £1.00 for postage. We can only accept payment by £ Sterling cheque drawn on a UK bank.

Don't want to buy a book just now? Simply send us your details and we'll mail you about new titles.

Subculture Order Form

I enclose a Cheque / Postal Order for **£7.95**, inclusive of postage & packing to UK addresses, payable to **Palmprint Publications** for one copy of Subculture by Sarah Veitch. Please send my copy to:

Name: ______________________________

Address: ______________________________

____

____

____

Postcode: ________________

☐ Please tick if you do **not** wish to be mailed when new titles are published. It is our policy **never** to pass your name and address to other organisations.

We aim to dispatch the day we receive your order but please allow up to 14 days for delivery. We are happy to receive a photocopy or handwritten order if you prefer not to tear out this form.
When completed please send to:

Palmprint Publications
PO Box 392, Weston-Super-Mare BS23 3ZS
United Kingdom www.palmprint.co.uk